DRAGONS

The Greatest Stories

Edited by

MARTIN H. GREENBERG

Published by MJF Books
Fine Communications
322 Eighth Avenue
New York, NY 10001

Library of Congress Catalog Card Number 97-70823
ISBN 1-56731-166-0
Dragons: The Greatest Stories
Copyright © 1997 by Tekno-Books

Manufactured in the United States of America on acid-free paper

MJF Books and the MJF colophon are trademarks of Fine Creative Media, Inc.

10 9 8 7 6 5 4 3 2

Contents

viii

Introduction

▢ ▢ ▢

Martin H. Greenberg

In the various forms of fantasy literature, mythological creatures have come to represent various ideals of cultures that created them. Unicorns, for example, usually represent purity and goodness. Elves are embodiments of nobility and immortality. Of course, the dark side of humankind has also been personified; spirits are often created out of the desire for revenge, and thus symbolize that aspect of humanity. The vampire, for instance, is world folklore's depiction of cruelty and evil.

Usually the creature in question bears at least a few similarities from one culture to another. The European unicorn and the Chinese Ki'rin are almost identical. Spirits and ghosts also share many characteristics all over the world. The vampires of the world may appear in different forms, but they always have a hunger for fresh blood, and are always evil.

However, the one creature that different cultures of the world cannot seem to agree on is the dragon. This greatest and most fearsome mythological creature has appeared in different incarnations all over the world, good as well as evil.

In Europe, the dragon has often been depicted as a cruel, treasure-hoarding beast. From the "monstrous fire-dragon" that was the death of the Geatish hero Beowulf, to the dragon that St. George battled, to the great and terrible Smaug of J.R.R. Tolkien's fiction, Europeans have illustrated dragons as creatures to be feared, attributing to them the greedy evil aspects of mankind. The dragon's role in Asia, however, is markedly different. Often represented by a wingless, four-legged cross between a lizard and a snake, Eastern dragons are usually the embodiment of wisdom and honor. They were believed to roam the sky, often by walking on the clouds, and delighted in watching and interacting with mortals.

In ancient Central America, the Aztecs worshipped a winged serpent named Quetzalcoatl as an incarnation of their sun god. This dragon was also benevolent, creating mankind from his own blood and providing food for his worshipers by stealing the first grain of maize from the ants.

Even within a single continent, the differences in dragon myths are many. In Europe, the form of the dragon changes from country to country. France, for example, has a popular folk tale about *La Tarasque*, a half-mammal, half-fish beast which crawled out of the ocean and ravaged the countryside until Saint Martha defeated it with the power of her faith. In Austria the dragon was called a *lindwurm* and was rumored to cause accidents and deaths on the river Glan. The Norse had their versions of dragons named *linnormr*, which periodically swooped down from the skies to kill and plunder.

Throughout the ages, the dragon has come to symbolize both the good and evil inherent in mankind. Sharing many of our own personality traits, their appearance is like nothing else in ancient or modern fantasy, and often corresponds to their natures. The Eastern dragons were often described as having beautiful metallic scales which gleamed in the sunlight, and faces that reflected their inner serenity and peace. Conversely, European dragons were the color of fire or night, their wings leathery and claw-tipped, and the only thing that gleamed in their face was a mouthful of fangs. Their souls were every bit as evil as their appearances.

Besides being a symbol of evil, dragons have also been an embodiment of the ultimate battle. In medieval times, there were few greater tests of heroism. From Beowulf to Cuchulain to St. George, history is filled with tales of heroes who have taken up the challenge. Some, like St. George, vanquished their foe, while others, like

Beowulf, slew the beast at the cost of their own life. Whether the hero survived or not, however, the dragon invariably lost.

The dragon is the only mythological creature to have so many different interpretations all over the world. Whether good or evil, the impact it has had on the mythology of ancient cultures is great, often representing what man would like to be or what he most fears becoming.

In today's fantasy fiction, both good and evil dragons appear. But even today, the forms of dragons vary depending on who is writing about them. From Anne McCaffrey's telepathic genetically-engineered dragons of Pern to Craig Shaw Gardner's title character of his magic realism trilogy *The Dragon Circle* to Margaret Weis and Tracy Hickman's bestselling *Dragonlance* books, the mightiest of mythological creatures is alive and well, if only in our imaginations.

The following stories collect the best and brightest fantasy authors and their versions of dragons. From stories combining fantasy dragons with science-fiction, such as Gordon Dickson's "Two Yards of Dragon" and Gregory Benford and Marc Laidlaw's "A Hiss of Dragon," to pure flights of fancy by Roger Zelazny and Orson Scott Card, all types of dragons are represented here.

No matter what shape it appears in, the dragon has inspired awe, fear, and courage for centuries. As these stories show, it's not hard to understand why.

The Dragon

◻ ◻ ◻

by Ray Bradbury

The night blew in the short grass on the moor; there was no other motion. It had been years since a single bird had flown by in the great blind shell of sky. Long ago a few small stones had simulated life when they crumbled and fell into dust. Now only the night moved in the souls of the two men bent by their lonely fire in the wilderness; darkness pumped quietly in their veins and ticked silently in their temples and their wrists.

Firelight fled up and down their wild faces and welled in their eyes in orange tatters. They listened to each other's faint, cool breathing and the lizard blink of their eyelids. At last, one man poked the fire with his sword.

"Don't, idiot; you'll give us away!"

"No matter," said the second man. "The dragon can smell us miles off anyway. God's breath, it's cold. I wish I was back at the castle."

"It's death, not sleep, we're after. . . ."

"Why? Why? The dragon never sets foot in the town!"

"Quiet, fool! He eats men traveling alone from our town to the next!"

"Let them be eaten and let us get home!"

"Wait now; listen!"

The two men froze.

They waited a long time, but there was only the shake of their horses' nervous skin like black velvet tambourines jingling the silver stirrup buckles, softly, softly.

"Ah." The second man sighed. "What a land of nightmares. Everything happens here. Someone blows out the sun; it's night. And then, and *then*, oh, God, listen! This dragon, they say his eyes are fire. His breath a white gas; you can see him burn across the dark lands. He runs with sulfur and thunder and kindles the grass. Sheep panic and die insane. Women deliver forth monsters. The dragon's fury is such that tower walls shake back to dust. His victims, at sunrise, are strewn hither thither on the hills. How many knights, I ask, have gone for this monster and failed, even as we shall fail?"

"Enough of that!"

"More than enough! Out here in this desolation I cannot tell what year this is!"

"Nine hundred years since the Nativity."

"No, no," whispered the second man, eyes shut. "On this moor is no Time, is only Forever. I feel if I ran back on the road the town would be gone, the people yet unborn, things changed, the castles unquarried from the rocks, the timbers still uncut from the forests; don't ask how I know; the moor knows and tells me. And here we sit alone in the land of the fire dragon, God save us!"

"Be you afraid, then gird on your armor!"

"What use? The dragon runs from nowhere; we cannot guess its home. It vanishes in fog; we know not where it goes. Aye, on with our armor, we'll die well dressed."

Half into his silver corselet, the second man stopped again and turned his head.

Across the dim country, full of night and nothingness from the heart of the moor itself, the wind sprang full of dust from clocks that used dust for telling time. There were black suns burning in the heart of this new wind and a million burnt leaves shaken from some autumn tree beyond the horizon. This wind melted landscapes, lengthened bones like white wax, made the blood roil and thicken to a muddy deposit in the brain. The wind was a thousand souls dying and all time confused and in transit. It was a fog inside of a mist inside of a darkness, and this place was no man's place and there was no year or hour at all, but only these men in a faceless emptiness of sudden frost, storm and white thunder which moved behind the great falling pane of green glass that was the lightning. A squall of rain drenched the turf; all faded away until there was unbreathing hush and the two men waiting alone with their warmth in a cool season.

"There," whispered the first man. "Oh, *there . . .*"

Miles off, rushing with a great chant and a roar—the dragon.

In silence the men buckled on their armor and mounted their horses. The midnight wilderness was split by a monstrous gushing as the dragon roared nearer, nearer; its flashing yellow glare spurted above a hill and then, fold on fold of dark body, distantly seen, therefore indistinct, flowed over that hill and plunged vanishing into a valley.

"Quick!"

They spurred their horses forward to a small hollow.

"This is where it passes!"

They seized their lances with mailed fists and blinded their horses by flipping the visors down over their eyes.

"Lord!"

"Yes, let us use His name."

On the instant, the dragon rounded a hill. Its monstrous amber eye fed on them, fired their armor in red glints and glitters. With a terrible wailing cry and a grinding rush it flung itself forward.

"Mercy, God!"

The lance struck under the unlidded yellow eye, buckled, tossed the man through the air. The dragon hit, spilled him over, down, ground him under. Passing, the black brunt of its shoulder smashed the remaining horse and rider a hundred feet against the side of a boulder, wailing, wailing, the dragon shrieking, the fire all about, around, under it, a pink, yellow, orange sun-fire with great soft plumes of blinding smoke.

"Did you *see* it?" cried a voice. "Just like I told you!"

"The same! The same! A knight in armor, by the Lord Harry! We *hit* him!"

"You goin' to stop?"

"Did once; found nothing. Don't like to stop on this moor. I get the willies. Got a *feel*, it has."

"But we hit *something!*"

"Gave him plenty of whistle; chap wouldn't budge!"

A steaming blast cut the mist aside.

"We'll make Stokely on time. More coal, eh, Fred?"

Another whistle shook dew from the empty sky. The night train, in fire and fury, shot through a gully, up a rise, and vanished away over cold earth toward the north, leaving black smoke and steam to dissolve in the numbed air minutes after it had passed and gone forever.

The Smallest Dragonboy

囗 囗 囗

by Anne McCaffrey

Although Keevan lengthened his walking stride as far as his legs would stretch, he couldn't quite keep up with the other candidates. He knew he would be teased again.

Just as he knew many things that his foster mother told him he ought not to know, Keevan knew that Beterli, the most senior of the boys, set that spanking pace just to embarrass him, the smallest dragonboy. Keevan would arrive, tail fork-end of the group, breathless, chest heaving, and maybe get a stern look from the instructing wingsecond.

Dragonriders, even if they were still only hopeful candidates for the glowing eggs which were hardening on the hot sands of the Hatching Ground cavern, were expected to be punctual and prepared. Sloth was not tolerated by the Weyrleader of Benden Weyr. A good record was especially important now. It was very near hatching time, when the baby dragons would crack their mottled shells, and stagger forth to choose their lifetime companions. The very thought of that glorious moment made Keevan's breath catch in his throat. To be chosen—to be a dragonrider! To sit astride the neck of a winged beast with jeweled eyes: to be his companion in good times and fighting extremes; to fly effortlessly over the lands of Pern! Or, thrillingly, *between* to any point anywhere on the world! Flying *between* was done on dragonback or not at all, and it was dangerous.

Keevan glanced upward, past the black mouths of the weyr caves in which grown dragons and their chosen riders lived, toward the Star Stones that crowned the ridge of the old volcano that was Benden Weyr. On the height, the blue watch dragon, his rider mounted on his neck, stretched the great transparent pinions that carried him on the winds of Pern to fight the evil Thread that fell at certain times from the skies. The many-faceted rainbow jewels of his eyes glistened fleetingly in the greeny sun. He folded his great wings to his back, and the watchpair resumed their statuelike pose of alertness.

Then the enticing view was obscured as Keevan passed into the Hatching Ground cavern. The sands underfoot were hot, even through heavy wher-hide boots. How the bootmaker had protested having to sew so small! Keevan was forced to wonder why being small was reprehensible. People were always calling him "babe" and shooing him away as being "too small" or "too young" for this or that. Keevan was constantly working, twice as hard as any other boy his age, to prove himself capable. What if his muscles weren't as big as Beterli's? They were just as hard. And if he couldn't overpower anyone in a wrestling match, he could outdistance everyone in a footrace.

"Maybe if you run fast enough," Beterli had jeered on the occasion when Keevan had been goaded to boast of his swiftness, " you could catch a dragon. That's the only way you'll make a dragonrider!"

"You just wait and see, Beterli, you just wait," Keevan had replied. He would have liked to wipe the contemptuous smile from Beterli's face, but the guy didn't fight fair even when a wingsecond was watching. "No one knows what Impresses a dragon!"

"They've got to be able to *find* you first, babe!"

Yes, being the smallest candidate was not an enviable position. It was therefore imperative that Keevan Impress a dragon in his first hatching. That would wipe the smile off every face in the cavern, and accord him the respect due any dragonrider, even the smallest one.

Besides, no one knew exactly what Impressed the baby dragons as they struggled from their shells toward their lifetime partners.

"I like to believe that dragons see into a man's heart," Keevan's foster mother, Mende, told him. "If they find goodness, honesty, a flexible mind, patience, courage—and you've got that in quantity, dear Keevan—that's what dragons look for. I've seen many a well-grown lad left standing on the sands, Hatching Day, in favor of someone not so strong or tall or handsome. And if my memory serves me"—which it usually did: Mende knew every word of every Harper's tale worth telling, Keevan did not interrupt her to say so— "I don't believe that F'lar, our Weyrleader, was all that tall when bronze Mnementh chose him. And Mnementh was the only bronze dragon of that hatching."

Dreams of Impressing a bronze were beyond Keevan's boldest reflections, although that goal dominated the thoughts of every other hopeful candidate. Green dragons were small and fast and more numerous. There was more prestige to Impressing a blue or brown than a green. Being practical, Keevan seldom dreamed as high as a big fighting brown, like Canth, F'nor's fine fellow, the biggest brown on all Pern. But to fly a bronze? Bronzes were almost as big as the queen, and only they took the air when a queen flew at mating time. A bronze rider could aspire to become Weyrleader! Well, Keevan would console himself, brown riders could aspire to become wingseconds, and that wasn't bad. He'd even settle for a green dragon: they were small, but so was he. No matter! He simply had to Impress a dragon his first time in the Hatching Ground. Then no one in the Weyr would taunt him anymore for being so small.

Shells, Keevan thought now, but the sands are hot!

"Impression time is imminent, candidates," the wingsecond was saying as everyone crowded respectfully close to him. "See the extent of the striations on this promising egg?" The stretch marks *were* larger than yesterday.

Everyone leaned forward and nodded thoughtfully. That particular egg was the one Beterli had marked as his own, and no other candidate dared, on pain of being beaten by Beterli at his first opportunity, to approach it. The egg was marked by a large yellowish splotch in the shape of a dragon back-winging to land, talons outstretched to grasp the rock. Everyone knew that bronze eggs bore distinctive markings. And naturally, Beterli, who'd been presented at eight Impressions already and was the biggest of the candidates, had chosen it.

"I'd say that the great opening day is almost upon us," the wingsecond went on, and then his face assumed a grave expression. "As we well know, there are only forty eggs and seventy-two candidates. Some of you may be disappointed on the great day. That doesn't necessarily mean you aren't dragonrider material, just that *the* dragon for you hasn't been shelled. You'll have other hatchings, and it's no disgrace to be left behind an Impression or two. Or more."

Keevan was positive that the wingsecond's eyes rested on Beterli, who'd been stood off at so many Impressions already. Keevan tried to squinch down so the wingsecond wouldn't notice him. Keevan had been reminded too often that he was eligible to be a candidate by one day only. He, of all the hopefuls, was most likely to be left standing on the great day. One more reason why he simply had to Impress at his first hatching.

"Now move about among the eggs," the wingsecond said. "Touch them. We don't know that it does any good, but it certainly doesn't do any harm."

Some of the boys laughed nervously, but everyone immediately began to circulate among the eggs. Beterli stepped up officiously to "his" egg, daring anyone to come near it. Keevan smiled, because he had already touched it—every inspection day, when the others were leaving the Hatching Ground and no one could see him crouch to stroke it.

Keevan had an egg he concentrated on, too, one drawn slightly to the far side of the others. The shell had a soft greenish-blue tinge with a faint creamy swirl design. The consensus was that this egg contained a mere green, so Keevan was rarely bothered by rivals. He was somewhat perturbed then to see Beterli wandering over to him.

"I don't know why you're allowed in this Impression, Keevan. There are enough of us without a babe," Beterli said, shaking his head.

"I'm of age." Keevan kept his voice level, telling himself not to be bothered by mere words.

"Yah!" Beterli made a show of standing on his toetips. "You can't even see over an egg; Hatching Day, you better get in front or the dragons won't see you at all. Course, you could get run down that way in the mad scramble. Oh, I forget, you can run fast, can't you?"

"You'd better make sure a dragon sees *you*, this time, Beterli," Keevan replied. "You're almost overage, aren't you?"

Beterli flushed and took a step forward, hand half-raised. Keevan stood his ground, but if Beterli advanced one more step, he would call the wingsecond. No one fought on the Hatching Ground. Surely Beterli knew that much.

Fortunately, at that moment, the wingsecond called the boys together and led them from the Hatching Ground to start on evening chores. There were "glows" to be replenished in the main kitchen caverns and sleeping cubicles, the major hallways, and the queen's apartment. Firestone sacks had to be filled against Thread attack, and black rock brought to the kitchen hearths. The boys fell to their chores, tantalized by the odors of roasting meat. The population of the Weyr began to assemble for the evening meal, and the dragonriders came in from the Feeding Ground on their sweep checks.

It was the time of day Keevan liked best: once the chores were done but before dinner was served, a fellow could often get close enough to the dragonriders to hear their talk. Tonight, Keevan's father, K'last, was at the main dragonriders' table. It puzzled Keevan how his father, a brown rider and a tall man, could *be* his father—because he, Keevan, was so small. It obviously puzzled K'last, too, when he deigned to notice his small son: "In a few more Turns, you'll be as tall as I am—or taller!"

K'last was pouring Benden wine all around the table. The dragonriders were relaxing. There'd be no Thread attack for three more days, and they'd be in the mood to tell tales, better than Harper yarns, about impossible maneuvers they'd done a-dragonback. When Thread attack was closer, their talk would change to a discussion of tactics or evasion, of going *between*, how long to suspend there until the burning but fragile Thread would freeze and crack and fall harmlessly off dragon and man. They would dispute the exact moment to feed firestone to the dragon so he'd have the best flame ready to sear Thread midair and render it harmless to ground—and man—below. There was such a lot to know and understand about being a drag-onrider that sometimes Keevan was overwhelmed. How would he ever be able to remember everything he ought to know at the right moment? He couldn't dare ask such a question: this would only have given additional weight to the notion that he was too young yet to be a dragonrider.

"Having older candidates makes good sense," L'vel was saying, as Keevan settled down near the table. "Why waste four to five years of a dragon's fighting prime until his rider grows up enough to stand the rigors?" L'vel had Impressed a blue of Ramoth's first clutch. Most of the candidates thought L'vel was marvelous because he spoke up in front of the older riders, who awed them. "That was well enough in the Interval when you didn't need to mount the full Weyr comple-ment to fight Thread. But not now. Not with more eligible candidates than ever. Let the babes wait."

"Any boy who is over twelve Turns has the right to stand in the Hatching Ground," K'last replied, a slight smile on his face. He never argued or got angry. Keevan wished he were more like his fa-ther. And oh, how he wished he were a brown rider! "Only a dragon—each particular dragon—knows what he wants in a rider. We certainly can't tell. Time and again the theorists," K'last's smile deepened as his eyes swept those at the table, "are surprised by dragon choice. *They* never seem to make mistakes, however."

"Now, K'last, just look at the roster this Impression. Seventy-two boys and only forty eggs. Drop off the twelve youngest, and there's still a good field for the hatchlings to choose from. Shells! There are a couple of weyrlings unable to see over a wher egg much less a dragon! And years before they can ride Thread."

"True enough, but the Weyr is scarcely under fighting strength, and if the youngest Impress, they'll be old enough to fight when the oldest of our current dragons go *between* from senility."

"Half the Weyr-bred lads have already been through several Impressions," one of the bronze riders said then. "I'd say drop some of *them* off this time."

"There's nothing wrong in presenting a clutch with as wide a choice as possible," said the Weyrleader, who had joined the table with Lessa, the Weyrwoman.

"Has there ever been a case," she said, smiling in her odd way at the riders, "where a hatchling didn't choose?"

Her suggestion was almost heretical and drew astonished gasps from everyone, including the boys.

F'lar laughed. "You say the most outrageous things, Lessa."

"Well, *has* there ever been a case where a dragon didn't choose?"

"Can't say as I recall one," K'last replied.

"Then we continue in this tradition," Lessa said firmly, as if that ended the matter.

But it didn't. The argument ranged from one table to the other all through dinner, with some favoring a weeding out of the candidates to the most likely, lopping off those who were very young or who had had multiple opportunities to Impress. All the candidates were in a swivet, though such a departure from tradition would be to the advantage of many. As the evening progressed, more riders were favoring eliminating the youngest and those who'd passed four or more Impressions unchosen. Keevan felt he could bear such a dictum only if Beterli were also eliminated. But this seemed less likely than that Keevan would be turfed out, since the Weyr's need was for fighting dragons and riders.

By the time the evening meal was over, no decision had been reached, although the Weyrleader had promised to give the matter due consideration.

He might have slept on the problem, but few of the candidates did. Tempers were uncertain in the sleeping caverns next morning as the boys were routed out of their beds to carry water and black rock and cover the "glows." Twice Mende had to call Keevan to order for clumsiness.

"Whatever is the matter with you, boy?" she demanded in exasperation when he tippled black rock short of the bin and sooted up the hearth.

"They're going to keep me from this Impression."

"What?" Mende stared at him. "Who?"

"You heard them talking at dinner last night. They're going to turf the babes from the hatching."

Mende regarded him a moment longer before touching his arm gently. "There's lots of talk around a supper table, Keevan. And it cools as soon as the supper. I've heard the same nonsense before every hatching, but nothing is ever changed."

"There's always a first time," Keevan answered, copying one of her own phrases.

"That'll be enough of that, Keevan. Finish your job. If the clutch does hatch today, we'll need full rock bins for the feast, and you won't be around to do the filling. All my fosterlings make dragonriders."

"The first time?" Keevan was bold enough to ask as he scooted off with the rockbarrow.

Perhaps, Keevan thought later, if he hadn't been on that chore just when Beterli was also fetching black rock, things might have turned out differently. But he had dutifully trundled the barrow to the outdoor bunker for another load just as Beterli arrived on a similar errand.

"Heard the news, babe?" Beterli asked. He was grinning from ear to ear, and he put an unnecessary emphasis on the final insulting word.

"The eggs are cracking?" Keevan all but dropped the loaded shovel. Several anxieties flicked through his mind then: he was black with rock dust—would he have time to wash before donning the white tunic of candidacy? And if the eggs were hatching, why hadn't the candidates been recalled by the wingsecond?

"Naw! Guess again!" Beterli was much too pleased with himself.

With a sinking heart, Keevan knew what the news must be, and he could only stare with intense desolation at the older boy.

"C'mon! Guess, babe!"

"I've no time for guessing games," Keevan managed to say with indifference. He began to shovel black rock into the barrow as fast as he could.

"I said guess." Beterli grabbed the shovel.

"And I said I have no time for guessing games."

Beterli wrenched the shovel from Keevan's hands.

"I'll have that shovel back, Beterli." Keevan straightened up but he didn't come to Beterli's bulky shoulder. From somewhere, other boys appeared, some with barrows, some mysteriously alerted to the prospect of a confrontation among their numbers.

"Babes don't give orders to candidates around here, babe!"

Someone sniggered and Keevan, incredulous, knew that he must've been dropped from the candidacy.

He yanked the shovel from Beterli's loosened grasp. Snarling, the older boy tried to regain possession, but Keevan clung with all his strength to the handle, dragged back and forth as the stronger boy jerked the shovel about.

With a sudden, unexpected movement, Beterli rammed the handle into Keevan's chest, knocking him over the barrow handles. Keevan felt a sharp, painful jab behind his left ear, an unbearable pain in his left shin, and then a painless nothingness.

Mende's angry voice roused him, and startled, he tried to throw back the covers, thinking he'd overslept. But he couldn't move, so firmly was he tucked into his bed. And then the constriction of a bandage on his head and the dull sickishness in his leg brought back recent occurrences.

"Hatching?" he cried.

"No, lovey," Mende said in a kind voice. Her hand was cool and gentle on his forehead. "Though there's some as won't be at any hatching again." Her voice took on a stern edge.

Keevan looked beyond her to see the Weyrwoman, who was frowning with irritation.

"Keevan, will you tell me what occurred at the black rock bunker?" asked Lessa in an even voice.

He remembered Beterli now and the quarrel over the shovel and . . . what had Mende said about some not being at any hatching? Much as he hated Beterli, he couldn't bring himself to tattle on Beterli and force him out of candidacy.

"Come, lad," and a note of impatience crept into the Weyrwoman's voice. "I merely want to know what happened from you, too. Mende said she sent you for black rock. Beterli—and every Weyrling in the cavern—seems to have been on the same errand. What happened?"

"Beterli took my shovel. I hadn't finished with it."

"There's more than one shovel. What did he *say* to you?"

"He'd heard the news."

"What news?" The Weyrwoman was suddenly amused.

"That . . . that . . . there'd been changes."

"Is that what he said?"

"Not exactly."

"What did he say? C'mon, lad, I've heard from everyone else, you know."

"He said for me to guess the news."

"And you fell for that old gag?" The Weyrwoman's irritation returned.

"Consider all the talk last night at supper, Lessa," Mende said. "Of course the boy would think he'd been eliminated."

"In effect, he is, with a broken skull and leg." Lessa touched his arm in a rare gesture of sympathy. "Be that as it may, Keevan, you'll have other Impressions. Beterli will not. There are certain rules that must be observed by all candidates, and his conduct proves him unacceptable to the Weyr."

She smiled at Mende and then left.

"I'm still a candidate?" Keevan asked urgently.

"Well, you are and you aren't, lovey," his foster mother said. "Is the numbweed working?" she asked, and when he nodded, she said, "You must rest. I'll bring you some nice broth."

At any other time in his life, Keevan would have relished such cosseting, but now he just lay there worrying. Beterli had been dismissed. Would the others think it was his fault? But everyone was there! Beterli provoked that fight. His worry increased, because although he heard excited comings and goings in the passageway, no one tweaked back the curtain across the sleeping alcove he shared with five other boys. Surely one of them would have to come in sometime. No, they were all avoiding him. And something else was wrong. Only he didn't know what.

Mende returned with broth and beachberry bread.

"Why doesn't anyone come see me, Mende? I haven't done anything wrong, have I? I didn't ask to have Beterli turfed out."

Mende soothed him, saying everyone was busy with noontime chores and no one was angry with him. They were giving him a chance to rest in quiet. The numbweed made him drowsy, and her words were fair enough. He permitted his fears to dissipate. Until he heard a hum. Actually, he felt it first, in the broken shin bone and his sore head. The hum began to grow. Two things registered suddenly in Keevan's groggy mind: the only white candidate's robe still on the pegs in the chamber was his; and the dragons hummed when a clutch was being laid or being hatched. Impression! And he was flat abed.

Bitter, bitter disappointment turned the warm broth sour in his belly. Even the small voice telling him that he'd have other opportunities failed to alleviate his crushing depression. *This* was the Impression that mattered! This was his chance to show *everyone*, from Mende to K'last to L'vel and even the Weyrleader, that he, Keevan, was worthy of being a dragonrider.

He twisted in bed, fighting against the tears that threatened to choke him. Dragonmen don't cry! Dragonmen learn to live with pain.

Pain? The leg didn't actually pain him as he rolled about on his bedding. His head felt sort of stiff from the tightness of the bandage. He sat up, an effort in itself since the numbweed made exertion difficult. He touched the splintered leg; the knee was unhampered. He had no feeling in his bone, really. He swung himself carefully to the side of his bed and stood slowly. The room wanted to swim about him. He closed his eyes, which made the dizziness worse, and he had to clutch the wall.

Gingerly, he took a step. The broken leg dragged. It hurt in spite of the numbweed, but what was pain to a dragonman?

No one had said he couldn't go to the Impression. "You are and you aren't" were Mende's exact words.

Clinging to the wall, he jerked off his bedshirt. Stretching his arm to the utmost, he jerked his white candidate's tunic from the peg. Jamming first one arm and then the other into the holes, he pulled it over his head. Too bad about the belt. He couldn't wait. He hobbled to the door, hung on to the curtain to steady himself. The weight on his leg was unwieldy. He wouldn't get very far without something to lean on. Down by the bathing pool was one of the long crook-necked poles used to retrieve clothes from the hot troughs. But it was down there, and he was on the level above. And there was no one nearby to come to his aid: everyone would be in the Hatching Ground right now, eagerly waiting for the first egg to crack.

The humming increased in volume and tempo, an urgency to which Keevan responded, knowing that his time was all too limited if he was to join the ranks of the hopeful boys standing around the cracking eggs. But if he hurried down the ramp, he'd fall flat on his face.

He could, of course, go flat on his rear end, the way crawling children did. He sat down, sending a jarring stab of pain through his leg and up to the wound on the back of his head. Gritting his teeth and blinking away tears, Keevan scrabbled down the ramp. He had to wait a moment at the bottom to catch his breath. He got to one knee, the injured leg straight out in front of him. Somehow he managed to push himself erect, though the room seemed about to tip over his ears. It wasn't far to the crooked stick, but it seemed an age before he had it in his hand.

Then the humming stopped!

Keevan cried out and began to hobble frantically across the cavern, out to the bowl of the Weyr. Never had the distance between living caverns and the Hatching Ground seemed so great. Never had the Weyr been so breathlessly silent. It was as if the multitude of people and dragons watching the hatching held every breath in suspense. Not even the wind muttered down the steep sides of the bowl. The only sounds to break the stillness were Keevan's ragged gasps and the thump-thud of his stick on the hard-packed ground. Sometimes he had to hop twice on his good leg to maintain his balance. Twice he fell into the sand and had to pull himself up on the stick, his white tunic no longer spotless. Once he jarred himself so badly he couldn't get up immediately.

Then he heard the first exhalation of the crowd, the oohs, the muted cheer, the susurrus of excited whispers. An egg had cracked, and the dragon had chosen his rider. Desperation increased Keevan's hobble. Would he never reach the arching mouth of the Hatching Ground?

Another cheer and an excited spate of applause spurred Keevan to greater effort. If he didn't get there in moments, there'd be no unpaired hatchling left. Then he was actually staggering into the Hatching Ground, the sands hot on his bare feet.

No one noticed his entrance or his halting progress. And Keevan could see nothing but the backs of the white-robed candidates, seventy of them ringing the area around the egg. Then one side would surge forward or back and there'd be a cheer. Another dragon had been Impressed. Suddenly a large gap appeared in the white human wall, and Keevan had his first sight of the eggs. There didn't seem to be *any* left uncracked, and he could see the lucky boys standing beside wobble-legged dragons. He could hear the unmistakable plaintive crooning of hatchlings and their squawks of protest as they'd fall awkwardly in the sand.

Suddenly he wished that he hadn't left his bed, that he'd stayed away from the Hatching Ground. Now everyone would see his ignominious failure. So he scrambled as desperately to reach the shadowy walls of the Hatching Ground as he struggled to cross the bowl. He mustn't be seen.

He didn't notice, therefore, that the shifting group of boys remaining had begun to drift in his direction. The hard pace he had set himself and his cruel disappointment took their double toll of Keevan. He tripped and collapsed sobbing to the warm sands. He didn't see the consternation in the watching Weyrfolk above the Hatching Ground, nor did he hear the excited whispers of speculation. He didn't know that the Weyrleader and Weyrwoman had dropped to the arena and were making their way toward the knot of boys slowly moving in the direction of the entrance.

"Never seen anything like it," the Weyrleader was saying. "Only thirty-nine riders chosen. And the bronze trying to leave the Hatching Ground without making Impression."

"A case in point of what I said last night," the Weyrwoman replied, "where a hatchling makes no choice because the right boy isn't there."

"There's only Beterli and K'last's young one missing. And there's a full wing of likely boys to choose from . . ."

"None acceptable, apparently. Where is the creature going? He's not heading for the entrance after all. Oh, what have we there, in the shadows?"

Keevan heard with dismay the sound of voices nearing him. He tried to burrow into the sand. The mere thought of how he would be teased and taunted now was unbearable.

Don't worry! Please don't worry! The thought was urgent, but not his own.

Someone kicked sand over Keevan and butted roughly against him.

"Go away. Leave me alone!" he cried.

Why? was the injured-sounding question inserted into his mind. There was no voice, no tone, but the question was there, perfectly clear, in his head.

Incredulous, Keevan lifted his head and stared into the glowing jeweled eyes of a small bronze dragon. His wings were wet, the tips drooping in the sand. And he sagged in the middle on his unsteady legs, although he was making a great effort to keep erect.

Keevan dragged himself to his knees, oblivious of the pain in his leg. He wasn't even aware that he was ringed by the boys passed over, while thirty-one pairs of resentful eyes watched him Impress the dragon. The Weyrmen looked on, amused, and surprised at the draconic choice, which could not be forced. Could not be questioned. Could not be changed.

Why? asked the dragon again. *Don't you like me?* His eyes whirled with anxiety, and his tone was so piteous that Keevan staggered forward and threw his arms around the dragon's neck, stroking his eye ridges, patting the damp, soft hide, opening the fragile-looking wings to dry them, and wordlessly assuring the hatchling over and over again that he was the most perfect, most beautiful, most beloved dragon in the Weyr, in all the Weyrs of Pern.

"What's his name, K'van?" asked Lessa, smiling warmly at the new dragonrider. K'van stared up at her for a long moment. Lessa would know as soon as he did. Lessa was the only person who could "receive" from all dragons, not only her own Ramoth. Then he gave her a radiant smile, recognizing the traditional shortening of his name that raised him forever to the rank of dragonrider.

My name is Heth, the dragon thought mildly, then hiccuped in sudden urgency. *I'm hungry.*

"Dragons are born hungry," said Lessa, laughing. "F'lar, give the boy a hand. He can barely manage his own legs, much less a dragon's."

K'van remembered his stick and drew himself up. "We'll be just fine, thank you."

"You may be the smallest dragonrider ever, young K'van," F'lar said, "but you're one of the bravest!"

And Heth agreed! Pride and joy so leaped in both chests that K'van wondered if his heart would burst right out of his body. He looped an arm around Heth's neck and the pair, the smallest dragonboy and the hatchling who wouldn't choose anybody else, walked out of the Hatching Ground together forever.

The Rule of Names

□ □ □

by Ursula K. Le Guin

Mr. Underhill came out from under his hill, smiling and breathing hard. Each breath shot out of his nostrils as a double puff of steam, snow-white in the morning sunshine. Mr. Underhill looked up at the bright December sky and smiled wider than ever, showing snow-white teeth. Then he went down to the village.

"Morning, Mr. Underhill," said the villagers as he passed them in the narrow street between houses with conical, overhanging roofs like the fat red caps of toadstools. "Morning, morning!" he replied to each. (It was, of course, bad luck to wish anyone a *good* morning; a simple statement of the time of day was quite enough, in a place so permeated with Influences as Sattins Island, where a careless adjective might change the weather for a week.) All of them spoke to him, some with affection, some with affectionate disdain. He was all the little island had in the way of a wizard, and so deserved respect—but how could you respect a little fat man of fifty who waddled along with his toes turned in, breathing steam and smiling? He was no great shakes as a workman either. His fireworks were fairly elaborate but his elixirs were weak. Warts he charmed off frequently reappeared after three days; tomatoes he enchanted grew no bigger than canteloupes; and those rare times when a strange ship stopped at Sattins harbor, Mr. Underhill always stayed under his hill—for fear, he explained, of the evil eye. He was, in other words, a wizard the way walleyed Gan was a carpenter: by default. The villagers made do with badly hung doors and inefficient spells, for this generation, and relieved their annoyance by treating Mr. Underhill quite familiarly, as a mere fellow-villager. They even asked him to dinner. Once he asked some of them to dinner, and served a splendid repast, with silver, crystal, damask, roast goose, sparkling Andrades '639, and plum pudding with hard sauce; but he was so nervous all through the meal that it took the joy out of it, and besides, everybody was hungry again half an hour afterward. He did not like anyone to visit his cave, not even the anteroom, beyond which in fact nobody had ever got. When he saw people approaching the hill he always came trotting to meet them. "Let's sit out here under the pine trees!" he would say, smiling and waving towards the fir-grover, or if it was raining, "Let's go have a drink at the inn, eh?" though everybody knew he drank nothing stronger than well-water.

Some of the village children, teased by the locked cave, poked and pried and made raids while Mr. Underhill was away; but the small door that led into the inner chamber was spell-shut, and it seemed for once to be an effective spell. Once a couple of boys, thinking the wizard was over on the West Shore curing Mrs. Ruuna's sick donkey, brought a crowbar and a hatchet up there, but at the first whack of the hatchet on the door there came a roar of wrath from inside, and a cloud of purple steam. Mr. Underhill had got home early. The boys fled. He did not come out, and the boys came to no harm, though they said you couldn't believe what a huge hooting howling hissing horrible bellow that little fat man could make unless you'd heard it.

His business in town this day was three dozen fresh eggs and a pound of liver; also a stop at Seacaptain Fogeno's cottage to renew the seeing-charm on the old man's eyes (quite useless when applied to a case of detached retina, but Mr. Underhill kept trying), and finally a chat with old Goody Guld the concertina-maker's widow. Mr. Underhill's friends were mostly old people. He was timid with the strong young men of the village, and girls were shy of him. "He makes me nervous, he smiles so much," they all said, pouting, twisting silky ringlets round a finger. "Nervous" was a newfangled word, and their mothers all replied grimly, "Nervous, my foot, silliness is the word for it. Mr. Underhill is a very respectable wizard!"

After leaving Goody Guld, Mr. Underhill passed by the school, which was being held this day out on the common. Since no one on Sattins Island was literate, there were no books to learn to read from and no desks to carve initials on and no blackboards to erase, and in fact no schoolhouse. On rainy days the children met in the loft of the Communal Barn, and got hay in their pants; on sunny days the schoolteacher, Palani, took them anywhere she felt like. Today, surrounded by thirty interested children under twelve and forty uninterested sheep under five, she was teaching an important item on the curriculum: the Rules of Names. Mr. Underhill, smiling shyly, paused to listen and watch. Palani, a plump, pretty girl of twenty, made a charming picture there in the wintry sunlight, sheep and children around her, a leafless oak above her, and behind her the dunes and sea and clear, pale sky. She spoke earnestly, her face flushed pink by wind and words. "Now you know the Rules of Names already, children. There are two, and they're the same on every island in the world. What's one of them?"

"It ain't polite to ask anybody what his name is," shouted a fat, quick boy, interrupted by a little girl shrieking, "You can't never tell your own name to nobody my ma says!"

"Yes, Suba. Yes, Popi dear, don't screech. That's right. You never ask anybody his name. You never tell your own. Now think about that a minute and then tell me why we call our wizard Mr. Underhill." She smiled across the curly heads and the woolly backs at Mr. Underhill, who beamed, and nervously clutched his sack of eggs.

" 'Cause he lives under a hill!" said half the children.

"But is it his truename?"

"No!" said the fat boy, echoed by little Popi shrieking, "No!

"How do you know it's not?"

" 'Cause he came here all alone and so there wasn't anybody knew his truename so they could not tell us, and *he* couldn't—"

"Very good, Suba. Popi, don't shout. That's right. Even a wizard can't tell his truename. When you children are through school and go through the Passage, you'll leave your childnames behind and keep only your truenames, which you must never ask for and never give away. Why is that the rule?"

The children were silent. The sheep bleated gently. Mr. Underhill answered the question: "Because the name is the thing," he said in his shy, soft, husky voice, "and the truename is the true thing. To speak the name is to control the thing. Am I right, Schoolmistress?"

She smiled and curtseyed, evidently a little embarrassed by his participation. And he trotted off towards his hill, clutching the eggs to his bosom. Somehow the minute spent watching Palani and the children had made him very hungry. He locked his inner door behind him with a hasty incantation, but there must have been a leak or two in the spell, for soon the bare anteroom of the cave was rich with the smell of frying eggs and sizzling liver.

The wind that day was light and fresh out of the west, and on it at noon a little boat came skimming the bright waves into Sattins harbor. Even as it rounded the point a sharp-eyed boy spotted it, and knowing, like every child on the island, every sail and spar of the forty boats of the fishing fleet, he ran down the street calling out, "A foreign boat, a foreign boat!" Very seldom was the lonely isle visited by a boat from some equally lonely isle of the East Reach, or an adventurous trader from the Archipelago. By the time the boat was at the pier half the village was there to greet it, and fishermen were following it homewards, and cowherds and clam-diggers and herbhunters were puffing up and down all the rocky hills, heading towards the harbor.

But Mr. Underhill's door stayed shut.

There was only one man aboard the boat. Old Seacaptain Fogeno, when they told him that, drew down a bristle of white brows over his unseeing eyes. "There's only one kind of man," he said, "that sails the Outer Reach alone. A wizard, or a warlock, or a Mage . . ."

So the villagers were breathless, hoping to see for once in their lives a Mage, one of the mighty White Magicians of the rich, towered, crowded inner islands of the Archipelago. They were disappointed, for the voyager was quite young, a handsome black-bearded fellow who hailed them cheerfully from his boat, and leaped ashore like any sailor glad to have made port. He introduced himself at once as a sea-pedlar. But when they told Seacaptain Fogeno that he carried an oaken walking-stick around with him, the old man nodded. "Two wizards in one town," he said. "Bad!" And his mouth snapped shut like an old carp's.

As the stranger could not give them his name, they gave him one right away: Blackbeard. And they gave him plenty of attention. He had a small mixed cargo of cloth and sandals and *piswi* feathers for trimming cloaks and cheap incense and levity stones and fine herbs and great glass beads from Venway—the usual pedlar's lot. Everyone on Sattins Island came to look, to chat with the voyager, and perhaps to buy something—"Just to remember him by!" cackled Goody Guld, who like all the women and girls of the village was smitten with Blackbeard's bold good looks. All the boys hung round him too, to hear him tell of his voyages to far, strange islands of the Reach or describe the great rich islands of the Archipelago, the Inner Lanes, the roadsteads white with ships, and the golden roofs of Havnor. The men willingly listened to his tales; but some of them wondered why a trader should sail alone, and kept their eyes thoughtfully upon his oaken staff.

But all this time Mr. Underhill stayed under his hill.

"This is the first island I've ever seen that had no wizard," said Blackbeard one evening to Goody Guld, who had invited him and her nephew and Palani in for a cup of rushwash tea. "What do you do when you get a toothache, or the cow goes dry?"

"Why, we've got Mr. Underhill!" said the old woman.

"For what that's worth," muttered her nephew Birt, and then blushed purple and spilled his tea. Birt was a fisherman, a large, brave, wordless young man. He loved the schoolmistress, but the nearest he had come to telling her of his love was to give baskets of fresh mackerel to her father's cook.

"Oh, you do have a wizard?" Blackbeard asked. "Is he invisible?"

"No, he's just very shy," said Palani. "You've only been here a week, you know, and we see so few strangers here . . ." She also blushed a little, but did not spill her tea.

Blackbeard smiled at her. "He's a good Sattinsman, then, eh?"

"No," said Goody Guld, "no more than you are. Another cup, nevvy? Keep it in the cup this time. No, my dear, he came in a little bit of a boat, four years ago was it? Just a day after the end of the shad run, I recall, for they was taking up the nets over in East Creek, and Pondi Cowherd broke his leg that very morning—five years ago it must be. No, four. No, five it is, 'twas the year the garlic didn't sprout. So he sails in on a bit of a sloop loaded full up with great chests and boxes and says to Seacaptain Fogeno, who wasn't blind then, though old enough goodness knows to be blind twice over, 'I hear tell,' he says, 'you've got no wizard nor warlock at all, might you be wanting one?'—'Indeed, if the magic's white!' says the Captain, and before you could say cuttlefish Mr. Underhill had settled down in the cave under the hill and was charming the mange off Goody Beltow's cat. Though the fur grew in gray, and 'twas an orange cat. Queer-looking thing it was after that. It died last winter in the cold spell. Goody Beltow took on so at that cat's death, poor thing, worse than when her man was drowned on the Long Banks, the year of the long herring-runs, when nevvy Birt here was but a babe in petticoats." Here Birt spilled his tea again, and Blackbeard grinned, but Goody Guld proceeded undismayed, and talked on till nightfall.

Next day Blackbeard was down at the pier, seeing after the sprung board in his boat which he seemed to take a long time fixing, and as usual drawing the taciturn Sattinsmen into talk. "Now which of these is your wizard's craft?" he asked. "Or has he got one of those the Mages fold up into a walnut shell when they're not using it?"

"Nay," said a stolid fisherman. "She's oop in his cave, under hill."

"He carried the boat he came in up to his cave?"

"Aye. Clear oop. I helped. Heavier as lead she was. Full oop with great boxes, and they full oop with books o' spells, he says. Heavier as lead she was." And the solid fisherman turned his back, signing stolidly. Goody Guld's nephew, mending a net nearby, looked up from his work and asked with equal stolidity, "Would ye like to meet Mr. Underhill, maybe?"

Blackbeard returned Birt's look. Clever black eyes met candid blue ones for a long moment; then Blackbeard smiled and said, "Yes. Will you take me up to the hill, Birt?"

"Aye, when I'm done with this," said the fisherman. And when the net was mended, he and the Archipelagan set off up the village street towards the high green hill above it. But as they crossed the common Blackbeard said, "Hold on a while, friend Birt. I have a tale to tell you, before we meet your wizard."

"Tell away," said Birt, sitting down in the shade of a live-oak.

"It's a story that started a hundred years ago, and isn't finished yet—though it soon will be, very soon . . . In the very heart of the Archipelago, where the island crowd thick as flies on honey, there's a little isle called Pendor. The sealords of Pendor were mighty men, in the old days of war before the League. Loot and ransom and tribute came pouring into Pendor, and they gathered a great treasure there, long ago. Then from somewhere away out in the West Reach, where dragons breed on the lava isles, came one day a very mighty dragon. Not one of those overgrown lizards most of you Outer Reach folk call dragons, but a big, black, winged, wise, cunning monster, full of strength and subtlety, and like all dragons loving gold and precious stones above all things. He killed the Sealord and his soldiers, and the people of Pendor fled in their ships by night. They all fled away and left the dragon coiled up in Pendor Towers. And there he stayed for a hundred years, dragging his scaly belly over the emeralds and sapphires and coins of gold, coming forth only once in a year or two when he must eat. He'd raid nearby islands for his food. You know what dragons eat?"

Birt nodded and said in a whisper, "Maidens."

"Right," said Blackbeard. "Well, that couldn't be endured forever, nor the thought of him sitting on all that treasure. So after the League grew strong, and the Archipelago wasn't so busy with wars and piracy, it was decided to attack Pendor, drive out the dragon, and get the gold and jewels for the treasury of the League. They're forever wanting money, the League is. So a huge fleet gathered from fifty islands, and seven Mages stood in the prows of the seven strongest ships, and they sailed toward Pendor . . . They got there. They landed. Nothing stirred. The houses all stood empty, the dishes on the tables full of a hundred years' dust. The bones of the old Sealord and his men lay about in the castle courts and on the stairs. And the tower rooms reeked of dragon. But there was no dragon. And no treasure, not a diamond the size of a poppy seed, not a single silver bead . . . Knowing that he couldn't stand up to seven Mages, the dragon had skipped out. They tracked him, and found he'd flown to a deserted island up north called Udrath; they followed his trail there, and what did they find? Bones again. His bones—the dragon's. But no treasure. A wizard, some unknown wizard from somewhere, must have met him singlehanded, and defeated him—and then made off with the treasure, right under the League's nose!"

The fisherman listened, attentive and expressionless.

"Now that must have been a powerful wizard and a clever one, first to kill a dragon, and second to get off without leaving a trace. The lords and Mages of the Archipelago couldn't track him at all, neither where he'd come from nor where he'd made off to. They were about to give up. That was last spring; I'd been off on a three-year voyage up in the North Reach, and got back about that time. And they asked me to help them find the unknown wizard. That was clever of them. Because I'm not only a wizard myself, as I think some of the oafs here have guessed, but I am also a descendant of the Lords of Pendor. That treasure is mine. It's mine, and knows that it's mine. Those fools of the League couldn't find it, because it's not theirs. It belongs to the House of Pendor, and the great emerald, the star of the hoard, Inalkil the Greenstone, knows its master. Behold!" Blackbeard raised his oaken staff and cried aloud, "Inalkil!" The tip of the staff began to glow green, a fiery green radiance, a dazzling haze the color of April grass, and at the same moment the staff tipped in the wizard's hand, leaning, slanting till it pointed straight at the side of the hill above them.

"It wasn't so bright a glow, far away in Havnor," Blackbeard murmured, "but the staff pointed true. Inalkil answered when I called.

The jewel knows its master. And I know the thief, and I shall conquer him. He's a mighty wizard, who could overcome a dragon. But I am mightier. Do you want to know why, oaf? Because I know his name!"

As Blackbeard's tone got more arrogant, Birt had looked duller and duller, blanker and blanker; but at this he gave a twitch, shut his mouth, and stared at the Archipelagan. "How did you . . . learn it?" he asked very slowly.

Blackbeard grinned, and did not answer.

"Black magic?"

"How else?"

Birt looked pale, and said nothing.

"I am the Sealord of Pendor, oaf, and I will have the gold my fathers won, and the jewels my mothers wore, and the Greenstone! For they are mine. Now, you can tell your village boobies the whole story after I have defeated this wizard and gone. Wait here. Or you can come and watch, if you're not afraid. You'll never get the chance again to see a great wizard in all his power." Blackbeard turned, and without a backward glance strode off up the hill towards the entrance to the cave.

Very slowly, Birt followed. A good distance from the cave he stopped, sat down under a hawthorn tree, and watched. The Archipelagan had stopped; a stiff, dark figure alone on the green swell of the hill before the gaping cave mouth, he stood perfectly still. All at once he swung his staff up over his head, and the emerald radiance shone about him as he shouted, "Thief, thief of the Hoard of Pendor, come forth!"

There was a crash, as of dropped crockery, from inside the cave, and a lot of dust came spewing out. Scared, Birt ducked. When he looked again he saw Blackbeard still standing motionless, and at the mouth of the cave, dusty and dishevelled, stood Mr. Underhill. He looked small and pitiful, with his toes turned in as usual, and his little bowlegs in black tights, and no staff—he never had had one, Birt suddenly thought. Mr. Underhill spoke. "Who are you?" he said in his husky little voice.

"I am the Sealord of Pendor, thief, come to claim my treasure!"

*   *   *

At that, Mr. Underhill slowly turned pink, as he always did when people were rude to him. But he then turned something else. He turned yellow. His hair bristled out, he gave a coughing roar—and was a yellow lion leaping down the hill at Blackbeard, white fangs gleaming.

But Blackbeard no longer stood there. A gigantic tiger, color of night and lightning, bounded to meet the lion . . .

The lion was gone. Below the cave all of a sudden stood a high grove of trees, black in the winter sunshine. The tiger, checking himself in mid-leap just before he entered the shadow of the trees, caught fire in the air, became a tongue of flame lashing out at the dry black branches . . .

But where the trees had stood a sudden cataract leaped from the hillside, an arch of silvery crashing water, thundering down upon the fire. But the fire was gone . . .

For just a moment before the fisherman's staring eyes two hills rose—the green one he knew, and a new one, a bare, brown hillock ready to drink up the rushing waterfall. That passed so quickly it made Birt blink, and after blinking he blinked again, and moaned, for what he saw now was a great deal worse. Where the cataract had been there hovered a dragon. Black wings darkened all the hill, steel claws reached groping, and from the dark, scaly, gaping lips fire and steam shot out.

Beneath the monstrous creature stood Blackbeard, laughing.

"Take any shape you please, little Mr. Underhill!" he taunted. "I can match you. But the game grows tiresome. I want to look upon my treasure, upon Inalkil. Now, big dragon, little wizard, take your true shape. I command you by the power of your truename—Yevaud!"

Birt could not move at all, not even to blink. He cowered staring whether he would or not. He saw the black dragon hang there in the air above Blackbeard. He saw the fire lick like many tongues from the scaly mouth, the steam jet from the red nostrils. He saw Blackbeard's face grow white, white as chalk, and the beard-fringed lips trembling.

"Your name is Yevaud!"

"Yes," said a great, husky, hissing voice. "My truename is Yevaud, and my true shape is this shape."

"But the dragon was killed—they found dragon-bones on Udrath Island—"

"That was another dragon," said the dragon, and then stooped like a hawk, talons outstretched. And Birt shut his eyes.

When he opened them the sky was clear, the hillside empty, except for a reddish-blackish, trampled spot, and a few talon-marks in the grass.

Birt the fisherman got to his feet and ran. He ran across the common, scattering sheep to right and left, and straight down the village street to Palani's father's house. Palani was out in the garden weeding the nasturtiums. "Come with me!" Birt gasped. She stared. He grabbed her wrist and dragged her with him. She screeched a little, but did not resist. He ran with her straight to the pier, pushed her into his fishing-sloop the *Queenie*, untied the painter, took up the oars and set off rowing like a demon. The last that Sattins Island saw of him and Palani was the *Queenie*'s sail vanishing in the direction of the nearest island westward.

The villagers thought they would never stop talking about it, how Goody Guld's nephew Birt had lost his mind and sailed off with the schoolmistress on the very same day that the pedlar Blackbeard disappeared without a trace, leaving all his feathers and beads behind. But they did stop talking about it, three days later. They had other things to talk about, when Mr. Underhill finally came out of his cave.

Mr. Underhill had decided that since his truename was no longer a secret, he might as well drop his disguise. Walking was a lot harder than flying, and besides, it was a long, long time since he had had a real meal.

St. Dragon and the George

□ □ □

by Gordon R. Dickson

I

A trifle diffidently, Jim Eckert rapped with his claw on the blue-painted door.

Silence.

He knocked again. There was the sound of a hasty step inside the small, oddly peak-roofed house and the door was snatched open. A thin-faced old man with a tall pointed cap and a long, rather dingy-looking white beard peered out, irritably.

"Sorry, not my day for dragons!" he snapped. "Come back next Tuesday." He slammed the door.

It was too much. It was the final straw. Jim Eckert sat down on his haunches with a dazed thump. The little forest clearing with its impossible little pool tinkling away like Chinese glass wind chimes in the background, its well-kept greensward with the white gravel path leading to the door before him, and the riotous flower beds of asters, tulips, zinnias, roses and lilies-of-the-valley all equally impossibly in bloom at the same time about the white fingerpost labelled S. CAR-OLINUS and pointing at the house—it all whirled about him. It was more than flesh and blood could bear. At any minute now he would go completely insane and imagine he was a peanut or a cocker spaniel. Grottwold Hanson had wrecked them all. Dr. Howells would have to get another teaching assistant for his English Department. Angie . . .

Angie!

Jim pounded on the door again. It was snatched open.

"Dragon!" cried S. Carolinus, furiously. "How would you like to be a beetle?"

"But I'm not a dragon," said Jim, desperately.

The magician stared at him for a long minute, then threw up his beard with both hands in a gesture of despair, caught some of it in his teeth as it fell down and began to chew on it fiercely.

"Now where," he demanded, "did a dragon acquire the brains to develop the imagination to entertain the illusion that he is *not* a dragon? Answer me, O Ye Powers!"

"The information is psychically, though not physiologically correct," replied a deep bass voice out of thin air beside them and some five feet off the ground. Jim, who had taken the question to be rhetorical, started convulsively.

"Is that so?" S. Carolinus peered at Jim with new interest. "Hmm." He spat out a hair or two. "Come in, Anomaly—or whatever you call yourself."

Jim squeezed in through the door and found himself in a large single room. It was a clutter of mismatched furniture and odd bits of alchemical equipment.

"Hmm," said S. Carolinus, closing the door and walking once around Jim, thoughtfully. "If you aren't a dragon, what are you?"

"Well, my real name's Jim Eckert," said Jim. "But I seem to be in the body of a dragon named Gorbash."

"And this disturbs you. So you've come to me. How nice," said the magician, bitterly. He winced, massaged his stomach and closed his eyes. "Do you know anything that's good for a perpetual stomach-ache? Of course not. Go on."

"Well, I want to get back to my real body. And take Angie with me. She's my fiancée and I can send her back but I can't send myself back at the same time. You see, this Grottwold Hanson—well, maybe I better start from the beginning."

"Brilliant suggestion, Gorbash," said Carolinus. "Or whatever your name is," he added.

"Well," said Jim. Carolinus winced. Jim hurried on. "I teach at a place called Riveroak College in the United States—you've never heard of it—"

"Go on, go on," said Carolinus.

"That is, I'm a teaching assistant. Dr. Howells, who heads the English Department, promised me an instructorship over a year ago. But he's never come through with it; and Angie—Angie Gilman, my fiancée—"

"You mentioned her."

"Yes—well, we were having a little fight. That is, we were arguing about my going to ask Howells whether he was going to give me the instructor's rating for next year or not. I didn't think I should; and she didn't think we could get married—well, anyway, in came Grottwold Hanson."

"In *where* came *who*?"

"Into the Campus Bar and Grille. We were having a drink there. Hanson used to go with Angie. He's a graduate student in psychology. A long, thin geek that's just as crazy as he looks. He's always getting wound up in some new odd-ball organization or other—"

"Dictionary!" interrupted Carolinus, suddenly. He opened his eyes as an enormous volume appeared suddenly poised in the air before him. He massaged his stomach. "Ouch," he said. The pages of the volume began to flip rapidly back and forth before his eyes. "Don't mind me," he said to Jim. "Go on."

"—This time it was the Bridey Murphy craze. Hypnotism. Well—"

"Not so fast," said Carolinus. "*Bridey Murphy . . . Hypnotism . . .* yes . . ."

"Oh, he talked about the ego wandering, planes of reality, on and on like that. He offered to hypnotize one of us and show us how it worked. Angie was mad at me, so she said yes. I went off to the bar. I was mad. When I turned around, Angie was gone. Disappeared."

"Vanished?" said Carolinus.

"Vanished. I blew my top at Hanson. She must have wandered, he said, not merely the ego, but all of her. Bring her back, I said. I can't, he said. It seemed she wanted to go back to the time of St. George and the Dragon. When men were men and would speak up to their bosses about promotions. Handson'd have to send someone else back to rehypnotize her and send her back home. Like an idiot I said I'd go. Ha! I might've known he'd goof. He couldn't do anything right if he was paid for it. I landed in the body of this dragon."

"And the maiden?"

"Oh, she landed here, too. Centuries off the mark. A place where there actually were such things as dragons—fantastic."

"Why?" said Carolinus.

"Well, I mean—anyway," said Jim, hurriedly. "The point is, they'd already got her—the dragons, I mean. A big brute named Anark had found her wandering around and put her in a cage. They were having a meeting in a cave about deciding what to do with her. Anark wanted to stake her out for a decoy, so they could capture a lot of the local people—only the dragons called people *georges*—"

"They're quite stupid, you know," said Carolinus, severely, looking up from the dictionary. "There's only room for one name in their head at a time. After the Saint made such an impression on them his name stuck."

"Anyway, they were all yelling at once. They've got tremendous voices."

"Yes, you have," said Carolinus, pointedly.

"Oh, sorry," said Jim. He lowered his voice. "I tried to argue that we ought to hold Angie for ransom—" He broke off suddenly. "Say," he said. "I never thought of that. Was I talking dragon, then? What am I talking now? Dragons don't talk English, do they?"

"Why not?" demanded Carolinus, grumpily. "If they're British dragons?"

"But I'm not a dragon—I mean—"

"But you *are* here!" snapped Carolinus. "You and this maiden of yours. Since all the rest of you was translated here, don't you suppose your ability to speak understandably was translated, too? Continue."

"There's not much more," said Jim, gloomily. "I was losing the argument and then this very big, old dragon spoke up on my side. Hold Angie for ransom, he said. And they listened to him. It seems he swings a lot of weight among them. He's a great-uncle of me—of this Gorbash who's body I'm in—and I'm his only surviving relative. They penned Angie up in a cave and he sent me off to the Tinkling Water here, to find you and have you open negotiations for ransom. Actually, on the side he told me to tell you to make the terms easy on the georges—I mean humans; he wants the dragons to work toward good relations with them. He's afraid the dragons are in danger of being wiped out. I had a chance to double back and talk to Angie alone. We thought you might be able to send us both back."

He stopped rather out of breath, and looked hopefully at Carolinus. The magician was chewing thoughtfully on his beard.

"Smrgol," he muttered. "Now there's an exception to the rule. Very bright for a dragon. Also experienced. Hmm."

"Can you help us?" demanded Jim. "Look, I can show you—"

Carolinus sighed, closed his eyes, winced and opened them again.

"Let me see if I've got this straight," he said. "You had a dispute with this maiden to whom you're betrothed. To spite you, she turned to this third-rate practitioner, who mistakenly exorcised her from the United States (wherever in the cosmos that is) to here, further compounding his error by sending you back in spirit only to inhabit the body of Gorbash. The maiden is in the hands of the dragons and you have been sent to me by your great-uncle Smrgol."

"That's sort of it," said Jim dubiously, "only—"

"You wouldn't," said Carolinus, "care to change your story to something simpler and more reasonable—like being a prince changed into a dragon by some wicked fairy stepmother? Oh, my poor stomach! No?" He sighed. "All right, that'll be five hundred pounds of gold, or five pounds of rubies, in advance."

"B-but—" Jim goggled at him. "But I don't have any gold—or rubies."

"What? What kind of a dragon are you?" cried Carolinus, glaring at him. "Where's your hoard?"

"I suppose this Gorbash has one," stammered Jim, unhappily. "But I don't know anything about it."

"Another charity patient!" muttered Carolinus, furiously. He shook his fist at empty space. "What's wrong with that auditing department? Well?"

"Sorry," said the invisible bass voice.

"That's the third in two weeks. See it doesn't happen again for another ten days." He turned to Jim. "No means of payment?"

"No. Wait—" said Jim. "This stomach-ache of yours. It might be an ulcer. Does it go away between meals?"

"As a matter of fact, it does. Ulcer?"

"High-strung people working under nervous tension get them back where I come from."

"People?" inquired Carolinus suspiciously. "Or dragons?"

"There aren't any dragons where I come from."

"All right, all right, I believe you," said Carolinus, testily. "You don't have to stretch the truth like that. How do you exorcise them?"

"Milk," said Jim. "A glass every hour for a month or two."

"Milk," said Carolinus. He held out his hand to the open air and received a small tankard of it. He drank it off, making a face. After a moment, the face relaxed into a smile.

"By the Powers!" he said. "By the Powers!" He turned to Jim, beaming. "Congratulations, Gorbash, I'm beginning to believe you about that college business after all. The bovine nature of the milk quite smothers the ulcer-demon. Consider me paid."

"Oh, fine. I'll go get Angie and you can hypnotize—"

"What?" cried Carolinus. "Teach your grandmother to suck eggs. Hypnotize! Ha! And what about the First Law of Magic, eh?"

"The what?" said Jim.

"The First Law—the First Law—didn't they teach you anything in that college? Forgotten it already, I see. Oh, this younger generation! The First Law: *for every use of the Art and Science, there is required a corresponding price.* Why do I live by my fees instead of by conjurations? Why does a magic potion have a bad taste? Why did this Hanson-amateur of yours get you all into so much trouble?"

"I don't know," said Jim. "Why?"

"No credit! No credit!" barked Carolinus, flinging his skinny arms wide. "Why, I wouldn't have tried what he did without ten years credit with the auditing department, and *I* am a Master of the Arts. As it was, he couldn't get anything more than your spirit back, after sending the maiden complete. And the fabric of Chance and History is all warped and ready to spring back and cause all kinds of trouble. We'll have to give a little, take a little—"

"GORBASH!" A loud thud outside competed with the dragon-bellow.

"And here we go, " said Carolinus dourly. "It's already starting." He led the way outside. Sitting on the greensward just beyond the flower beds was an enormous old dragon Jim recognized as the great-uncle of the body he was in—Smrgol.

"Greetings, Mage!" boomed the old dragon, dropping his head to the ground in salute. "You may not remember me. Name's Smrgol— you remember the business about that ogre I fought at Gormely Keep? I see my grandnephew got to you all right."

"Ah, Smrgol—I remember," said Carolinus. "That was a good job you did."

"He had a habit of dropping his club head after a swing," said Smrgol. "I noticed it along about the fourth hour of battle and the next time he tried it, went in over his guard. Tore up the biceps of his right arm. Then—"

"I remember," Carolinus said. "So this is your nephew."

"Grandnephew," corrected Smrgol. "Little thick-headed and all that," he added apologetically, "but my own flesh and blood, you know."

"You may notice some slight improvement in him," said Carolinus, dryly.

"I hope so," said Smrgol, brightening. "Any change, a change for the better, you know. But I've bad news, Mage. You know that inch-worm of an Anark?"

"The one that found the maiden in the first place?"

"That's right. Well, he's stolen her again and run off."

"*What?*" cried Jim.

He had forgotten the capabilities of a dragon's voice. Carolinus tottered, the flowers and grass lay flat, and even Smrgol winced.

"My boy," said the old dragon reproachfully. "How many times must I tell you not to shout. I said, Anark stole the george."

"He means Angie!" cried Jim desperately to Carolinus.

"I know," said Carolinus, with his hands over his ears.

"You're sneezing again," said Smrgol, proudly. He turned to Carolinus. "You wouldn't believe it. A dragon hasn't sneezed in a hundred and ninety years. This boy did it the first moment he set eyes on the george. The others couldn't believe it. Sign of brains, I said. Busy brains make the nose itch. Our side of the family—"

"*Angie!*"

"See there? All right now, boy, you've shown us you can do it. Let's get down to business. How much to locate Anark and the george, Mage?"

They dickered like rug-pedlars for several minutes, finally settling on a price of four pounds of gold, one of silver, and a flawed emerald. Carolinus got a small vial of water from the Tinkling Spring and searched among the grass until he found a small sandy open spot. He bent over it and the two dragons sat down to watch.

"Quiet now," he warned. "I'm going to try a watch-beetle. Don't alarm it."

Jim held his breath. Carolinus tilted the vial in his hand and the crystal water fell in three drops—*Tink! Tink!* And again—*Tink!* The sand darkened with the moisture and began to work as if something was digging from below. A hole widened, black insect legs busily in action flickered, and an odd-looking beetle popped itself halfway out of the hole. Its forelimbs waved in the air and a little squeaky voice, like a cracked phonograph record repeating itself far away over a bad telephone connection, came to Jim's ears.

"*Gone to the Loathly Tower! Gone to the Loathly Tower! Gone to the Loathly Tower!*"

It popped back out of sight. Carolinus straightened up and Jim breathed again.

"The Loathly Tower!" said Smrgol. "Isn't that that ruined tower to the west, in the fens, Mage? Why, that's the place that loosed the blight on the mere-dragons five hundred years ago."

"It's a place of old magic," said Carolinus, grimly. "These places are like ancient sores on the land, scabbed over for a while but always breaking out with new evil when—the twisting of the Fabric by these two must have done it. The evilness there has drawn the evil in Anark to it—lesser to greater, according to the laws of nature. I'll meet you two there. Now, I must go set other forces in motion."

He began to twirl about. His speed increased rapidly until he was nothing but a blur. Then suddenly, he faded away like smoke; and was gone, leaving Jim staring at the spot where he had been.

A poke in the side brought Jim back to the ordinary world.

"Wake up, boy. Don't dally!" the voice of Smrgol bellowed in his ear. "We got flying to do. Come on!"

II

The old dragon's spirit was considerably younger than his body. It turned out to be a four-hour flight to the fens on the west seacoast. For the first hour or so Smrgol flew along energetically enough, meanwhile tracing out the genealogy of the mere-dragons and their relationship to himself and Gorbash; but gradually his steady flow of chatter dwindled and became intermittent. He tried to joke about his long-gone battle with the Ogre of Gormely Keep, but even this was too much and he fell silent with labored breath and straining wings. After a short but stubborn argument, Jim got him to admit that he would perhaps be better off taking a short breather and then coming on a little later. Smrgol let out a deep gasping sigh and dropped away from Jim in weary spirals. Jim saw him glide to an exhausted landing amongst the purple gorse of the moors below and lie there, sprawled out.

Jim continued on alone. A couple of hours later the moors dropped down a long land-slope to the green country of the fenland. Jim soared out over its spongy, grass-thick earth, broken into causeways and islands by the blue water, which in shallow bays and inlets was itself thick-choked with reeds and tall marsh grass. Flocks of water fowl rose here and there like eddying smoke from the glassy surface of one mere and drifted over to settle on another a few hundred yards away. Their cries came faintly to his dragon-sensitive ears and a line of heavy clouds was piling up against the sunset in the west.

He looked for some sign of the Loathly Tower, but the fenland stretched away to a faint blue line that was probably the sea, without showing sign of anything not built by nature. Jim was beginning to wonder uneasily if he had not gotten himself lost when his eye was suddenly caught by the sight of a dragon-shape nosing at something on one of the little islands amongst the meres.

Anark! he thought. And Angie!

He did not wait to see more. He nosed over and went into a dive like a jet fighter, sights locked on Target Dragon.

It was a good move. Unfortunately Gorbash-Jim, having about the weight and wingspread of a small flivver airplane, made a comparable amount of noise when he was in a dive, assuming the plane's motor to be shut off. Moreover, the dragon on the ground had evidently had experience with the meaning of such a sound; for, without even looking, he went tumbling head over tail out of the way just as Jim slammed into the spot where, a second before, he had been.

The other dragon rolled over onto his feet, sat up, took one look at Jim, and began to wail.

"It's not fair! It's not fair!" he cried in a (for a dragon) remarkably high-pitched voice. "Just because you're bigger than I am. And I'm all horned up. It's the first good one I've been able to kill in months and you don't need it, not at all. You're big and fat and I'm so weak and thin and hungry—"

Jim blinked and stared. What he had thought to be Angie, lying in the grass, now revealed itself to be an old and rather stringy-looking cow, badly bitten up and with a broken neck.

"It's just my luck!" the other dragon was weeping. He was less than three-quarters Jim's size and so emaciated he appeared on the verge of collapse. "Everytime I get something good, somebody takes it away. All I ever get to eat is fish—"

"Hold on," said Jim.

"Fish, fish, fish. Cold, nasty fi—"

"Hold on, I say! SHUT UP!" bellowed Jim, in Gorbash's best voice.

The other dragon stopped his wailing as suddenly as if his switch had been shut off.

"Yes, sir," he said, timidly.

"What's the matter? I'm not going to take this from you."

The other dragon tittered uncertainly.

"I'm not," said Jim. "It's your cow. All yours."

"He-he-he!" said the other dragon. "You certainly are a card, your honor."

"Blast it, I'm serious!" cried Jim. "What's your name, anyway?"

"Oh, well—" the other squirmed. "Oh well, you know—"

"*What's your name?*"

"Secoh, your worship!" yelped the dragon, frightenedly. "Just Secoh. Nobody important. Just a little, unimportant mere-dragon, your highness, that's all I am. Really!"

"All right, Secoh, dig in. All I want is some directions."

"Well—if your worship really doesn't . . ." Secoh had been sidling forward in fawning fashion. "If you'll excuse my table manners, sir. I'm just a mere-dragon—" and he tore into the meat before him in sudden, terrified, starving fashion.

Jim watched. Unexpectedly, his long tongue flickered out to lick his chops. His belly rumbled. He was astounded at himself. Raw meat? Off a dead animal—flesh, bones, hide and all? He took a firm grip on his appetites.

"Er, Secoh," he said. "I'm a stranger around these parts. I suppose you know the territory . . . Say, how does that cow taste, anyway?"

"Oh, terrubble—mumpf—" replied Secoh, with his mouth full. "Stringy—old. Good enough for a mere-dragon like myself, but not—"

"Well, about these directions—"

"Yes, your highness?"

"I think . . . you know it's your cow . . ."

"That's what your honor said," replied Secoh, cautiously.

"But I just wonder . . . you know I've never tasted a cow like that."

Secoh muttered something despairingly under his breath.

"What?" said Jim.

"I said," said Secoh, resignedly, "wouldn't your worship like to t-taste it—"

"Not if you're going to cry about it," said Jim.

"I bit my tongue."

"Well, in that case . . ." Jim walked up and sank his teeth in the shoulder of the carcass. Rich juices trickled enticingly over his tongue . . .

Some little time later he and Secoh sat back polishing bones with the rough uppers of their tongues which were as abrasive as steel files.

"Did you get enough to eat, Secoh?" asked Jim.

"More than enough, sir," replied the mere-dragon, staring at the white skeleton with a wild and famished eye. "Although, if your exaltedness doesn't mind, I've a weakness for marrow . . ." He picked up a thighbone and began to crunch it like a stick of candy.

"Now," said Jim. "About this Loathly Tower. Where is it?"

"The wh-what?" stammered Secoh, dropping the thighbone.

"The Loathly Tower. It's in the fens. You know of it, don't you?"

"Oh, sir! Yes, sir. But you wouldn't want to go there, sir! Not that I'm presuming to give your lordship advice—" cried Secoh, in a suddenly high and terrified voice.

"No, no," soothed Jim. "What are you so upset about?"

"Well—of course I'm only a timid little mere-dragon. But it's a terrible place, the Loathly Tower, your worship, sir."

"How? Terrible?"

"Well—well, it just is." Secoh cast an unhappy look around him. "It's what spoiled all of us, you know, five hundred years ago. We used to be like other dragons—oh, not so big and handsome as you, sir. Then, after that, they say it was the Good got the upper hand and the Evil in the Tower was vanquished and the Tower itself ruined. But it didn't help us mere-dragons any, and I wouldn't go there if I was your worship, I really wouldn't."

"But what's so bad? What sort of thing is it?"

"Well, I wouldn't say there was any real *thing* there. Nothing your worship could put a claw on. It's just strange things go to it and strange things come out of it; and lately . . ."

"Lately what?"

"Nothing—nothing, really, your excellency!" cried Secoh. "Your illustriousness shouldn't catch a worthless little mere-dragon up like that. I only meant, lately the Tower's seemed more fearful than ever. That's all."

"Probably your imagination," said Jim, shortly. "Anyway, where is it?"

"You have to go north about five miles." While they had eaten and talked, the sunset had died. It was almost dark now; and Jim had to strain his eyes through the gloom to see the mere-dragon's foreclaw, pointing away across the mere. "To the Great Causeway. It's a wide lane of solid ground running east and west through the fens. You follow it west to the Tower. The Tower stands on a rock overlooking the sea-edge."

"Five miles . . ." said Jim. He considered the soft grass on which he lay. His armored body seemed undisturbed by the temperature, whatever it was. "I might as well get some sleep. See you in the morning, Secoh." He obeyed a sudden, birdlike instinct and tucked his ferocious head and long neck back under one wing.

"Whatever your excellency desires . . ." the mere-dragon's muffled voice came distantly to his ear. "Your excellency has only to call and I'll be immediately available . . ."

The words faded out on Jim's ear, as he sank into sleep like a heavy stone into deep, dark waters.

When he opened his eyes, the sun was up. He sat up himself, yawned, and blinked.

Secoh was gone. So were the leftover bones.

"Blast!" said Jim. But the morning was too nice for annoyance. He smiled at his mental picture of Secoh carefully gathering the bones in fearful silence, and sneaking them away.

The smile did not last long. When he tried to take off in a northerly direction, as determined by reference to the rising sun, he found he had charley horses in both the huge wing-muscles that swelled out under the armor behind his shoulders. The result, of course, of yesterday's heavy exercise. Grumbling, he was forced to proceed on foot; and four hours later, very hot, muddy and wet, he pulled his weary body up onto the broad east-and-west-stretching strip of land which must, of necessity, be the Great Causeway. It ran straight as a Roman road through the meres, several feet higher than the rest of the fenland, and was solid enough to support good-sized trees. Jim collapsed in the shade of one with a heartfelt sigh.

He awoke to the sound of someone singing. He blinked and lifted his head. Whatever the earlier verses of the song had been, Jim had missed them; but the approaching baritone voice now caroled the words of the chorus merrily and clearly to his ear:

> *"A right good sword, a constant mind,*
> *A trusty spear and true!*
> *The dragons of the mere shall find*
> *What Nevile-Smythe can do!"*

The tune and words were vaguely familiar. Jim sat up for a better look and a knight in full armor rode into view on a large white horse through the trees. Then everything happened at once. The knight saw him, the visor of his armor came down with a clang, his long spear seemed to jump into his mailed hand and the horse under him leaped into a gallop, heading for Jim. Gorbash's reflexes took over. They hurled Jim straight up into the air, where his punished wing-muscles cracked and faltered. He was just able to manage enough of a fluttering flop to throw himself into the upper branches of a small tree nearby.

The knight skidded his horse to a stop below and looked up through the spring-budded branches. He tilted his visor back to reveal a piercing pair of blue eyes, a rather hawk-like nose and a jutting generous chin, all assembled into a clean-shaven young-man's face. He looked eagerly up at Jim.

"Come down," he said.

"No thanks," said Jim, hanging firmly to the tree. There was a slight pause as they both digested the situation.

"Dashed caitiff mere-dragon!" said the knight finally, with annoyance.

"I'm not a mere-dragon," said Jim,

"Oh, don't talk rot!" said the knight.

"I'm not," repeated Jim. He thought a minute. "I'll bet you can't guess who I really am."

The knight did not seem interested in guessing who Jim really was. He stood up in his stirrups and probed through the branches with his spear. The point did not quite reach Jim.

"Damn!" Disappointedly, he lowered the spear and became thoughtful. "I can climb the dashed tree," he muttered to himself. "But then what if he flies down and I have to fight him unhorsed, eh?"

"Look," called Jim, peering down—the knight looked up eagerly—"if you'll listen to what I've to say, first."

The knight considered.

"Fair enough," he said, finally. "No pleas for mercy, now!"

"No, no," said Jim.

"Because I shan't grant them, dammit! It's not in my vows. Widows and orphans and honorable enemies on the field of battle. But not dragons."

"No. I just want to convince you who I really am."

"I don't give a blasted farthing who you really are."

"You will," said Jim. "Because I'm not really a dragon at all. I've just been—uh—enchanted into a dragon."

The man on the ground looked skeptical.

"Really," said Jim, slipping a little in the tree. "You know S. Carolinus, the magician? I'm as human as you are."

"Heard of him, " grunted the knight. "You say *he* put you under?"

"No, he's the one who's going to change me back—as soon as I can find the lady I'm—er—betrothed to. A real dragon ran off with her. I'm after him. Look at me. Do I look like one of these scrawny mere-dragons?"

"Hmm," said the knight. He rubbed his hooked nose thoughtfully.

"Carolinus found she's at the Loathly Tower. I'm on my way there."

The knight stared.

"The Loathly Tower?" he echoed.

"Exactly," said Jim, firmly. "And now you know, your honor as knight and gentleman demands you don't hamper my rescue efforts."

The knight continued to think it over for a long moment or two. He was evidently not the sort to be rushed into things.

"How do I know you're telling the truth!" he said at last.

"Hold your sword up. I'll swear on the cross of its hilt."

"But if you're a dragon, what's the good in that? Dragons don't have souls, dammit!"

"No," said Jim, "but a Christian gentleman has; and if I'm a Christian gentleman, I wouldn't dare forswear myself like that, would I?"

The knight struggled visibly with this logic for several seconds. Finally, he gave up.

"Oh, well . . ." He held up his sword by the point and let Jim swear on it. Then he put the sword back in its sheath as Jim descended. "Well," he said, still a little doubtfully, "I suppose, under the circumstances, we ought to introduce ourselves. You know my arms?"

Jim looked at the shield which the other swung around for his inspection. It showed a wide X of silver—like a cross lying over sideways—on a red background and above some sort of black animal in profile which seemed to be lying down between the X's bottom legs.

"The gules, a saltire argent, of course," went on the knight, "are the Nevile of Raby arms. My father, as a cadet of the house, differenced with a hart lodged sable—you see it there at the bottom. Naturally, as his heir, I carry the family arms."

"Nevile-Smythe," said Jim, remembering the name from the song.

"Sir Reginald, knight bachelor. And you, sir?"

"Why, uh . . ." Jim clutched frantically at what he knew of heraldry. "I bear—in my proper body, that is—"

"Quite."

"A . . . gules, a typewriter argent, on a desk sable. Eckert, Sir James—uh—knight bachelor. Baron of—er—Riveroak."

Nevile-Smythe was knitting his brows.

"Typewriter . . ." he was muttering, "typewriter . . ."

"A local beast, rather like a griffin," said Jim, hastily. "We have a lot of them in Riveroak—that's in America, a land over the sea to the west. You may not have heard of it."

"Can't say that I have. Was it there you were enchanted into this dragon-shape?"

"Well, yes and no. I was transported to this land by magic as was the uh—Lady Angela. When I woke here I was bedragoned."

"Were you?" Sir Reginald's blue eyes bulged a little in amazement. "Angela—fair name, that! Like to meet her. Perhaps after we get this muddle cleared up, we might have a bit of a set-to on behalf of our respective ladies."

Jim gulped slightly.

"Oh, you've got one, too?"

"Absolutely. And she's tremendous. The Lady Elinor—" The knight turned about in his saddle and began to fumble about his equipment. Jim, on reaching the ground, had at once started out along the causeway in the direction of the Tower, so that the knight happened to be pacing alongside him on horseback when he suddenly went into these evolutions. It seemed to bother his charger not at all. "Got her favor here someplace—half a moment—"

"Why don't you just tell me what it's like?" said Jim, sympathetically.

"Oh, well," said Nevile-Smythe, giving up his search, "it's a kerchief, you know. Monogrammed. E. d'C. She's a deChauncy. It's rather too bad, though. I'd have liked to show it to you since we're going to the Loathly Tower together."

"We are?" said Jim, startled. "But—I mean, it's my job. I didn't think you'd want—"

"Lord, yes," said Nevile-Smythe, looking somewhat startled himself. "A gentleman of coat-armor like myself—and an outrage like this taking place locally. I'm no knight-errant, dash it, but I *do* have a decent sense of responsibility."

"I mean—I just meant—" stumbled Jim. "What if something happened to you? What would the Lady Elinor say?"

"Why, what could she say?" replied Nevile-Smythe in plain astonishment. "No one but an utter rotter dodges his plain duty. Besides, there may be a chance here for me to gain a little worship. Elinor's keen on that. She wants me to come home safe."

Jim blinked.

"I don't get it," he said.

"Beg pardon?"

Jim explained his confusion.

"Why, how do you people do things overseas?" said Nevile-Smythe. "After we're married and I have lands of my own, I'll be expected to raise a company and march out at my lord's call. If I've no name as a knight, I'll be able to raise nothing but bumpkins and clodpoles who'll desert at the first sight of steel. On the other hand, if I've a name, I'll have good men coming to serve under my banner; because, you see, they know I'll take good care of them; and by the same token they'll take good care of me—I say, isn't it getting dark rather suddenly?"

Jim glanced at the sky. It was indeed—almost the dimness of twilight although it could, by rights, be no more than early afternoon yet. Glancing ahead up the Causeway, he became aware of a further phenomenon. A line seemed to be cutting across the trees and grass and even extending out over the waters of the meres on both sides. Moreover, it seemed to be moving toward them as if some heavy, invisible fluid was slowly flooding out over the low country of the fenland.

"Why—" he began. A voice wailed suddenly from his left to interrupt him.

"No! No! Turn back, your worship. Turn back! It's death in there!"

They turned their heads sharply. Secoh, the mere-dragon, sat perched on a half-drowned tussock about forty feet out in the mere.

"Come here, Secoh!" called Jim.

"No! No!" The invisible line was almost to the tussock. Secoh lifted heavily into the air and flapped off, crying. "Now it's loose! It's broken loose again. And we're all lost . . . lost . . . lost . . ."

His voice wailed away and was lost in the distance. Jim and Nevile-Smythe looked at each other.

"Now, that's one of our local dragons for you!" said the knight disgustedly. "How can a gentleman of coat armor gain honor by slaying a beast like that? The worst of it is when someone from the Midlands compliments you on being a dragonslayer and you have to explain—"

At that moment either they both stepped over the line, or the line moved past them—Jim was never sure which; and they both stopped, as by one common, instinctive impulse. Looking at Sir Reginald, Jim could see under the visor how the knight's face had gone pale.

"In manus tuas Domine," said Nevile-Smythe, crossing himself.

About and around them, the serest gray of winter light lay on the fens. The waters of the meres lay thick and oily, still between the shores of dull green grass. A small, cold breeze wandered through the tops of the reeds and they rattled together with a dry and distant sound like old bones cast out into a forgotten courtyard for the wind to play with. The trees stood helpless and still, their new, small leaves now pinched and faded like children aged before their time while all about and over all the heaviness of dead hope and bleak despair lay on all living things.

"Sir James," said the knight, in an odd tone and accents such as Jim had not heard him use before, "wot well that we have this day set our hands to no small task. Wherefore I pray thee that we should push forward, come what may, for my heart faileth and I think me that it may well hap that I return not, ne no man know mine end."

Having said this, he immediately reverted to his usual cheerful self and swung down out of his saddle. "Clairvaux won't go another inch, dash it!" he said. "I shall have to lead him—by the bye, did you know that mere-dragon?"

Jim fell into step beside him and they went on again, but a little more slowly, for everything seemed an extra effort under this darkening sky.

"I talked to him yesterday," said Jim. "He's not a bad sort of dragon."

"Oh, I've nothing against the beasts, myself. But one slays them when one finds them, you know."

"An old dragon—in fact he's the granduncle of this body I'm in," said Jim, "thinks that dragons and humans really ought to get together. Be friends, you know."

"Extraordinary thought!" said Nevile-Smythe, staring at Jim in astonishment.

"Well, actually," said Jim, "why not?"

"Well, I don't know. It just seems like it wouldn't do."

"He says men and dragons might find common foes to fight together."

"Oh, that's where he's wrong, though. You couldn't trust dragons to stick by you in a bicker. And what if your enemy had dragons of his own? They wouldn't fight each other. No. No."

They fell silent. They had moved away from the grass onto flat sandy soil. There was a sterile, flinty hardness to it. It crunched under the hooves of Clarivaux, at once unyielding and treacherous.

"Getting darker, isn't it?" said Jim, finally.

The light was, in fact, now down to a grayish twilight, through which it was impossible to see more than a dozen feet. And it was dwindling as they watched. They had halted and stood facing each other. The light fled steadily, and faster. The dimness became blacker, and blacker—until finally the last vestige of illumination was lost and blackness, total and complete, overwhelmed them. Jim felt a gauntleted hand touch one of his forelimbs.

"Let's hold together," said the voice of the knight. "Then whatever comes upon us, must come upon us all at once."

"Right," said Jim. But the word sounded cold and dead in his throat.

They stood, in silence and in lightlessness, waiting for they did not know what. And the blankness about them pressed further in on them, now that it had isolated them, nibbling at the very edges of their minds. Out of the nothingness came nothing material, but from within them crept up one by one, like blind white slugs from some bottomless pit, all their inner doubts and fears and unknown weaknesses, all the things of which they had been ashamed and which they had tucked away to forget, all the maggots of their souls.

Jim found himself slowly, stealthily beginning to withdraw his forelimb from under the knight's touch. He no longer trusted Nevile-Smythe—for the evil that must be in the man because of the evil he knew to be in himself. He would move away . . . off into the darkness alone . . .

"Look!" Nevile-Smythe's voice cried suddenly to him, distant and eerie, as if from someone already a long way off. "Look back the way we came."

Jim turned about. Far off in the darkness, there was a distant glimmer of light. It rolled toward them, growing as it came. They felt its power against the power of lightlessness that threatened to overwhelm them; and the horse Clarivaux stirred unseen beside them, stamped his hooves on the hard sand, and whinnied.

"This way!" called Jim.

"This way!" shouted Nevile-Smythe.

The light shot up suddenly in height. Like a great rod it advanced toward them and the darkness was rolling back, graying, disappearing. They heard a sound of feet close, and a sound of breathing, and then—

It was daylight again.

And S. Carolinus stood before them in tall hat and robes figured with strange images and signs. In his hand upright before him—as if it was blade and buckler, spear and armor all in one—he held a tall carven staff of wood.

"By the Powers!" he said. "I was in time. Look there!"

He lifted the staff and drove it point down into the soil. It went in and stood erect like some denuded tree. His long arm pointed past them and they turned around.

The darkness was gone. The fens lay revealed far and wide, stretching back a long way, and up ahead, meeting the thin dark line of the sea. The Causeway had risen until they now stood twenty feet above the mere-waters. Ahead to the west, the sky was ablaze with sunset. It lighted up all the fens and the end of the Causeway leading onto a long and bloody-looking hill, whereon—touched by that same dying light—there loomed above and over all, amongst great tumbled boulders, the ruined, dark and shattered shell of a Tower as black as jet.

III

"—why didn't you wake us earlier, then?" asked Jim.

It was the morning after. They had slept the night within the small circle of protection afforded by Carolinus' staff. They were sitting up now and rubbing their eyes in the light of a sun that had certainly been above the horizon a good two hours.

"Because," said Carolinus. He was sipping at some more milk and he stopped to make a face of distaste. "Because we had to wait for them to catch up with us."

"Who? Catch up?" asked Jim.

"If I knew *who*," snapped Carolinus, handing his empty milk tankard back to emptier air, "I would have said *who*. All I know is that the present pattern of Chance and History implies that two more will join our party. The same pattern implied the presence of this knight and—oh, so that's who they are."

Jim turned around to follow the magician's gaze. To his surprise, two dragon shapes were emerging from a clump of brush behind them.

"Secoh!" cried Jim. "And—Smrgol! Why—" His voice wavered and died. The old dragon, he suddenly noticed, was limping and one wing hung a little loosely, half-drooping from its shoulder. Also, the eyelid on the same side as the loose wing and stiff leg was sagging more or less at half-mast. "Why, what happened?"

"Oh, a bit stiff from yesterday," huffed Smrgol, bluffly. "Probably pass off in a day or two."

"Stiff nothing!" said Jim, touched in spite of himself. "You've had a stroke."

"Stroke of bad luck, *I'd* say," replied Smrgol, cheerfully, trying to wink his bad eye and not succeeding very well. "No, boy, it's nothing. Look who I've brought along."

"I—I wasn't too keen on coming," said Secoh, shyly, to Jim. "But your granduncle can be pretty persuasive, your wo—you know."

"That's right!" boomed Smrgol. "Don't you go calling anybody your worship. Never heard of such stuff!" He turned to Jim. "And letting a george go in where he didn't dare go himself! Boy, I said to him, don't give me this *only a mere-dragon* and *just a mere-dragon*. Mere's got nothing to do with what kind of dragon you are. What kind of a world would it be if we were all like that?" Smrgol mimicked (as well as his dragon-basso would let him) someone talking in a high, simpering voice. "Oh, I'm just a plowland-and-pasture dragon—you'll have to excuse me, I'm only a halfway-up-the-hill dragon—*Boy!*" bellowed Smrgol, "I said, you're a *dragon!* Remember that. And a dragon acts like a dragon or he doesn't act at all!"

"Hear! Hear!" said Nevile-Smythe, carried away by enthusiasm.

"Hear that, boy? Even the george here knows that. Don't believe I've met you, george," he added, turning to the knight.

"Nevile-Smythe, Sir Reginald. Knight bachelor."

"Smrgol. Dragon."

"Smrgol? You aren't the—but you couldn't be. Over a hundred years ago."

"The dragon who slew the Ogre of Gormely Keep? That's who I am, boy—george, I mean."

"By Jove! Always thought it was a legend, only."

"Legend? Not on your honor, george! I'm old—even for a dragon, but there was a time—well, well, we won't go into that. I've something more important to talk to you about. I've been doing a lot of thinking the last decade or so about us dragons and you georges getting together. Actually, we're really a lot alike—"

"If you don't mind, Smrgol," cut in Carolinus, snappishly, "we aren't out here to hold a parlement. It'll be noon in—when will it be noon, you?"

"Four hours, thirty-seven minutes, twelve seconds at the sound of the gong," replied the invisible bass voice. There was a momentary pause, and then a single mellow, chimed note. "Chime, I mean," the voice corrected itself.

"Oh, go back to bed!" cried Carolinus furiously.

"I've been up for hours," protested the voice, indignantly.

Carolinus ignored it, herding the party together and starting them off for the Tower. The knight fell in beside Smrgol.

"About this business of men and dragons getting together," said

Nevile-Smythe. "Confess I wasn't much impressed until I heard your name. D'you think it's possible?"

"Got to make a start sometime, george." Smrgol rumbled on. Jim, who had moved up to the head of the column to walk beside Carolinus, spoke to the magician.

"What lives in the Tower?"

Carolinus jerked his fierce old bearded face around to look at him. "What's *living* there?" he snapped. "I don't know. We'll find out soon enough. What *is* there—neither alive nor dead, just in existence at the spot—is the manifestation of pure evil."

"But how can we do anything against that?"

"We can't. We can only contain it. Just as you—if you're essentially a good person—contain the potentialities for evil in yourself, by killing its creatures, your evil impulses and actions."

"Oh?" said Jim.

"Certainly. And since evil opposes good in like manner, its creatures, the ones in the Tower, will try to destroy us."

Jim felt a cold lump in his throat. He swallowed.

"Destroy us?"

"Why no, they'll probably just invite us to tea—" The sarcasm in the old magician's voice broke off suddenly with the voice itself. They had just stepped through a low screen of bushes and instinctively checked to a halt.

Lying on the ground before them was what once had been a man in full armor. Jim heard the sucking intake of breath from Nevile-Smythe behind him.

"A most foul death," said the knight softly, "most foul . . ." He came forward and dropped clumsily to his armored knees, joining his gauntleted hands in prayer. The dragons were silent. Carolinus poked with his staff at a wide trail of slime that led around and over the body and back toward the Tower. It was the sort of trail a garden slug might have left—if this particular garden slug had been two or more feet wide where it touched the ground.

"A Worm" said Carolinus. "But Worms are mindless. No Worm killed him in such cruel fashion." He lifted his head to the old dragon.

"I didn't say it, Mage," rumbled Smrgol, uneasily.

"Best none of us say it until we know for certain. Come on." Carolinus took up the lead and led them forward again.

They had come up off the Causeway onto the barren plain that sloped up into a hill on which stood the Tower. They could see the wide fens and the tide flats coming to meet them in the arms of a small bay—and beyond that the sea, stretching misty to the horizon.

The sky above was blue and clear. No breeze stirred; but, as they looked at the Tower and the hill that held it, it seemed that the azure above had taken on a metallic cast. The air had a quivering unnaturalness like an atmosphere dancing to heat waves, though the day was chill; and there came on Jim's ears, from where he did not know, a high-pitched dizzy singing like that which accompanies delirium, or high fever.

The Tower itself was distorted by these things. So that although to Jim it seemed only the ancient, ruined shell of a building, yet, between one heartbeat and the next, it seemed to change. Almost, but not quite, he caught glimpses of it unbroken and alive and thronged about with fantastic, half-seen figures. His heart beat stronger with the delusion; and its beating shook the scene before him, all the hill and Tower, going in and out of focus, in and out, *in* and *out* . . .

. . . And there was Angie, in the Tower's doorway, calling him . . .

"*Stop!*" shouted Carolinus. His voice echoed like a clap of thunder in Jim's ears; and Jim awoke to his senses, to find himself straining against the barrier of Carolinus' staff, that barred his way to the Tower like a rod of iron. "By the Powers!" said the old magician, softly and fiercely. "Will you fall into the first trap set for you?"

"Trap?" echoed Jim, bewilderedly. But he had no time to go further, for at that moment there rose from among the giant boulders at the Tower's base the heavy, wicked head of a dragon as large as Smrgol.

The thunderous bellow of the old dragon beside Jim split the unnatural air.

"*Anark!* Traitor—thief—inchworm! Come down here!"

Booming dragon-laughter rolled back an answer.

"Tell us about Gormely Keep, old bag of bones! Ancient mud-puppy, fat lizard, scare us with words!"

Smrgol lurched forward; and again Carolinus' staff was extended to bar the way.

"Patience," said the magician. But with one wrenching effort, the old dragon had himself under control. He turned, panting, to Carolinus.

"What's hidden, Mage?" he demanded.

"We'll see." Grimly, Carolinus brought his staff, endwise, three times down upon the earth. With each blow the whole hill seemed to shake and shudder.

Up among the rocks, one particularly large boulder tottered and rolled aside. Jim caught his breath and Secoh cried out, suddenly.

In the gap that the boulder revealed, a thick, slug-like head was lifting from the ground. It reared, yellow-brown in the sunlight, its two sets of horns searching and revealing a light external shell, a platelet with a merest hint of spire. It lowered its head and slowly, inexorably, began to flow downhill toward them, leaving its glistening trail behind it.

"Now—" said the knight. But Carolinus shook his head. He struck at the ground again.

"Come forth!" he cried, his thin, old voice piping on the quivering air. "By the Powers! Come forth!"

And then they saw it.

From behind the great barricade of boulders, slowly, there reared first a bald and glistening dome of hairless skin. Slowly this rose, revealing two perfectly round eyes below which they saw, as the whole came up, no proper nose, but two airslits side by side as if the whole of the bare, enormous skull was covered with a simple sheet of thick skin. And rising still further, this unnatural head, as big around as a beach ball, showed itself to possess a wide and idiot-grinning mouth, entirely lipless and revealing two jagged, matching rows of yellow teeth.

Now, with a clumsy, studied motion, the whole creature rose to its feet and stood knee-deep in the boulders and towering above them. It was manlike in shape, but clearly nothing ever spawned by the human race. A good twelve feet high it stood, a rough patchwork kilt of untanned hides wrapped around its thick waist—but this was not the extent of its differences from the race of Man. It had, to begin with, no neck at all. That obscene beachball of a hairless, near-featureless head balanced like an apple on thick, square shoulders of gray, coarse-looking skin. Its torso was one straight trunk, from which its arms and legs sprouted with a disproportionate thickness and roundness, like sections of pipe. Its knees were hidden by its kilt and its further legs by the rocks; but the elbows of its oversize arms had unnatural hinges to them, almost as if they had been doubled, and the lower arms were almost as large as the upper and near-wrist-less, while the hands themselves were awkward, thick-fingered parodies of the human extremity, with only three digits, of which one was a single, opposed thumb.

The right hand held a club, bound with rusty metal, that surely not even such a monster should have been able to lift. Yet one grotesque hand carried it lightly, as lightly as Carolinus had carried his staff. The monster opened its mouth.

"He!" it went. "He! He!"

The sound was fantastic. It was a bass titter, if such a thing could be imagined. Though the tone of it was as low as the lowest note of a good operatic basso, it clearly came from the creature's upper throat and head. Nor was there any real humor in it. It was an utterance with a nervous, habitual air about it, like a man clearing his throat. Having sounded, it fell silent, watching the advance of the great slug with its round, light blue eyes.

Smrgol exhaled slowly.

"Yes," he rumbled, almost sadly, almost as if to himself. "What I was afraid of. An ogre."

In the silence that followed, Nevile-Smythe got down from his horse and began to tighten the girths of its saddle.

"So, so, Clarivaux," he crooned to the trembling horse. "So ho, boy."

The rest of them were looking all at Carolinus. The magician leaned on his staff, seeming very old indeed, with the deep lines carven in the ancient skin of his face. He had been watching the ogre, but now he turned back to Jim and the other two dragons.

"I had hoped all along," he said, "that it needn't come to this. However," he crackled sourly, and waved his hand at the approaching Worm, the silent Anark and the watching ogre, "as you see . . . The world goes never the way we want it by itself, but must be haltered and led." He winced, produced his flask and cup, and took a drink of milk. Putting the utensils back, he looked over at Nevile-Smythe, who was now checking his weapons. "I'd suggest, Knight, that you take the Worm. It's a poor chance, but your best. I know you'd prefer that renegade dragon, but the Worm is the greater danger."

"Difficult to slay, I imagine?" queried the knight.

"Its vital organs are hidden deep inside it," said Carolinus, "and being mindless, it will fight on long after being mortally wounded. Cut off those eye-stalks and blind it first, if you can—"

"Wait!" cried Jim, suddenly. He had been listening bewilderedly. Now the word seemed to jump out of his mouth. "What're we going to do?"

"Do?" said Carolinus, looking at him. "Why, fight, of course."

"But," stammered Jim, "wouldn't it be better to go get some help? I mean—"

"Blast it, boy!" boomed Smrgol. "We can't wait for that! Who knows what'll happen if we take time for something like that? Hell's bells, Gorbash, lad, you got to fight your foes when you meet them, not the next day, or the day after that."

"Quite right, Smrgol," said Carolinus, dryly. "Gorbash, you don't understand this situation. Every time you retreat from something like this, it gains and you lose. The next time the odds would be even worse against us."

They were all looking at him. Jim felt the impact of their curious glances. He did not know what to say. He wanted to tell them that he was not a fighter, that he did not know the first thing to do in this sort of battle, that it was none of his business anyway and that he would not be here at all, if it were not for Angie. He was, in fact, quite humanly scared, and floundered desperately for some sort of strength to lean on.

"What—what am I supposed to do?" he said.

"Why, fight the ogre, boy! Fight the ogre!" thundered Smrgol—and the inhuman giant up on the slope, hearing him, shifted his gaze suddenly from the Worm to fasten it on Jim. "And I'll take on that louse of an Anark. The george here'll chop up the Worm, the Mage'll hold back the bad influences—and there we are."

"Fight the ogre . . ." If Jim had still been possessed of his ordinary two legs, they would have buckled underneath him. Luckily his dragon-body knew no such weakness. He looked at the overwhelming bulk of his expected opponent, contrasted the ogre with himself, the armored, ox-heavy body of the Worm with Nevile-Smythe, the deep-chested over-size Anark with the crippled old dragon beside him—and a cry of protest rose from the very depths of his being. "But we can't win!"

He turned furiously on Carolinus, who, however, looked at him calmly. In desperation he turned back to the only normal human he could find in the group.

"Nevile-Smythe," he said. "You don't need to do this."

"Lord, yes," replied the knight, busy with his equipment. "Worms, ogres—one fights them when one runs into them, you know." He considered his spear and put it aside. "Believe I'll face it on foot," he murmured to himself.

"Smrgol!" said Jim. "Don't you see—can't you understand? Anark is a lot younger than you. And you're not well—"

"Er . . ." said Secoh, hesitantly.

"Speak up, boy!" rumbled Smrgol.

"Well," stammered Secoh, "it's just . . . what I mean is, I couldn't bring myself to fight that Worm or that ogre—I really couldn't. I just sort of go to pieces when I think of them getting close to me. But I *could*—well, fight another dragon. It wouldn't be quite so bad, if you know what I mean, if that dragon up there breaks my neck—" He broke down and stammered incoherently. "I know I sound awfully silly—"

"Nonsense! Good lad!" bellowed Smrgol. "Glad to have you. I—

er—can't quite get into the air myself at the moment—still a bit stiff. But if you could fly over and work him down this way where I can get a grip on him, we'll stretch him out for the buzzards." And he dealt the mere-dragon a tremendous thwack with his tail by way of congratulation, almost knocking Secoh off his feet.

In desperation, Jim turned back to Carolinus.

"There is no retreat," said Carolinus, calmly, before Jim could speak. "This is a game of chess where if one piece withdraws, all fall. Hold back the creatures, and I will hold back the forces—for the creatures will finish me, if you go down, and the forces will finish you if they get me."

"Now, look here, Gorbash!" shouted Smrgol in Jim's ear. "That Worm's almost here. Let me tell you something about how to fight ogres, based on experience. You listening, boy?"

"Yes," said Jim, numbly.

"I know you've heard the other dragons calling me an old wind-bag when I wasn't around. But I *have* conquered an ogre—the only one in our race to do it in the last eight hundred years—and they haven't. So pay attention, if you want to win your own fight."

Jim gulped.

"All right," he said.

"Now, the first thing to know," boomed Smrgol, glancing at the Worm who was now less than fifty yards distant, "is about the bones in an ogre—"

"Never mind the details!" cried Jim. "What do I do?"

"In a minute," said Smrgol. "Don't get excited, boy. Now, about the bones in an ogre. The thing to remember is that they're big—matter of fact in the arms and legs, they're mainly bone. So there's no use trying to bite clear through, if you get a chance. What you try to do is get at the muscle—that's tough enough as it is—and hamstring. That's point one." He paused to look severely at Jim.

"Now, point two," he continued, "also connected with bones. Notice the elbows on that ogre. They aren't like a george's elbows. They're what you might call double-jointed. I mean, they have two joints where a george has just the one. Why? Simply because with the big bones they got to have and the muscle on them, they'd never be able to bend an arm more than halfway up before the bottom part'd bump the top if they had a george-type joint. Now, the point of all this is that when it swings that club, it can only swing in one way with that elbow. That's up and down. If it wants to swing it side to side, it's got to use its shoulder. Consequently if you can catch it with its club down and to one side of the body, you got an advantage; because it takes two motions to get it back up and in line again—instead of one, like a george."

"Yes, yes," said Jim, impatiently, watching the advance of the Worm.

"Don't get impatient, boy. Keep cool. Keep cool. Now, the knees don't have that kind of joint, so if you can knock it off its feet you got a real advantage. But don't try that, unless you're sure you can do it; because once it gets you pinned, you're a goner. The way to fight it is in-and-out—fast. Wait for a swing, dive in, tear him, get back out again. Got it?"

"Got it," said Jim, numbly.

"Good. Whatever you do, don't let it get a grip on you. Don't pay attention to what's happening to the rest of us, no matter what you hear or see. It's every one for himself. Concentrate on your own foe; and *keep your head*. Don't let your dragon instinct get in there and slug run away with you. That's why the georges have been winning against us as they have. Just remember you're faster than that ogre and your brains'll win for you if you stay clear, keep your head and don't rush. I tell you, boy—"

He was interrupted by a sudden cry of joy from Nevile-Smythe, who had been rummaging around Clarivaux's saddle.

"I say!" shouted Nevile-Smythe, running up to them with surprising lightness, considering his armor. "The most marvelous stroke of luck! Look what I found." He waved a wispy stretch of cloth at them.

"What?" demanded Jim, his heart going up in one sudden leap.

"Elinor's favor! And just in time, too. Be a good fellow, will you," went on Nevile-Smythe, turning to Carolinus, "and tie it about my vambrance here on the shield arm. Thank you, Mage."

Carolinus, looking grim, tucked his staff into the crook of his arm and quickly tied the kerchief around the armor of Nevile-Smythe's lower left arm. As he tightened the final knot and let his hands drop away, the knight caught up his shield into position and drew his sword with his other hand. The bright blade flashed like a sudden streak of lightning in the sun, he leaned forward to throw the weight of his armor before him, and with a shout of "*A Nevile-Smythe! Elinor! Elinor!*" he ran forward up the slope toward the approaching Worm.

Jim heard, but did not see, the clash of shell and steel that was their coming together. For just then everything began to happen at once. Up on the hill, Anark screamed suddenly in fury and launched himself down the slope in the air, wings spread like some great bomber gliding in for a crash landing. Behind Jim, there was the frenzied flapping of leathery wings as Secoh took to the air to meet him—but this was drowned by a sudden short, deep-chested cry, like a wordless shout; and, lifting his club, the ogre stirred and stepped clear of the boulders, coming forward and straight down the hill with huge, ground-covering strides.

"Good luck, boy," said Smrgol, in Jim's ear. "And Gorbash—" Something in the old dragon's voice made Jim turn his head to look at Smrgol. The ferocious red mouth-pit and enormous fangs were frighteningly open before him, but behind it Jim read a strange affection and concern in the dark dragon-eyes. "—Remember," said the old dragon, almost softly, "that you are a descendant of Ortosh and Agtval, and Gleingul who slew the sea serpent on the tide-banks of the Gray Sands. And be therefore valiant. But remember, too, that you are my only living kin and the last of our line . . . and be careful."

Then Smrgol's head was jerked away, as he swung about to face the coming together of Secoh and Anark in mid-air and bellowed out his own challenge. While Jim, turning back toward the Tower, had only time to take to the air before the rush of the ogre was upon him.

He had lifted on his wings without thinking—evidently this was dragon instinct when attacked. He was aware of the ogre suddenly before him, checking now, with its enormous hairy feet digging deep into the ground. The rust-bound club flashed before Jim's eyes and he felt a heavy blow high on his chest that swept him backward through the air.

He flailed with his wings to regain balance. The over-size idiot face was grinning only a couple of yards off from him. The club swept up for another blow. Panicked, Jim scrambled aside, and saw the ogre sway forward a step. Again the club lashed out—*quick!*— how could something so big and clumsy-looking be so quick with its hands? Jim felt himself smashed down to earth and a sudden lance of bright pain shot through his right shoulder. For a second, a gray, thick-skinned forearm loomed over him and his teeth met in it without thought.

He was shaken like a rat by a rat terrier and flung clear. His wings beat for the safety of altitude, and he found himself about twenty feet off the ground, staring down at the ogre, which grunted a wordless sound and shifted the club to strike upward. Jim cupped air with his wings, to fling himself backward and avoid the blow. The club whistled through the unfeeling air; and, sweeping forward, Jim ripped at one great blocky shoulder and beat clear. The ogre spun to face him, still grinning. But now blood welled and trickled down where Jim's teeth had gripped and torn, high on the shoulder.

—And suddenly, Jim realized something:

He was no longer afraid. He hung in the air, just out of the ogre's reach, poised to take advantage of any opening; and a hot sense of excitement was coursing through him. He was discovering the truth about fights—and about most similar things—that it is only the beginning that is bad. Once the chips are down, several million years of instinct take over and there is no time for thought for anything but confronting the enemy. So it was with Jim—and then the ogre moved in on him again; and that was his last specific intellectual thought of the fight, for everything else was drowned in his overwhelming drive to avoid being killed and, if possible, to kill, himself. . . .

IV

It was a long, blurred time, about which later Jim had no clear memory. The sun marched up the long arc of the heavens and crossed the nooning point and headed down again. On the torn-up sandy soil of the plain he and the ogre turned and feinted, smashed and tore at each other. Sometimes he was in the air, sometimes on the ground. Once he had the ogre down on one knee, but could not press his advantage. At another time they had fought up the long slope of the hill almost to the Tower and the ogre had him pinned in the cleft between two huge boulders and had hefted its club back for the final blow that would smash Jim's skull. And then he had wriggled free between the monster's very legs and the battle was on again.

Now and then throughout the fight he would catch brief kaleidoscopic glimpses of the combats being waged about him: Nevile-Smythe now wrapped about by the blind body of the Worm, its eyestalks hacked away—and striving in silence to draw free his sword-arm, which was pinned to his side by the Worm's encircling body. Or there would roll briefly into Jim's vision a tangled roaring tumble of flailing leathery wings and serpentine bodies that was Secoh, Anark and old Smrgol. Once or twice he had a momentary view of Carolinus, still standing erect, his staff upright in his hand, his long white beard flowing forward over his blue gown with the cabalistic golden signs upon it, like some old seer in the hour of Armageddon. Then the gross body of the ogre would blot out his vision and he would forget all but the enemy before him.

The day faded. A dank mist came rolling in from the sea and fled in little wisps and tatters across the plain of battle. Jim's body ached and slowed, and his wings felt leaden. But the ever-grinning face and sweeping club of the ogre seemed neither to weaken nor to tire. Jim drew back for a moment to catch his breath; and in that second, he heard a voice cry out.

"Time is short!" it cried, in cracked tones. "We are running out of time. The day is nearly gone!"

It was the voice of Carolinus. Jim had never heard him raise it before with just such a desperate accent. And even as Jim identified the voice, he realized that it came clearly to his ears—and that for some-time now upon the battlefield, except for the ogre and himself, there had been silence.

He shook his head to clear it and risked a quick glance about him.

He had been driven back almost to the neck of the Causeway itself, where it entered onto the plain. To one side of him, the snapped strands of Clarivaux's bridle dangled limply where the terrified horse had broken loose from the earth-thrust spear to which Nevile-Smythe had tethered it before advancing against the Worm on foot. A little off from it stood Carolinus, upheld now only by his staff, his old face shrunken and almost mummified in appearance, as if the life had been all but drained from it. There was nowhere else to retreat to; and Jim was alone.

He turned back his gaze to see the ogre almost upon him. The heavy club swung high, looking gray and enormous in the mist. Jim felt in his limbs and wings a weakness that would not let him dodge in time; and, with all his strength, he gathered himself, and sprang instead, up under the monster's guard and inside the grasp of those cannon-thick arms.

The club glanced off Jim's spine. He felt the arms go around him, the double triad of bone-thick fingers searching for his neck. He was caught, but his rush had knocked the ogre off his feet. Together they went over and rolled on the sandy earth, the ogre gnawing with his jagged teeth at Jim's chest and striving to break a spine or twist a neck, while Jim's tail lashed futilely about.

They rolled against the spear and snapped it in half. The ogre found its hold and Jim felt his neck begin to be slowly twisted, as if it were a chicken's neck being wrung in slow motion. A wild despair flooded through him. He had been warned by Smrgol never to let the ogre get him pinned. He had disregarded that advice and now he was lost, the battle was lost. *Stay away*, Smrgol had warned, *use your brains* . . .

The hope of a wild chance sprang suddenly to life in him. His head was twisted back over his shoulder. He could see only the gray mist above him, but he stopped fighting the ogre and groped about with both forelimbs. For a slow moment of eternity, he felt nothing, and then something hard nudged against his right foreclaw, a glint of bright metal flashed for a second before his eyes. He changed his grip on what he held, clamping down on it as firmly as his clumsy foreclaws would allow—

—and with every ounce of strength that was left to him, he drove the fore-part of the broken spear deep into the middle of the ogre that sprawled above him.

The great body bucked and shuddered. A wild scream burst from the idiot mouth alongside Jim's ear. The ogre let go, staggered back and up, tottering to its feet, looming like the Tower itself above him. Again, the ogre screamed, staggering about like a drunken man, fumbling at the shaft of the spear sticking from him. It jerked at the shaft, screamed again, and, lowering its unnatural head, bit at the wood like a wounded animal. The tough ash splintered between its teeth. It screamed once more and fell to its knees. Then slowly, like a bad actor in an old-fashioned movie, it went over on its side, and drew up its legs like a man with the cramp. A final scream was drowned in bubbling. Black blood trickled from its mouth and it lay still.

Jim crawled slowly to his feet and looked about him.

The mists were drawing back from the plain and the first thin light of late afternoon stretching long across the slope. In its rusty illumination, Jim made out what was to be seen there.

The Worm was dead, literally hacked in two. Nevile-Smythe, in bloody, dinted armor, leaned wearily on a twisted sword not more than a few feet off from Carolinus. A little farther off, Secoh raised a torn neck and head above the intertwined, locked-together bodies of Anark and Smrgol. He stared dazedly at Jim. Jim moved slowly, painfully over to the mere-dragon.

Jim came up and looked down at the two big dragons. Smrgol lay with his eyes closed and his jaws locked in Anark's throat. The neck of the younger dragon had been broken like the stem of a weed.

"Smrgol . . ." croaked Jim.

"No—" gasped Secoh. "No good. He's gone. . . . I led the other one to him. He got his grip—and then he never let go. . . ." The mere-dragon choked and lowered his head.

"He fought well," creaked a strange harsh voice which Jim did not at first recognize. He turned and saw the Knight standing at his shoulder. Nevile-Smythe's face was white as sea-foam inside his helmet and the flesh of it seemed fallen in to the bones, like an old man's. He swayed as he stood.

"We have won," said Carolinus, solemnly, coming up with the aid of his staff. "Not again in our lifetimes will evil gather enough strength in this spot to break out." He looked at Jim. "And now," he said, "the balance of Chance and History inclines in your favor. It's time to send you back."

"Back?" said Nevile-Smythe.

"Back to his own land, Knight," replied the magician. "Fear not, the dragon left in this body of his will remember all that happened and be your friend."

"Fear!" said Nevile-Smythe, somehow digging up a final spark of energy to expend on hauteur. "I fear no dragon, dammit. Besides, in respect to the old boy here"—he nodded at the dead Smrgol—"I'm going to see what can be done about this dragon-alliance business."

"He was great!" burst out Secoh, suddenly, almost with a sob. "He—he made me strong again. Whatever he wanted, I'll do it." And the mere-dragon bowed his head.

"You come along with me then, to vouch for the dragon end of it," said Nevile-Smythe. "Well," he turned to Jim, "it's goodby, I suppose, Sir James."

"I suppose so," said Jim. "Goodby to you, too, I—" Suddenly he remembered.

"Angie!" he cried out, spinning around. "I've got to go get Angie out of that Tower!"

Carolinus put his staff out to halt Jim.

"Wait," he said. "Listen . . ."

"Listen?" echoed Jim. But just at that moment, he heard it, a woman's voice calling, high and clear, from the mists that still hid the Tower.

"*Jim! Jim, where are you?*"

A slight figure emerged from the mist, running down the slope toward them.

"Here I am!" bellowed Jim. And for once he was glad of the capabilities of his dragon-voice. "Here I am, Angie—"

—but Carolinus was chanting in a strange, singing voice, words without meaning, but which seemed to shake the very air about them. The mist swirled, the world rocked and swung. Jim and Angie were caught up, were swirled about, were spun away and away down an echoing corridor of nothingness . . .

. . . and then they were back in the Grille, seated together on one side of the table in the booth. Hanson, across from them, was goggling like a bewildered accident victim.

"Where—where am I?" he stammered. His eyes suddenly focused on them across the table and he gave a startled croak. "Help!" he cried, huddling away from them. "Humans!"

"What did you expect?" snapped Jim. "Dragons?"

"No!" shrieked Hanson. "Watch-beetles—like me!" And, turning about, he tried desperately to burrow his way through the wood seat of the booth to safety.

V

It was the next day after that Jim and Angie stood in the third floor corridor of Chumley Hall, outside the door leading to the office of the English Department.

"Well, are you going in or aren't you?" demanded Angie.

"In a second, in a second," said Jim, adjusting his tie with nervous fingers. "Just don't rush me."

"Do you suppose he's heard about Grottwold?" Angie asked.

"I doubt it," said Jim. "The Student Health Service says Hanson's already starting to come out of it—except that he'll probably always have a touch of amnesia about the whole afternoon. Angie!" said Jim, turning on her. "Do you suppose, all the time we were there, Hanson was actually being a watch-beetle underground?"

"I don't know, and it doesn't matter," interrupted Angie, firmly. "Honestly, Jim, now you've finally promised to get an answer out of Dr. Howells about a job, I'd think you'd want to get it over and done with, instead of hesitating like this. I just can't understand a man who can go about consorting with dragons and fighting ogres and then—"

"—still not want to put his boss on the spot for a yes-or-no answer," said Jim. "Hah! Let me tell you something." He waggled a finger in front of her nose. "Do you know what all this dragon-ogre business actually taught me? It wasn't to be scared, either."

"All right," said Angie, with a sigh. "What was it then?"

"I'll tell you," said Jim. "What I found out . . ." He paused. "What I found out was not, not to be scared. It was that scared or not doesn't matter; because you just go ahead, anyway."

Angie blinked at him.

"And that," concluded Jim, "is why I agreed to have it out with Howells, after all. Now you know."

He yanked Angie to him, kissed her grimly upon her startled lips, and, letting go of her, turned about. Giving a final jerk to his tie, he turned the knob of the office door, opened it, and strode valiantly within.

The Champion of Dragons

🀀 🀀 🀀

by Mickey Zucker Reichert

The rising sun haloed a red-tiered fortress on the mountain's highest peak. Far below, in a glade partially covered by mats of woven grass, Miura Usashibo and Otake Nakamura knelt in silence, chests rising and falling from the strain of mock combat. Nearby, their sensei watched, stroking his wispy beard.

Usashibo closed his eyes, and a familiar quiet darkness overcame his world. His heart pounded from a mixture of exertion and excitement. Sweat rolled down his face. The reed mats cut their regular pattern into his knees, and the euphoric afterglow of combat consumed him. Victory no longer granted him the unbridled sense of triumph it had scarcely a year ago. Winning had become mundane. But the physical and emotional peak attained in combat never dulled. It seemed as if no reality existed beyond the feelings of inner peace and power he could reach only through all-consuming violence.

Usashibo turned his thoughts to the dragon that Sensei had chosen and trained him to fight. Sensei either would not or could not describe the creature and its method of combat. His initial explanation detailed all he would reveal of Usashibo's enemy. "Every ten years the Master and I select a champion to seek out and slay the dragon. We train him to reach beyond his limitations and drive him until he surpasses even the Master. We have chosen you, Miura Usashibo, as the fourteenth champion of dragons. The others never returned." Yet, despite this grim appraisal, the possibility of failure never occurred to Usashibo. *In the quiet of my soul, I am invincible. I will return.*

A sharp handclap snapped Usashibo's attention back to his surroundings. Sensei bowed, signaling an end to Usashibo's last practice session before setting out to destroy the dragon. As the old man turned, his linen jacket and pants hissed gently. Pausing, he bowed to the shrine of the mountain's spirit and climbed the long flight of stone steps which led to the Master's fortress.

Otake Nakamura remained kneeling where Usashibo had landed what Sensei had judged a killing blow. The interlocking squares of his abdominal muscles rose and fell, and blood beaded from the vertical red line where the champion of dragons' wooden sword had cut his stomach. Silently, he stared at the mats before him. Usashibo searched Nakamura's face for signs of the friendship they had shared a little over a year ago, but none survived. Usashibo studied his old companion, hungry for recognition that he was still a human being if no longer a friend.

Nakamura touched his forehead to the ground, then rose. "May you return from tomorrow's battle victorious and the gods of the winds and the mountains watch over you." Etiquette demanded Nakamura remain until Usashibo responded to his overly formal gesture.

Usashibo shifted uncomfortably, recalling the many times he had tried to force Nakamura to acknowledge how close they had been in friendship. But the mountains they had climbed together, the girls they had known, and the fights they had started became distant memories. Early in his training, Usashibo vented his frustration and loneliness on Nakamura during their practice sessions, battering him until he could barely walk. As he withdrew further, Usashibo's anger lessened. But the feeling of betrayal remained. The soul mate who would have urged Usashibo to rip the dragon's ugly head off was gone, and Usashibo missed him.

Usashibo rose and pressed wrinkles from his pants with the palms of his hands. He replied with exaggerated formality. "Thank you,

Otake." Usashibo dismissed his sparring partner, anxious for the solace of being alone.

Nakamura turned and followed Sensei up the stone staircase, apparently unable to understand the inspired madness that goaded Usashibo to consecrate his life to a goal no one had ever achieved and the fleeting glance at immortality it offered. As boys, Nakamura and Usashibo had shared visions of greatness, but it seemed Nakamura dreamed with his mouth instead of his heart.

Over the years of training, Usashibo had paid a high price for his dream. He denied himself many of the indulgences of youth, gradually surrendering pieces of himself to his art until only the warrior survived. Only one aspect of life remained inviolate: his love for his wife, Rumiko. He knew she fought to maintain the spark of desire within him. He wished her task was easier. Usashibo turned toward the narrow path which led to the village of Miyamoto and resolved to grant Rumiko the only gift which remained his to give: the last night he knew he would be alive.

At the edge of the rice mats, Usashibo slipped his feet into his sandals and slid his swords through his belt. Despite his melancholia, his mind entered his familiar regimen of imaginary combat. As he walked, he consciously controlled each step and shift of balance. His left hand rested on his scabbarded sword, draped over the handguard. He recalled Sensei's words at times when he had doubted his purpose: *Once a raindrop begins to fall, it must continue to fall or it is no longer even a drop of rain. A man must finish his journey once the first step is taken.* Usashibo laughed to himself and wished Sensei spoke more directly.

As Usashibo entered Miyamoto, he tried to close his mind against the ordeal mingling with its citizenry presented. The townspeople regarded him as the epitome of virtue or the target of envy, not as human. Soon, peasants and the rough wooden huts of the village surrounded him. Although people jammed the streets, the throng parted before him. Young girls leered invitations, and men he had known since childhood pretended not to notice him with exaggerated indifference. A child asked him if he could really slay the dragon, only to be snatched away by an embarrassed mother before Usashibo could answer. He felt the tension of hastily averted stares.

Stories of Usashibo's feats, provided and embellished by Naka-mura, endeared the teller but not the subject. Many attributed Us-ashibo's prowess to magic or unwholesome herbs. Others sought tricks to make his accomplishments fall within their narrow view of possibility. Even those people who dismissed Nakamura's tales as lies managed to attribute the blame for the deception to Usashibo.

Quickly, Usashibo crossed the town and traversed the white gravel path through his garden to his cottage. He paused before the faded linen door and removed his sandals. Closing his eyes to help escape the cruel reality of Miyamoto, he stepped through the curtain. The starchy smell of boiling rice mingled with the pine scent of charcoal and the musky aroma of freshly cut reeds. Rice paper walls shielded him from the attentions of people who believed him either more or less than human. Gradually, Sensei's demands and the unattainable goals the peasants projected onto him were borne away on the breeze as wisps of smoke. His own aspirations still burned obsessively in his mind like an endless fire in a swordsmith's forge. He basked in the feeling of power it inspired. He accepted the flame he knew he could never entirely escape or extinguish. Without the desire it inspired, he would not be Miura Usashibo. He opened his eyes.

A ceramic pot rested on a squat, black hibachi. Steam and smoke rose, darkening the tan walls and ceiling. Rumiko knelt on the pol-ished wood floor, and the brush in her hand darted over a sheet of paper. The soft beauty in her round face and dark eyes belied a wit that could cut as quickly and deeply as his sword and a strength which, in many ways, surpassed his own. The rice pot's lid rattled. White froth poured over the sides and hissed as it struck the charcoal. Rumiko rose, turned toward the hibachi, removed the lid, and stared into the boiling rice. Quietly, Usashibo waited for her to meet his gaze.

The steam freed several strands from Rumiko's tightly coiffed hair. Her face reddened. Droplets of sweat beaded on her upper lip, but she did not look up.

Tension filled the room. It seemed almost tangible, as it does when a delicate glass bottle has fallen but not yet shattered on the floor. He could deal with Rumiko momentarily, but Usashibo knew his swords demanded their proper respect. In four strides, he crossed the room and knelt before a black, lacquered stand. He withdrew the longer sword from his cloth belt, applied a thin coating of clove oil, blotted it nearly dry with powder, and delicately placed it in the stand. He slid the companion sword free, repeated the process, and hung it above the mate. Respectfully, he bowed, then rose.

Rumiko stood, stiff-backed, stirring the rice. Her wooden spoon moved in precise circles.

As Usashibo walked, the green reed mats crackled beneath his feet. He stopped behind Rumiko, swearing he would allow nothing to spoil this night for her. With a finger, he traced a stray lock of hair along her neck and trailed off across her shoulder. His hand discovered taut muscles beneath her thin robe. Confusion and concern mingled within Usashibo. "Rumiko?"

The faint, hissing explosions of Rumiko's tears striking the charcoal punctuated the silence. Usashibo's grip on her arms hardened, as if to lend her his own strength.

Rumiko shifted uneasily in his grasp. "Always the swords first. If you loved me as much as you love them, you'd stay. Let someone else try to kill the dragon."

Usashibo snapped Rumiko toward him and wrapped his arms around her. She braced her elbows against his chest. Carefully, Usashibo pulled her to him, despite her resistance, and buried his face in her hair. "Ah, Rumiko. I will return. You must believe."

Rumiko ceased struggling. Usashibo relaxed his arms and dropped them to her waist. She leaned away from him and stared through red-laced eyes. "Do you really believe the thirteen others thought they would lose? Why risk your life here with me to fight a dragon that never hurts anyone who doesn't attack it? Stay. Please."

Usashibo had never questioned his reason to slay the dragon. The thought of surrendering his dream seemed so alien it did not merit consideration, but her words raised doubt. *Perhaps the dragon could kill me as it did all the others.* After so many consecutive victories, the thought of defeat appalled Usashibo. He knew he must fight the dragon, if only to prove himself invincible. If he quit now, all his striving and sacrifice meant nothing. One moment of weakness would make him and everything he believed in a deadly joke. *Ideals are worth dying for. I have trained my entire life for this one fight. If I cannot win, I deserve to die. Once a raindrop begins to fall, it must continue to fall, or it is no longer even a drop of rain. I've lied to myself; Rumiko never understood my dream. She is the same as all the others.*

Usashibo recalled a clear winter day half a year and a lifetime ago. His first sensei, the consummate warrior in action and spirit, had died in his sleep. He had much left to teach, and Usashibo had much he still wanted to learn. It seemed unfair for Sensei to die as quietly as a peasant. Shortly after learning of his teacher's death, Usashibo fought with Rumiko over how the rice was prepared and left her.

Then, distraught, Usashibo had walked to the falls north of Miyamoto and sat on the crest, watching water crash to the rocks below. Mist swirled around him as he folded a small square of paper into a swan. He tossed the bird over the precipice as a gift to the god of the cascade. It spiraled gently downward until it struck the water. Then it plummeted and disappeared beneath the foam. He had seen his future as a warrior perish with old Sensei, and he had lost Rumiko, too. At that time, he realized he wanted to follow his swan over the falls.

A hand had touched Usashibo's arm. He spun, drew his sword instinctively, stood, and faced Rumiko. Resheathing his sword, he had turned back to the waterfall. She stood beside him, and forced him to face her. He felt tears run down his face, and Rumiko smiled sadly. Her presence spoke more deeply than words. He thought he sensed an understanding and similarity of purpose that transcended love.

But the love Usashibo had believed in was a lie. Now, the muscles at the corners of his jaw tightened as well as his grip. Rumiko winced and twisted, pushing desperately at his hands. He released her, and she retreated, kneading bruised arms. "Go now. I refuse to spend the night with a man who would rather die alone than live with me."

Rage and self-pity warred within Usashibo. His stomach clenched, and thoughts raced through his mind. He was truly alone. Sweat formed on his forehead, and he walked mechanically from Rumiko. He stooped, lifted the swords from their stand, and returned each to his belt. The familiarity of his weapons became an anchor for his troubled thoughts. In the past year they had cost him much, but they had returned far more in a way no one seemed to understand. While the world changed, they remained reassuringly constant. Though they tested him unmercifully, they never doubted or judged. *Rumiko cannot force me to give up the direction that shaped my life. I refuse to become her servant.* He dropped his left hand to his long sword and sprinted for the door.

The linen curtain enwrapped Usashibo like a net. His momentum carried him blindly through, tearing cloth from the doorway. Anger and frustration exploded within him. He shredded the faded linen. When the cloth fell away, he snatched up his sandals and resumed running.

Stones crunched beneath Usashibo's tread. Their sharp edges bit into his feet, and he sought the physical pain to replace the hurt Rumiko's betrayal had caused. He burst from his garden and into the street. He crashed into a young man and both sprawled in the dust. The man rose, swearing viciously. But when he recognized Usashibo, he broke off and apologized for his own clumsiness. *The bastards won't even curse me.* Unconsciously, Usashibo placed his right hand on his hilt. *The dragon won't single me out as different.*

Usashibo leapt to his feet and raced down the street, knocking peasants aside when they did not dodge quickly enough. Soon, they cleared a lane before him, and he ran between walls of people to meet the dragon.

The damp warmth of the pine forest surrounded Usashibo. He scrambled across a small waterfall. Thick boughs shielded him from the sun and freed the ground from undergrowth. The terrain remained level, and Usashibo quickly neared the isolated clearing where legend claimed the dragon lived. In the three days since he had left Rumiko, he existed only to slay the dragon. The rigor of solitary sword practice and travel occupied every waking moment, though Rumiko haunted his dreams.

Stray beams of sunlight pierced the forest's canopy. In the distance, a head-high wall of brambles signaled an end to the trees, the edge of the dragon's clearing. Usashibo squatted near the base of a tree. The muscles at the nape of his neck tightened. A wave of warmth passed through him. His chest prickled with the first drops of sweat.

The scene was a sharp contrast to Usashibo's imaginings. The hollow whistle of a songbird echoed from the edge of the clearing. A brown and black beetle peered cautiously from beneath a loose curl of bark above his shoulder. No evil presence exerted its control over the woodlands. But perhaps the clearing would be different.

Usashibo's left hand rested on the mouth of his scabbard, and his thumb overlapped the sword's guard. He crept from tree to tree, paused, and peeked through the wall of briars. In the center of the clearing stood a cottage surrounded by a garden similar to his own. Usashibo stared, unable to believe that anyone would dare to live this close to the dragon.

Usashibo circled the clearing, searching for a gap in the wall of thorns. At the far edge, he found a path that led through the garden to the cottage. He pushed through the briars and emerged into the sun. As he blinked, eyes adjusting to the light, a man stepped through the cottage's door. Although Usashibo had never seen this man before, much about him seemed familiar. The powerful shoulders and mocking eyes marked him as a warrior, even without the two swords resting in his belt. Usashibo's left hand resumed its position at the mouth of his scabbard. The two men stared at each other in silence, mirror images separated by clusters of red and gold blossoms.

Wind ruffled the strange man's wide black pants. Slowly, he moved toward Usashibo, feet skimming the ground but never losing contact. Just beyond sword range, he stopped and met Usashibo's stare. He grinned, and the creases that formed at the corners of his eyes made him look immeasurably older. "A champion of dragons. Ten years so soon."

Usashibo forced himself to relax; tension would slow his reactions. From the combination of ease and precision that permeated the man's movements, Usashibo knew he followed the way of the sword with a dedication most men cannot imagine. He knew this man shared his obsession to master his sword and himself and the isolation it brought. Curiosity broke through the strange feelings of companionship welling in Usashibo's mind. "How did you know I am a champion of dragons?"

A smile again crossed the man's face. "The way you walk, the way you hold your shoulders, and the unconquerable look in your eye. The last man I fought recognized me as I now recognize you. I was the last champion of dragons."

Usashibo's eyes narrowed accusingly. He feigned wiping sweat from his palm on the left side of his jacket to bring his hand nearer the hilt of his sword. "The last champion died fighting the dragon. He never returned."

The man's hand also casually drifted to his sword. "And you saw the body? Why should I return to people who inspired me, drove me to achieve beyond their dreams, then condemned me as different. They made me become the dragon, as shall you if you survive me." The man unsheathed his sword slowly and raised the blade, hilt gripped two-handed near his shoulder. "You cannot escape them. I've lived many places. All people are the same. It's easier being alone."

Usashibo drew both his swords and retreated two steps. His short blade hovered at waist height, the long one poised above it. The thought of killing the only person who truly understood the hell he survived appalled him. "I don't want to fight you."

The man lowered the tip of his sword until it nearly touched the ground. "You don't need to know who'd win? If you're afraid, you're a disgrace to the swords you carry."

The possibility of losing this combat had never occurred to Usashibo. Surrender would render the years of training and self-denial meaningless. The minutes of immortality during this fight had cost too much to be given up now. After sacrificing Rumiko's love, one man's life would not keep Usashibo from his goal. Despite the bond he shared with this man, or because of it, Usashibo knew he must kill the dragon he faced. *In the quiet of my soul, I am invincible.*

Usashibo thrust with both swords. The man dodged and retreated.

The two men circled. They probed each others' defenses without fully attacking. The man struck for Usashibo's forward leg. Usashibo leapt above the attack. The man lunged again. Usashibo batted the blade aside with his short sword. He countercut at the man's wrists. The man jerked his sword back and caught Usashibo's blow near his hilt. Spinning away, he cut beneath Usashibo's guard. Pain seared Usashibo's thigh. Reflexively, he lowered both swords to block the blow which had already landed. The man's sword arched toward Usashibo's undefended head.

Usashibo dropped his short sword and pivoted away. As the blow descended, Usashibo blended with the man's movement. His free hand caught his opponent's hilt and continued the forward motion. Pulled off-balance, the man stumbled. Usashibo drove his long sword into his opponent's chest. He continued the cut as his blade slid free. The man dropped to the ground.

Red froth bubbled from the man's mouth as he clutched the wound. "Brother, you did not disappoint me." A final smile crossed his face before death glazed his features.

A horse's whicker snapped Usashibo's attention from the man he had killed. Snatching up his short sword, he whirled, poised for combat.

Rumiko sat astride a dun stallion at the edge of the clearing, bow in hand, arrow nocked. She answered Usashibo's question before he asked it. "If he'd won, I'd have killed him."

Usashibo lowered his swords and stared at his wife, puzzled. The entire situation confounded him, and the burning cut on his thigh clouded thought further. One question pressed foremost in his thoughts. "Why didn't you shoot him before the fight?"

A shy smile lit Rumiko's face. "When I heard him talk, I knew he was right. You had to fight." She shrugged. "That's the way Miura Usashibo is."

Suddenly, Usashibo realized the force that had driven and shaped his life had disappeared. The dragon was dead. The joy he should have felt at Rumiko's revelation lost itself in the void the dragon had filled. For the first time in Usashibo's life, he experienced panic. Tears welled in his eyes.

Rumiko's grin broadened as her horse danced sideways. "I understand Mimasaka has been plagued by a demon for three hundred years."

An inner warmth and new sense of purpose suffused Usashibo. *There are many dragons and only one Rumiko.* "Let's go home."

Take Me Out To the Ball Game

◻ ◻ ◻

by Esther M. Friesner

Explain it to me again, O Master," said the dragon. With a single golden claw it prodded the mystic deck spread out before it. Curls of violet smoke crept from its nostrils to wreath the images of lewd and diabolical beings unscrolled against the walls of the wizard's chamber.

"It's simple," replied the mortal who, despite his puny size and unassuming appearance, was undisputed master of the great Worm's every action while residing in this bubble of a here-and-now. A scholar's hand—soft, womanish, the nails badly bitten and begrimed with ink—jabbed down to pinpoint one specific effigy from among the many similar pasteboards laid at the dragon's feet. "This is Billy Jim-Bob Borden, number eight for the Mets. When he comes out of the bull pen to pitch against the Cubs, you eat him."

"Cubs," the dragon mused, stroking the orange barbels depending from its scaly chin. "I have eaten cubs before this, of many sorts: Wolf, bear, lion, gryphon. . . ."

"No, no, no! Not the *Cubs*! You don't eat the *Cubs*! It's the Mets I want you to devour, dammit!"

"What? All of them?" Beautifully articulated five-toed paws folded themselves across a belly luminous as the full moon and nearly as vast. "Even in my greedygut youth I could not manage to consume more than three princesses daily without getting a case of the Jabderi Turnabouts, and I have no idea if these creatures you call Mets are more or less digestible than royalty. I fear I will be ill if I obey you, O Master, and I assure you, even a mage of your doubtless powers would not be happy trying to command an ailing dragon." Something in the way the beast's eyes narrowed when it said that left little space for debate.

Very patiently the wizard explained, "I don't want you to eat *all* the Mets; just a *few* Mets."

"Fewmets?" The dragon's indignation and revulsion flared up with a corresponding augmentation of body heat, causing paint to peel from the walls. "Am I summoned to this miserable ratfart world that I might use my gifts for the processing of mere sewage? Fewmets, forsooth!"

"Oh, jeez, I didn't mean—I just want you to—the *pitcher* for the Mets!" the wizard groaned. "That's all I want you to eat, okay? Just the pitcher, see?"

"I see." The dragon made a face. "Will it be crockery or metal?"

"Will what be?"

"The pitcher. The one you want me to eat. I pray it be not glass, which repeats on me like a curse. If you could see your way clear to arranging matters so that it is porcelain, O Master, I would be eternally grateful. And I do mean eternally."

The wizard jammed his Chicago Cubs cap down hard over his eyes, flung himself on his bed, and began to sob. The dragon observed this display with scarlet eyes made dispassionate by the inexorable roll of countless centuries and ate a Metallica poster off the wall.

"I never said it was going to be easy, Larry," said the wizard's apprentice from her place by the PC. She was a whole lot better-looking than the usual run of *aides-de-grammarye*, and had a way of making her sigil-strewn robes pooch out in a manner that had caused Wizard Larry to forget about the Cubs' league standings for all of fifteen minutes at a stretch. This was not one of those times.

"Yeah, Shannon, but you said it was going to *work!*" he countered.

A bitter man is not a pretty sight, but one who has had his innate bitterness refined by long years of backing the Cubs is about as ugly as a Gorgon with PMS.

Ever reasonable (and for that very quality Larry vowed to kill her some day) Shannon replied, "I said the *incantation* would be easy. Did I lie? It was easy as pie, once we got that virgin's blood."

For some reason, at mention of the blood, Larry turned sullen. More sullen.

"There, there, O Master," the dragon said, helping itself to a big glossy of David Lee Roth. A titanic paw patted the wizard's back with enough companionability to dislocate several vertebrae. "I'm sure you have a great personality."

"*You* be quiet!" Larry roared at the monster. "And *you*—" he whirled on Shannon, "—you mention that vir—vir—that blood stuff one more time and I tell Rover over here to warm up by eating *you*! You got that?"

The dragon dipped its horned head until those leathery lips were within whispering distance of Shannon's delicate ear and confided, "No wonder he can't get a date." Shannon just nodded. "What's a nice piece of ya-ha like you doing wasting your time in this blob-tail's company anyway? Apart from needing a dependable source of virgin's blood."

"Oh, he's okay, really," Shannon responded. "You should've known him in college, the way I did. With a good job like he got—computers, of course—why he ever had to move back in with his mother—"

"Since college?"

"Four years ago, yup."

The dragon was dumbfounded. "He has known a morsel of your evident relishability for at least four years and he is still a vir—?"

Before Shannon could respond, Larry picked up his genuine replica St. Louis slugger with the authentic ersatz Mickey Mantle autograph decal and poked the great beast hard amidships. Well, hard for Larry. The dragon barely noticed the impact until the little wizard screamed, "Hey! Pay attention to me! I'm the master here!"

Shannon's adorable mouth curved into that most goading of female expressions, the skeptical smile. "So you keep telling us. Okay. Master something. But before you start throwing your cosmic weight around, Larry dear, just remember this: You're in charge on *my* sufferance. I showed you the book." Here she patted the right hip pocket of the designer jeans now peeping from beneath the silky folds of her robe. "*I* suggested ways we might modernize the incantations. *I* cleaned up after you wet yourself at the thought of actually trying to summon a beast from the Beyond. *I*—"

"I did not!" Larry protested. He leveled a badly shaking finger at Shannon's smug face. "I never wet myself! You were here—" he appealed to the dragon. "You saw. I struck fear into your heart with my very presence! I was superb! I was commanding! I was—I was masterful! I was—I was—" His voice and his certainty drained away with equal rapidity. "Wasn't I?"

The dragon sighed and fumbled around the many creases of its iridescent hide until, from some bizarre, biological equivalent of a pocket, it withdrew a much-crumpled parchment. "Look, O Master, all I know is you were the one who uttered the key phrase of summoning, and its says right here in the regs (paragraph XVII, section C, subheading 83f) that my end of the deal is to appear and fulfill your desires for the span of fifty-two *uribets*. Once that span has passed, if you have not already dismissed me by the potency of your sorcerous spells—" here the dragon did its best to conceal a sarcastic snort, "—anything goes. Including you. Now, would you care to get *on* with it?" An ominous ticking filled the bedroom, although no timepiece was visible. The very rock-star posters on the walls seemed to pulse with the regular, inexorable beat of passing *uribets*.

"How long is that in real time?" Larry inquired with understandable concern.

Dragons lack shoulders and cannot shrug effectively, yet the Worm still managed to convey the sentiment *beats the hell out of me* without recourse to speech. "What good would it do you did you know that, O Master?" He waved the parchment about so that it rustled loudly. "As any fool can see, paragraph LXIV, section G, subheading 6i, codicil t4 expressly forbids me from giving you that information."

In the great tradition of the otherwise resourceless, Larry whined, "But that's not *fair!*" His appeal to good sportsmanship cut no tofu with the dragon.

"*Que voulez-vous? Quien Sabe? Cui bono?*" the beast replied, showing off the fabled encyclopedic wisdom of Worms everywhere. "*Nu*? Is it fair for lowly vermin such as yourself to yank beings of my grand and immortal breed from the pressing business of our normal lives, just to feed your piddling egos and do your scutwork? Therefore, that the greedy may know and tremble, the regs do decree a finite timespan to our servitude, yet keep full knowledge of that span from you. Thus you must use our powers judiciously and quickly, lest the allotted time pass and we munch your—"

"Point taken, point taken." Larry shooed the dreadful thought away. "Hey, I'm no time waster. Haven't I been trying to make you understand what I want for the past hour?"

"Greed," opined the dragon, "is sometimes less of a problem than incompetence. Neither, however, is *my* problem. I do what I am told. Now, you said there was this flask full of bearcub fewmets you wanted me to—"

"Don't scream like that, Larry," said Shannon. "Your mother will come upstairs to see if I'm having my will with you." The look on her face added a silent *you wish*, with perhaps a hint of *I wish, too*, thrown in for honesty's sake. She tossed the dog-eared paperback onto the bed. "If you'd done your homework, you'd see that there's no reason to go to pieces over this. It says right there that dragons are very old and very wise. And very acquisitive—treasure hordes, and all that—but that's beside the point. Because they're so wise, they never undertake a task until they understand it fully, and because they're so old, they've got all the time in the world to figure it out. You want fast service, you're going to have to explain things carefully, completely, literally, and in detail."

"Super," Larry grumped. "Explain everything there is to know about baseball? The season will be over by then."

"The allotted *uribets* may be over even sooner," the dragon mused.

"Ah, shoot, it'd be easier to—to—"

A frightening expression slowly spread itself across Larry's sallow features, a look of revelation and renewed zeal that signals danger in a sane man and absolute Armageddon-a-brewin' in a diehard Cubs fan. Shannon saw, and knew, and trembled.

Somewhere, somehow, someone was going to have to pay the price for Larry's unheralded brainstorm.

"Why did *I* have to pay for the tickets?" Shannon growled as they sidled their way into the stadium seats.

"Because I'm the wizard and you're just the apprentice," Larry returned smugly.

"It was *my* book. It was *my* idea."

"And it was *my* blood. As you keep reminding me every chance you get. So I might as well get some satisfaction out of it."

"The day you get any satisfaction . . ."

"Don't snarl, Shannon." Larry was practically beaming. "Next time I'll let you do the summoning."

Shannon's dangerously glittering eyes could have forewarned Larry that any dragons his lovely apprentice summoned would be given one command right off the bat, and it wouldn't be one he'd live to appreciate. But for the nonce, Larry wasn't in a reflective mood. His step was light and his heart was high. He was about to give the dragon a paws-on lesson, as it were, in the Great American Pastime. And then there would be no linguistic confusion whatsoever when he issued his "devour" directive. Billy Jim-Bob Borden didn't know it yet, but he was as good as Worm Chow right now.

"Excuse me. Pardon me. Oh, was that your foot? A thousand pardons," said the dragon, wriggling its scaly rump past the other spectators in the row until it reached its seat. A gusty sigh, garnished by whirlwinds of pale purple steam, escaped through the creature's nostrils as it plopped down and remarked, "So this is baseball. I like it."

"You ain't seen nothing yet," Larry promised it.

That much was true. It was a clear, hot July day at Wrigley, perfect baseball weather. The teams hadn't taken the field yet, but the newscasters and sportswriters were already at their posts, ready to verbally bludgeon the upcoming contest into more-or-less immortality. An insert in the program book informed the Gentle Spectator that today's game was special in that a large delegation of Japanese businessmen would be present in the same box with the sportscasters and writers, honored guests of the Management. Whether they were there with an eye to buying Wrigley, the journalists, or Chicago itself remained to be seen. No one with an ounce of business acumen ever dreamed they were there to purchase the Cubs.

The crowd was enthusiastic, even if more of their optimistic spirit sprang from the huge paper cups of beer in their hands than from any hope of seeing the Cubs win one. The smell of hot dogs was heavy on the air. Larry felt a drop of something thick and wet soak his shoulder. He looked up and saw the dragon was drooling.

It was while the dragon was stuffing the fourteenth red-hot-with-everything down its gullet that Shannon leaned over and whispered, "They really don't see it, do they?"

Larry shrugged. "They see it enough to hand it a weiner and charge it admission."

"You know what I mean by *see* it!" Shannon snapped. "And they don't. How come?"

"Beats me. You could look it up. It's *your* book," Larry reminded her nastily.

"The book tells about the characteristics of dragons and how to summon them from one plane of reality to another. It doesn't say much about their effect on people, aside from the section on diet and digestive problems. Ogres give them the colic."

"So we won't let it eat any Republicans." Larry rested his minuscule chin in his hand, thinking over the rest of what she'd said. "Maybe people just see what they want to," he concluded. "If it doesn't make sense to them, they refuse to admit it's real."

"You mean 'I'll believe it when I see it' really ought to be 'I'll see it *if* I believe it'?" Shannon asked. Larry nodded. With rather needless malice she added, "Like the Cubs winning a game."

That smarted. Larry shot her the briefest of stink-eyes, then threw himself back into explaining baseball to the reptile with renewed zeal.

The problem with such a state of spiritual frenzy is that certain details often go unexplained as being too obvious for elucidation. This most egregiously overlooks the fact that there is no such thing as *too obvious* to a dragon, with the exception of . . .

"Diamonds?" The fringed skin of the creature's brow ridges rose. "It is played on diamonds?"

"Yeah, right, like I just said. Anyway, that mound in the middle of the field—"

"A field of diamonds . . ." the Worm breathed, and closed its glittering eyes in reflective ecstasy.

By the time the Cubs and the Braves got out there ("This is a battle of the giants, ladies and gentlemen!" shouted ace sportscaster Gregory Hughes. The Japanese were the only ones present polite enough not to laugh out loud.) the dragon was well enough versed in the gentle art of horsehide slamming for Larry's purposes.

Or so Larry thought.

"That is the pitcher?" the dragon asked, indicating the young man occupying the mound.

"That's Carl Watson, pitcher for the Braves. You don't wanna eat him."

"I don't?" Only one brow ridge lifted this time. "Why don't I? I'm hungry."

"Because he's no threat to the Cubs and if you're hungry I'll get you another foot-long with everything. Now *pay attention*! You will eat the Mets pitcher and the Mets pitcher only. To be more specific, you will eat *this* Mets pitcher." He flipped a baseball card out of the pack he always carried in his shirt pocket, tucked in snugly right behind the calculator and the leaky Bic pens.

With surprising delicacy, the dragon took the card between two claws, the better to examine it. "Your pardon, O Master, but full sunlight does not suit my vision." It brought the pasteboard to the very tip of its nose, only to have the constant curls of violet smoke emanating from its nostrils obscure it. Out of patience, the dragon snorted to clear the air and sparks flew, several coming perilously near the card.

"Hey! Watch it! That's valuable!" Larry squawked, wigwagging his arms.

"What is?" asked the dragon with what Shannon might have recognized as dangerous interest. Shannon, however, had gone to the ladies' room and, if the lines were as usual, wasn't expected back that decade.

"That card, you 'gator farm reject."

The dragon regarded the sputtering little man that an ungenerous Fate had made its temporary Master, then glanced back at the card. "It's paper," it commented. "Not even of the sort your kind use for currency, debauched and metal-poor creatures that you are. It is *not* valuable. I should know. Valuable is my life."

"Oh, for—! Look, I admit it's not as rare as a Honus Wagner card, but there are plenty of people out there ready and willing to pay five bucks cash money for a Billy Jim-Bob Borden card in good condition."

"Bucks?"

Larry leapt in quickly to untangle any linguistic snarls that might compel the dragon to ask about does, fawns, and other non-negotiable cervines. "Dollars. The green paper we use as currency. Enough to buy you a couple more red-hots-with-everything, at least."

"With everything?" The dragon licked its chops. "For this?" It tilted the card this way and that before its beady eyes. "And how many red-hots might I obtain for this Honus Wagner you mentioned?"

"Red-hots? Ha! A Honus Wagner is worth—it's worth—" Larry groped for the hot-dog-equivalency-table value of the most prized baseball card of all time and failed. "A Honus Wagner's worth a blipping king's ransom!"

The dragon was telling Larry that where it came from, kings did not blip, when Shannon came back, bearing beer.

"I sneaked into the men's room. How's it going with the education of Godzilla Kaplan?"

"Who?"

"Not bad," Larry admitted. "I think we're halfway home."

"Home plate," said the dragon, and Larry beamed. The beast handed him back the card. "So that is my meal-to-be. And when may I have the pleasure—?"

"When he steps out onto that mound right there to pitch against my Cubs exactly one week from today. Got that?"

"Got it." The dragon helped itself to Shannon's beer and guzzled it noisily, dribbling most of the brew down onto poor Larry. "Sorry," it said. "It's difficult to be neat when you don't have lips."

"I dated someone like that once," Shannon mused, hailing the vendor for refills across the board. The dragon did for five more measures of the foamy; its belch rattled windows up and down the length of Michigan Avenue.

"Oh, great!" Larry threw his hands up in disgust. "I bet that Richter Scale ripper knocked everything I've already told you clean out of your narrow little skull."

The dragon took umbrage. "It did not. I have my orders. I am to devour one Billy Jim-Bob Borden, pitcher for the Mets, on this very site in one week's time. That *is* all you wish me to do for you, is it not, O Master?"

"Yes, yes, thank God *yes!*" Larry let his head droop with relief. "That's it, that's all, that is absolutely the whole shebang, my one and only desire, after which you may take yourself back to whatever backed-up drainpipe of reality spawned you."

"Good," said the dragon. "You have spoken, O Master, and I shall obey." Whereupon it spread its huge, leathery blue wings, caught a wayward breeze off the lake, and soared into the clouds. It returned in a swoop of such glorious grace that its sheer immanence caused the whole of Wrigley Field's audience to rise to their feet and collectively accept the fact that yes, Chicago, there *was* a real dragon.

The fact that it ate Steve Donahue, the lead hitter for the Cubs right off the bat, as it were, was also pretty darned persuasive.

"What is it doing? What-is-it-*doing*?" Larry shrilled, ripping the Cubs cap from his head and following it with several handfuls of hair.

"Well, it *did* ask you if all you wanted it to do was eat Borden in a week's time, and you *did* say yes, it was your sole desire," Shannon reminded him. "So I guess it figures that until then, it's a free agent."

Panic. Turmoil. Lots of shouting in Japanese. The scene down on the field and up in the stands was that uncomfortable amalgam of good old American survival instinct versus good old American rub-berneckers' death-wish. Larry and Shannon both leapt up to stand on their seats, the better to avoid being trampled by the thundering hordes of escaping spectators, only to discover that none of the thundering hordes were in any hurry to escape. Not when it looked like there was a pretty good chance of making it onto the evening news.

"Henry! Henry, let's get out of here!" shouted one matron from her place a few seats down from Larry and Shannon.

"You nuts, Darlene?" her mate replied. "We're right in a line with that lizard and the T.V. cameras. Hey! Hey, up here!" he shouted, waving a huge green foam-rubber hand, index finger extended, at the gentlemen of the electronic press. "We're number *one*! We're number *one*!"

The newshounds could not have cared less. It was dog-eat-dog on the Wrigley turf, as well as dragon-eat-Donahue. After the initial shock cooled, old reflexes kicked in hard. Orders were barked in the press box, phones seized, backup videocams dragooned into service as the journalists descended, bag and baggage, upon the playing field. The cohort of Japanese businessmen came trotting after in closed phalanx, for reasons known only to themselves.

There was chaos in the trenches, for the dugouts had been trans-formed from congenial shelters sacred to ump-cursing and crotch-scratching into military strongholds. Feelings ran high among the Cubs, many of whom seized their heaviest bats and swore to avenge poor Donahue's death upon the dragon's very skull. Their manager, Tommy Adano, had his hands full trying to restrain them. On the other side, the Braves might have no such personal stake in matters, but with the cameras on them they were constrained to live up to their name, at the least, and rouse a monster-threatening rhubarb for the benefit of the fans back home.

As for the dragon, it gobbled up its prey in two squirty bites, spit-ting out Donahue's cleats and cap like watermelon seeds. Then it looked around at the milling throng surrounding it and shook its head as if deploring so many snacks, so little time.

"They're nuts," Larry said to no one in particular. "They're out of their minds. Why don't they run away?"

"They're media," Shannon answered.

"They're meat."

His words proved true, with benefit of dragon. The newsmen were intent on giving the public what the public wanted, and the only thing that all members of the public there present wanted was their fifteen minutes of fame. As they swarmed about it, the dragon watched their shenanigans with that fine detachment usually exhibited by patrons of the better class of dessert trolleys.

Its hauteur was deceitfully encouraging to the bolder newshawks as well as to the more war-minded among the players. They mistook it for the state of somnolent sluggishness that common reptiles display after gorging themselves. How tragic, such careless generalizations. How sad that they could not do the simple, lifesaving arithmetic to prove that a single ingested ballplayer was hardly sufficient to glut even one of the dragon's bellies.

Carl Watson leapt from the dugout, brandishing a baseball bat to which he had affixed some especially sharp spikes. A frothing Tommy Adano pounded after, showing absolutely no concern for his star pitcher's morale to judge by the names he was calling him.

Gregory Hughes, with a fine "once more into the breech" spirit, led a head-on, mikes-foremost charge of two backup "color commentary" ex-jocks, three cameramen, and an assistant makeup girl who thought she was joining an escape party. Several of the Japanese businessmen jogged behind, perhaps under the impression that the Honorable Hughes-san was the closest thing they had to an official host and that it would be impolite to abandon him.

This turned out to be providential. The dragon was not full and ultimately not fussy, except when it came to munching electronic equipment.

Shiro Matsuhito managed to retrieve the rejected comm-unit and relayed the unfortunate news that the dragon was systematically consuming all comers.

"Yes, yes, yes!" he shouted into the mouthpiece. "He is doing what I tell you! Everybody, everybody he is eating, one after the next!"

"Waitaminnit," barked the harried anchorman still safe at Gregory Hughes' home station. "Slow down, okay? Where's Hughes?"

"Where I tell you!" Mr. Matsuhito insisted. "The dragon, it eats Hughes-san first. Watson second, and third—" he looked up to doublecheck "—Adano."

He wondered why the honorable gentleman with whom he spoke groaned so loudly. He marveled even more at the death-threats he received when he passed on the news that the dragon had just devoured the assistant makeup girl, whose name happened to be Tamara, and one of his own colleagues, the honorable Mr. Todai.

Up in the stands, Larry had gone so far as to tear his Cubs cap from his fevered brow and fling it down amid the puddles of spilled soda pop and crushed hot dog stubbins. "Gimme the book!" he bellowed at Shannon.

Dutifully she passed him the dog-eared paperback guide to matters occult. The price sticker from that strange little used-books store in Schaumberg still covered over part of the words *For Funne & Prophette* in the title. Larry flipped through the pages like a madman until he found the section he was looking for.

" 'To Banish Ye Dragonne . . .' " he read aloud. "Thank God!" With the look of a man possessed, or at least determined, he jammed his Cubs cap back on, settled it at a this-means-business angle, and stalked down onto the field. Shannon remained behind in nearly the same pose as a thousand pink-gowned princesses on a thousand fairy tale battlements. Her expression, however, was less *My Hero!* than *We're All Going to Die, and You First, Larry, Which is Kinda Too Bad Because I Kinda Like You and I Wish You Didn't Live with Your Mother.* Then she sighed, shrugged, and trotted down to the field herself, the better to pick up the pieces.

She did not reach the diamond as quickly as he did, owing to a slight touch of myopia that made her very cautious when confronted with large quantities of descending stairs. She held onto the railings and for the most part kept her eyes fixed on her feet, with occasional upward glances to see how things were going. Halfway there, she thought she heard Larry's shrill voice shouting, "Let me through! I'm a wizard!" Three-quarters of the way down she caught sight of the crowd parting so that he might approach the monster. She paused only long enough to see him raise a commanding hand at the dragon while the other thumbed awkwardly through the book. A series of eldritch and arcane syllables thundered from lips never meant to thunder anything—a sound quickly swallowed by the sonic boom of a dragon laughing. Shannon didn't know whether to redouble her pace to reach the field and stand by her man, or just give the whole thing up as too little, too late. When she had no more than a handful of steps left, there came the unmistakable *vroosh*! of flame and a nasty, burning smell. It seemed as if her decision had been made for her.

Strange to say, there were no Bits-O'-Larry to pop into a body bag, but his Cubs cap was a goner. The little man staggered into Shannon's arms and collapsed. She cradled his head in her lap and reflected that he looked rather sweet when barbecued. The layer of charcoal on his person was about analogous to that on a piece of Mother's Day breakfast toast as made by an ambitious three-year-old. A few fingerlings of smoke wafted up from his singed hair. A quick triage on Shannon's part revealed that the dragon was indeed a lizard of exceptional control and an artist among its kind. The damage to Larry was purely superficial, done more for dramatic effect than earnest destruction.

Oddly enough, the dragon's assault on Larry had effectively put its other plans for extended carnage and havoc on Hold. The great Worm yawned, snorted at the milling throng, curled up on the pitcher's mound and went to sleep with its forepaws hugging some particularly gory leftovers. From outside the stadium came the sound of police sirens approaching, but the dragon paid them no mind. It could fricassee Chicago's Finest before they were halfway through reading it its rights, and it knew it.

Shannon took advantage of the lull to tend to Larry. She found a half-empty cup of beer and used it to bring her knight in Extra Crispy armor around. "You're alive," she told him when he opened his eyes.

"The hell you say," he replied, sitting up suddenly, and kissed her so long and hard and true and honest that for a moment Shannon wondered as to the wisdom of letting nice guys read Hemingway. Then she settled down to enjoy it.

When at last the liplock let go, Shannon managed to pant, "So . . . the incantation didn't work?"

"Does it look like it did?" Larry returned. "Dragons are worse than kids when it comes to holding you to your word. Uh—you did say you wanted to have kids, didn't you?"

"Three," Shannon affirmed.

"Okay, one of each, then. Anyway, *it* said it'd gotten its assignment and if it could fulfill it before the *uribets* hit the fan, or whatever, then it was free to do anything it wanted until then because *I'd* said eating the Mets' pitcher was the only thing I wanted it to do. I had, in effect, waived my power over it in all other matters, including the consumption and/or incineration of other baseball players, reporters, and digestible bystanders."

"What if the time-limit runs out before it can eat the Mets' pitcher?" Shannon asked. "Can you banish it then?"

Larry held up a wad of blackened, curling sheets of paper that still smelled faintly of sulfur, chili-dogs, and beer. "It was your book. How good is your memory?" Shannon groaned; Larry comforted her. Thoroughly.

"If we survive," she said after awhile, "I'd like a church wedding."

"We might not," Larry reminded her, a canny look in his eye. "Care to cut to the honeymoon? It's not as if we're ever going to need any more of my blood—except to get the marriage license, and they don't care if I'm still a vir—"

"*Here?*" Shannon was scandalized. "You want us to make love *here?* On a field where the *Cubs* play?" The lady's resentment was understandable. "And you said I was special!"

But Larry chuckled. A brush with flaming death often wields transforming powers, and for some reason nerds cook up better than most other folk, developing a much-needed layer of crust where lesser men crumble. "But this isn't just a field where the Cubs play, darling," he said. "I'll bet there isn't a more priceless *lit d'amour* anywhere in the world than this field right here. If you believe the dragon, I mean."

"Larry, baby, I love you," Shannon remarked. "And because I love you I feel compelled to point out that I think the dragon sizzled up a great big dollop of your gray matter."

"I'm not nuts, Shannon. I'm just saying that the reason the dragon isn't going anywhere is that when I told it baseball is played on diamonds, it took it literally. Now it's convinced that under that dirt—"

"Astroturf," Shannon corrected. "I think."

"Whatever. Anyway, *under* it are the *real* diamonds. And you know how dragons are about sleeping on treasure. It told me it's not going anywhere, not even after the fifty-two *uribets* are up."

"You're kidding! I mean, I can understand relocating to Chicago, but voluntarily choosing to stay anywhere near the Cubs—" Shannon spread her hands, helpless to comprehend the ways of Worms.

"A nice, comfy bed to sleep on, a populace with no licensed or experienced dragon-slayers, and the equivalent of room service meals? Yeah, I think the greedy son-of-a-suitcase knows what it's doing." Larry looked thoughtful. "Greed . . . One thing I do recall from your book, Shannon, is where it said that dragons are very old, and very wise, and very acquisitive. Which is a nice way of calling them just as big pigs as us."

"So?" Shannon inquired.

"So . . ."

So, some time later, as the remains of three police cars smoldered on the outfield and the dragon sat picking its teeth with a nightstick, Larry once more sallied forth onto the turf. He had driven home, showered and picked up a change of clothes, but no weapons, sorcerous or mundane. Most of the spectators had retreated far from the line of very real fire, although Authorities demanding that they vacate the stadium were ignored. It mattered not that the dragon had given a whole new twist to the term Sudden Death Overtime. They had paid their money and, by God, so long as they had a fighting chance of living through this, they were going to get their money's worth.

"Ahem," said Larry.

The dragon put down the nightstick. "Yes?" it drawled.

"Shouldn't that be 'Yes, O Master?' " Larry prompted.

"Hardly." The dragon's jaws gaped in a mammoth yawn. "You

stopped being my Master about two *uribets*, seventeen-and-a-half *divblas* ago."

"Yeah? Well, you still owe me *something*. What about eating Billy Jim-Bob Borden?" Larry asked, pretending great annoyance.

"So sorry, O Former Master. Had the opportunity presented itself within my time limit, I would have been pleased to oblige you. Now, however . . ." Unable to shrug, the dragon was not all hampered when it came to giving the old Bronx cheer. When done with a forked tongue, it was twice as messy.

Larry wiped dragon-spit from his face. "You never said that my desires had to be fulfillable within your time limit."

"You never asked me."

"If your time is up, why are you still here?"

"I like it here," the Worm replied, and enumerated the very same reasons Larry himself had elucidated for Shannon's benefit earlier. In conclusion it said, "So you see, you risk more than you know in coming along and bothering me this way now. Nothing compels me to obey you at all, and you remain unscalded where you stand only upon my sufferance. Call me a sentimental fool, but when a Former Master has as many strikes against him as you do, I just can't bear to finish him off."

"Strikes against me? You *did* say strikes against me?" Larry beamed. "I may not be a great wizard, but at least I managed to teach you a thing or two about baseball."

"Lovely game," said the dragon. It was caught off guard by a sudden belch and a Cubs cap flew out of its mouth. "I am very fond of it. But I am fonder of the diamonds upon which it is played. Diamonds by themselves, however, do not make for an entirely satisfactory bed. If you want real sleepable softness and slumber support, you need an assortment of gemstones plus the more popular precious metals. As soon as I have rested I intend to issue an ultimatum to the citizens of this town."

"Oh?"

"Yes; they must bring hither all their gold, jewels, and other valuables at once, to add to my bed, else see their city burned to the ground around them!"

"It's been done already," Larry said. He reached into the left pocket of his chinos and took out a blue disposable butane lighter. "By a cow." He flicked it on. "Belonged to a Mrs. O'Leary." He reached into his right pocket and took out a something thin, flat, oblong, and fairly fragile-looking. "Or so they say." He held the little pasteboard three inches above the flame.

"What's that?" the dragon asked.

"A baseball card," Larry said in an offhanded manner. "Nowadays they come in waxed paper-wrapped packs, just the cards alone. Before that, you had to buy them with bubblegum that was so bad, chewing the cards was better. But 'way back when, you got 'em with cigarettes. Smoking's a filthy habit, don't you think?"

The dragon gave a suspicious growl and sent up small, involuntary puffs through its nostrils.

"Okay, so you disagree. But there was this one ballplayer back then who didn't. He wasn't a smoker himself and he thought tobacco was a health hazard and he figured that having his picture used as a promotional gimmick for cigarettes was wrong, so he demanded that the company withdraw it at once. Only a few of those cards ever went public, which is what makes them so valuable."

The dragon's eyes lit up like furnaces at the v-word.

"Yessir," Larry went on, letting the lighter rise about an inch nearer the pasteboard. "You sure have to admire that Honus Wagner for being a man of principle."

Dawn hit the dragon right between the eyes. It uttered a horrified shriek, made all the more terrible by the fact that so few things can horrify a dragon. "That's a Honus Wagner!" it cried. "By the Egg, be careful, you mortal fool! Its value is incalculable!"

"I know how valuable a Honus Wagner is," Larry replied. "I was the one who taught you that, remember?"

"And you will burn up such a treasure?"

"Right before your beady little eyes, yup."

The dragon snarled. "Do so and die."

"How?" Larry smirked. "By fire?"

The dragon's snarl went deep into its chest and rumbled loud its helpless frustration. A huge paw armed with fearsome golden talons raised itself above Larry's head, but the little man just brought the card close enough to the flame so that any impact strong enough to jostle him would mean its immediate, fiery destruction. The paw lowered, the talons drummed an angry tattoo on the playing field.

"All right; it's your card," the dragon grumbled. "Deal."

"It's simple. I give you the card, you leave our world and return to your own."

"Agreed," said the dragon a trifle too readily.

"*And* you swear by whatever oath you hold most sacred that you will never, never, *never* come back here!" Larry plugged the obvious loophole solidly.

The dragon's head drooped. "I cannot promise that. Some powers are greater than my own. What if you summon me here again?"

"I'd call the odds on that mighty slim. You smashed the book, remember? And I don't think Waldenbooks or B. Dalton's has it on permanent re-order."

"The book?" A glimmer of cunning came into the dragon's eye. "Oh, but a mage of your inherent gifts does not need all that folderol to summon a Worm. In truth, you have but to speak aloud the cantrip—" here the dragon lowered its voice and whispered a short series of syllables which, by a happy coincidence, just happened to be the easily remembered brand names of Larry's favorite chocolate syrup, deodorant, and steak knives not available in any store "—let fall the requisite five drops of virgin's blood, and I shall appear to do your slightest bidding."

"What makes you think I'm dumb enough to make the same mistake twice?"

"No mistake, O Potential Master, if your first request is that I give you the mystic words to send me home again once our business is done. Think of all I could do for you. Think of the wealth I could fetch you, the enemies I could slay for you, the power I could bring you, the bevies of beautiful, sloe-eyed women I could deliver to your doorstep, piping hot." The dragon showed more teeth than a platoon of life insurance salesmen and said, "Trust me."

"I'll think about it. Meanwhile, do we have a bargain?"

The dragon raised its right forepaw. "I do swear most mightily by the sacred Egg of my forebears; we do." Larry handed over the card, which the dragon snatched up eagerly. Holding it near its eyes, the Worm remarked, "Honus Wagner looks rather young."

"Clean living," Larry supplied. "And just think: If a Honus Wagner card is worth so much *here* for its rarity, imagine how valuable it'll be in your home world where they don't have any baseball cards at all!"

"Say, you're right!" The dragon actually wagged its tail. "And to think that old Grythphulc was lording it over the rest of us because *he* owns the bones of a pedigreed albino swordsman! I can hardly wait to see his face when he beholds my Honus!" Gloating nastily, the dragon launched itself skyward until, reaching the proper altitude for such things, it vanished.

It was in a lull between press conferences, civic banquets, parades, and his induction as an honorary member of the Baseball Hall of Fame that Larry was finally able to steal a few moments alone with Shannon. The rendezvous took place in his room because, as his mother reminded him, receiving the plaudits of a grateful city was no excuse for not cleaning out his closet.

"Maybe I should call the dragon back," Larry grumbled. "Let *him* clean out the closet."

"And the rest of Chicago for lunch, while he's at it." Shannon kicked off her shoes. "Dragons are sly. No matter what he promised you, he'd find a way to get out of it if you bring him back. And once he's back, how long do you think it'll take before he finds out that was no Honus Wagner; that was a wallet-size fake baseball card of you when you played Little League? Boy, talk about dead meat!"

"Oh, yeah? Well, maybe it'd be worth the risk. Just a few fast magical words, five drops of virgin's blood, and next thing I know I'll have wealth, power, more hordes of gorgeous women than I'll know what to do with—"

"Probably true." Shannon sighed and yanked him out of the closet by the neck of his honest-to-sweat Cubs shirt. "Absolute power corrupts. I can see I've got my work cut out for me."

"What work?" asked Larry as she shoved him in the direction of the bed.

"Saving you from corruption." She sat down beside him. "By re-moving the temptation to resummon the dragon." She threw her arms around his neck. "By removing the means to resummon it."

Later, Larry's mother pounded on the door and demanded what on earth he was thinking of, making all that racket.

"Baseball scores, Mom!" he shouted back. "I'm thinking of base-ball scores!" Well, he *was*.

Lethal Perspective

◻ ◻ ◻

by Alan Dean Foster

They assembled in the Special Place. Though a considerable amount of time had passed, none forgot the date and none lost their way. It took more than several days for all to arrive, but they were very long lived and none took umbrage at another's delay.

It was the very end of the season and a small team of climbers from France was exploring a new route up the south col of K5 when one happened to look up instead of down. He shouted as loud as he could, but the wind was blowing and it took a moment before he could get the attention of the woman directly ahead of him. By the time she tilted her head back to scan the sky, the apparition had vanished. She studied her climbing companion warily and then smiled. So did the others, when they were informed.

They put it down to momentary snow blindness, and the climber who'd looked up didn't press the point. He was a realist and knew he had no chance of convincing the least skeptical of his friends. But to his dying day he would know in his heart that what he'd seen that frigid morning just east of Everest was not an accident of snow blindness, or a patrolling eagle, or a figment of his imagination.

The Special Place was filling up. Legendary nemesis of the subcontinent, Videprasa had the least distance to travel and arrived first. Old Kurenskaya the Terrible appeared next, making good time despite his age and the need to avoid the limited air defense radar based in southern Kazahkistan.

O'mou'iroturotu showed up still damp from hours of flying through the biggest typhoon the South China Sea had experienced in a decade, and Booloongatta the Night soon after. They were followed by Cracuti from central Europe, Al-Methzan ras-Shindar from out of the Empty Quarter, and Nhauantehotec from the green depths of Central America.

It grew crowded in the Special Place as more of the Kind arrived. They jostled for space, grumbling and rumbling until the vast ancient cavern resounded like the Infinite Drum. Though solitary by nature, all gathered eagerly at this singular predetermined time.

Despite the incredible altitude and the winter storm which had begun to rage outside, conditions within the Special Place remained comfortable. Creatures that are capable of spontaneous internal combustion do not suffer the cold.

As the Elder Dominant, Old Kurenskaya performed the invocation. This was concluded with a binding, concerted blast of flame the largest napalm ordnance in the American armory could not have matched, resulting in a massive avalanche outside the Special Place as a great sheet of ice and snow was loosened from beneath. The French climbing team far to the west heard but did not witness it.

"It is the time," Kurenskaya announced. He was very old and most of his back scales had shaded from red to silver. But he could still ravage and destroy with the best of them. Only these days, like the others, he had to be more circumspect in his doings.

He glanced around the crowded cavern, vertical yellow pupils narrowing. "I do not see As'ah'mi among us." There was a moment of confusion until Nhauantehotec spoke up. "He will not be joining us."

Kurenskaya bared snaggle teeth. "Why not? What has happened?"

Nhauantehotec sighed and black smoke crept from his nostrils. "He was not careful. As we must all be careful these days. I think he forgot to soar in the stealthy manner and was picked up on U.S. Border Patrol radar. Not surprisingly, they mistook him for a drug runner's plane and shot him down. I heard him curse his forgetfulness as he fell and altered my path to see if I could help, but by the time I arrived he was but combusting brimstone and sulfur on the ground."

A smoky murmur filled the cavern. Old Kurenskaya raised both clawed forefeet for silence. "Such is the fate of those who let time master their minds. We sorrow for one of our own who forgot. But the rest are come, healthy and well." He gestured to the one next to him with a clawed foot the size of a steam-shovel bucket. "As first to arrive it falls to you, Videprasa, to regale us with tales of your accomplishments."

She nodded deferentially to the Elder Dominant and instinctively flexed vast, membranous wings. "I have since the last gathering kept myself properly hidden, emerging only to wreak appropriate havoc through the stealth we have had to adopt since humans developed advanced technologies." Raising a forefoot and looking thoughtful, she began ticking off disasters on her thick, clawed fingers.

"Eleven years ago there was a train wreck north of New Delhi. The devastating avalanche in Bhutan I instigated twenty years ago. There was the plastics plant explosion in Uttar Pradesh and the sinking of the small freighter during the typhoon that struck Bangladesh only a few years past." She smiled, showing cutlery that would have been the envy of a dozen crocodiles.

"I am particularly proud of the chemical plant damage in Bhopal that killed so many."

Al-Methzan ras-Shindar snorted fire. "That was very subtly done. You are to be commended." He straightened proudly, thrusting out his scaly chest and glaring around the cavern. "You all know what I have been up to lately." Quong the Magnificent flicked back the tendrils that lined his head and jaws. "You were fortunate to find yourself in so efficacious a situation."

Snakelike, Al-Methzan's head whipped around. "I do not deny it, but it required skill to take advantage." Eyes capable of striking terror into the bravest man glittered with the memory. "It was purest pleasure. I struck and ripped and tore and was not noticed. The humans were too busy amongst themselves. And around me, around me every day, were those wonderful burning wells to dance about and dart through and tickle my belly against." Al-Methzan ras-Shindar stretched luxuriously, the tips of his great wings scraping the ceiling.

"I haven't felt this clean in centuries."

There was a concerted murmur of envious delight from the others, and Old Kurenskaya nodded approvingly. "You did well. How else have you fulfilled the mandate?"

Al-Methzan ras-Shindar resumed the recitation of his personal tales of mayhem and destruction. He was followed by Booloongatta the Night and then the rest. The hours and the days passed in pleasant companionship, reminiscence, and safety, as the storm howled outside the gathering place. They were safe here. The Roof of the World saw few humans in the best of times, and in the winter was invariably little visited.

There was more to the gathering than mere camaraderie, however. More to the boasting of accomplishments than a desire simply to impress others of one's kind. For the gathering and the telling constituted also a competition. For approval, surely, and for admiration, truly. But there was more at stake than that.

There was the Chalice.

It hung 'round Old Kurenskaya's neck, suspended from a woven rope of pure asbestos fiber, thick as a man's arm. It was large for a human drinking utensil, tiny by the standards of the Kind. The great Berserker Jaggskrolm had taken the prize from the human Gunnar Rakeiennen in 1029, in a battle atop Mt. Svodmaggen that had lasted for four days and rent the air with fire and fury. When all had done and the killer Rakeiennen lay dead, his fortress razed, his golden horde taken, his women ravished (the great Jaggskrolm having been ritually mindful of the traditions), practically nothing remained unburned save the jewel-studded, golden chalice with which the most beauteous of Rakeiennen's women had bought her freedom (not to mention saving herself from a rough evening).

Ever since it had been a symbol of dominance, of the most effective and best applied skills of the Kind. Old Kurenskaya had won it during the last Tatar invasion of his homeland and had kept it ever since, having last been awarded it by acclamation (the only way it could be awarded) for his work among the humans during the purges and famines of the 1920s and 30s. Admittedly, he'd had human help, but his fellows did not feel cheated. Such assistance was to be welcomed, and cleverly used. As Al-Methzan ras-Shindar had utilized events so recently.

It seemed truly that because of his most recent accomplishments ras-Shindar had the inside track on securing the Chalice. Nhauante-hotec had been working particularly hard, and the devastating achievements of skillful Mad Sunabaya of the Deep impressed all the assembled with their breadth and thoroughness. Despite his years, Old Kurenskaya wasn't about to give up the Chalice without a fight, and it had to be admitted that his brief but critical presence at Chernobyl would go down as a hallmark accomplishment of modern times.

When at last all had concluded their recitative, and waited content and with satisfaction for the vote of acclamation, Old Kurenskaya was pleased. It had been a gathering free of discord, unlike some in the past, and had demonstrated conclusively that the Kind could not only survive but prosper in their efforts despite the technical exploits of their old enemy, humankind. He was elated, and ready. All, in fact, were anxious for the choosing, so they could be on their way. Though all had enjoyed the gathering, they preferred to keep to themselves, and by now were growing irritable.

"If, then, each has stipulated and declaimed their deeds, and retold their tales, I will name names, and call for the choosing." He raised a clawed forefoot to begin.

Only to be interrupted.

"Wait, please! I have not spoken."

Dire reptilian heads swiveled in the direction of the voice. It was so slight as to be barely intelligible, and those of the Kind with smaller hearing organs than their more floridly earred brethren had to strain to make out individual words. But it was one of them, no doubt of that, for it spoke in the secret and ancient language known only to the Kind.

Something like a small, scaly hummingbird appeared in the air before Old Kurenskaya and hovered there noiselessly.

"What is this?" Videprasa emitted a smoky burst of flame and laughter. "A bird has slipped in among us, to be out of the storm, no doubt!"

"No," roared Cracuti, the sharp spines of her back flexing with amusement, "this is not a bird, but a bug!"

The minuscule speaker whirled angrily. "I am Nomote, of the Kind." Laughter and smoke filled the gathering place. "I demand to be heard!"

Old Kurenskaya raised both clawed forefeet and the ferocious, terrific laughter gradually died down. He scowled at the tiny visitor. "There are three recent-born among us. I did not know of a fourth."

"Who would admit to birthing *this*?" snorted Videprasa, and another round of awesome laughter shook rock from the walls of the cavern.

Old Kurenskaya looked around reprovingly. "This Nomote is of the Kind—if . . . somewhat lesser than most of us. Give to him the deference he deserves, as befits the traditions." An abashed silence settled over the gathering.

The Elder Dominant nodded to the hovering mite. "Speak to us then of your exploits." One of the assembled sniggered but went quiet when Old Kurenskaya glared threateningly in his direction. "Tell of what you have done to fulfill the traditions of the Kind." He sat back on his hindquarters, his leathery, age-battered wings rumpled elegantly about him.

"I am young and have not the experience or strength of others who have accomplished so much." A few murmurs of grudging approval sounded among the assembled. "I have had to study our ancient adversaries and to learn. I have struggled to master the stealthy ways needed to carry out the work without being noticed by the humans and their clever new machines." It hesitated, wee wings beating furiously to keep it in place.

"Alas, I have had not the skill, nor the strength, nor the prowess to do as so many of you have done. I have done but one thing, and it, like myself, is small."

Nomote's humbleness and modesty had by now won for him some sympathy among the assembled, for who among them could not save for the intervention of fortuitous fate imagine himself in such a poignant condition.

"Tell us of what you have done and what you do," said Old Kurenskaya encouragingly. He glared warningly one more time, but by now the gathering was subdued. "None of the Kind will laugh, I promise it. Any offender will have to deal with *me*." At that moment Old Kurenskaya did not look so old.

Nomote blinked bright, tiny eyes. A small puff of dark smoke emerged from the tip of his snout. "I go invisibly among those humans who are ready and those who are reluctant, I breathe the addiction into their nostrils and their mouths, and then when they weaken and are susceptible, I light their cigarettes."

They gave him the Chalice, which was too large for him to carry, much less wear around his neck. But Nhauantehotec moved it to a convenient lair for him, and though he could not fly with it shining broadly against his chest as had his glorious predecessors, it made a most excellent bath in which to relax upon returning from a good day's work among the execrable humans.

The Storm King

🔲 🔲 🔲

by Joan D. Vinge

They said that in those days the lands were cursed that lay in the shadow of the Storm King. The peak thrust up from the gently rolling hills and fertile farmlands like an impossible wave cresting on the open sea, a brooding finger probing the secrets of heaven. Once it had vomited fire and fumes, ash and molten stone had poured from its throat; the distant forerunners of the people who lived beneath it now had died of its wrath. But the Earth had spent Her fury in one final cataclysm, and now the mountain lay quiet, dark, and cold, its mouth choked with congealed stone.

And yet still the people lived in fear. No one among them remembered having seen its summit, which was always crowned by cloud; lightning played in the purple, shrouding robes, and distant thunder filled the dreams of the folk who slept below with the roaring of dragons.

For it was a dragon who had come to dwell among the crags: that elemental focus of all storm and fire carried on the wind, drawn to a place where the Earth's fire had died, a place still haunted by ancient grief. And sharing the spirit of fire, the dragon knew no law and obeyed no power except its own. By day or night it would rise on furious wings of wind and sweep over the land, inundating the crops with rain, blasting trees with its lightning, battering walls and tearing away rooftops; terrifying rich and poor, man and beast, for the sheer pleasure of destruction, the exaltation of uncontrolled power. The people had prayed to the new gods who had replaced their worship of the Earth to deliver them; but the new gods made Their home in the sky, and seemed to be beyond hearing.

By now the people had made Their names into curses, as they pried their oxcarts from the mud or looked out over fields of broken grain and felt their bellies and their children's bellies tighten with hunger. And they would look toward the distant peak and curse the Storm King, naming the peak and the dragon both; but always in whispers and mutters, for fear the wind would hear them, and bring the dark storm sweeping down on them again.

The storm-wracked town of Wyddon and its people looked up only briefly in their sullen shaking-off and shoveling-out of mud as a stranger picked his way among them. He wore the woven leather of a common solider, his cloak and leggings were coarse and ragged, and he walked the planks laid down in the stinking street as though determination alone kept him on his feet. A woman picking through baskets of stunted leeks in the marketplace saw with vague surprise that he had entered the tiny village temple; a man putting fresh thatch on a torn-open roof saw him come out again, propelled by the indignant, orange-robed priest.

"If you want witchery, find yourself a witch! This is a holy place; the gods don't meddle in vulgar magic!"

"I can see that," the stranger muttered, staggering in ankle-deep mud. He climbed back onto the boards with some difficulty and obvious disgust. "Maybe if they did you'd have streets and not rivers of muck in this town." He turned away in anger, almost stumbled over a mud-colored girl blocking his forward progress on the boardwalk.

"You priests should bow down to the Storm King!" the girl postured insolently, looking toward the priest. "The dragon can change all our lives more in one night than your gods have done in a lifetime."

"Slut!" The priest shook his carven staff at her; its necklace of golden bells chimed like absurd laughter. "There's a witch for you, beggar. If you think she can teach you to tame the dragon, then go with her!" He turned away, disappearing into the temple. The stranger's body jerked, as though it strained against his control, wanting to strike at the priest's retreating back.

"You're a witch?" The stranger turned and glared down at the bony figure standing in his way, found her studying him back with obvious skepticism. He imagined what she saw—a foreigner, his straight black hair whacked off like a serf's, his clothes crawling with filth, his face grimed and gaunt and set in a bitter grimace. He frowned more deeply.

The girl shook her head. "No. I'm just bound to her. You have business to take up with her, I see—about the Storm King." She smirked, expecting him to believe she was privy to secret knowledge.

"As you doubtless overheard, yes." He shifted his weight from one leg to the other, trying fruitlessly to ease the pain in his back.

She shrugged, pushing her own tangled brown hair back from her face. "Well, you'd better be able to pay for it, or you've come a long way from Kwansai for nothing."

He started, before he realized that his coloring and his eyes gave that much away. "I can pay." He drew his dagger from its hidden sheath, the only weapon he had left, and the only thing of value. He let her glimpse the jeweled hilt before he pushed it back out of sight.

Her gray eyes widened briefly. "What do I call you, Prince of Thieves?" with another glance at his rags.

"Call me Your Highness," not lying, and not quite joking.

She looked up into his face again, and away. "Call me Nothing, Your Highness. Because I am nothing." She twitched a shoulder at him. "And follow me."

They passed the last houses of the village without further speech, and followed the mucky track on into the dark, dripping forest that lay at the mountain's feet. The girl stepped off the road and into the trees without warning; he followed her recklessly, half angry and half afraid that she was abandoning him. But she danced ahead of him through the pines, staying always in sight, although she was plainly impatient with his lagging pace. The dank chill of the sunless wood gnawed his aching back and swarms of stinging gnats feasted on his exposed skin; the bare-armed girl seemed as oblivious to the insects as she was to the cold.

He pushed on grimly, as he had pushed on until now, having no choice but to keep on or die. And at last his persistence was rewarded; he saw the forest rise ahead, and buried in the flank of the hillside among the trees was a mossy hut linteled by immense stones.

The girl disappeared into the hut as he entered the clearing before it. He slowed, looking around him at the clusters of carven images pushing up like unnatural growths from the spongy ground, or dangling from tree limbs. Most of the images were subtly or blatantly obscene. He averted his eyes and limped between them to the hut's entrance.

He stepped through the doorway without waiting for an invitation, to find the girl crouched by the hearth in the cramped interior, wearing the secret smile of a cat. Beside her an incredibly wrinkled, ancient woman sat on a three-legged stool. The legs were carved into shapes that made him look away again, back at the wrinkled face and the black, buried eyes that regarded him with flinty bemusement. He noticed abruptly that there was no wall behind her: the far side of the hut melted into the black volcanic stone, a natural fissure opening into the mountain's side.

"So, Your Highness, you've come all the way from Kwansai seeking the Storm King, and a way to tame its power?"

He wrapped his cloak closely about him and grimaced, the nearest thing to a smile of scorn that he could manage. "Your girl has a quick tongue. But I've come to the wrong place, it seems, for real power."

"Don't be so sure!" The old woman leaned toward him, shrill and spiteful. "You can't afford to be too sure of anything, Lassan-din. You were prince of Kwansai, you should have been king there when your father died, and overlord of these lands as well. And now you're nobody and you have no home, no friends, barely even your life. Nothing is what it seems to be . . . it never is."

Lassan-din's mouth went slack; he closed it, speechless at last. *Nothing is what it seems.* The girl called Nothing grinned up at him from the floor. He took a deep breath, shifting to ease his back again.

"Then you know what I've come for, if you already know that much, witch."

The hag half-rose from her obscene stool; he glimpsed a flash of color, a brighter, finer garment hidden beneath the drab outer robe she wore—the way the inner woman still burned fiercely bright in her eyes, showing through the wasted flesh of her ancient body. "Call me no names, you prince of beggars! I am the Earth's Own. Your puny Kwansai priests, who call my sisterhood 'witch,' who destroyed our holy places and drove us into hiding, know nothing of power. They're fools, they don't believe in power and they are powerless, charlatans. You know it or you wouldn't be here!" She settled back, wheezing. "Yes, I could tell you what you want; but suppose you tell me."

"I want what's mine! I want my kingdom." He paced restlessly, two steps and then back. "I know of elementals, all the old legends. My people say that dragons are stormbringers, born from a joining of Fire and Water and Air, three of the four Primes of Existence. Nothing but the Earth can defy their fury. And I know that if I can hold a dragon in its lair with the right spells, it must give me what I want, like the heroes of the Golden Time. I want to use its power to take back my lands."

"You don't want much, do you?" The old woman rose from her seat and turned her back on him, throwing a surreptitious handful of something into the fire, making it flare up balefully. She stirred the pot that hung from a hook above it; spitting five times into the noxious brew as she stirred. Lassan-din felt his empty stomach turn over. "If you want to challenge the Storm King, you should be out there climbing, not here holding your hand out to me."

"Damn you!" His exasperation broke loose, and his hand wrenched her around to face him. "I need some spell, some magic, some way to pen a dragon up. I can't do it with my bare hands!"

She shook her head, unintimidated, and leered toothlessly at him. "My power comes to me through my body, up from the Earth Our Mother. She won't listen to a man—especially one who would destroy her worship. Ask your priests who worship the air to teach you their empty prayers."

He saw the hatred rising in her, and felt it answered: The dagger was out of its hidden sheath and in his hand before he knew it, pressing the soft folds of her neck. "I don't believe you, witch. See this dagger—" quietly, deadly. "If you give me what I want, you'll have the jewels in its hilt. If you don't, you'll feel its blade cut your throat."

"All right, all right!" She strained back as the blade's tip began to bite. He let her go. She felt her neck; the girl sat perfectly still at their feet, watching. "I can give you something, a spell. I can't guarantee She'll listen. But you have enough hatred in you for ten men—and maybe that will make your man's voice loud enough to penetrate Her skin. This mountain is sacred to Her, She still listens through its ears, even if She no longer breathes here."

"Never mind the superstitious drivel. Just tell me how I can keep the dragon in without it striking me dead with its lightning. How I can fight fire with fire—"

"You don't fight fire with fire. You fight fire with water."

He stared at her; at the obviousness of it, and the absurdity—"The dragon is the creator of storm. How can mere water—?"

"A dragon is anathema. Remember that, prince who would be king. It is chaos, power uncontrolled; and power always has a price. That's the key to everything. I can teach you the spell for controlling the waters of the Earth; but you're the one who must use it."

He stayed with the women through the day, and learned as the hours passed to believe in the mysteries of the Earth. The crone spoke words that brought water fountaining up from the well outside her door while he looked on in amazement, his weariness and pain forgotten. As he watched she made a brook flow upstream; made crystal droplets beading the forest pines join in a diadem to crown his head, and then with a word released them to run cold and helpless as tears into the collar of his ragged tunic.

She seized the fury that rose up in him at her insolence, and challenged him to do the same. He repeated the ungainly, ancient spellwords defiantly, arrogantly—and nothing happened. She scoffed, his anger grew; she jeered and it grew stronger. He repeated the spell again, and again, and again . . . until at last he felt the terrifying presence of an alien power rise in his body, answering the call of his blood. The droplets on the trees began to shiver and commingle; he watched an eddy form in the swift clear water of the stream—. The Earth had answered him.

His anger failed him at the unbelievable sight of his success . . . and the power failed him too. Dazed and strengthless, at last he knew his anger for the only emotion with the depth or urgency to move the body of the Earth, or even his own. But he had done the impossible— made the Earth move to a man's bidding. He had proved his right to be a king, proved that he could force the dragon to serve him as well. He laughed out loud. The old woman moaned and spat, twisting her hands that were like gnarled roots, mumbling curses. She shuffled away toward the woods as though she were in a trance; turned back abruptly as she reached the trees, pointing past him at the girl standing like a ghost in the hut's doorway. "You think you've known the Earth; that you own Her, now. You think you can take anything and make it yours. But you're as empty as that one, and as powerless!" And she was gone.

Night had fallen through the dreary wood without his realizing it. The girl Nothing led him back into the hut, shared a bowl of thick, strangely herbed soup and a piece of stale bread with him. He ate gratefully but numbly, the first warm meal he had eaten in weeks; his mind drifted into waking dreams of banqueting until dawn in royal halls.

When he had eaten his share, wiping the bowl shamelessly with a crust, he stood and walked the few paces to the hut's furthest corner. He lay down on the hard stone by the cave mouth, wrapping his cloak around him, and closed his eyes. Sleep's darker cloak settled over him.

And then, dimly, he became aware that the girl had followed him, stood above him looking down. He opened his eyes unwillingly, to see her unbelt her tunic and pull it off, kneel down naked at his side. A piece of rock crystal, perfectly transparent, perfectly formed, hung glittering coldly against her chest. He kept his eyes open, saying nothing.

"The Old One won't be back until you're gone; the sight of a man calling on the Earth was too strong for her." Her hand moved insinuatingly along his thigh.

He rolled away from her, choking on a curse as his back hurt him sharply. "I'm tired. Let me sleep."

"I can help you. She could have told you more. I'll help you tomorrow . . . if you lie with me tonight."

He looked up at her, suddenly despairing. "Take my body, then; but it won't give you much pleasure." He pulled up the back of his tunic, baring the livid scar low on his spine. "My uncle didn't make a cripple of me —but he might as well have." When he even thought of a woman there was only pain, only rage . . . only that.

She put her hand on the scar with surprising gentleness. "I can help that too . . . for tonight." She went away, returned with a small jar of ointment and rubbed the salve slowly into his scarred back. A strange, cold heat sank through him; a sensuous tingling swept away the grinding ache that had been his only companion through these long months of exile. He let his breath out in an astonished sigh, and the girl lay down beside him, pulling at his clothes.

Her thin body was as hard and bony as a boy's, but she made him forget that. She made him forget everything, except that tonight he was free from pain and sorrow, tonight he lay with a woman who desired him, no matter what her reason. He remembered lost pleasure, lost joy, lost youth, only yesterday . . . until yesterday became tomorrow.

In the morning he woke, in pain, alone and fully clothed, aching on the hard ground. *Nothing* . . . He opened his eyes and saw her standing at the fire, stirring a kettle. A *dream*—? The cruel betrayal that was reality returned tenfold.

They ate together in a silence that was sullen on his part, and inscrutable on hers. After last night it seemed obvious to him that she was older than she looked—as obvious as the way he himself had changed from boy to old man in a span of months. And he felt an insubstantiality about her that he had not noticed before, an elusiveness that might only have been an echo of his dream. "I dreamed, last night . . ."

"I know." She climbed to her feet, cutting him off, combing her snarled hair back with her fingers. "You dream loudly." Her face was closed.

He felt a frown settle between his eyes again. "I have a long climb. I'd better get started." He pushed himself up and moved stiffly toward the doorway. The old hag still had not returned.

"Not that way," the girl said abruptly. "This way." She pointed as he turned back, toward the cleft in the rock.

He stood still. "That will take me to the dragon?"

"Only part way. But it's easier by half. I'll show you." She jerked a brand out of the fire and started into the maw of darkness.

He went after her with only a moment's uncertainty. He had lived in fear for too long; if he was afraid to follow this witch-girl into her Goddess's womb, then he would never have the courage to challenge the Storm King.

The low-ceilinged cleft angled steeply upward, a natural tube formed millennia ago by congealing lava. The girl began to climb confidently, as though she trusted some guardian power to place her hands and feet surely—a power he could not depend on as he followed her up the shaft. The dim light of day snuffed out behind him, leaving only her torch to guide them through utter blackness, over rock that was alternately rough enough to flay the skin from his hands and slick enough to give him no purchase at all. The tunnel twisted like a worm, widening, narrowing, steepening, folding back on itself in an agony of contortion. His body protested its own agony as he dragged it up handholds in a sheer rock face, twisted it, wrenched it, battered it against the unyielding stone. The acrid smoke from the girl's torch stung his eyes and clogged his lungs; but it never seemed to slow her own tireless motion, and she took no pity on his weakness. Only the knowledge of the distance he had come kept him from demanding that they turn back; he could not believe that this could possibly be an easier way than climbing the outside of the mountain. It began to seem to him that he had been climbing through this foul blackness for all of eternity, that this was another dream like his dream last night, but one that would never end.

The girl chanted softly to herself now; he could just hear her above his own labored breathing. He wondered jealously if she was drawing strength from the very stone around them, the body of the Earth. He could feel no pulse in the cold heart of the rock; and yet after yesterday he did not doubt its presence, even wondering if the Earth sapped his own strength with preternatural malevolence. *I am a man, I will be king!* he thought defiantly. And the way grew steeper, and his hands bled.

"Wait —!" He gasped out the word at last, as his feet went out from under him again and he barely saved himself from sliding back down the tunnel. "I can't go on."

The girl, crouched on a level spot above him, looked back and down at him and ground out the torch. His grunt of protest became a grunt of surprise as he saw her silhouetted against a growing gray-brightness. She disappeared from his view; the brightness dimmed and then strengthened.

He heaved himself up and over the final bend in the wormhole, into a space large enough to stand in if he had had the strength. He crawled forward hungrily into the brightness at the cave mouth, found the girl kneeling there, her face raised to the light. He welcomed the fresh air into his lungs, cold and cleansing; looked past her—and down.

They were dizzyingly high on the mountain's side, above the treeline, above a sheer unscalable face of stone. A fast-falling torrent of water roared on their left, plunging out and down the cliff-face. The sun winked at him from the cloud-wreathed heights; its angle told him they had climbed for the better part of the day. He looked over at the girl.

"You're lucky," she said, without looking back at him. Before he could even laugh at the grotesque irony of the statement she raised her hand, pointing on up the mountainside. "The Storm King sleeps—another storm is past. I saw the rainbow break this sunrise."

He felt a surge of strength and hope, absorbed the indifferent blessing of the Holy Sun. "How long will it sleep?"

"Two more days, perhaps. You won't reach its den before night. Sleep here, and climb again tomorrow."

"And then?" He looked toward her expectantly.

She shrugged.

"I paid you well," not certain in what coin, anymore. "I want a fair return! How do I pen the beast?"

Her hand tightened around the crystal pendant hanging against her tunic. She glanced back into the cave mouth. "There are many waters flowing from the heights. One of them might be diverted to fall past the entrance of its lair."

"A waterfall? I might as well hold up a rose and expect it to cower!"

"Power always has its price; as the Old One said." She looked directly at him at last. "The storm rests here in mortal form—the form of the dragon. And like all mortals, it suffers. Its strength lies in the scales that cover its skin. The rain washes them away—the storm is agony to the stormbringer. They fall like jewels, they catch the light as they fall, like a trail of rainbow. It's the only rainbow anyone here has ever seen . . a sign of hope, because it means an end to the storm; but a curse, too, because the storm will always return, endlessly."

"Then I could have it at my mercy . . ." He heard nothing else.

"Yes. If you can make the Earth move to your will." Her voice was flat.

His hands tightened. "I have enough hate in me for that."

"And what will you demand, to ease it?" She glanced at him again, and back at the sky. "The dragon is defiling this sacred place; it should be driven out. You could become a hero to my people, if you forced the dragon to go away—a god. They need a god who can do them some good . . ."

He felt her somehow still watching him, measuring his response, even though she had looked away. "I came here to solve my problem, not yours. I want my own kingdom, not a kingdom of mud-men. I need the dragon's power—I didn't come here to drive that away."

The girl said nothing, still staring at the sky.

"It's a simple thing for you to move the waters—why haven't you driven the dragon away yourself, then?" His voice rasped in his parched throat, sharp with unrecognized guilt.

"I'm Nothing. I have no power—the Old One holds my soul." She looked down at the crystal.

"They why won't the Old One do it?"

"She hates, too. She hates what our people have become under the new gods, your gods. That's why she won't."

"I'd think it would give her great pleasure to prove the impotence of the new gods." His mouth stretched sourly.

"She wants to die in the Earth's time, not tomorrow." The girl folded her arms, and her own mouth twisted.

He shook his head. "I don't understand that . . . why you didn't destroy our soldiers, our priests, with your magic?"

"The Earth moves slowly to our bidding, because She is eternal. An arrow is small—but it moves swiftly."

He laughed once, appreciatively. "I understand."

"There's a cairn of stones over there." She nodded back into the darkness. "Food is under it." He realized that this must have been a place of refuge for the women in times of persecution. "The rest is up to you." She turned, merging abruptly into the shadows.

"Wait!" he called, surprising himself. "You must be tired."

She shook her head, a deeper shadow against darkness.

"Stay with me—until morning." It was not quite a demand, not quite a question.

"Why?" He thought he saw her eyes catch light and reflect it back at him, like a wild thing's.

Because I had a dream. He did not say it, did not say anything else.

"Our debts have balanced." She moved slightly, and something landed on the ground at his feet; his dagger. The hilt was pockmarked with empty jewel settings; stripped clean. He leaned down to pick it up. When he straightened again she was gone.

"You need a light—!" He called after her again.

Her voice came back to him, from a great distance: "May you get what you deserve!" And then silence, except for the roaring of the falls.

He ate, wondering whether her last words were a benediction or a curse. He slept, and the dreams that came to him were filled with the roaring of dragons.

With the light of a new day he began to climb again, following the urgent river upward toward its source that lay hidden in the waiting crown of clouds. He remembered his own crown, and lost himself in memories of the past and future, hardly aware of the harsh sobbing of his breath, of flesh and sinew strained past a sane man's endurance. Once he had been the spoiled child of privilege, his father's only son—living in the world's eye, his every whim a command. Now he was as much Nothing as the witch-girl far down the mountain. But he would live the way he had again, his every wish granted, his power absolute—he *would* live that way again, if he had to climb to the gates of heaven to win back his birthright.

The hours passed, endlessly, inevitably, and all he knew was that slowly, slowly, the sky lowered above him. At last the cold, moist edge of clouds enfolded his burning body, drawing him into another world of gray mist and gray silences; black, glistening surfaces of rock; the white sound of the cataract rushing down from even higher above. Drizzling fog shrouded the distances any way he turned, and he realized that he did not know where in this layer of cloud the dragon's den lay. He had assumed that it would be obvious, he had trusted the girl to tell him all he needed to know . . . Why had he trusted her? That pagan slut—his hand gripped the rough hilt of his dagger; dropped away, trembling with fatigue. He began to climb again, keeping the sound of falling water nearby for want of any other guide. The light grew vaguer and more diffuse, until the darkness falling in the outer world penetrated the fog world and the haze of his exhaustion. He lay down at last, unable to go on, and slept beneath the shelter of an overhang of rock.

He woke stupefied by daylight. The air held a strange acridness that hurt his throat, that he could not identify. The air seemed almost to crackle; his hair ruffled, although there was no wind. He pushed himself up. He knew this feeling now: a storm was coming. A storm coming . . . a storm, here? Suddenly, fully awake, he turned on his knees, peering deeper beneath the overhang that sheltered him. And in the light of dawn he could see that it was not a simple overhang, but another opening into the mountain's side—a wider, greater one, whose depths the day could not fathom. But far down in the blackness a flickering of unnatural light showed. His hair rose in the electric breeze, he felt his skin prickle. *Yes . . . yes!* A small cry escaped him. He had found it! Without even knowing it, he had slept in the mouth of the dragon's lair all night. Habit brought a thanks to the gods to his lips, until he remembered—He muttered a *thank you* to the Earth beneath him before he climbed to his feet. A brilliant flash silhouetted him; a rumble like distant thunder made the ground vibrate, and he froze. Was the dragon waking—?

But there was no further disturbance, and he breathed again. Two days, the girl had told him, the dragon might sleep. And now he had reached his final trial, the penning of the beast. Away to his right he could hear the cataract's endless song. But would there be enough water in it to block the dragon's exit? Would that be enough to keep it prisoner, or would it strike him down in lightning and thunder, and sweep his body from the heights with torrents of rain? . . . Could he even move one droplet of water, here and now? Or would he find that all the thousand doubts that gnawed inside him were not only useless but pointless?

He shook it off, moving out and down the mist-dim slope to view the cave mouth and the river tumbling past it. A thin stream of water already trickled down the face of the opening, but the main flow was diverted by a folded knot of lava. If he could twist the water's course and hold it, for just long enough . . .

He climbed the barren face of stone at the far side of the cave mouth until he stood above it, confronting the sinuous steel and flashing white of the thing he must move. It seemed almost alive, and he felt weary, defeated, utterly insignificant at the sight of it. But the mountain on which he stood was a greater thing than even the river, and he knew that within it lay power great enough to change the water's course. But he was the conduit, his will must tap and bend the force that he had felt stir in him two days ago.

He braced his legs apart, gathered strength into himself, trying to recall the feel of magic moving in him. He recited the spell-words, the focus for the willing of power—and felt nothing. He recited the words again, putting all his concentration behind them. Again nothing. The Earth lay silent and inert beneath his feet.

Anger rose in him, at the Earth's disdain, and against the strange women who served Her—the jealous, demanding anger that had opened him to power before. And this time he did feel the power stir in him, sluggishly, feebly. But there was no sign of any change in the water's course. He threw all his conscious will toward change, *change, change*—but still the Earth's power faltered and mocked him. He let go of the ritual words at last, felt the tingling promise of energy die, having burned away all his own strength.

He sat down on the wet stone, listened to the river roar with laughter. He had been so sure that when he got here the force of his need would be strong enough . . . *I have enough hate in me*, he had told the girl. But he wasn't reaching it now. Not the real hatred that had carried him so far beyond the limits of his strength and experience. He began to concentrate on that hatred, and the reasons behind it; the loss, the pain, the hardship and fear . . .

His father had been a great ruler over the lands that his ancestors had conquered. And he had loved his queen, Lassan-din's mother. But when she died, his unhealing grief had turned him ruthless and ironwilled. He had become a despot, capricious, cruel, never giving an inch of his power to another man—even his spoiled and insecure son. Disease had left him wasted and witless in the end. And Lassan-din, barely come to manhood, had been helpless, unable to block his jealous uncle's treachery. He had been attacked by his own guard as he prayed in the temple (*In the temple*—his mouth pulled back), and maimed, barely escaping with his life, to find that his entire world had come to an end. He had become a hunted fugitive in his own land, friendless, trusting no one—forced to lie and steal and grovel to survive. He had eaten scraps thrown out to dogs and lain on hard stones in the rain, while the festering wound in his back kept him from any rest . . .

Reliving each day, each moment, of his suffering and humiliation, he felt his rage and his hunger for revenge grow hotter. The Earth hated this usurper of Her holy place, the girl had said . . . but no more than he hated the usurper of his throne. He climbed to his feet again, every muscle on fire, and held out his hands. He shouted the incantation aloud, as though it could carry all the way to his homeland. *His homeland:* he would see it again, make it his own again—

The power entered him as the final word left his mouth, paralyzing every nerve, stopping even the breath in his throat. Fear and elation were swept up together into the maelstrom of his emotions, and power exploded like a sun behind his eyes. But through the fiery haze that blinded him, he could still see the water heave up from its bed—a steely wall crowned with white, crumbling over and down on itself. It swept toward him, a terrifying cataclysm, until he thought that he would be drowned in the rushing flood. But it passed him by where he stood, plunging on over the outcropping roof of the cave below. Eddies of foam swirled around his feet, soaking his stained leggings.

The power left him like the water's surge falling away. He took a deep breath, and another, backing out of the flood. His body moved sluggishly; drained, abandoned, an empty husk. But his mind was full with triumph and rejoicing.

The ground beneath his feet shuddered, jarring his elation, dropping him giddily back into reality. He pressed his head with his hands as pain filled his senses, a madness crowding out coherent thought— a pain that was not his own.

(Water . . . !) Not a plea, but outrage and confusion, a horror of being trapped in a flood of molten fire. *The dragon.* He realized suddenly what had invaded his mind; realized that he had never stopped to wonder how a storm might communicate with a man: not by human speech, but by stranger, more elemental means. Water from the fall he had created must be seeping into its lair . . . His face twisted with satisfaction. "Dragon!" He called it with his mind and his voice together.

(Who calls? Who tortures me? Who fouls my lair? Show yourself, slave!)

"Show yourself to me, Storm King! Come out of your cave and

destroy me—if you can!" The wildness of his challenge was tinged with terror.

The dragon's fury filled his head until he thought that it would burst; the ground shook beneath his feet. But the rage turned to frustration and died, as though the gates of liquid iron had bottled it up with its possessor. He gulped air, holding his body together with an effort of will. The voice of the dragon pushed aside his thoughts again, trampled them underfoot; but he knew that it could not reach him, and he endured without weakening.

(Who are you, and why have you come?) He sensed a grudging resignation in the formless words, the feel of a ritual as eternal as the rain.

"I am a man who should have been a king. I've come to you, who are King of Storms, for help in regaining my own kingdom."

(You ask me for that? Your needs mean nothing, human. You were born to misery, born to crawl, born to struggle and be defeated by the powers of Air and Fire and Water. You are meaningless, you are less than nothing to me!)

Lassan-din felt the truth of his own insignificance, the weight of the dragon's disdain. "That may be," he said sourly. "But this insignificant human has penned you up with the Earth's blessing, and I have no reason to ever let you go unless you pledge me your aid."

The rage of the storm beast welled up in him again, so like his own rage; it rumbled and thundered in the hollow of the mountain. But again a profound agony broke its fury, and the raging storm subsided. He caught phantom images of stone walls lit by shifting light, the smell of water.

(If you have the strength of the Earth with you, why bother me for mine?)

"The Earth moves too slowly," *and too uncertainly*, but he did not say that. "I need a fury to match my own."

(Arrogant fool,) the voice whispered, (you have no measure of my fury.)

"Your fury can crumble walls and blast towers. You can destroy a fortress castle—and the men who defend it. I know what you can do," refusing to be cowed. "And if you swear to do it for me, I'll set you free."

(You want a castle ruined. Is that all?) A tone of false reason crept into the intruding thoughts.

"No. I also want for myself a share of your strength—protection from my enemies." He had spent half a hundred cold, sleepless nights planning these words; searching his memory for pieces of dragon-lore, trying to guess the limits of its power.

(How can I give you that? I do not share my power, unless I strike you dead with it.)

"My people say that in the Golden Times the heroes wore mail made from dragon scales, and were invincible. Can you give me that?" He asked the question directly, knowing that the dragon might evade the truth, but that it was bound by immutable natural law, and could not lie.

(I can give you that,) grudgingly. (Is that all you ask of me?)

Lassan-din hesitated. "No. One more thing." His father had taught him caution, if nothing else. "One request to be granted at some future time—a request within your power, but one you must obey."

The dragon muttered, deep within the mountainside, and Lassan-din sensed its growing distress as the water poured into the cave. (If it is within my power, then, yes!) Dark clouds of anger filled his mind. (Free me, and you will have everything you ask!) *And more—* Did he heard that last, or was it only the echoing of his own mind? (Free me, and enter my den.)

"What I undo, I can do again." He spoke the warning more to reassure himself than to remind the dragon. He gathered himself mentally, knowing this time what he was reaching toward with all his strength, made confident by his success. And the Earth answered him once more. He saw the river shift and heave again like a glistening serpent, cascading back into its original bed; opening the cave mouth to his sight, fanged and dripping. He stood alone on the hillside, deafened by his heartbeat and the crashing absence of the river's voice. And then, calling his own strength back, he slid and clambered down the hillside to the mouth of the dragon's cave.

The flickering illumination of the dragon's fire led him deep into the maze of stone passageways, his boots slipping on the wet rock. His hair stood on end and his fingertips tingled with static charge, the air reeked of ozone. The light grew stronger as he rounded a final corner of rock; blazed up, echoing and reechoing from the walls. He shouted in protest as it pinned him like a creeping insect against the cave wall.

The light faded gradually to a tolerable level, letting him observe as he was observed, taking in the towering, twisted black-tar formations of congealed magma that walled this cavern . . . the sudden, heart-stopping vision they enclosed. He looked on the Storm King in silence for a time that seemed endless.

A glistening layer of cast-off scales was its bed, and he could scarcely tell where the mound ceased and the dragon's own body began. The dragon looked nothing like the legends described, and yet just as he had expected it to (and somehow he did not find that strange): Great mailed claws like crystal kneaded the shifting opalescence of its bed; its forelegs shimmered with the flexing of its muscles. It had no hindquarters, its body tapered into the fluid coils of a snake's form woven through the glistening pile. Immense segmented wings, as leathery as a bat's, as fragile as a butterfly's, cloaked its monstrous strength. A long sinuous neck stretched toward him, red faceted eyes shone with inner light from a face that was closest to a cat's face of all the things he knew, but fiercely fanged and grotesquely distorted. The horns of a stag sprouted from its forehead, and foxfire danced among the spines. The dragon's size was a thing that he could have described easily, and yet it was somehow immeasurable, beyond his comprehension.

This was the creature he had challenged and brought to bay with his feeble spell-casting . . . this boundless, pitiless, infinite demon of the air. His body began to tremble, having more sense than he did. But he *had* brought it to bay, taken its word-bond, and it had not blasted him the moment he entered its den. He forced his quavering voice to carry boldly, "I'm here. Where is my armor?"

(Leave your useless garments and come forward. My scales are my strength, lie among them and cover yourself with them. But remember when you do that if you wear my mail, and share my power, you may find them hard to put off again. Do you accept that?)

"Why would I ever want to get rid of power? I accept it! Power is the center of everything."

(But power has its price, and we do not always know how high it will be.) The dragon stirred restlessly, remembering the price of power as the water still pooling on the cavern's floor seeped up through its shifting bed.

Lassan-din frowned, hearing a deceit because he expected one. He stripped off his clothing without hesitation and crossed the vast, shadow-haunted chamber to the gleaming mound. He lay down below the dragon's baleful gaze and buried himself in the cool, scintillating flecks of scale. They were damp and surprisingly light under his touch, adhering to his body like the dust rubbed from a moth's wing. When he had covered himself completely, until even his hair glistened with myriad infinitesimal lights, the dragon bent its head until the horrible mockery of a cat's face loomed above him. He cringed back as it opened its mouth, showing him row behind row of inward-turning teeth, and a glowing forge of light. It let its breath out upon him, and his sudden scream rang darkly in the chamber as lightning wrapped his unprotected body.

But the crippling lash of pain was gone as quickly as it had come; and looking at himself he found the coating of scales fused into a film of armor as supple as his own skin, and as much a part of him now. His scale-gloved hands met one another in wonder, the hands of an alien creature.

(Now come.) A great glittering wing extended, inviting him to climb. (Cling to me as your armor clings to you, and let me do your bidding and be done with it.)

He mounted the wing with elaborate caution, and at last sat astride the reptilian neck, clinging to it with an uncertainty that did not fully acknowledge its reality.

The dragon moved under him without ceremony or sign, slithering down from its dais of scales with a hiss and rumble that trembled the closed space. A wind rose around them with the movement; Lassan-din felt himself swallowed into a vortex of cold, terrifying force that took his breath away, blinding and deafening him as he was sucked out of the cave-darkness and into the outer air.

Lightning cracked and shuddered, penetrating his closed lids, splitting apart his consciousness; thunder clogged his chest, reverberating through his flesh and bones like the crashing fall of an avalanche. Rain lashed him, driving into his eyes, swallowing him whole but not dissolving or dissipating his armor of scales.

In the first wild moments of storm he had been piercingly aware of an agony that was not his own, a part of the dragon's being tied into his consciousness, while the fury of rain and storm fed back on their creator. But now there was no pain, no awareness of anything tangible; even the substantiality of the dragon's existence beneath him had faded. The elemental storm was all that existed now, he was aware only of its raw, unrelenting power surrounding him, sweeping him on to his destiny.

After an eternity lost in the storm he found his sight again, felt the dragon's rippling motion beneath his hands. The clouds parted and as his vision cleared he saw, ahead and below, the gray stone battlements of the castle fortress that had once been his . . . and was about to become his again. He shouted in half-mad exultation, feeling the dragon's surging, unconquerable strength become his own. He saw from his incredible height the tiny, terrified forms of those men who had defeated and tormented him, saw them cowering like worms before the doom descending upon them. And then the vision was torn apart again in a blinding explosion of energy, as lightning struck the stone towers again and again, and the screams of the fortress's defenders were lost in the avalanche of thunder. His own senses reeled, and he felt the dragon's solidness dissolve beneath him once more; with utter disbelief felt himself falling, like the rain . . . "No! No—!"

But his reeling senses righted abruptly, and he found himself standing solidly on his own feet, on the smoking battlements of his castle. Storm and flame and tumbled stone were all around him, but the blackened, fear-filled faces of the beaten defenders turned as one to look up at his; their arms rose, pointing, their cries reached him dimly. An arrow struck his chest, and another struck his shoulder, staggering him; but they fell away, rattling harmlessly down his scaled body to his feet. A shaft of sunlight broke the clouds, setting afire the glittering carapace of his armor. Already the storm was beginning to dissipate; above him the dragon's retreat stained the sky with a band of rainbow scales falling. The voice of the storm touched his mind a final time, (You have what you desire. May it bring you the pleasure you deserve.)

The survivors began, one by one, to fall to their knees below him.

Lassan-din had ridden out of exile on the back of the whirlwind, and his people bowed down before him, not in welcome but in awe and terror. He reclaimed his birthright and his throne, purging his realm of those who had overthrown it with vengeful thoroughness, but never able to purge himself of the memories of what they had done to him. His treacherous uncle had been killed in the dragon's attack, robbing Lassan-din of his longed-for retribution, the payment in kind for his own crippling wound. He wore his bitterness like the glittering dragonskin, and he found that like the dragonskin it could never be cast off again. His people hated and feared him for his shining alienness; hated him all the more for his attempts to secure his place as their ruler, seeing in him the living symbol of his uncle's inhumanity, and his father's. But he knew no other way to rule them; he could only go on, as his father had done before him, proving again and again to his people that there was no escaping what he had become. Not for them, not for himself.

They called him the Storm King, and he had all the power he had ever dreamed of—but it brought him no pleasure, no ease, no escape from the knowledge that he was hated or from the chronic pain of his maimed back. He was both more and less than a man, but he was no longer a man. Lying alone in his chambers between silken sheets he dreamed now that he still slept on stones; and dreamed the dream he had had long ago in a witch's hut, a dream that might have been something more . . . And when he woke he remembered the witch-girl's last words to him, echoed by the storm's roaring—"May you get what you deserve."

At last he left his fortress castle, where the new stone of its mending showed whitely against the old; left his rule in the hands of ad-

visers cowed by threats of the dragon's return; left his homeland
again for the dreary, gray-clad land of his exile.

He did not come to the village of Wydden as a hunted exile this time,
but as a conqueror gathering tribute from his subject lands. No one
there recognized the one in the other, or knew why he ordered the village priest thrown bodily out of his wretched temple into the muddy
street. But on the dreary day when Lassan-din made his way at last
into the dripping woods beneath the ancient volcanic peak, he made
the final secret journey not as a conqueror.

He came alone to the ragged hut pressed up against the brooding
mountain wall, suffering the wet and cold, like a friendless stranger.
He came upon the clearing between the trees with an unnatural sud-
denness, to find a figure in mud-stained, earth-brown robes standing
by the well, waiting, without surprise. He knew instantly that it was
not the old hag; but it took him a longer moment to realize who it
was: The girl called Nothing stood before him, dressed as a woman
now, her brown hair neatly plaited on top of her head and bearing
herself with a woman's dignity. He stopped, throwing back the hood
of his cloak to let her see his own glittering face—though he was certain she already knew him, had expected him.

She bowed to him with seeming formality. "The Storm King hon-
ors my humble shrine." Her voice was not humble in the least.

"Your shrine?" He moved forward. "Where's the old bitch?"

She folded her arms as though to ward him off. "Gone forever. As
I thought you were. But I'm still here, and I serve in her place; I am
Fallatha, the Earth's Own, now. And your namesake still dwells in
the mountain, bringing grief to all who live in its cloud-shadow . . . I
thought you'd taken all you could from us, and gained everything
you wanted. Why have you come back, and come like a beggar?"

His mouth thinned. But this once he stopped the arrogant response
that came too easily to his lips—remembering that he had come here
the way he had, to remind himself that he must ask, and not demand.
"I came because I need your help again."

"What could I possibly have to offer our great ruler? My spells are nothing compared to the storm's wrath. And you have no use for my poor body—"

He jerked at the mocking echo of his own thoughts. "Once I had, on that night we both remember—that night you gave me back the use of mine." He gambled with the words. His eyes sought the curve of her breasts, not quite hidden beneath her loose outer robe.

"It was a dream, a wish; no more. It never happened." She shook her head, her face still expressionless. But in the silence that fell between them he heard a small, uncanny sound that chilled him: somewhere in the woods a baby was crying.

Fallatha glanced unthinkingly over her shoulder, toward the hut, and he knew then that it was her child. She made a move to stop him as he started past her; let him go, and followed resignedly. He found the child inside, an infant squalling in a blanket on a bed of fragrant pine boughs. Its hair was midnight black, its eyes were dark, its skin dusky; his own child, he knew with a certainty that went beyond simply what his eyes showed him. He knelt, unwrapping the blanket— let it drop back as he saw the baby's form. "A girl-child," dull with disappointment.

Fallatha's eyes said that she understood the implications of his disappointment. "Of course. I have no more use for a boy-child than you have for this one. Had it been a male child, I would have left it in the woods."

His head came up angrily, and her gaze slapped him with his own scorn. He looked down again at his infant daughter, feeling ashamed. "Then it did happen . . ." His hands tightened by his knees. "Why?" looking up at her again.

"Many reasons, and many you couldn't understand . . . But one was to win my freedom from the Old One. She stole my soul, and hid it in a tree to keep me her slave. She might have died without telling me where it was. Without a soul I had no center, no strength, no reality. So I brought a new soul into myself—this one's," smiling suddenly at the wailing baby, "and used its focus to make her give me back my own. And then with two souls," the smile hardened, "I took hers away. She wanders the forest now searching for it. But she won't find it." Fallatha touched the pendant of rock crystal that hung against her breast; what had been ice clear before was now a deep, smoky gray color.

Lassan-din suppressed a shudder. "But why *my* child?" *My child.* His own gaze would not stay away from the baby for long. "Surely any village lout would have been glad to do you the service."

"Because you have royal blood, you were a king's son—you are a king."

"That's not necessarily proof of good breeding." He surprised himself with his own honesty.

"But you called on the Earth, and She answered you. I have never seen Her answer a man before, or since . . . And because you were in need." Her voice softened unexpectedly. "An act of kindness begets a kind soul, they say."

"And now you hope to beget some reward for it, no doubt." He spoke the words with automatic harshness. "Greed and pity—a fitting set of god-parents, to match her real ones."

She shrugged. "You will see what you want to see, I suppose. But even a blind man could see more clearly." A frown pinched her forehead. "You've come here to me for help, Lassan-din; I didn't come to you."

He rubbed his scale-bright hands together, a motion that had become a habit long since; they clicked faintly. "Does—does the baby have a name?"

"Not yet. It is not our custom to name a child before its first year. Too often they die. Especially in these times."

He looked away from her eyes. "What will you do with—our child?" Realizing suddenly that it mattered a great deal to him.

"Keep her with me, and raise her to serve the Earth, as I do."

"If you help me again, I'll take you both back to my own lands, and give you anything you desire." He searched her face for a response.

"I desire to be left in peace with my child and my goddess." She leaned down to pick the baby up, let it seek her breast.

His inspiration crystallized: "Damn it, I'll throw my own priests out, I'll make your goddess the only one and you her high priestess!"

Her eyes brightened, and faded. "A promise easily spoken, and difficult to keep."

"What do you want, then?" He got to his feet, exasperated.

"You have a boon left with the dragon, I know. Make it leave the mountain. Send it away."

He ran his hands through his glittering hair. "No. I need it. I came here seeking help for myself, not your people."

"They're your people now—they *are* you. Help them and you help yourself! Is that so impossible for you to see?" Her own anger blazed white, incandescent with frustration.

"If you want to be rid of the dragon so much, why haven't you sent it away yourself, witch?"

"I would have." She touched the baby's tiny hand, its soft black hair. "Long ago. But until the little one no longer suckles my strength away, I lack the power to call the Earth to my purpose."

"Then you can't help me, either." His voice was flat and hopeless.

"I still have the salve that eased your back; but it won't help you now, it won't melt away your dragon's skin . . . I couldn't help your real needs, even if I had all my power."

"What do you mean?" He thrust his face at her. "Are you saying you couldn't ever undo this scaly hide of mine, that protects me from my people's hatred—and makes me a monster in their eyes? You think that's really why I've come to you? What makes you think I'd ever want to give up *my* power, my protection?" He clawed at his arms.

"It's not a man's skin that makes him a monster, or a god," Fallatha said quietly. "It's what lies beneath the skin, behind the eyes— his actions, not his face. You've lost your soul, as I lost mine; and only you know where to find it . . . But perhaps it would do you good to shed that skin that keeps you safe from hatred; and from love and joy and mercy, all the other feelings that might pass between human beings, between your people and their king."

"Yes! Yes, I want to be free of it, by the Holy Sun!" His face collapsed under the weight of his despair. "I thought my power would give me everything. But behind this armor I'm still nothing; less than that crippled wretch you took pity on!" He realized at last that he had come here this time to rid himself of the same things he had come to rid himself of—and to find—before. "I have a last boon due me from the dragon. It made me as I am; it can unmake me." He ran his hands down his chest, feeling the slippery, unyielding scales hidden beneath the rich cloth of his shirt.

"You mean to seek it out again, then?"

He nodded, and his hands made fists.

She carried the baby with her to the shelf above the crooked window, took down a small earthenware pot. She opened it and held it close to the child's face still buried at her breast; the baby sagged into sleep in the crook of her arm. She turned back to his uncomprehending face. "The little one will sleep now until I wake her. We can take the inner way, as we did before."

"You're coming? Why?"

"You didn't ask me that before. Why ask it now?"

He wasn't sure whether it was a question or an answer. Feeling as though not only his body but his mind was an empty shell, he only shrugged and kept silent.

They made the nightmare climb into blackness again, worming their way upward through the mountain's entrails; but this time she did not leave him where the mountain spewed them out, close under the weeping lid of the sky. He rested the night with the mother of his only child, the two of them lying together but apart. At dawn they pushed on, Lassan-din leading now, following the river's rushing torrent upward into the past.

They came to the dragon's cave at last, gazed on it for a long while in silence, having no strength left for speech.

"Storm King!" Lassan-din gathered the rags of his voice and his concentration for a shout. "Hear me! I have come for my last request!"

There was an alien stirring inside his mind; the charge in the air and the dim flickering light deep within the cave seemed to intensify.

(So you have returned to plague me.) The voice inside his head cursed him, with the weariness of the ages. He felt the stretch and play of storm-sinews rousing; remembered suddenly, dizzily, the feel of his ride on the whirlwind. (Show yourself to me.)

They followed the winding tunnel as he had done before to an audience in the black hall radiant with the dust of rainbows. The dragon crouched on its scaly bed, its glowering ruby eye fixed on them. Lassan-din stopped, trying to keep a semblance of self-possession. Fallatha drew her robes close together at her throat and murmured something unintelligible.

(I see that this time you have the wisdom to bring your true source of power with you . . . though she has no power in her now. Why have you come to me again? Haven't I given you all that you asked for?)

"All that and more," he said heavily. "You've doubled the weight of the griefs I brought with me before."

(I?) The dragon bent its head; its horns raked them with clawfingered shadows in the sudden, swelling brightness. (I did nothing to you. Whatever consequences you've suffered are no concern of mine.)

Lassan-din bit back a stinging retort; said, calmly, "But you remember that you owe me one final boon. You know that I've come to collect it."

(Anything within my power.) The huge cat-face bowed ill-humoredly; Lassan-din felt his skin prickle with the static energy of the moment.

"Then take away these scales you fixed on me, that make me invulnerable to everything human!" He pulled off his drab, dark cloak and the rich royal clothing of red and blue beneath it, so that his body shone like an echo of the dragon's own.

The dragon's faceted eyes regarded him without feeling. (I cannot.)

Lassan-din froze as the words out of his blackest nightmares turned him to stone. "What—what do you mean, you cannot? You did this to me—you can undo it!"

(I cannot. I can give you invulnerability, but I cannot take it away from you. I cannot make your scales dissolve and fall away with a breath any more than I can keep the rain from dissolving mine, or causing me exquisite pain. It is in the nature of power that those who wield it must suffer from it, even as their victims suffer. That is power's price—I tried to warn you. But you didn't listen . . . none of them have ever listened.) Lassan-din felt the sting of venom, and the ache of an ageless empathy.

He struggled to grasp the truth, knowing that the dragon could not lie. He swayed, as belief struck him at last like a blow. "Am I . . . am I to go through the rest of my life like this, then? Like a monster?" He rubbed his hands together, a useless, mindless washing motion.

(I only know that it is not in my power to give you freedom from yourself.) The dragon wagged its head, its face swelling with light, dazzling him. (Go away, then,) the thought struck him fiercely, (and suffer elsewhere!)

Lassan-din turned away; stumbling like a beaten dog. But Fallatha caught at his glittering, naked shoulder, shook him roughly. "Your boon! It still owes you one—ask it!"

"Ask for what?" he mumbled, barely aware of her. "There's nothing I want."

"There is! Something for your people, for your child—even for you. Ask for it! Ask!"

He stared at her, saw her pale, pinched face straining with suppressed urgency and desire. He saw in her eyes the endless sunless days, the ruined crops, the sodden fields—the mud and hunger and misery the Storm King had brought to the lands below for three times her lifetime. And the realization came to him that even now, when he had lost control of his own life, he still had the power to end this land's misery. Understanding came to him at last that he had been given an opportunity to use his power positively, unselfishly, for the good of the people he ruled . . . for his own good. That it meant a freer choice, and perhaps a truer humanity, than anything he had ever done. That his father had lost something many years ago which he had never known was missing from his own life, until now. He turned back into the view of the dragon's hypnotically swaying head. "My last boon, then, is something else; something I know to be within your power, stormbringer. I want you to leave this mountain, leave these lands, and never return. I want you to travel seven days on your way before you seek a new settling place, if you ever do.

Travel as fast as you can, and as far, without taking retribution from the lands below. That is the final thing I ask of you."

The dragon spat in blinding fury. He shut his eyes, felt the ground shudder and roll beneath him. (You dare to command me to leave my chosen lands? You dare?)

"I claim my right!" He shouted it, his voice breaking. "Leave these lands alone—take your grief elsewhere and be done with them, and me!"

(As you wish, then—) The Storm King swelled above them until it filled the cave-space, its eyes a garish hellshine fading into the night-blackness of storm. Lightning sheeted the closing walls, thunder rumbled through the rock, a screaming whirlwind battered them down against the cavern floor. Rain poured over them until there was no breathing space, and the Storm King roared its agony inside their skulls as it suffered for its own revenge. Lassan-din felt his senses leaving him, with the knowledge that the storm would be the last thing he ever knew, the end of the world . . .

But he woke again, to silence. He stirred sluggishly on the wet stone floor, filling his lungs again and again with clear air, filling his empty mind with the awareness that all was quiet now, that no storm raged for his destruction. He heard a moan, not his own, and coughing echoed hollowly in the silence. He raised his head, reached out in the darkness, groping, until he found her arm. "Fallatha—?"

"Alive . . . praise the Earth."

He felt her move, sitting up, dragging herself toward him. The Earth, the cave in which they lay, had endured the storm's rage with sublime indifference. They helped each other up, stumbled along the wall to the entrance tunnel, made their way out through the blackness onto the mountainside.

They stood together, clinging to each other for support and reassurance, blinking painfully in the glaring light of early evening. It took him long moments to realize that there was more light than he remembered, not less.

"Look!" Fallatha raised her arm, pointing. Water dripped in a silver line from the sleeve of her robe. "The sky! The sky—" She laughed, a sound that was almost a sob.

He looked up into the aching glare, saw patches that he took at first for blackness, until his eyes knew them finally for blue. It was still raining lightly, but the clouds were parting, the tyranny of gray was broken at last. For a moment he felt her joy as his own, a fleeting, wild triumph—until looking down, he saw his hands again, and his shimmering body still scaled, monstrous, untransformed . . . "Oh, gods—!" His fists clenched at the sound of his own curse, a useless plea to useless deities.

Fallatha turned to him, her arm still around his shoulder, her face sharing his despair. "Lassan-din. I always knew that you were a good man, even though you have done evil things . . . You have reclaimed your soul today—remember that, and remember that my people will love you for your sacrifice. The world exists beyond yourself, and you will see that how you make your way through it matters." She touched his scaled cheek hesitantly, a promise.

"But all they'll ever see is how I look! And no matter what I do from now on, when they see the mark of damnation on me, they'll only remember why they hated me." He caught her arms in a bruising grip. "Fallatha, help me, please—I'll give you anything you ask!"

She shook her head, biting her lips, "I can't, Lassan-din. No more than the dragon could. You must help yourself, change yourself—I can't do that for you."

"How? How can I rid myself of this skin, if all the magic of Earth and Sky can't do it?" He sank to his knees, feeling the rain strike the opalescent scales and trickle down—feeling lit dimly, barely, as though the rain fell on someone else. Remorse and regret filled him now, as rage had filled him on this spot once before. Tears welled in his eyes and spilled over, in answer to the calling-spell of grief; ran down his face, mingling with the rain. He put up his hands, sobbing uncontrollably, unselfconsciously, as though he were the last man alive in the world, and alone forever.

And as he wept he felt a change begin in the flesh that met there, face against hands. A tingling and burning, the feel of skin sleep-deadened coming alive again. He lowered his hands wonderingly,

saw the scales that covered them dissolving, the skin beneath them
his own olive-brown, supple and smooth. He shouted in amazement,
and wept harder, pain and joy intermingled, like the tears and rain
that melted the cursed scales from his body and washed them away.

He went on weeping until he had cleansed himself in body and
spirit, freed himself from the prison of his own making. And then,
exhausted and uncertain, he climbed to his feet again, meeting the
calm, gray gaze of the Earth's gratitude in Fallatha's eyes. He smiled
and she smiled; the unexpectedness of the expression, and the sight
of it, resonated in him.

Sunlight was spreading across the patchwork land far below,
dressing the mountain slope in royal greens, although the rain still
fell around them. He looked up almost unthinkingly, searching—
found what he had not realized he sought. Fallatha followed his
glance and found it with him. Her smile widened at the arching band
of colors, the rainbow; not a curse any longer, or a mark of pain, but
once again a promise of better days to come.

Dragon's Teeth

▢ ▢ ▢

by David Drake

The sound of squealing axles drifted closer on the freezing wind. The watching Roman raised his eyes an inch above the rim of his brush-screened trench. A dozen Sarmatian wagons were hulking toward him into the twilight. Their wheels of uncured oak, gapped and irregular at the fellies, rumbled complainingly as they smashed stiff grass and bushes into the unyielding soil.

A smile of grim satisfaction brushed Vettius's lips as the Sarmatians approached. He did not touch the bow that lay beside him; it was still too soon.

The enormous weight of the wagons turned every finger's breadth of rise into a steep escarpment up which the oxen had to plod. They grunted out great plumes of breath as they threw their weight into the traces. Sexless, almost lifeless in their poses of stolid acceptance, the drivers hunched on the high wagon seats. Like the oxen, they had been at their killing work since dawn. The wind slashed and eddied about the canopies of aurochs hide that covered the boxes. Tendrils of smoke from heating fires within squirmed through the peaks. They hung for a moment in the sunset before scudding off into invisibility.

The last of the wagons was almost within the defile, Vettius noted. It would be very soon now.

Among the Sarmatians the whole family traveled together, even to war. The children and nursing mothers huddled inside the wagons.

So did the warriors; their work, like that of the horses tethered behind each wain, was yet to come. Soon the wagons would halt and laager up in the darkness. Using night as a shroud, the reivers would mount and thunder across the frozen Danube. Laughingly they would return before dawn with booty and fresh Roman ears.

The only picket Vettius could see from where he lay was a single rider slightly ahead and to the left of the wagons. Earlier in the day he might have been guide or outrider. Hours had passed. Wagons had bunched or straggled according to the strength of their teams and the temper of their drivers. Now, while the sun bled like an open wound in the western sky, the rider was almost a part of the jumbled line and no protection for it. Vettius smiled again, and his hand was on the bow.

The wind that moaned around the wagons scuffed up crystals from the snow crusts lying in undulant rills among the brush. The shaggy pony's rump and belly sparkled. The beast's torso, like its rider's, was hidden under armor of broad horn scales, each one painstakingly sewn onto a leather backing by the women of the family. Across his pommel rested a slender lance more than eighteen feet long. The Sarmatian fondled its grip as he nodded over his mount's neck, neglecting to watch the bushes that clawed spike shadows from the sun.

A sound that trickled through the wind made him straighten; unexpected movement caught his eye. Then the Roman archer rose up from behind a bush far too small to conceal a man the way it had. The Sarmatian, spurring his horse in incredulous panic, heard the slap of the bowstring, heard the loud pop as one scale of his cuirass shattered. After the bodkin-pointed arrow ripped through his chest he heard nothing at all.

"Let's get 'em!" Vettius shouted, nocking another arrow as his first target pitched out of the saddle. The trumpeter crouching behind him set the silver-mounted warhorn to his lips and blasted out the attack. Already the shallow hillsides were spilling soldiers down on the unprepared Sarmatians.

The driver of the lead wagon stood up, screaming a warning. The nearest Roman thrust her through the body with his spear. With two slashes of his shortsword, the legionary cut open the canopy behind her and plunged inside with a howl of triumph.

Sarmatians leaped out the back of the second wagon, trying to reach their horses. Three legionaries met them instead. Vettius had set fifty men in ambush, all picked veterans in full armor. None of the others had bows—the legate had feared a crossfire in the dusk— but sword and spear did the butcher's work on the startled nomads. The Sarmatians were dressed for war in armor of boiled leather or aurochs horn, but they had no shields and their light swords were no match for the heavy Roman cut-and-thrust blades. One at a time the nomads jumped down to be stretched on the ground by a stab, a quick chop, or even the heavy smash of a shield rim. Death trebled, the legionaries stood waiting for each victim. The fading sunlight gleamed from their polished helmets and greaves and touched with fire the wheels of bronze and vermilioned leather that marked their shields.

The legate's practiced eye scanned the fighting. The wrack showed the Sarmatians had battled with futile desperation. A baby lay beside the fourth wagon. Its skull had been dashed in on the wagon box but its nails were stained with Roman blood. The oxen bellowed, hamstrung in the yoke. One was spurting black jets through a heart-deep channel. This day was Rome's vengeance; retribution for a thousand sudden raids, a thousand comrades crumpled from a chance arrow or a dagger thrust in the night.

Only toward the rear where three wagons had bunched together was there real fighting. Vettius ran down the line of wagons though his quiver was almost emptied when he saw one of his men hurtle through the air in a lifeless somersault. The legionary crashed to the ground like a load of scrap metal. His whole chest and body armor had been caved in by an enormous blow. Measurably later the man's sword completed its own parabola and clanked thirty feet away.

"Get back!" Vettius shouted when he saw the windrow of ruined bodies strewn in front of him. "Stand clear!" Before he could say more, the killer was lumbering toward him around the back of the wagon.

The horsehair crest wobbling in the waning sunlight increased the figure's titanic height, but even bareheaded the giant would have been half again as tall as the six-foot soldier. Worse, he was much heavier-built than a man, a squat dwarf taller than the wagon. Though he carried no shield, his whole body shone with a covering of smooth bronze plates. Both gauntleted hands gripped the haft of an iron-headed mace. The six-foot helve was as thick as a man's calf and the head could have served as an anvil.

The giant strode toward Vettius with terrifying agility.

Vettius arced his bow. The shaft of his arrow splintered on the monster's breastplate. It left only a bright scar on the metal. Vettius stepped back, nocking another missile and shifting his aim to the oddly sloped helmet. The face was completely covered except for a T-shaped slot over the eyes and nose. The light was very dim but the narrow gap stood out dead black against the helmet's luster. As the giant started to swing his mace parallel to the ground, Vettius shot again.

The arrow glanced off the bronze and howled away into the darkness.

Vettius leaped upward and fell across the wagon seat as the giant's mace hurtled toward him. The spiked head smashed into a wheel with awesome force, scattering fragments of wood and making the whole wagon shudder. As it rocked, the driver's hacked corpse tumbled to the ground, leaving the Roman alone on the seat as he sighted along his last arrow. He released it.

The giant had reversed his grip on the mace. Now he swung his weapon upward with no more effort than a man with a flywhisk. As the head came level with the giant's hips, the mace slipped from his fingers to fly forward and burst through the side of the wagon. The titan reeled backwards. A small tuft of feathers was barely visible where the helmet slot crossed the bridge of his nose.

The earth trembled when he fell.

Shaking with reaction himself, Vettius dropped his now-useless bow and craned his neck to peer over the wagon's canopy at the remaining fighting. Some of the wains were already burning. Confusion or the victors had spilled the heating fires from their earthenware pots and scattered coals in the cloth and straw of the bed-ding.

"Save me a prisoner!" Vettius bellowed against the wind. "For Mithra's sake, save me a prisoner!"

He jumped to the ground and cautiously approached the fallen giant. The helmet came off easily when he grasped it by the crest and yanked. Beneath the bronze the face was almost human. The jaw was square and massive; death's rictus had drawn thin lips back from leo-nine tushes, yellowed and stark. The nose squatted centrally like a smashed toad, and from it the face rose past high flat eyesockets to enormous ridges of bone. There was virtually no forehead, so that the brows sloped shallowly to a point on the back of the skull. Only their short tight coils distinguished the eyebrows from the black strands that covered the rest of the head.

No wonder the helmet looked odd, Vettius thought bleakly. He would believe in the face, in a man so large, because they were there for him to touch; but he would have called another man a liar for claiming the existence of something so impossible. Perhaps believ-ing in the impossible was the secret of the success of the Christians whose god, dead three hundred years, was now beginning to rule the Empire.

The trumpeter approached from behind with his horn slung and a bloody sword in his right hand. The torque he now wore was of gold so pure and soft that he had spread it by hand to get it off a dead nomad and rebent it around his own neck.

"Sir!" he called, "are you all right?"

"Give me a hand here," Vettius grunted unresponsively as he tugged at the mace. Together the men pulled the weapon from the fabric of the wagon. Vettius gave a curt order and hefted it alone as his subordinate stepped back. "Ha!" he snorted in disbelief. The mace weighed at least two talents, the weight of a small man or a fair-sized woman.

He let it thud to the ground and walked away from it. "May the Bull bugger me if I don't learn more about this," he swore.

*   *   *

The doorkeeper had difficulty slamming the door against the gust of wind that followed Vettius into the anteroom. Moist air from the baths within condensed to bead the decorated tiles and rime the soldier's cape of black bearskin. He wore the bear's head as a cowl. The beast's glass eyes usually glared out above Vettius's own; now they too were frosted and the doorkeeper, turning, shuddered at the look of blank agony they gave him.

Vettius shrugged off the cape and stamped his muddy boots on the floor. The doorkeeper sighed inwardly and picked up his twig broom. The damned man had been stomping through the muck like a common solider instead of riding decently in a litter as befit his rank. The slave said nothing aloud as he swept, though; the legate had a reputation for violence and he already wore a dark glower this afternoon.

Walking through the door of the changing room, Vettius tossed his cape to one of the obsequious attendants and began to unlace his boots. While he sat on a bench and stripped off his thick woolen leggings, the other attendant looked delicately at the miry leather and asked with faint disdain, "Will you have these cleaned while you bathe, sir?"

"Dis, why should I?" the soldier snarled. "I've got to wear them out of here, don't I?"

The attendant started at his tone. Vettius chuckled at the man's fear and threw the filthy leggings in his face. Laying both his tunics on the bench, he surveyed the now apprehensive slaves and asked, "Either of you know where Dama is?"

"The Legate Vettius?" called a voice from the inner hallway. A third attendant poked his head into the changing room. "Sir? If you will follow me . . ."

The attendant's sandals slapped nervously down the hallway past steam rooms on the right and the wall of the great pool on the left. Tiles of glaucous gray covered the floors and most of the walls, set off by horizontal bands of mosaic. A craftsman of Naisso who had never been to the coast had inset octopi and dolphins cavorting on a bright green sea. The civilization I protect, Vettius thought disgustedly. The reason I bow to fat fools.

At the corner of the hall the attendant stopped and opened one of the right-hand doors. Steam puffed out. Vettius peered in with his hand on the jamb to keep from slipping on the slick tile. Through the hot fog he could make out the figure of the small man who lay on one of the benches.

"Dama?" the soldier called uncertainly.

"Come on in, Lucius," invited the other. He rose to his elbow and the light on his head of tight blond curls identified him. "How did it go?"

"The interrogation was fine," Vettius answered; but his tone was savage, that of a man used to taking out his frustrations in slaughter and very close to the point of doing so again. "We didn't need much persuasion to get the prisoner to tell us everything he knew about the giant. It came from a tent village called Torgu, and he says the shaman running the place has ten more just like it."

"If one, why not eleven?" Dama mused. "But I didn't think the Sarmatians ever made a shaman chief."

"I didn't either," Vettius agreed darkly, "and that wasn't the last strange thing he told us about this wizard, this Hydaspes. He was at Torgu when the family we ambushed got there late in the fall, nervous as the Emperor's taster and fussing around the village to look over each new arrival. He wasn't claiming much authority, either. Then about two months ago a horseman rode in from the east. Our prisoner didn't talk with the fellow but he saw him give a package the size of his fist to Hydaspes. That was what the wizard had been waiting for. He laughed and capered all the way to his tent and didn't come out again for a week. When he did, he started giving orders like a king. Since now he had a nine-foot giant behind him, everyone obeyed. In back of Hydaspes's tent there was a long trench in the frozen ground and a lot of dirt was missing. Nobody the prisoner knew hung about behind there to see if the wizard really was digging up giants there night after night—they were all scared to death by then."

"So a one-time hedge wizard gets a giant bodyguard," the merchant said softly, "and he unites a tribe under him. If he can do that, he may just as easily become king of the whole nation. What would happen, Lucius, if the Sarmatians got a real king, a real leader who stopped their squabbling and sent them across the Danube together?"

The white fear that had been shimmering around the edges of Vettius's mind broke through again and tensed all his muscles. "A century ago the Persians unified Mesopotamia against us," he said. "Constant fighting. Some victories, more losses. But we could accept that on one frontier—it's a big empire. On two at the same time . . . I can't say what would happen."

"We'd better deal with Hydaspes soon," Dama summarized flatly, "or Hydaspes will deal with us. Have you told Celsus?"

"Oh, I told the Count," Vettius snapped, "but he didn't believe me—and besides, he was too busy reaming me out for leading the ambush myself. It was *undignified* for a legate, he said."

Dama crowed, trying to imagine Vettius too dignified for a fight.

"That's the sort he is," the soldier agreed with a rueful smile. "He expects me to keep my cutthroats in line without dirtying my boots. A popular attitude this side of the river, it seems."

Knuckles slammed on the steam-room door. Both men looked up sharply.

"Sirs, quickly!" the attendant hissed from outside.

Dama threw the door open, his face blank.

"Sirs," the frightened slave explained, "the Count has come for the legate Vettius. I misdirected him, thinking you might want to prepare, but he'll be here any moment."

"I'll put on a tunic and meet him in the changing room," the soldier decided. "I've no desire to be arrested in the nude."

The frightened changing room attendants had disappeared into the far reaches of the building, leaving the friends to pull on their linen tunics undisturbed. Celsus burst in on them without ceremony, followed by two of his runners. *He's not here to charge me after all,* Vettius thought, not without at least a squad of troops. Though Mithra knew, his wishes would have supported a treason indictment.

"Where have you been?" the official stormed. His round face was almost the color of his toga's broad maroon hem.

"Right here in the bath, your excellency," Vettius replied without difference.

"Word just came by heliograph," the Count sputtered. "There were ten attacks last night, *ten!* Impregnable monsters leading them— Punicum, Novae, Farsuli, Anarti—posts wiped out!"

"I told you there were other attacks planned," the soldier replied calmly. "None of them was in my sector. I told you the why of that, too."

"But you lied when you said you killed a monster, didn't you?" accused Calsus, stamping his foot. "At Novae they hit one with a catapult and the bolt only bounced off!"

"Then they didn't hit him squarely," Vettius retorted. "The armor isn't that heavy. And I told you, I shot mine through the viewslit in his helmet."

The Count motioned his runners away. Noticing Dama for the first time he screamed, "Get out! Get out!"

The merchant bowed and exited behind the runners. He stood near the door.

"Listen," Celsus whispered, plucking at the soldier's sleeve to bring his ear lower, "you've got to do something about the giants. It'll look bad if these raids continue."

"Fine," Vettius said in surprise. "Give me my regiment and the Fifth Macedonian, and some cavalry—say the Old Germans. I'll level Torgu and everyone in it."

"Oh no," his pudgy superior gasped, "not so much! The Emperor will hear about it and the gods know what he'll think. Oh, no—fifty men, that was enough before."

"Are you—" Vettius began, then rephrased his thought. "This isn't an ambush for one family, your excellency. This is disposing of a powerful chief and maybe a thousand of his followers, a hundred miles into Sarmatia. I might as well go alone as with fifty men."

"Fifty men," Celsus repeated. Then, beaming as if he were making a promise, he added, "You'll manage, I'm sure."

The two riders were within a few miles of Torgu before they were noticed.

"I shouldn't have let you come," Vettius grumbled to his companion. "Either I should have gone myself or else marched my regiment in and told Celsus to bugger himself."

Dama smiled. "You don't have any curiosity, Lucius. You only see the job to be done. Myself, I want to know where a nine-foot giant comes from."

They eyed the sprawling herd of black cattle finding some unimaginable pasturage beneath the snow crust. Perhaps they were stripping bark from the brush that scarred the landscape with its black rigidity. A cow scented the unfamiliar horses approaching it. The animal blatted and scrambled to its feet, splashing dung behind it. When it had bustled twenty feet away, the cow regained enough composure to turn and stare at the riders, focusing the ripple of disturbance that moved sluggishly through other bovine minds. Face after drooling, vacant face rotated toward them; after long moments, even the distant herdsman looked up from where he huddled over his fire in the lee of a hill.

Dama's chest grew tight. There was still another moment's silence while the Sarmatian made up his mind that there really were Romans riding through his herd toward Torgu. When at last he grasped that fact, he leaped to his feet yipping his amazement. For an instant he crouched bowlegged, waiting for a hostile move. When the intruders ignored him, the Sarmatian scampered to his horse and lashed it into a startled gallop for home.

The merchant chewed at his cheeks, trying to work saliva into a mouth that had gone dry when he realized they would be noticed. He'd known they were going to meet Sarmatians: that was their whole purpose. But now it was too late to back out. "About time we got an escort," he said with false bravado. "I'm surprised the Sarmatians don't patrol more carefully."

"Why should they?" Vettius snorted. "They know they're safe over here so long as a brainless scut like Celsus is in charge of the border."

They jogged beyond the last of the cattle. Without the Sarmatian's presence the beasts were slowly drifting away from the trampled area where they had been herded. If they wandered far they would be loose at night when the wolves hunted.

"Cows," Vettius muttered. "It's getting hard to find men, my friend."

Half a mile away on the top of the next rolling hill an armored horseman reined up in a spatter of snow. He turned his head and gave a series of short yelps that carried over the plain like bugle calls. Moments later a full score of lancers topped the brow of the hill and pounded down toward the interlopers.

"I think we'll wait here," the soldier said.

"Sure, give them a sitting target," Dama agreed with a tense smile.

Seconds short of slaughter, the leading Sarmatian raised his lance. The rest of the troop followed his signal. The whole group swept around Vettius and Dama to halt in neighing, skidding chaos. One horse lost its footing and spilled its rider on the snow with a clatter of weapons. Cursing, the disgruntled Sarmatian lurched toward the Romans with his short, crooked sword out. From behind Dama, the leader barked a denial and laid his lance in front of the man. The merchant breathed deeply but did not relax his grip on the queerly shaped crossbow resting on his saddle until the glowering Sarmatian had remounted.

The leader rode alongside Vettius and looked up at the soldier on his taller horse. "You come with us to Torgu," he ordered in passable Greek.

"That's right," Vettius agreed in Sarmatian. "We're going to Torgu to see Hydaspes."

There was a murmur from the Sarmatians. One of them leaned forward to shake an amulet bag in the soldier's face, gabbling something too swiftly to be understood.

The leader had frowned when Vettius spoke. He snapped another order and kicked his horse forward. Romans and Sarmatians together jogged up the hill, toward the offal and frozen muck of Torgu.

On the back of a nameless, icebound stream stood the village's central hall and only real building. Dama glanced at it as they rode past. Its roughly squared logs were gray and streaked with odd splits along the twisted grain. Any caulking there might have been in the seams had fallen out over the years. The sides rose to a flaring roof of scummed thatch, open under the eaves to emit smoke and the stink of packed bodies. The hall would have seemed crude in the most stagnant backwaters of the Empire; the merchant could scarcely believe there could be a threat from a people to whom it was the height of civilization.

Around the timber structure sprawled the nomad wagons in filthy confusion. Their sloping canopies were shingled with cow droppings set out to dry in the wan sunlight before being burned for fuel. The light soot that had settled out of thousands of cooking fires permeated the camp with an unclean, sweetish odor. Nothing in the village but the untethered horses watching the patrol looked cared for.

Long lances had been butted into the ground beside each wagon. As he stared back at the flat gazes directed at him by idle Sarmatians, Dama realized what was wrong with the scene. Normally, only a handful of each family group would have been armored lancers. The rest would be horse archers, able to afford only a bow and padded linen protection. Most of their escort hung cased bows from their saddles, but all bore the lance and most wore scale mail.

"Lucius," the merchant whispered in Latin, "are all of these nobles?"

"You noticed that," Vettius replied approvingly. "No, you can see from their looks that almost all of them were merely herdsmen recently. Somebody made them his retainers, paid for their equipment and their keep."

"Hydaspes?" the merchant queried.

"I guess. He must have more personal retainers than the king, then."

"You will be silent!" ordered the Sarmatian leader.

They had ridden almost completely through the camp and were approaching a tent of gaily pennoned furs on the edge of the plains. At each corner squatted an octagonal stump of basalt a few feet high. The stones were unmarked and of uncertain significance, altars or boundary markers or both. No wains had been parked within fifty paces of the tent. A pair of guards stood before its entrance. Dama glanced at the streamers and said, "You know, there really is a market for silk in this forsaken country. A shame that—"

"Silence!" the Sarmatian repeated as he drew up in front of the tent. He threw a rapid greeting to the guards, one of whom bowed and ducked inside. He returned quickly, followed by a tall man in a robe of fine black Spanish wool. The newcomer's face was thin for a Sarmatian and bore a smile that mixed triumph—and something else. On his shoulder, covered by the dark hood, clung a tiny monkey with great brown eyes. From time to time it put its mouth to its master's ear and murmured secretly.

"Hydaspes," Vettius whispered. "He always wears black."

"Have they been disarmed?" the wizard questioned. The escort's leader flushed in embarrassment at his oversight and angrily demanded the Romans' weapons. Vettius said nothing as he handed over his bow and the long cavalry sword he carried even now that he commanded an infantry unit. The merchant added his crossbow and a handful of bolts to the collection.

"What is that?" Hydaspes asked, motioning his man to hand him the crossbow.

"It comes from the east where I get my silk," Dama explained, speaking directly to the wizard. "You just drop a bolt into the tall slot on top. That holds it while you pull back on the handle, cocking and firing it all in one motion."

"From the east? I get weapons from the east," the Sarmatian said with a nasty quirk of his lip. "But this, this is only a toy, surely? The arrow is so light and scarcely a handspan long. What could a man do with such a thing?"

Dama shrugged. "I'm not a warrior. For my own part, I wouldn't care to be shot with this or anything else."

The wizard gestured an end to the conversation, setting the weapon inside his tent for later perusal. "Dismount, gentlemen, dismount," he continued in excellent Greek. "Perhaps you have heard of me?"

"Hydaspes the wizard. Yes," Vettius lied, "even within the Empire we think of you when we think of a powerful sorcerer. That's why we've come for help."

"In whose name?" the Sarmatian demanded. "Constantius the emperor?"

"Celsus, Count of Dacia," Vettius snapped back. "The Empire has suffered the bloody absurdities of Constantius and his brothers long enough. Eunuchs run the army, priests rule the state, and the people pray to the tax gatherers. We'll have support when we get started, but first we need some standard to rally to, something to convince everyone that we have more than mere hopes behind us. We want your giants, and we'll pay you a part of the Empire to get them."

"And you, little man?" Hydaspes asked the merchant unexpectedly.

Dama had been imagining the Count's face if he learned his name was being linked with raw treason, but he recovered swiftly and fumbled at his sash while replying, "We merchants have little cause to love Constantius. The roads are ruinous, the coinage base, and the rapacity of local officials leaves little profit for even the most daring adventure."

"So you came to add your promise of future gain?"

"Future? Who knows the future?" Dama grunted. Gold gleamed in his hand. A shower of coins arced unerringly from his right palm to his left and back again. "If you can supply what we need, you'll not lament your present payment."

"Ho! Such confidence," the wizard said, laughing cheerfully. The monkey chittered, stroking its master's hair with bulbous fingertips. "You really believe that I can raise giants from the past?

"I can!"

Hydaspes's face became a mask of unreason. Dama shifted nervously from one foot to the other, realizing that the wizard was far from the clever illusionist they had assumed back at Naisso he must be. This man wasn't sane enough to impose successfully on so many people, even ignorant barbarians. Or was the madness a recent thing?

"Subradas, gather the village behind my tent," Hydaspes ordered abruptly, "but leave space in the middle as wide and long as the tent itself."

The leader of the escort dipped his lance in acknowledgment. "The women, Lord?"

"All—women, slaves, everyone. I'm going to show you how I raise the giants."

"Ho!" gasped the listening Sarmatians. The leader saluted again and rode off shouting. Hydaspes turned to re-enter his tent, then paused. "Take the Romans, too," he directed the guards. "Put them by the flap and watch them well.

"Yes," he continued, glancing back at Vettius, "it is a very easy thing to raise giants, if you have the equipment and the knowledge. Like drawing a bow for a man like you."

The Hell-lit afterimage of the wizard's eyes continued to blaze in the soldier's mind when the furs had closed behind the black figure.

As the rest of the Sarmatians dismounted and began to jostle them around the long tent, Dama whispered, "This isn't working. If it gets too tight, break for the tent. You know about my bow?"

Vettius nodded, but his mind was chilled by a foretaste of death.

As the prisoner had said, eleven long trenches bristled outward from the wall of Hydaspes's tent. Each was shallow but too extensive for the wizard to have dug it in the frozen ground in one night. Dama disliked the way the surface slumped over the ditches, as if enormous corpses had clawed their way out of the graves . . .

Which was what the wizard seemed to claim had happened.

The guards positioned the two Romans at the center of the back wall of the tent where laces indicated another entrance. Later comers crowded about anxiously, held back in a rough circle by officers with drawn swords. Twenty feet to either side of the Romans stretched the straight walls of the tent paralleled by a single row of warriors. From the basalt posts at either corner curved the rest of the tribe in milling excitement, warriors in front and women and children squirming as close as they could get before being elbowed back.

The Sarmatians were still pushing for position when Hydaspes entered the cleared space, grinning ironically at Vettius and Dama as he stepped between them. A guard laced the tent back up. In the wizard's left hand was a stoppered copper flask; his right gripped a small packet of supple cowhide.

"The life!" Hydaspes shouted to the goggle-eyed throng, waving the flask above his head from the center of the circle. He set the vessel down on the dirt and carefully unrolled the leather wrappings from the other objects.

"And the seed!" the wizard cried at last. In his palm lay a pair of teeth. They were a dull, stony gray without any of the sheen of ivory. One was a molar, human but inhumanly large. The other tooth, even less credible, seemed to be a canine fully four inches long. With one tooth in either hand, Hydaspes goat-footed about the flask in an impromptu dance of triumph.

His monkey rider clacked its teeth in glee.

The wizard stopped abruptly and faced the Romans. "Oh, yes. The seed. I got them, all thirteen teeth, from the Chinese—the people who sell you your silk, merchant. Dragons' teeth they call them—hee hee! And I plant them just like Cadmus did when he built Thebes. But I'm the greater prince, oh yes, for I'll build an *empire* where he built a city."

Dama licked his lips. "We'll help you build your empire," he began, but the wizard ignored him and spoke only to Vettius.

"You want my giants, Roman, my darlings? Watch!"

Hydaspes plucked a small dagger from his sash and poked a hole in the ground. Like a farmer planting a nut, the wizard popped the molar into the hole and patted the earth back down. When he straightened he shouted a few words at the sky. The villagers gasped, but Dama doubted whether they understood any more of the invocation than he did. Perhaps less—the merchant thought he recognized the language, at least, one he had heard chanted on the shores of the Persian Gulf on a dead, starless night. He shuddered.

Now the wizard was unstoppering his flask and crooning under his breath. His cowl had fallen back to display the monkey clinging fiercely to his long oily hair. When the wizard turned, Dama could see the beast's lips miming its master obscenely.

Droplets spattered from the flask, bloody red and glowing. The merchant guessed wine or blood, changed his mind when the fluid popped and sizzled on the ground. The frozen dirt trembled like a stricken gong.

The monkey leaped from Hydaspes's shoulder, strangely unaffected by the cold. It faced the wizard across the patch of fluid-scarred ground. It was chanting terrible squeaky words that thundered back from Hydaspes.

The ground split.

The monkey collapsed. Hydaspes leaped over the earth's sudden gape and scooped up the little creature, wrapping it in his cloak.

Through the crack in the soil thrust an enormous hand. Earth heaved upward again. The giant's whole torso appeared, dribbling dirt back into the trench. Vettius recognized the same thrusting jaw, the same high flat eyesockets, as those of the giant he had killed.

The eyes were Hydaspes's own.

"Oh yes, Roman," the wizard cackled. "The life and the seed—and the mind too, hey? There must be the mind."

The giant rose carefully in a cascade of earth. Even standing in the trench left by his body, he raised his pointed skull eight feet into the air.

"My mind!" Hydaspes shrieked, oblivious to everyone but the soldier. "Part of me in each of my darlings, you see? Flowing from me through my pet here to them."

One of the wizard's hands caressed the monkey until it murmured lasciviously. The beast's huge eyes were seas of steaming brown mud, barely flecked by pinpoint pupils.

"You said you knew me," continued the wizard. "Well, I know you too, Lucius Vettius. I saw you bend your bow, I saw you kill my darling—

"I saw you kill me, Roman!"

Vettius unclasped his cape, let it slip to the ground. Hydaspes wiped a streak of spittle from his lips and stepped back to lay a hand on the giant's forearm. "Kill me again, Roman," the wizard said softly. "Go ahead; no one will interfere. But this time you don't have a bow. Watch the little one!" he snapped to the guard on Dama's right.

The Sarmatian gripped the merchant's shoulder.

Then the giant charged.

Vettius dived forward at an angle, rolling beyond the torn-up section of the clearing. The giant spun, stumbling in a ditch that had cradled one of his brothers. The soldier had gained the room he wanted in the center of the open space and waited in a loosearmed crouch. The giant sidled toward him splay-footed.

"Hey!" the Roman shouted and lunged for his opponent's dangling genitalia. The giant struck with shocking speed, swatting Vettius in midair like a man playing handball. Before the Roman's thrusting fingers could make contact, the giant's open-handed blow had crashed into his ribs and hurled him a dozen feet away. Only the giant's clumsy rush saved Vettius from being pulped before he could jump to his feet again. The soldier was panting heavily but his eyes were fixed on the giant's. A thread of blood dribbled off the point of his jaw. Only a lip split on the hard ground—thus far.

The giant charged.

Two faces in the crowd were not fixed on the one-sided battle. Dama fingered the hem of his cloak unobtrusively, following the fight only from the corners of his eyes. It would be pointless to watch his friend die. Instead the merchant eyed Hydaspes, who had dug another hole across the clearing and inserted the last and largest tooth into it. The wizard seemed to ignore the fighting. If he watched at all, it was through the giant's eyes as he claimed; surely, mad as he was Hydaspes would not otherwise have turned his back on his revenge. For the first time Dama thought he recognized an unease about the monkey that rode again on the wizard's shoulder. It might only have been fatigue. Certainly Hydaspes seemed to notice nothing unusual as he tamped down the soil and began his thirteenth invocation.

Dama's guard was wholly caught up in the fight. He began to pound the merchant on the back in excitement, yelling bloodthirsty curses at Vettius. Dama freed the slender stiletto from his cloak and palmed it. He did not turn his head lest the movement catch the guard's attention. Instead he raised his hand to the Sarmatian's neck, delicately fingered his spine. Before the moth-light touch could register on the enthusiastic Sarmatian, Dama slammed the thin blade into the base of his brain and gave it a twist. The guard died instantly. The merchant supported the slumping body, guiding it back against the tent. Hydaspes continued chanting a litany with the monkey, though the noise of the crowd drowned out his words. The wizard formed the inaudible syllables without noticing either Dama or the stumbling way his beast answered him. There was a look of puzzlement, almost fear, in the monkey's eyes. The crowd continued to cheer as the merchant opened the flap with a quick slash and backed inside Hydaspes's tent.

Inside a pair of chalcedony oil lamps burned with tawny light. The floor was covered with lush furs, some of which draped wooden benches. On a table at one end rested a pair of human skulls, unusually small but adult in proportions. More surprising were the cedar book chests holding parchments and papyri and even the strange pleated leaf-books of India. Dama's crossbow stood beside the front entrance. He ran to it and loosed the bundle of stubby, unfletched darts beside it. From his wallet came a vial of pungent tarry matter into which he jabbed the head of each dart. The uncovered portions of the bronze points began to turn green. Careful not to touch the smears of venom, the merchant slipped all ten missiles into the crossbow's awkward vertical magazine.

Only then did he peer through the tent flap.

Vettius leaped sideways, kicking at the giant's knee. The ragged hobnails scored his opponent's calf, but the giant's deceptively swift hand closed on the Roman's outer tunic. For a heartsick instant the heavy fabric held; then it ripped and Vettius tumbled free. The giant lunged after him. Vettius backpedaled and, as his enemy straightened, launched himself across the intervening space. The heel of his outstretched boot slammed into the pit of the giant's stomach. Again the iron nails made a bloody ruin of the skin. The titan's breath whooshed out, but its half-ton bulk did not falter at the blow. Vettius, thrown back by the futile impact, twisted away from the giant's unchecked rush. The creature's heels grazed past, thudded with mastodonic force. The soldier took a shuddering breath and lurched to his feet. A long arm clawed for his face. The Roman staggered back; barely clear of the spadelike talons. The monster pressed after him relentlessly, and Vettius was forced at last to recognize what should have been hopelessly obvious from the first: he could not possibly kill the giant with his bare hands.

A final strategem took shape. With desperate purpose Vettius began to circle and retreat before his adversary. He should have planned it, measured it, but now he could only trust to luck and the giant's incredible weight. Backed almost against a corner post, he

crouched and waited. Arms wide, the giant hesitated—then rushed in
for the kill. Vettius met him low, diving straight at his opponent instead of making a vain effort to get clear again. The Roman's arms
locked about the great ankles and the giant wavered, then began to
topple forward. As he fell his taloned fingers clamped crushingly on
Vettius's ribs.

The unyielding basalt altar met the giant's skull with shattering
force. Bone slammed dense rock with the sound of a maul on a
wedge. Warm fluids spattered the snow while the Sarmatians
moaned in disbelief. Hydaspes knelt screaming on the ground, his
fists pummeling terror from a mind that had forgotten even the invocation it had just completed. The earth began pitching like an un-
mastered horse. It split in front of the wizard where the tooth had
been planted. The crack raced jaggedly through the crowd and beyond.

"Lucius!" Dama cried, lifting the corner of the tent.

The soldier pulled his leg free from the giant's pinioning body and
rolled toward the voice, spilling endwise the only Sarmatian alert
enough to try to stop him. Dama dropped the tent wall and nodded
toward the front, his hands full of crossbow.

"There're horses waiting out there. I'll slow them up."

Vettius stamped on a hand that thrust into the tent.

"Get out, damn you!" the merchant screamed. "There aren't any
more weapons in here."

A Sarmatian rolled under the furs with a feral grimace and a dagger in his hand. The soldier hefted a full case of books and hurled it
at his chest. Wood and bone splintered loudly. Vettius turned and ran
toward the horses.

The back flap ripped apart in the haste of the Sarmatians who had
remembered its existence. The first died with a dart through his eye
as Dama jerked the cocking handle of his weapon. The next missile
fell into position. The merchant levered back the bow again. At full
cock the sear released, snapped the dart out into the throat of the next
man. The Sarmatian's life dissolved in a rush of red flame as the bolt
pricked his carotid to speed its load of poison to the brain. The third
man stumbled over his body, screamed. Two darts pinged off his mail

before one caught the armpit he bared when he threw his hands over his face.

Relentless as a falling obelisk, Dama stroked out the full magazine of lethal missiles, shredding six screaming victims in the space of a short breath. The entrance was plugged by a clot of men dying in puling agony. Tossing his empty bow at the writhing chaos behind him, Dama ran through the front flap and vaulted onto his horse.

"We'll never get clear!" Vettius shouted as he whipped his mount. "They'll run us down in relays before we reach the Danube."

Wailing Sarmatians boiled around both ends of the tent, shedding helmets, weapons—any encumbrance. Their voices honed a narrow blade of terror.

"The control," Dama shouted back as the pair dodged among the crazy pattern of wagon tongues. "He used his own mind and a monkey's to control something not quite a man."

"So what?"

"That last tooth didn't come from a man. It didn't come from anything like a man."

Something scaly, savage and huge towered over the wreckage of the tent. It cocked its head to glare at the disappearing riders while scrabbling with one stubby foreleg to stuff a black-robed figure farther into its maw. Vettius twisted in his saddle to stare in amazement at the coffin-long jaws gaping twenty feet in the air and the spined backfin like that of no reptile of the past seventy million years.

The dragon hissed, leaving a scarlet mist of blood to hang in the air as it ducked its head for another victim.

Two Yards
of Dragon

▢ ▢ ▢

by L. Sprague de Camp

Eudoric Dambertson, Esquire, rode home from his courting of Lusina, daughter of the enchanter Baldonius, with a face as long as an olifant's nose. Eudoric's sire, Sir Dambert, said:
"Well, how fared thy suit, boy? Ill, eh?"

"I—" began Eudoric.

"I told you 'twas an asinine notion, eh? Was I not right? When Baron Emmerhard has more daughters than he can count, any one of which would fetch a pretty parcel of land with her, eh? Why, why answerest not?"

"I—" said Eudoric.

"Come on, lad, speak up!"

"How can he, when ye talk all the time?" said Eudoric's mother, the Lady Aniset.

"Oh," said Sir Dambert. "Your pardon, son. Moreover and furthermore as I've told you, an' ye were Emmerhard's son-in-law, he'd use his influence to get you your spurs. Here ye be, a strapping youth of three-and-twenty, not yet knighted. 'Tis a disgrace to our lineage."

"There are no wars toward, to afford opportunity for deeds of knightly dought," said Eudoric.

"Aye, 'tis true. Certes, we all hail the blessings of peace, which the

wise governance of our sovran emperor hath given us for lo these
thirteen years. Howsomever, to perform a knightly deed, our young
men must needs waylay banditti, disperse rioters, and do suchlike
fribbling feats."

As Sir Dambert paused, Eudoric interjected, "Sir, that problem
now seems on its way to solution."

"How meanest thou?"

"If you'll but hear me, Father! Doctor Baldonius has set me a task,
ere he'll bestow Lusina on me, which should fit me for knighthood
in any jurisdiction."

"And that is?"

"He's fain to have two square yards of dragon hide. Says he needs
'em for his magical mummeries."

"But there have been no dragons in these parts for a century or
more!"

"True; but, quoth Baldonius, the monstrous reptiles still abound
far to eastward, in the lands of Pathenia and Pantorozia. Forsooth,
he's given me a letter of introduction to his colleague, Doctor Raspiudus, in Pathenia."

"What?" cried the Lady Aniset. "Thou, to set forth on some year-
long journey to parts unknown, where, 'tis said, men hop on a single
leg or have faces in their bellies? I'll not have it! Besides, Baldonius
may be privy wizard to Baron Emmerhard, but 'tis not to be denied
that he is of no gentle blood."

"Well," said Eudoric, "so who was gentle when the Divine Pair
created the world?"

"Our forebears were, I'm sure, whate'er were the case with those
of the learned Doctor Baldonius. You young people are always full
of idealistic notions. Belike thou'lt fall into heretical delusions, for I
hear that the Easterlings have not the true religion. They falsely believe that God is one, instead of two as we truly understand."

"Let's not wander into the mazes of theology," said Sir Dambert,
his chin to his fist. "To be sure, the paynim Southrons believe that
God is three, an even more pernicious notion than that of the Easterlings."

"An' I meet God in my travels, I'll ask him the truth o't," said Eudoric.

"Be not sacrilegious, thou impertinent whelp! Still and all and notwithstanding, Doctor Baldonius were a man of influence to have in the family, be his origin never so humble. Methinks I could prevail upon him to utter spells to cause my crops, my neat, and my villeins to thrive, whilst casting poxes and murrains on my enemies. Like that caitiff Rainmar, eh? What of the bad seasons we've had? The God and Goddess know we need all the supernatural help we can get to keep us from penury. Else we may some fine day awaken to find that we've lost the holding to some greasy tradesman with a purchased title, with pen for lance and tally sheet for shield."

"Then I have your leave, sire?" cried Eudoric, a broad grin splitting his square, bronzed young face.

The Lady Aniset still objected, and the argument raged for another hour. Eudoric pointed out that it was not as if he were an only child, having two younger brothers and a sister. In the end, Sir Dambert and his lady agreed to Eudoric's quest, provided he return in time to help with the harvest, and take a manservant of their choice.

"Whom have you in mind?" asked Eudoric.

"I fancy Jillo the trainer," said Sir Dambert.

Eudoric groaned. "That old mossback, ever canting and haranguing me on the duties and dignities of my station?"

"He's but a decade older than ye," said Sir Dambert. "Moreover and furthermore, ye'll need an older man, with a sense of order and propriety, to keep you on the path of a gentleman. Class loyalty above all, my boy! Young men are wont to swallow every new idea that flits past, like a frog snapping at flies. Betimes they find they've engulfed a wasp, to their scathe and dolor."

"He's an awkward wight, Father, and not overbrained."

"Aye, but he's honest and true, no small virtues in our degenerate days. In my sire's time there was none of this newfangled saying the courteous 'ye' and 'you' even to mere churls and scullions. 'Twas always 'thou' and 'thee.' "

"How you do go on, Dambert dear," said the Lady Aniset.

"Aye, I ramble. 'Tis the penalty of age. At least, Eudoric, the faithful Jillo knows horses and will keep your beasts in prime fettle." Sir Dambert smiled. "Moreover and furthermore, if I know Jillo God-marson, he'll be glad to get away from his nagging wife for a spell."

So Eudoric and Jillo set forth to eastward, from the knight's hold-ing of Arduen, in the barony of Zurgau, in the county of Treveria, in the kingdom of Locania, in the New Napolitanian Empire. Eudoric— of medium height, powerful build, dark, with square-jawed but oth-erwise undistinguished features—rode his palfrey and led his mighty destrier Morgrim. The lank, lean Jillo bestrode another palfrey and led a sumpter mule. Morgrim was piled with Eudoric's panoply of plate, carefully nested into a compact bundle and lashed down under a canvas cover. The mule bore the rest of their supplies.

For a fortnight they wended uneventfully through the duchies and counties of the Empire. When they reached lands where they could no longer understand the local dialects, they made shift with Hel-ladic; the tongue of the Old Napolitanian Empire, which lettered men spoke everywhere.

They stopped at inns where inns were to be had. For the first fort-night, Eudoric was too preoccupied with dreams of his beloved Lusina to notice the tavern wenches. After that, his urges began to fever him, and he bedded one in Zerbstat, to their mutual satisfaction. Thereafter, however, he forebore, not as a matter of sexual morals but as a matter of thrift.

When benighted on the road, they slept under the stars—or, as be-fell them on the marches of Avaria, under a rain-dripping canopy of clouds. As they bedded down in the wet, Eudoric asked his compan-ion:

"Jillo, why did you not remind me to bring a tent?"

Jillo sneezed. "Why, sir, come rain, come snow, I never thought that so sturdy a springald as ye be would ever need one. The heroes in the romances never travel with tents."

"To the nethermost hell with heroes of the romances! They go clat-tering around on their destriers for a thousand cantos. Weather is ever fine. Food, shelter, and a change of clothing appear, as by magic, whenever desired. Their armor never rusts. They suffer no tisics and fluxes. They pick up no fleas or lice at the inns. They're never swindled by merchants, for none does aught so vulgar as buying and selling."

"If ye'll pardon me, sir," said Jillo, "that were no knightly way to speak. It becomes not your station."

"Well, to the nethermost hells with my station, too! Wherever these paladins go, they find damsels in distress to rescue, or have other agreeable, thrilling and sanitary adventures. What adventures have we had? The time we fled from robbers in the Turonian Forest. The time I fished you out of the Albis half drowned. The time we ran out of food in the Asciburgi Mountains and had to plod fodderless over those hair-raising peaks for three days on empty stomachs."

"The Divine Pair do but seek to try the mettle of a valorous aspirant knight, sir. Ye should welcome these petty adversities as a chance to prove your manhood."

Eudoric made a rude noise with his mouth. "That for my manhood! Right now, I'd fainer have a stout roof overhead, a warm fire before me, and a hot repast in my belly. An' ever I go on such a silly jaunt again, I'll find one of those versemongers—like that troubadour, Landwin of Kromnitch, that visited us yesteryear—and drag him along, to show him how little real adventures are like those of the romances. And if he fall into the Albis, he may drown, for all of me. Were it not for my darling Lusina—"

Eudoric lapsed into gloomy silence, punctuated by sneezes.

They plodded on until they came to the village of Liptai, on the border of Pathenia. After the border guards had questioned and passed them, they walked their animals down the deep mud of the main street. Most of the slatternly houses were of logs or of crudely hewn planks, innocent of paint.

"Heaven above!" said Jillo. "Look at that, sir!"

"That" was a gigantic snail shell, converted into a small house.

"Knew you not of the giant snails of Pathenia?" asked Eudoric. "I've read of them in Doctor Baldonius' encyclopedia. When full grown, they—or rather their shells—are ofttimes used for dwellings in this land."

Jillo shook his head. " 'Twere better had ye spent more of your

time on your knightly exercises and less on reading. Your sire had
never learnt his letters, yet he doth his duties well enow."

"Times change, Jillo. I may not clang rhymes so featly as Doctor
Baldonius, or that ass Landwin of Kromnitch; but in these days a
stroke of the pen were oft more fell than the slash of a sword. Here's
a hostelry that looks not too slummocky. Do you dismount and inquire within as to their tallage."

"Why, sir?"

"Because I am fain to know, ere we put our necks in the noose! Go
ahead. An' I go in, they'll double the scot at sight of me."

When Jillo came out and quote prices, Eudoric said, "Too dear.
We'll try the other."

"But, Master! Mean ye to put us in some flea-bitten hovel, like
that which we suffered in Bitava?"

"Aye. Didst not prate to me on the virtues of petty adversity in
strengthening one's knightly mettle?"

" 'Tis not that, sir."

"What, then?"

"Why, when better quarters are to be had, to make do with the
worse were an insult to your rank and station. No gentleman—"

"Ah, here we are!" said Eudoric. "Suitably squalid, too! You see,
good Jillo, I did but yester'een count our money, and lo! more than
half is gone, and our journey not yet half completed."

"But, noble Master, no man of knightly mettle would so debase
himself as to tally his silver, like some base-born commercial—"

"Then I must needs lack true knightly mettle. Here we be!"

For a dozen leagues beyond Liptai rose the great, dense Motolian
Forest. Beyond the forest lay the provincial capital of Velitchovo.
Beyond Velitchovo, the forest thinned out *gradatim* to the great
grassy plains of Pathenia. Beyond Pathenia, Eudoric had been told,
stretched the boundless deserts of Pantorozia, over which a man
might ride for months without seeing a city.

Yes, the innkeeper told them, there were plenty of dragons in the
Motolian Forest. "But fear them not," said Kasmar in broken Helladic. "From being hunted, they have become wary and even timid.

An' ye stick to the road and move yarely, they'll pester you not unless ye surprise or corner one."

"Have any dragons been devouring maidens fair lately?" asked Eudoric.

Kasmar laughed. "Nay, good Master. What were maidens fair doing, traipsing round the woods to stir up the beasties? Leave them be, I say, and they'll do the same by you."

A cautious instinct warned Eudoric not to speak of his quest. After he and Jillo had rested and had renewed their equipment, they set out, two days later, into the Motolian Forest. They rode for a league along the Velitchovo road. Then Eudoric, accoutered in full plate and riding Morgrim, led his companion off the road into the woods to southward. They threaded their way among the trees, ducking branches, in a wide sweep around. Steering by the sun, Eudoric brought them back to the road near Liptai.

The next day they did the same, except that their circuit was to the north of the highway.

After three more days of this exploration, Jillo became restless. "Good Master, what do we, circling round and about so bootlessly? The dragons dwell farther east, away from the haunts of men, they say."

"Having once been lost in the woods," said Eudoric, "I would not repeat the experience. Therefore do we scout our field of action, like a general scouting a future battlefield."

" 'Tis an arid business," said Jillo with a shrug. "But then, ye were always one to see further into a millstone than most."

At last, having thoroughly committed the byways of the nearer forest to memory, Eudoric led Jillo farther east. After casting about, they came at last upon the unmistakable tracks of a dragon. The animal had beaten a path through the brush, along which they could ride almost as well as on the road. When they had followed this track for above an hour, Eudoric became aware of a strong, musky stench.

"My lance, Jillo!" said Eudoric, trying to keep his voice from rising with nervousness.

The next bend in the path brought them into full view of the dragon, a thirty-footer facing them on the trail.

"Ha!" said Eudoric. "Meseems 'tis a mere cockadrill, albeit longer of neck and of limb than those that dwell in the rivers of Agisymba—if the pictures in Doctor Baldonius' books lie not. Have at thee, vile worm!"

Eudoric couched his lance and put spurs to Morgrim. The destrier bounded forward.

The dragon raised its head and peered this way and that, as if it could not see well. As the hoofbeats drew nearer, the dragon opened its jaws and uttered a loud, hoarse, groaning bellow.

At that, Morgrim checked his rush with stiffened forelegs, spun ponderously on his haunches, and veered off the trail into the woods. Jillo's palfrey bolted likewise, but in another direction. The dragon set out after Eudoric at a shambling trot.

Eudoric had not gone fifty yards when Morgrim passed close aboard a massive old oak, a thick limb of which jutted into their path. The horse ducked beneath the bough. The branch caught Eudoric across the breastplate, flipped him backward over the high cantle of his saddle, and swept him to earth with a great clatter.

Half stunned, he saw the dragon trot closer and closer—and then lumber past him, almost within arm's length, and disappear on the trail of the fleeing horse. The next that Eudoric knew, Jillo was bending over him, crying:

"Alas, my poor heroic Master! Be any bones broke, sir?"

"All of them, methinks," groaned Eudoric. "What's befallen Morgrim?"

"That I know not. And look at this dreadful dent in your beauteous cuirass!"

"Help me out of the thing. The dent pokes most sorely into my ribs. The misadventures I suffer for my dear Lusina!"

"We must get your breastplate to a smith to have it hammered out and filed smooth again."

"Fiends take the smiths! They'd charge half the cost of a new one. I'll fix it myself, if I can find a flat rock to set it on and a big stone wherewith to pound it."

"Well, sir," said Jillo, "ye were always a good man of your hands.

But the mar will show, and that were not suitable for one of your quality."

"Thou mayst take my quality and stuff it!" cried Eudoric. "Canst speak of nought else? Help me up, pray." He got slowly to his feet, wincing, and limped a few steps.

"At least," he said, "nought seems fractured. But I misdoubt I can walk back to Liptai."

"Oh, sir, that were not to be thought of! Me allow you to wend afoot whilst I ride? Fiends take the thought!" Jillo unhitched the palfrey from the tree to which he had tethered it and led it to Eudoric.

"I accept your courtesy, good Jillo, only because I must. To plod the distance afoot were but a condign punishment for so bungling my charge. Give me a boost, will you?" Eudoric grunted as Jillo helped him into the saddle.

"Tell me, sir," said Jillo, "why did the beast ramp on past you without stopping to devour you as ye lay helpless? Was't that Morgrim promised a more bounteous repast? Or that the monster feared that your plate would give him a disorder of the bowels?"

"Meseems 'twas neither. Marked you how gray and milky appeared its eyes? According to Doctor Baldonius' book, dragons shed their skins from time to time, like serpents. This one neared the time of its skin change, wherefore the skin over its eyeballs had become thickened and opaque, like glass of poor quality. Therefore it could not plainly discern objects lying still, and pursued only those that moved."

They got back to Liptai after dark. Both were barely able to stagger Eudoric from his sprains and bruises and Jillo footsore from the unaccustomed three-league hike.

Two days later, when they had recovered, they set out on the two palfreys to hunt for Morgrim. "For," Eudoric said, "that nag is worth more in solid money than all the rest of my possessions together."

Eudoric rode unarmored save for a shirt of light mesh mail, since the palfrey could not carry the extra weight of the plate all day at a brisk pace. He bore his lance and sword, however, in case they should again encounter a dragon.

They found the site of the previous encounter, but no sign either of the dragon or of the destrier. Eudoric and Jillo tracked the horse by its prints in the soft mold for a few bowshots, but then the slot faded out on harder ground.

"Still, I misdoubt Morgrim fell victim to the beast," said Eudoric. "He could show clean heels to many a steed of lighter build, and from its looks the dragon was no courser."

After hours of fruitless searching, whistling, and calling, they returned to Liptai. For a small fee, Eudoric was allowed to post a notice in Helladic on the town notice board, offering a reward for the return of his horse.

No words, however, came of the sighting of Morgrim. For all that Eudoric could tell, the destrier might have run clear to Velitchovo.

"You are free with advice, good Jillo," said Eudoric. "Well, rede me this riddle. We've established that our steeds will bolt from the sight and smell of dragon, for which I blame them little. Had we all the time in the world, we could doubtless train them to face the monsters, beginning with a stuffed dragon, and then, perchance, one in a cage in some monarch's menagerie. But our lucre dwindles like the snow in spring. What's to do?"

"Well, if the nags won't stand, needs we must face the worms on foot," said Jillo.

"That seems to me to throw away our lives to no good purpose, for these vasty lizards can outrun and outturn us and are well harnessed to boot. Barring the luckiest of lucky thrusts with the spear—as, say, into the eye or down the gullet—that fellow we erst encountered could make one mouthful of my lance and another of me."

"Your knightly courage were sufficient defense, sir. The Divine Pair would surely grant victory to the right."

"From all I've read of battles and feuds," said Eudoric, "methinks the Holy Couple's attention oft strays elsewhither when they should be deciding the outcome of some mundane fray."

"That is the trouble with reading; it undermines one's faith in the True Religion. But ye could be at least as well armored as the dragon, in your panoply of plate."

"Aye, but then poor Daisy could not bear so much weight to the site—or, at least, bear it thither and have breath left for a charge. We must be as chary of our beasts' welfare as of our own, for without them 'tis a long walk back to Trevaria. Nor do I deem that we should like to pass our lives in Liptai."

"Then, sir, we could pack the armor on the mule, for you to do on in dragon country."

"I like it not," said Eudoric. "Afoot, weighted down by that lobster's habit, I could move no more spryly than a tortoise. 'Twere small comfort to know that if the dragon ate me, he'd suffer indigestion afterward."

Jillo sighed. "Not the knightly attitude, sir, if ye'll pardon my saying so."

"Say what you please, but I'll follow the course of what meseems were common sense. What we need is a brace of those heavy steel crossbows for sieges. At close range, they'll punch a hole in a breastplate as 'twere a sheet of papyrus."

"They take too long to crank up," said Jillo. "By the time ye've readied your second shot, the battle's over."

"Oh, it would behoove us to shoot straight the first time; but better one shot that pierces the monster's scales than a score that bounce off. Howsomever, we have these fell little hand catapults not, and they don't make them in this barbarous land."

A few days later, while Eudoric still fretted over the lack of means to his goal, he heard a sudden sound like a single thunderclap from close at hand. Hastening out from Kasmar's Inn, Eudoric and Jillo found a crowd of Pathenians around the border guard's barracks.

In the drill yard, the guard was drawn up to watch a man demonstrate a weapon. Eudoric, whose few words of Pathenian were not up to conversation, asked among the crowd for somebody who could speak Helladic. When he found one, he learned that the demonstrator was a Pantorozian. The man was a stocky, snub-nosed fellow in a bulbous fur hat, a jacket of coarse undyed wool, and baggy trousers tucked into soft boots.

"He says the device was invented by the Sericans," said the villager. "They live half a world away, across the Pantorozian deserts. He puts some powder into that thing, touches a flame to it, and *boom!* it spits a leaden ball through the target as neatly as you please."

The Pantorozian demonstrated again, pouring black powder from the small end of a horn down his brass barrel. He placed a wad of rag over the mouth of the tube, then a leaden ball, and pushed both ball and wad down the tube with a rod. He poured a pinch of powder into a hole on the upper side of the tube near its rear, closed end.

Then he set a forked rest in the ground before him, rested the barrel in the fork, and took a small torch that a guardsman handed him. He pressed the wooden stock of the device against his shoulder, sighted along the tube, and with his free hand touched the torch to the touchhole. Ffft, *bang!* A cloud of smoke, and another hole appeared in the target.

The Pantorozian spoke with the captain of the guard, but they were too far for Eudoric to hear, even if he could have understood their Pathenian. After a while, the Pantorozian picked up his tube and rest, slung his bag of powder over his shoulder, and walked with downcast air to a cart hitched to a shade tree.

Eudoric approached the man, who was climbing into his cart. "God den, fair sir!" began Eudoric, but the Pantorozian spread his hands with a smile of incomprehension.

"Kasmar!" cried Eudoric, sighting the innkeeper in the crowd. "Will you have the goodness to interpret for me and this fellow?"

"He says," said Kasmar, "that he started out with a wainload of these devices and has sold all but one. He hoped to dispose of his last one in Liptai, but our gallant Captain Boriswaf will have nought to do with it."

"Why?" asked Eudoric. "Meseems 'twere a fell weapon in practiced hands."

"That is the trouble, quoth Master Vlek. Boriswaf says that should so fiendish a weapon come into use, 'twill utterly extinguish the noble art of war, for all men will down weapons and refuse to fight rather than face so devilish a device. Then what should he, a lifelong soldier, do for his bread? Beg?"

"Ask Master Vlek where he thinks to pass the night."

"I have already persuaded him to lodge with us, Master Eudoric."

"Good, for I would fain have further converse with him."

Over dinner, Eudoric sounded out the Pantorozian on the price he asked for his device. Acting as translator, Kasmar said, "If ye strike a bargain on this, I should get ten per centum as a broker's commission, for ye were helpless without me."

Eudoric got the gun, with thirty pounds of powder and a bag of leaden balls and wadding, for less than half of what Vlek had asked of Captain Boriswaf. As Vlek explained, he had not done badly on this peddling trip and was eager to get home to his wives and children.

"Only remember," he said through Kasmar, "overcharge it not, lest it blow apart and take your head off. Press the stock firmly against your shoulder, lest it knock you on your arse like a mule's kick. And keep fire away from the spare powder, lest it explode all at once and blast you to gobbets."

Later, Eudoric told Jillo, "That deal all but wiped out our funds."

"After the tradesmanlike way ye chaffered that barbarian down?"

"Aye. The scheme had better work, or we shall find ourselves choosing betwixt starving and seeking employment as collectors of offal or diggers of ditches. Assuming, that is, that in this rocky place they even bother to collect offal."

"Master Eudoric!" said Jillo. "Ye would not really lower yourself to accept menial wage labor?"

"Sooner than starve, aye. As Helvolius the philosopher said, no rider wears sharper spurs than Necessity."

"But if 'twere known at home, they'd hack off your gilded spurs, break your sword over your head, and degrade you to base varlet!"

"Well, till now I've had no knightly spurs to hack off, but only the plain silvered ones of an esquire. For the rest, I count on you to see that they don't find out. Now go to sleep and cease your grumbling."

The next day found Eudoric and Jillo deep into the Motolian Forest. At the noonday halt, Jillo kindled a fire. Eudoric made a small torch of a stick whose end was wound with a rag soaked in bacon fat. Then he loaded the device as he had been shown how to do and fired three balls at a mark on a tree. The third time, he hit the mark squarely, although the noise caused the palfreys frantically to tug and rear.

They remounted and went on to where they had met the dragon.

Jillo rekindled the torch, and they cast up and down the beast's trail. For two hours they saw no wildlife save a fleeing sow with a farrow of piglets and several huge snails with boulder-sized shells.

Then the horses became unruly. "Methinks they scent our quarry," said Eudoric.

When the riders themselves could detect the odor and the horses became almost unmanageable, Eudoric and Jillo dismounted.

"Tie the nags securely," said Eudoric. " 'Twould never do to slay our beast and then find that our horses had fled, leaving us to drag this land cockadrill home afoot."

As if in answer, a deep grunt came from ahead. While Jillo secured the horses, Eudoric laid out his new equipment and methodically loaded his piece.

"Here it comes," said Eudoric. "Stand by with that torch. Apply it not ere I give the word!"

The dragon came in sight, plodding along the trail and swinging its head from side to side. Having just shed its skin, the dragon gleamed in a reticular pattern of green and black, as if it had been freshly painted. Its great, golden, slit-pupiled eyes were now keen.

The horses screamed, causing the dragon to look up and speed its approach.

"Ready?" said Eudoric, setting the device in its rest.

"Aye, sir. Here goeth!" Without awaiting further command, Jillo applied the torch to the touchhole.

With a great boom and a cloud of smoke, the device discharged, rocking Eudoric back a pace. When the smoke cleared, the dragon was still rushing upon them, unharmed.

"Thou idiot!" screamed Eudoric. "I told thee not to give fire until I commanded! Thou has made me miss it clean!"

"I'm s-sorry, sir. I was palsied with fear. What shall we do now?"

"Run, fool!" Dropping the device, Eudoric turned and fled.

Jillo also ran. Eudoric tripped over a root and fell sprawling. Jillo stopped to guard his fallen master and turned to face the dragon. As Eudoric scrambled up, Jillo hurled the torch at the dragon's open maw.

The throw fell just short of its target. It happened, however, that the dragon was just passing over the bag of black powder in its charge. The whirling torch, descending in its flight beneath the monster's head, struck this sack.

BOOM!

When the dragon hunters returned, they found the dragon writhing in its death throes. Its whole underside had been blown open, and blood and guts spilled out.

"Well!" said Eudoric, drawing a long breath. "That is enough knightly adventure to last me for many a year. Fall to; we must flay the creature. Belike we can sell that part of the hide that we take not home ourselves."

"How do ye propose to get it back to Liptai? Its hide alone must weigh in the hundreds."

"We shall hitch the dragon's tail to our two nags and lead them, dragging it behind. 'Twill be a weary swink, but we must needs recover as much as we can to recoup our losses."

An hour later, blood-splattered from head to foot, they were still struggling with the vast hide. Then, a man in forester's garb, with a large gilt medallion on his breast, rode up and dismounted. He was a big, rugged-looking man with a rattrap mouth.

"Who slew this beast, good my sirs?" he inquired.

Jillo spoke: "My noble master, the squire Eudoric Dambertson here. He is the hero who hath brought this accursed beast to book."

"Be that sooth?" said the man to Eudoric.

"Well, ah," said Eudoric, "I must not claim much credit for the deed."

"But ye were the slayer, yea? Then, sir, ye are under arrest."

"What? But wherefore?"

"Ye shall see." From his garments, the stranger produced a length of cord with knots at intervals. With this he measured the dragon from nose to tail. Then the man stood up again.

"To answer your question, on three grounds: *imprimis,* for slaying a dragon out of lawful season; *secundus,* for slaying a dragon below the minimum size permitted; and *tertius,* for slaying a female dragon, which is protected the year round."

"You say this is a female?"

"Aye, 'tis as plain as the nose on your face."

"How does one tell with dragons?"

"Know, knave, that the male hath small horns behind the eyes, the which this specimen patently lacks."

"Who are you anyway?" demanded Eudoric.

"Senior game warden Voytsik of Prath, at your service. My credentials." The man fingered his medallion. "Now, show me your licenses, pray!"

"Licenses?" said Eudoric blankly.

"Hunting licenses, oaf!"

"None told us that such were required, sir," said Jillo.

"Ignorance of the law is no pretext; ye should have asked. That makes four counts of illegality."

Eudoric said, "But why—why in the name of the God and Goddess—"

"Pray, swear not by your false, heretical deities."

"Well, why should you Pathenians wish to preserve these monstrous reptiles?"

"*Imprimis*, because their hides and other parts have commercial value, which would perish were the whole race extirpated. *Secundus*, because they help to maintain the balance of nature by devouring the giant snails, which otherwise would issue forth nightly from the forest in such numbers as to strip bare our crops, orchards, and gardens and reduce our folk to hunger. And *tertius*, because they add a picturesque element to the landscape, thus luring foreigners to visit our land and spend their gold therein. Doth that explanation satisfy you?"

Eudoric had a fleeting thought of assaulting the stranger and either killing him or rendering him helpless while Eudoric and Jillo salvaged their prize. Even as he thought, three more tough-looking fellows, clad like Voytsik and armed with crossbows, rode out of the trees and formed up behind their leader.

"Now come along, ye two," said Voytsik.

"Whither?" asked Eudoric.

"Back to Liptai. On the morrow, we take the stage to Velitchovo, where your case will be tried."

"Your pardon, sir; we take the what?"

"The stagecoach."

"What's that, good my sir?"

"By the only God, ye must come from a barbarous land indeed! Ye shall see. Now come along, lest we be benighted in the woods."

The stagecoach made a regular round trip between Liptai and Velitchovo thrice a sennight. Jillo made the journey sunk in gloom, Eudoric kept busy viewing the passing countryside and, when opportunity offered, asking the driver about his occupation: pay, hours, fares, the cost of the vehicle, and so forth. By the time the prisoners reached their destination, both stank mightily because they had had no chance to wash the dragon's blood from their blood-soaked garments.

As they neared the capital, the driver whipped up his team to a gallop. They rattled along the road beside the muddy river Pshora until the river made a bend. Then they thundered across the planks of a bridge.

Velitchovo was a real city, with a roughly paved main street and an onion-domed, brightly colored cathedral of the One God. In a massively timbered municipal palace, a bewhiskered magistrate asked, "Which of you two aliens truly slew the beast?"

"The younger, hight Eudoric," said Voytsik.

"Nay, Your Honor, 'twas I!" said Jillo.

"That is not what he said when we came upon them red-handed from their crime," said Voytsik. "This lean fellow plainly averred that his companion had done the deed, and the other denied it not."

"I can explain that," said Jillo. "I am the servant of the most worshipful squire Eudoric Dambertson of Arduen. We set forth to slay the creature, thinking this a noble and heroic deed that should redound to our glory on earth and our credit in Heaven. Whereas we both had a part in the act, the fatal stroke was delivered by your humble servant here. Howsomever, wishing like a good servant for all the glory to go to my master, I gave him the full credit, not knowing that this credit should be counted as blame."

"What say ye to that, Master Eudoric?" asked the judge.

"Jillo's account is essentially true," said Eudoric. "I must, however, confess that my failure to slay the beast was due to mischance and not want of intent."

"Methinks they utter a pack of lies to confuse the court," said Voytsik. "I have told Your Honor of the circumstances of their arrest, whence ye may judge how matters stand."

The judge put his fingertips together. "Master Eudoric," he said, "ye may plead innocent, or as incurring sole guilt, or as guilty in company with your servant. I do not think that you can escape some guilt, since Master Jillo, being your servant, acted under your orders. Ye be therefore responsible for his acts and at the very least a factor of dragocide."

"What happens if I plead innocent?" said Eudoric.

"Why, in that case, an' ye can find an attorney, ye shall be tried in due course. Bail can plainly not be allowed to foreign travelers, who can so easily slip through the law's fingers."

"In other words, I needs must stay in jail until my case comes up. How long will that take?"

"Since our calendar be crowded, 'twill be at least a year and a half. Whereas, an' ye plead guilty, all is settled in a trice."

"Then I plead sole guilt," said Eudoric.

"But, dear Master—" wailed Jillo.

"Hold thy tongue, Jillo. I know what I do."

The judge chuckled. "An old head on young shoulders, I perceive. Well, Master Eudoric. I find you guilty on all four counts and amerce you the wonted fine, which is one hundred marks on each count."

"Four hundred marks!" exclaimed Eudoric. "Our total combined wealth at this moment amounts to fourteen marks and thirty-seven pence, plus some items of property left with Master Kasmar in Liptai."

"So, ye'll have to serve out the corresponding prison term, which comes to one mark a day—unless ye can find someone to pay the balance of the fine for you. Take him away, jailer."

"But, Your Honor!" cried Jillo, "what shall I do without my noble master? When shall I see him again?"

"Ye may visit him any day during the regular visiting hours. It were well if ye brought him somewhat to eat, for our prison fare is not of the daintiest."

At the first visiting hour, when Jillo pleaded to be allowed to share Eudoric's sentence, Eudoric said, "Be not a bigger fool than thou canst help! I took sole blame so that ye should be free to run mine errands; whereas had I shared my guilt with you, we had both been mewed up here. Here, take this letter to Doctor Raspiudus; seek him out and acquaint him with our plight. If he be in sooth a true friend of our own Doctor Baldonius, belike he'll come to our rescue."

Doctor Raspiudus was short and fat, with a bushy white beard to his waist. "Ah, dear old Baldonius!" he cried in good Helladic. "I mind me of when we were lads together at the Arcane College of Saalingen University! Doth he still string verses together?"

"Aye, that he does," said Eudoric.

"Now, young man, I daresay that your chiefest desire is to get out of this foul hole, is't not?"

"That, *and* to recover our three remaining animals and other possessions left behind in Liptai, *and* to depart with the two square yards of dragon hide that I've promised to Doctor Baldonius, with enough money to see us home."

"Methinks all these matters were easily arranged, young sir. I need only your power of attorney to enable me to go to Liptai, recover the objects in question and return hither to pay your fine and release you. Your firearm is, I fear, lost to you, having been confiscated by the law."

" 'Twere of little use without a new supply of the magical powder," said Eudoric. "Your plan sounds splendid. But, sir, what do you get out of this?"

The enchanter rubbed his hands together. "Why, the pleasure of favoring an old friend—and also the chance to acquire a complete dragon hide for my own purposes. I know somewhat of Baldonius' experiments. As he can do thus and so with two yards of dragon, I can surely do more with a score."

"How will you obtain this dragon hide?"

"By now the foresters will have skinned the beast and salvaged the other parts of monetary worth, all of which will be put up at auction for the benefit of the kingdom. And I shall bid them in." Raspiudus chuckled. "When the other bidders know against whom they bid, I think not that they'll force the price up very far."

"Why can't you get me out of here now and then go to Liptai?"

Another chuckle. "My dear boy, first I must see that all is as ye say in Liptai. After all, I have only your word that ye be in sooth the Eudoric Dambertson of whom Baldonius writes. So bide ye in patience a few days more. I'll see that ye be sent better aliment than the slop they serve here. And now, pray, your authorization. Here are pen and ink."

To keep from starvation, Jillo got a job as a paver's helper and worked in hasty visits to the jail during his lunch hour. When a fortnight had passed without word from Doctor Raspiudus, Eudoric told Jillo to go to the wizard's home for an explanation.

"They turned me away at the door," reported Jillo. "They told me that the learned doctor had never heard of us."

As the import of this news sank in, Eudoric cursed and beat the wall in his rage. "That filthy, treacherous he-witch! He gets me to sign that power of attorney; then, when he has my property in his grubby paws, he conveniently forgets about us! By the God and Goddess, if ever I catch him—"

"Here, here, what's all this noise?" said the jailer. "Ye disturb the other prisoners."

When Jillo explained the cause of his master's outrage, the jailer laughed. "Why, everyone knows that Raspiudus is the worst skinflint and treacher in Velitchovo! Had ye asked me, I'd have warned you."

"Why has none of his victims slain him?" asked Eudoric.

"We are a law-abiding folk, sir. We do not permit private persons to indulge their feuds on their own, and we have some *most* ingenious penalties for homicide."

"Mean ye," said Jillo, "that amongst you Pathenians a gentleman may not avenge an insult by the gage of battle?"

"Of course not! We are not bloodthirsty barbarians."

"Ye mean there are no true gentlemen amongst you," sniffed Jillo.

"Then, Master Tiolkhof," said Eudoric, calming himself by force of will, "am I stuck here for a year or more?"

"Aye, but ye may get time off for good behavior at the end—three or four days, belike."

When the jailer had gone, Jillo said, "When ye get out, Master, ye must needs uphold your honor by challenging this runagate to the trial of battle, to the death."

Eudoric shook his head. "Heard you not what Tiolkhof said? They deem dueling barbarous and boil the duelists in oil, or something equally entertaining. Anyway, Raspiudus could beg off on grounds of age. We must, instead, use what wits the Holy Couple gave us. I wish now that I'd sent you back to Liptai to fetch our belongings and never meddled with his rolypoly sorcerer."

"True, but how could ye know, dear Master? I should probably have bungled the task in any case, what with my ignorance of the tongue and all."

After another fortnight, King Vladmor of Pathenia died. When his son Yogor ascended the throne, he declared a general amnesty for all crimes less than murder. Thus Eudoric found himself out in the street again, but without horse, armor, weapons, or money beyond a few marks.

"Jillo," he said that night in their mean little cubicle, "we must needs get into Raspiudus' house somehow. As we saw this afternoon, 'tis a big place with a stout, high wall around it."

"An' ye could get a supply of that black powder, we could blast a breach in the wall."

"But we have no such stuff, nor means of getting it, unless we raid the royal armory, which I do not think we can do."

"Then how about climbing a tree near the wall and letting ourselves down by ropes inside the wall from a convenient branch?"

"A promising plan, *if* there were such an overhanging tree. But there isn't, as you saw as well as I when we scouted the place. Let me think. Raspiudus must have supplies borne into his stronghold from time to time. I misdoubt his wizardry is potent enough to conjure foodstuffs out of air."

"Mean ye that we should gain entrance as, say, a brace of chicken farmers with eggs to sell?"

"Just so. But nay, that won't do. Raspiudus is no fool. Knowing of this amnesty that enlarged me, he'll be on the watch for such a trick. At least, so should I be, in his room, and I credit him with no less wit than mine own. . . . I have it! What visitor would logically be likely to call upon him now, whom he will not have seen for many a year and whom he would hasten to welcome?"

"That I know not, sir."

"Who would wonder what had become of us and, detecting our troubles in his magical scryglass, would follow upon our track by uncanny means?"

"Oh, ye mean Doctor Baldonius!"

"Aye. My whiskers have grown nigh as long as his since last I shaved. And we're much of a size."

"But I never heard that your old tutor could fly about on an enchanted broomstick, as some of the mightiest magicians are said to do."

"Belike he can't, but Doctor Raspiudus wouldn't know that."

"Mean ye," said Jillo, "that ye've a mind to play Doctor Baldonius? Or to have me play him? The latter would never do."

"I know it wouldn't, good my Jillo. You know not the learned patter proper to wizards and other philosophers."

"Won't Raspiudus know you, sir? As ye say he's a shrewd old villain."

"He's seen me but once, in that dark, dank cell, and that for a mere quarter hour. You he's never seen at all. Methinks I can disguise myself well enough to befool him—unless you have a better notion."

"Alack, I have none! Then what part shall I play?"

"I had thought of going in alone."

"Nay, sir, dismiss the thought! Me let my master risk his mortal body and immortal soul in a witch's lair without my being there to help him!"

"If you help me the way you did by touching off that firearm whilst our dragon was out of range—"

"Ah, but who threw the torch and saved us in the end? What disguise shall I wear?"

"Since Raspiudus knows you not, there's no need for any. You shall be Baldonius' servant, as you are mine."

"Ye forget, sir, that if Raspiudus knows me not, his gatekeepers might. Forsooth, they're likely to recall me because of the noisy protests I made when they barred me out."

"Hm. Well, you're too old for a page, too lank for a bodyguard, and too unlearned for a wizard's assistant. I have it! You shall go as my concubine!"

"Oh, Heaven above, sir, not that! I am a normal man! I should never live it down!"

To the massive gate before Raspiudus' house came Eudoric, with a patch over one eye, and his beard, uncut for a month, dyed white. A white wig cascaded down from under his hat. He presented a note, in a plausible imitation of Baldonius' hand, to the gatekeeper:

> Doctor Baldonius of Treveria presents his compliments to his old friend and colleague Doctor Raspiudus of Velitchovo, and begs the favor of an audience to discuss the apparent disappearance of two young protégés of his.

A pace behind, stooping to disguise his stature, slouched a rouged and powdered Jillo in woman's dress. If Jillo was a homely man, he made a hideous woman, least as far as his face could be seen under the headcloth. Nor was his beauty enhanced by the dress, which Eudoric had stitched together out of cheap cloth. The garment looked like what it was: the work of a rank amateur at dressmaking.

"My master begs you to enter," said the gatekeeper.

"Why, dear old Baldonius!" cried Raspiudus, rubbing his hands together. "Ye've not changed a mite since those glad, mad days at Saalingen! Do ye still string verses?"

"Ye've withstood the ravages of time well yourself, Raspiudus," said Eudoric, in an imitation of Baldonius' voice.

" 'As fly the years, the geese fly north in spring; Ah, would the years, like geese, return awing!' "

Raspiudus roared with laughter, patting his paunch. "The same old Baldonius! Made ye that one up?' "

Eudoric made a deprecatory motion. "I am a mere poetaster; but had not the higher wisdom claimed my allegiance, I might have made my mark in poesy."

"What befell your poor eye?"

"My own carelessness in leaving a corner of a pentacle open. The demon got in a swipe of his claws ere I could banish him. But now, good Raspiudus, I have a matter to discuss whereof I told you in my note."

"Yea, yea, time enow for that. Be ye weary from the road? Need ye baths? Aliment? Drink?"

"Not yet, old friend. We have but now come from Velitchovo's best hostelry."

"Then let me show you my house and grounds. Your lady . . . ?"

"She'll stay with me. She speaks nought but Treverian and fears being separated from me among strangers. A mere swineherd's chick, but a faithful creature. At my age, that is of more moment than a pretty face."

Presently, Eudoric was looking at his and Jillo's palfreys and their sumpter mule in Raspiudus' stables. Eudoric made a few hesitant efforts, as if he were Baldonius seeking his young friends, to inquire after their disappearance. Each time Raspiudus smoothly turned the question aside, promising enlightenment later.

An hour later, Raspiudus was showing off his magical sanctum. With obvious interest, Eudoric examined a number of squares of dragon hide spread out on a workbench. He asked:

"Be this the integument of one of those Pathenian dragons, whereof I have heard?"

"Certes, good Baldonius. Are they extinct in your part of the world?"

"Aye. 'Twas for that reason that I sent my young friend and former pupil, of whom I'm waiting to tell you, eastward to fetch me some of this hide for use in my work. How does one cure this hide?"

"With salt, and—*unh!*"

Raspiudus collapsed, Eudoric having just struck him on the head with a short bludgeon that he whisked out of his voluminous sleeves.

"Bind and gag him and roll him behind the bench!" said Eudoric.

"Were it not better to cut his throat, sir?" said Jillo.

"Nay. The jailor told us that they have ingenious ways of punishing homicide, and I have no wish to prove them by experiment."

While Jillo bound the unconscious Raspiudus, Eudoric chose two pieces of dragon hide, each about a yard square. He rolled them together into a bundle and lashed them with a length of rope from inside his robe. As an afterthought, he helped himself to the contents of Raspiudus' purse. Then he hoisted the roll of hide to his shoulder and issued from the laboratory. He called to the nearest stableboy.

"Doctor Raspiudus," he said, "asks that ye saddle up those two nags." He pointed. "Good saddles, mind you! Are the animals well shod?"

"Hasten, sir," muttered Jillo. "Every instant we hang about here—"

"Hold thy peace! The appearance of haste were the surest way to arouse suspicion." Eudoric raised his voice. "Another heave on that girth, fellow! I am not minded to have my aged bones shattered by a tumble into the roadway."

Jillo whispered, "Can't we recover the mule and your armor, to boot?"

Eudoric shook his head. "Too risky," he murmured. "Be glad if we get away with whole skins."

When the horses had been saddled to his satisfaction, he said, "Lend me some of your strength in mounting, youngster." He groaned as he swung awkwardly into the saddle. "A murrain on thy master, to send us off on this footling errand—me that hasn't sat a horse in years! Now hand me that accursed roll of hide. I thank thee, youth; here's a little for thy trouble. Run ahead and tell the gatekeeper to have his portal well opened. I fear that if this beast pulls up of a sudden, I shall go flying over its head!"

A few minutes later, when they had turned a corner and were out of sight of Raspiudus' house, Eudoric said, "Now, trot!"

"If I could but get out of this damned gown," muttered Jillo. "I can't ride decently in it."

"Wait till we're out of the city gate."

When Jillo had shed the offending garment, Eudoric said, "Now ride, man, as never before in your life!"

They pounded off on the Liptai road. Looking back, Jillo gave a screech. "There's a thing flying after us! It looks like a giant bat!"

"One of Raspiudus' sendings," said Eudoric. "I knew he'd get loose. Use your spurs! Can we but gain the bridge . . ."

They fled at a mad gallop. The sending came closer and closer, until Eudoric thought he could feel the wind of its wings.

Then their hooves thundered across the bridge over the Pshora.

"Those things will not cross running water," said Eudoric, looking back. "Slow down, Jillo. These nags must bear us many leagues, and we must not founder them at the start."

". . . so here we are," Eudoric told Doctor Baldonius.

"Ye've seen your family, lad?"

"Certes. They thrive, praise to the Divine Pair. Where's Lusina?"

"Well—ah—ahem—the fact is, she is not here."

"Oh? Then where?"

"Ye put me to shame, Eudoric. I promised you her hand in return for the two yards of dragon hide. Well, ye've fetched me the hide, at no small effort and risk, but I cannot fulfill my side of the bargain."

"Wherefore?"

"Alas! My undutiful daughter ran off with a strolling player last summer, whilst ye were chasing dragons—or perchance 'twas the other way round. I'm right truly sorry. . . ."

Eudoric frowned silently for an instant, then said, "Fret not, esteemed Doctor. I shall recover from the wound—provided, that is, that you salve it by making up my losses in more materialistic fashion."

Baldonius raised bushy gray brows. "So? Ye seem not so grief-stricken as I should have expected, to judge from the lover's sighs and tears wherewith ye parted from the jade last spring. Now ye'll accept money instead?"

"Aye, sir. I admit that my passion had somewhat cooled during our long separation. Was it likewise with her? What said she of me?"

"Aye, her sentiments did indeed change. She said you were too much an opportunist altogether to please her. I would not wound your feelings. . . ."

Eudoric waved a deprecatory hand. "Continue, pray. I have been somewhat toughened by my months in the rude, rough world, and I am interested."

"Well, I told her she was being foolish; that ye were a shrewd lad who, an' ye survived the dragon hunt, would go far. But her words were: 'That is just the trouble, Father. He is too shrewd to be very lovable.' "

"Hmph," grunted Eudoric. "As one might say: I am a man of enterprise, thou art an opportunist, he is a conniving scoundrel. 'Tis all in the point of view. Well, if she prefers the fools of this world, I wish her joy of them. As a man of honor, I would have wedded Lusina had she wished. As things stand, trouble is saved all around."

"To you, belike, though I misdoubt my headstrong lass'll find the life of an actor's wife a bed of violets:

Who'd wed on a whim is soon filled to the brim
Of worry and doubt, till he longs for an out.
So if ye would wive, beware of the gyve
Of an ill-chosen mate; 'tis a harrowing fate.

But enough of that. What sum had ye in mind?"

"Enough to cover the cost of my good destrier Morgrim and my panoply of plate, together with lance and sword, plus a few other chattels and incidental expenses of travel. Fifteen hundred marks should cover the lot."

"Fif-teen *hundred!* Whew! I could ne'er afford—nor are these moldy patches of dragon hide worth a fraction of the sum."

Eudoric sighed and rose. "You know what you can afford, good my sage." He picked up the roll of dragon hide. "Your colleague Doctor Calporio, wizard to the Count of Treveria, expressed a keen interest in this material. In fact, he offered me more than I have asked of you, but I thought it only honorable to give you the first chance."

"What!" cried Baldonius. "That mountebank, charlatan, that faker? Misusing the hide and not deriving a tenth of the magical benefits from it that I should? Sit down, Eudoric; we will discuss these things."

An hour's haggling got Eudoric his fifteen hundred marks. Baldonius said, "Well, praise the Divine Couple that's over. And now, beloved pupil, what are your plans?"

"Would ye believe it, Doctor Baldonius," said Jillo, "that my poor, deluded master is about to disgrace his lineage and betray his class by a base commercial enterprise?"

"Forsooth, Jillo? What's this?"

"He means my proposed coach line," said Eudoric.

"Good Heaven, what's that?"

"My plan to run a carriage on a weekly schedule from Zurgau to Kromnitch, taking all who can pay the fare, as they do in Pathenia. We can't let the heathen Easterlings get ahead of us."

"What an extraordinary idea! Need ye a partner?"

"Thanks, but nay. Baron Emmerhard has already thrown in with me. He's promised me my knighthood in exchange for the partnership."

"There is no nobility anymore," said Jillo.

Eudoric grinned. "Emmerhard said much the same sort of thing, but I convinced him that anything to do with horses is a proper pursuit for a gentleman. Jillo, you can spell me at driving the coach, which will make you a gentleman, too!"

Jillo sighed. "Alas! The true spirit of knighthood is dying in this degenerate age. Woe is me that I should live to see the end of chivalry! How much did ye think of paying me, sir?"

Chinese Puzzle

◻ ◻ ◻

by John Wyndham

The parcel, waiting provocatively on the dresser, was the first
thing that Hwyl noticed when he got in from work.

"From Dai, is it?" he inquired of his wife.

"Yes, indeed. Japanese the stamps are," she told him.

He went across to examine it. It was the shape a small hatbox
might be, about ten inches each way perhaps. The address: Mr. &
Mrs. Hwyl Hughes, Ty Derwen, Llynllawn, Llangolwgcoch,
Brecknockshire, S.Wales, was lettered carefully, for the clear understanding of foreigners. The other label, also hand-lettered, but
in red, was quite clear too. It said: EGGS—Fragile—With great
CARE.

"There is funny to send eggs so far," Hwyl said. "Plenty of eggs
we are having. Might be chocolate eggs, I think?"

"Come you to your tea, man," Bronwen told him. "All day I have
been looking at that old parcel, and a little longer it can wait now."

Hwyl sat down at the table and began his meal. From time to time,
however, his eyes strayed again to the parcel.

"If it is real eggs they are, careful you should be," he remarked.
"Reading in a book I was once how in China they keep eggs for
years. Bury them in the earth, they do, for a delicacy. There is strange
for you, now. Queer they are in China, and not like Wales, at all."

Bronwen contented herself with saying that perhaps Japan was not like China, either.

When the meal had been finished and cleared, the parcel was transferred to the table. Hwyl snipped the string and pulled off the brown paper. Within was a tin box which, when the sticky tape holding its lid had been removed, proved to be full to the brim with sawdust. Mrs. Hughes fetched a sheet of newspaper and prudently covered the table top. Hwyl dug his fingers into the sawdust.

"Something there, there is," he announced.

"There is stupid you are. Of course there is something there," Bronwen said, slapping his hand out of the way.

She trickled some of the sawdust out onto the newspaper, and then felt inside of the box herself. Whatever it was, it felt much too large for an egg. She poured out more sawdust and felt again. This time her fingers encountered a piece of paper. She pulled it out and laid it on the table: a letter in Dafydd's handwriting. Then she put in her hand once more, got her fingers under the object, and lifted it gently out.

"Well, indeed! Look at that now! Did you ever?" she exclaimed. "Eggs, he was saying, is it?"

They both regarded it with astonishment for some moments.

"So big it is. Queer, too," said Hwyl at last.

"What kind of bird to lay such an egg?" said Bronwen.

"Ostrich, perhaps?" suggested Hwyl.

But Bronwen shook her head. She had once seen an ostrich's egg in a museum, and remembered it well enough to know that it had little in common with this. The ostrich's egg had been a little smaller, with a dull, sallow-looking, slightly dimpled surface. This was smooth and shiny, and by no means had the same dead look: it had a luster to it, a nacreous kind of beauty.

"A pearl, could it be?" she said, in an awed voice.

"There is silly you are," said her husband. "From an oyster as big as Llangolwgcoch Town Hall, you are thinking?"

He burrowed into the tin again, but "Eggs," it seemed, had been a manner of speaking: there was no other, nor room for one.

Bronwen put some of the sawdust into one of her best vegetable dishes, and bedded the egg carefully on top of it. Then they sat down to read their son's letter:

S.S. Tudor Maid,
Kobe.

Dear Mam and Dad,

I expect you will be surprised about the enclosed I was too. It is a funny looking thing I expect they have funny birds in China after all they have Pandas so why not. We found a small sampan about a hundred miles off the China coast that had bust its mast and should never have tried and all except two of them were dead they are all dead now. But one of them that wasn't dead then was holding this egg-thing all wrapped up in a padded coat like it was a baby only I didn't know it was an egg then not till later. One of them died coming aboard but this other one lasted two days longer in spite of all I could do for him which was my best. I was sorry nobody here can speak Chinese because he was a nice little chap and lonely and knew he was a goner but there it is. And when he saw it was nearly all up he gave me this egg and talked very faint but I'd not have understood anyway. All I could do was take it and hold it careful the way he had and tell him I'd look after it which he couldn't understand either. Then he said something else and looked very worried and died poor chap.

So here it is. I know it is an egg because when I took him a boiled egg once he pointed to both of them to show me but nobody on board knows what kind of egg. But seeing I promised him I'd keep it safe I am sending it to you to keep for me as this ship is no place to keep anything safe anyway and hope it doesn't get cracked on the way too.

Hoping this finds you as it leaves me and love to all and you special.

Dai.

"Well, there is strange for you now," said Mrs. Hughes, as she finished reading. "And *looking* like an egg it is, indeed—the shape of it," she conceded. "But the colors are not. There is pretty they are. Like you see when oil is on the road in the rain. But never an egg like that have I seen in my life. Flat the color is on eggs, and not to shine."

Hwyl went on looking at it thoughtfully.

"Yes. There is beautiful," he agreed, "but what use?"

"Use, is it, indeed!" said his wife. "A trust, it is, and sacred, too. Dying the poor man was, and our Dai gave him his word. I am thinking of how we will keep it safe for him till he will be back, now."

They both contemplated the egg awhile.

"Very far away, China is," Bronwen remarked, obscurely.

Several days passed, however, before the egg was removed from display on the dresser. Word quickly went round the valley about it, and the callers would have felt slighted had they been unable to see it. Bronwen felt that continually getting it out and putting it away again would be more hazardous than leaving it on exhibition.

Almost everyone found the sight of it rewarding. Idris Bowen who lived three houses away was practically alone in his divergent view.

"The shape of an egg, it has," he allowed. "But careful you should be, Mrs. Hughes. A fertility symbol it is, I am thinking, and stolen, too, likely."

"Mr. Bowen—" began Bronwen, indignantly.

"Oh, by the men in that boat, Mrs. Hughes. Refugees from China they would be, see. Traitors to the Chinese people. And running away with all they could carry, before the glorious army of the workers and peasants could catch them, too. Always the same, it is, as you will be seeing when the revolution comes to Wales."

"Oh, dear, dear! There is funny you are, Mr. Bowen. Propaganda you will make out of an old boot, I think," said Bronwen.

Idris Bowen frowned.

"Funny I am not, Mrs. Hughes. And propaganda there is in an honest boot, too," he told her as he left with dignity.

By the end of a week practically everyone in the village had seen the egg and been told no, Mrs. Hughes did not know what kind of a creature had laid it, and the time seemed to have come to store it away safely against Dafydd's return. There were not many places in the house where she could feel sure that it would rest undisturbed, but, on consideration, the airing-cupboard seemed as likely as any, so she put it back on what sawdust was left in the tin, and stowed it in there.

It remained there for a month, out of sight and pretty much out of mind until a day when Hwyl returning from work discovered his wife sitting at the table with a disconsolate expression on her face and a bandage on her finger. She looked relieved to see him.

"Hatched, it is," she observed.

The blankness of Hwyl's expression was irritating to one who had had a single subject on her mind all day.

"Dai's egg," she explained. "Hatched out, it is, I am telling you."

"Well, there is a thing for you, now!" said Hwyl. "A nice little chicken, is it?"

"A chicken it is not, at all. A monster, indeed, and biting me it is, too." She held out her bandaged finger.

She explained that this morning she had gone to the airing-cupboard to take out a clean towel, and as she put her hand in, something had nipped her finger, painfully. At first she had thought that it might be a rat that had somehow got in from the yard, but then she had noticed that the lid was off the tin, and the shell of the egg there was all broken to pieces.

"How is it to see?" Hwyl asked.

Bronwen admitted that she had not seen it well. She had had a glimpse of a long, greeny-blue tail protruding from behind a pile of sheets, and then it had looked at her over the top of them, glaring at her from red eyes. On that, it had seemed to her more the kind of a job a man should deal with, so she had slammed the door and gone to bandage her finger.

"Still there, then, is it?" said Hwyl.

She nodded.

"Right you. Have a look at it, we will, now then," he said decisively.

He started to leave the room, but on second thoughts turned back to collect a pair of heavy work gloves. Bronwen did not offer to accompany him.

Presently there was a scuffle of his feet, an exclamation or two, then his tread descending the stairs. He came in, shutting the door behind him with his foot. He set the creature he was carrying down on the table, and for some seconds it crouched there, blinking, but otherwise unmoving.

"Scared, he was, I think," Hwyl remarked.

In the body, the creature bore some resemblance to a lizard—a large lizard, over a foot long. The scales of its skin, however, were much bigger, and some of them curled up and stood out here and there, in a finlike manner. And the head was quite unlike a lizard's, being much rounder, with a wide mouth, broad nostrils, and, over all, a slightly pushed-in effect, in which were set a pair of goggling red eyes. About the neck, and also making a kind of mane, were curious, streamer-like attachments with the suggestion of locks of hair which had permanently cohered. The color was mainly green, shot with blue and having a metallic shine to it, but there were brilliant red markings about the head and in the lower parts of the locks. There were touches of red, too, where the legs joined the body and on the feet, where the toes finished in sharp yellow claws. Altogether, a surprisingly vivid and exotic creature.

It eyed Bronwen Hughes for a moment, turned a baleful look on Hwyl, and then started to run about the table top, looking for a way off. The Hugheses watched it for a moment or two, and then regarded one another.

"Well, there is nasty for you, indeed," observed Bronwen.

"Nasty it may be. But beautiful it is, too, look," said Hwyl.

"Ugly old face to have," Bronwen remarked.

"Yes, indeed. But fine colors, too, see. Glorious, they are, like technicolor, I am thinking," Hwyl said.

The creature appeared to have half a mind to leap from the table. Hwyl leaned forward and caught hold of it. It wriggled, and tried to get its head round to bite him, but discovered he was holding it too near the neck for that. It paused in its struggles. Then, suddenly, it snorted. Two jets of flame and a puff of smoke came from its nostrils. Hwyl dropped it abruptly, partly from alarm but more from surprise. Bronwen gave a squeal, and climbed hastily onto her chair.

The creature itself seemed a trifle astonished. For a few seconds it stood turning its head and waving the sinuous tail that was quite as long as its body. Then it scuttled across to the hearthrug, and curled itself up in front of the fire.

"By dammo! There was a thing for you!" Hwyl exclaimed, regarding it a trifle nervously. "Fire there was with it, I think. I will like to understand that, now."

"Fire indeed, and smoke, too," Bronwen agreed. "There is shocking it was, and not natural, at all."

She looked uncertainly at the creature. It had so obviously settled itself for a nap that she risked stepping down from the chair, but she kept on watching it, ready to jump up again if it should move. Then:

"Never did I think I will see one of those. And not sure it is right to have in the house, either," she said.

"What is it you are meaning, now?" Hwyl asked, puzzled.

"Why, a dragon, indeed," Bronwen told him.

Hwyl stared at her.

"Dragon!" he exclaimed. "There is foolish—" Then he stopped. He looked at it again, and then down at the place where the flame had scorched his glove. "No, by dammo!" he said. "Right you. A dragon it is, I believe."

They both regarded it with some apprehension.

"Glad I am, not to live in China," observed Bronwen.

Those who were privileged to see the creature during the next day or two supported almost to a man the theory that it was a dragon. This they established by poking sticks through the wire netting of the hutch that Hwyl had made for it, until it obliged with a resentful huff of flame. Even Mr. Jones, the Chapel, did not doubt its authenticity, though on the propriety of its presence in his community he preferred to reserve judgment for the present.

After a short time, however, Bronwen Hughes put an end to the practice of poking it. For one thing, she felt responsible to Dai for its well-being, for another, it was beginning to develop an irritable disposition and a liability to emit flame without cause; for yet another, and although Mr. Jones's decision on whether it could be considered as one of God's creatures or not was still pending, she felt that in the meantime it deserved equal rights with other dumb animals. So she put a card on the hutch saying: PLEASE NOT TO TEASE, and most of the time was there to see that it was heeded.

Almost all Llynllawn, and quite a few people from Llangolwg-coch, too, came to see it. Sometimes they would stand for an hour or more, hoping to see it huff. If it did, they went off satisfied that it was a dragon; but if it maintained a contented, non-fire-breathing mood, they went and told their friends that it was really no more than a little old lizard, though big, mind you.

Idris Bowen was an exception to both categories. It was not until his third visit that he was privileged to see it snort, but even then he remained unconvinced.

"Unusual, it is, yes," he admitted. "But a dragon it is not. Look you at the dragon of Wales, or the dragon of St. George, now. To huff fire is something, I grant you, but wings, too, a dragon must be having, or a dragon he is not."

But that was the kind of caviling that could be expected from Idris, and disregarded.

After ten days or so of crowded evenings, however, interest slackened. Once one had seen the dragon and exclaimed over the brilliance of its coloring, there was little to add, beyond being glad that it was in the Hughes's house rather than one's own, and wondering how big it would eventually grow. For really, it did not do much but sit and blink, and perhaps give a little huff of flame if you were lucky. So presently the Hughes's home became more their own again.

And, no longer pestered by visitors, the dragon showed an equable disposition. It never huffed at Bronwen, and seldom at Hwyl. Bronwen's first feeling of antagonism passed quickly, and she found herself growing attached to it. She fed it and looked after it, and found that on a diet consisting chiefly of minced horseflesh and dog biscuits it grew with astonishing speed. Most of the time she let it run free in the room. To quiet the misgivings of callers she would explain:

"Friendly, he is, and pretty ways he has with him, if there is not teasing. Sorry for him, I am, too, for bad it is to be an only child, and an orphan worse still. And less than an orphan, he is, see. Nothing of his own sort he is knowing, nor likely, either. So very lonely he is being, poor thing, I think."

But inevitably, there came an evening when Hwyl, looking thoughtfully at the dragon, remarked:

"Outside you, soon. There is too big for the house you are getting, see."

Bronwen was surprised to find how unwilling she felt about that.

"Very good and quiet, he is," she said. "There is clever he is to tuck his tail away not to trip people, too. And clean with the house he is, also, and no trouble. Always out to the yard at proper times. Right as clockwork."

"Behaving well, he is, indeed," Hwyl agreed. "But growing so fast, now. More room he will be needing, see. A fine hutch for him in the yard, and with a run to it, I think."

The advisability of that was demonstrated a week later when Bronwen came down one morning to find the end of the wooden hutch charred away, the carpet and rug smoldering, and the dragon comfortably curled up in Hwyl's easy chair.

"Settled, it is, and lucky not to burn in our bed. Out you," Hwyl told the dragon. "A fine thing to burn a man's house for him, and not grateful, either. For shame, I am telling you."

The insurance man who came to inspect the damage thought similarly.

"Notified, you should have," he told Bronwen. "A fire risk, he is, you see."

Bronwen protested that the policy made no mention of dragons.

"No, indeed," the man admitted, "but a normal hazard he is not, either. Inquire, I will, from Head Office how it is, see. But better to turn him out before more trouble, and thankful, too."

So a couple of days later the dragon was occupying a larger hutch, constructed of asbestos sheets, in the yard. There was a wire-netted run in front of it, but most of the time Bronwen locked the gate and left the back door of the house open so that he could come and go as he liked. In the morning he would trot in and help Bronwen by huffing the kitchen fire into a blaze, but apart from that he had learned not to huff in the house. The only times he was any bother to anyone were the occasions when he set his straw on fire in the night so that the neighbors got up to see if the house was burning, and were somewhat short about it the next day.

Hwyl kept a careful account of the cost of feeding him, and hoped that it was not running into more than Dai would be willing to pay. Otherwise, his only worries were his failure to find a cheap, noninflammable bedding stuff, and speculation on how big the dragon was likely to grow before Dai should return to take him off their hands. Very likely all would have gone smoothly until that happened, but for the unpleasantness with Idris Bowen.

The trouble which blew up unexpectedly one evening was really of Idris' own finding. Hwyl had finished his meal and was peacefully enjoying the last of the day beside his door, when Idris happened along, leading his whippet on a string.

"Oh, hullo you, Idris," Hwyl greeted him amiably.

"Hullo you, Hwyl," said Idris. "And how is that phony dragon of yours, now then?"

"Phony, is it, you are saying?" repeated Hwyl, indignantly.

"Wings a dragon is wanting, to be a dragon," Idris insisted, firmly.

"Wings to hell, man! Come you and look at him now then, and please to tell me what he is if he is no dragon."

He waved Idris into the house, and led him through into the yard. The dragon, reclining in its wired run, opened an eye at them, then closed it again.

Idris had not seen it since it was lately out of the egg. Its growth impressed him.

"There is big he is now," he conceded. "Fine, the colors of him, and fancy, too. But still no wings to him, so a dragon he is not."

"What, then, is it he is?" demanded Hwyl.

How Idris would have replied to this difficult question was never to be known, for at that moment the whippet jerked its string free from his fingers, and dashed, barking, at the wire netting. The dragon was startled out of its snooze. It sat up suddenly, and snorted with surprise. There was a yelp from the whippet, which bounded into the

air and then set off round and round the yard, howling. At last Idris
managed to corner it and pick it up. All down the right side its hair
had been scorched off, making it look very peculiar. Idris' eyebrows
lowered.

"Trouble you want, is it? And trouble you will be having, by
God!" he said.

He put the whippet down again, and began to take off his coat.

It was not clear whether he had addressed, and meant to fight,
Hwyl or the dragon, but either intention was forestalled by Mrs.
Hughes, coming to investigate the yelping.

"Oh! Teasing the dragon, is it!" she said. "There is shameful, indeed. A lamb the dragon is, as people know well. But not to tease. It
is wicked you are, Idris Bowen, and to fight does not make right, either. Go you from here, now then."

Idris began to protest, but Bronwen shook her head and set her
mouth.

"Not listening to you, I am, see. A fine brave man, to tease a helpless dragon. Not for weeks now has the dragon huffed. So go you,
and quick."

Idris glowered. He hesitated, and pulled on his jacket again. He
collected his whippet and held it in his arms. After a final disparag-
ing glance at the dragon, he turned.

"Law I will have of you," he announced ominously, as he left.

Nothing more, however, was heard of legal action. It seemed as if
Idris had either changed his mind or been advised against it, and that
the whole thing would blow over. But three weeks later was the night
of the Union Branch Meeting.

It had been a dull meeting, devoted chiefly to passing a number of
resolutions suggested to it by its headquarters, as a matter of course.
Then, just at the end, when there did not seem to be any other business, Idris Bowen rose.

"Stay, you!" said the chairman to those who were preparing to
leave, and he invited Idris to speak.

Idris waited for persons who were half in and half out of their
overcoats to subside, then:

"Comrades—" he began.

There was immediate uproar. Through the mingled approbation and cries of "Order" and "Withdraw" the chairman smote energetically with his gavel until quiet was restored.

"Tendentious, that is," he reproved Idris. "Please to speak halfway, and in good order."

Idris began again:

"Fellow workers. Sorry indeed, I am, to have to tell you of a discovery I am making. A matter of disloyalty, I am telling you: grave disloyalty to good friends and com—and fellow workers, see." He paused, and went on:

"Now every one of you is knowing of Hwyl Hughes's dragon, is it? Seen him for yourselves you have likely, too. Seen him myself, I have, and saying he was no dragon. But now then, I am telling you, wrong I was, wrong, indeed. A dragon he is, and not to doubt, though no wings.

"I am reading in the encyclopedia in Merthyr Public Library about two kinds of dragons, see. Wings the European dragon has, indeed. But wings the Oriental dragon has not. So apologizing now to Mr. Hughes, I am, and sorry."

A certain restiveness becoming apparent in the audience was quelled by a change in his tone.

"*But*—" he went on, "but another thing, too, I am reading there, and troubled inside myself with it, I am. I will tell you. Have you looked at the feet of this dragon, is it? Claws there is, yes, and nasty, too. But how many, I am asking you? And five, I am telling you. Five with each foot." He paused dramatically, and shook his head. "Bad, is that, bad indeed. For look you, Chinese a five-toed dragon is, yes—but five-toed is not a Republican dragon, five-toed is not a People's dragon; five-toed is an *Imperial* dragon, see. A symbol, it is, of the oppression of Chinese workers and peasants. And shocking to think that in our village we are keeping such an emblem. What is it that the free people of China will be saying of Llynllawn when they will hear of this, I am asking? What is it Mao Tse Tung, glorious leader of the heroic Chinese people in their magnificent fight for peace, will be thinking of South Wales and this imperialist dragon—?" he was continuing, when differences of view in the audience submerged his voice.

Again the chairman called the meeting to order. He offered Hwyl the opportunity to reply, and after the situation had been briefly explained, the dragon was, on a show of hands, acquitted of political implication by all but Idris' doctrinaire faction, and the meeting broke up.

Hwyl told Bronwen about it when he got home.

"No surprise there," she said. "Jones the Post is telling me, telegraphing Idris has been."

"Telegraphing?" inquired Hwyl.

"Yes, indeed. Asking the *Daily Worker,* in London, how is the party line on imperialist dragons, he was. But no answer yet, though."

A few mornings later the Hugheses were awakened by a hammering on their door. Hwyl went to the window and found Idris below. He asked what the matter was.

"Come you down here, and I will show you," Idris told him.

After some argument, Hwyl descended. Idris led the way round to the back of his own house, and pointed.

"Look you there, now," he said.

The door of Idris' henhouse was hanging by one hinge. The remains of two chickens lay close by. A large quantity of feathers was blowing about the yard.

Hwyl looked at the henhouse more closely. Several deep-raked scores stood out white on the creosoted wood. In other places there were darker smears where the wood seemed to have been scorched. Silently Idris pointed to the ground. There were marks of sharp claws, but no imprint of a whole foot.

"There is bad. Foxes, is it?" inquired Hwyl.

Idris choked slightly.

"Foxes, you are saying. Foxes, indeed! What will it be but your dragon? And the police to know it, too."

Hwyl shook his head.

"No," he said.

"Oh," said Idris. "A liar, I am, is it? I will have the guts from you, Hwyl Hughes, smoking hot, too, and glad to do it."

"You talk too easy, man," Hwyl told him. "Only how the dragon is still fast in his hutch, I am saying. Come you now, and see."

They went back to Hwyl's house. The dragon was in his hutch, sure enough, and the door of it was fastened with a peg. Furthermore, as Hwyl pointed out, even if he had left it during the night, he could not have reached Idris' yard without leaving scratches and traces on the way, and there were none to be found.

They finally parted in a state of armistice. Idris was by no means convinced, but he was unable to get round the facts, and not at all impressed with Hwyl's suggestion that a practical joker could have produced the effect on the henhouse with a strong nail and a blowtorch.

Hwyl went upstairs again to finish dressing.

"There is funny it is, all the same," he observed to Bronwen. "Not seeing, that Idris was, but scorched the peg is, on the *outside* of the hutch. And how should that be, I wonder?"

"Huffed four times in the night the dragon has, five, perhaps," Bronwen said. "Growling, he is, too, and banging that old hutch about. Never have I heard him like that before."

"There is queer," Hwyl said, frowning. "But never out of his hutch, and that to swear to."

Two nights later Hwyl was awakened by Bronwen shaking his shoulder.

"Listen, now then," she told him.

There was an unmistakable growling going on at the back of the house, and the sound of several snorts.

"Huffing, he is, see," said Bronwen, unnecessarily.

There was a crash of something thrown with force, and the sound of a neighbor's voice cursing. Hwyl reluctantly decided that he had better get up and investigate.

Everything in the yard looked as usual, except for the presence of a large tin can which was clearly the object thrown. There was, however, a strong smell of burning, and a thudding noise, recognizable as the sound of the dragon tramping round and round in his hutch to stamp out the bedding caught alight again. Hwyl went across and opened the door. He raked out the smoldering straw, fetched some fresh, and threw it in.

"Quiet, you," he told the dragon. "More of this, and the hide I will have off you, slow and painful, too. Bed, now then, and sleep."

He went back to bed himself, but it seemed as if he had only just laid his head on the pillow when it was daylight, and there was Idris Bowen hammering on the front door again.

Idris was more than a little incoherent, but Hwyl gathered that something further had taken place at his house, so he slipped on jacket and trousers, and went down. Idris led the way down beside his own house, and threw open the yard door with the air of a conjurer. Hwyl stared for some moments without speaking.

In front of Idris' henhouse stood a kind of trap, roughly contrived of angle iron and wire netting. In it, surrounded by chicken feathers and glaring at them from eyes like live topazes, sat a creature, blood-red all over.

"Now, there is a dragon for you, indeed," Idris said. "Not to have colors like you see on a merry-go-round at a circus, either. A serious dragon, that one, and proper—wings, too, see?"

Hwyl went on looking at the dragon without a word. The wings were folded at present, and the cage did not give room to stretch them. The red, he saw now, was darker on the back and brighter beneath, giving it the rather ominous effect of being lit from below by a blast-furnace. It certainly had a more practical aspect than his own dragon, and a fiercer look about it altogether. He stepped forward to examine it more closely.

"Careful, man," Idris warned him, laying a hand on his arm.

The dragon curled back its lips, and snorted. Twin flames a yard long shot out of its nostrils. It was a far better huff than the other dragon had ever achieved. The air was filled with a strong smell of burnt feathers.

"A fine dragon, that is," Idris said again. "A real Welsh dragon for you. Angry he is, see, and no wonder. A shocking thing for an imperialist dragon to be in his country. Come to throw him out, he has, and mincemeat he will be making of your namby-pamby, best-parlor dragon, too."

"Better for him not to try," said Hwyl, stouter in word than heart.

"And another thing, too. Red this dragon is, and so a real People's dragon, see."

"Now then. Now then. Propaganda with dragons again, is it? Red the Welsh dragon has been two thousand years, and a fighter, too, I grant you. But a fighter for Wales, look; not just a loudmouth talker of fighting for peace, see. If it is a good red Welsh dragon he is, then out of some kind of egg laid by your Uncle Joe, he is not; and thankful, too, I think," Hwyl told him. "And look you," he added as an afterthought, "this one it is who is stealing your chickens, not mine, at all."

"Oh, let him have the old chickens, and glad," Idris said. "Here he is come to chase a foreign imperialist dragon out of his rightful territory, and a proper thing it is, too. None of your D.P. dragons are we wanting round Llynllawn, or South Wales, either."

"Get you to hell, man," Hwyl told him. "Sweet-dispositioned my dragon is, no bother to anyone, and no robber of henhouses, either. If there is trouble at all, the law I will be having of you and your dragon for disturbing of the peace, see. So I am telling you. And goodbye, now."

He exchanged another glance with the angry-looking, topaz eyes of the red dragon, and then stalked away, back to his own house.

That evening, just as Hwyl was sitting down to his meal, there was a knock at the front door. Bronwen went to answer it, and came back.

"Ivor Thomas and Dafydd Ellis wanting you. Something about the Union," she told him.

He went to see them. They had a long and involved story about dues that seemed not to have been fully paid. Hwyl was certain that he was paid-up to date, but they remained unconvinced. The argument went on for some time before, with headshaking and reluctance, they consented to leave. Hwyl returned to the kitchen. Bronwen was waiting, standing by the table.

"Taken the dragon off, they have," she said flatly.

Hwyl stared at her. The reason why he had been kept at the front door in pointless argument suddenly came to him. He crossed to the window and looked out. The back fence had been pushed flat, and a crowd of men carrying the dragon's hutch on their shoulders was already a hundred yards beyond it. Turning round, he saw Bronwen standing resolutely against the back door.

"Stealing, it is, and you not calling," he said accusingly.

"Knocked you down, they would, and got the dragon just the same," she said. "Idris Bowen and his lot, it is."

Hwyl looked out of the window again.

"What to do with him, now then?" he asked.

"Dragon fight, it is," she told him. "Betting, they were. Five to one on the Welsh dragon, and sounding very sure, too."

Hwyl shook his head.

"Not to wonder, either. There is not fair, at all. Wings, that Welsh dragon has, so air attacks he can make. Unsporting, there is, and shameful indeed."

He looked out of the window again. More men were joining the party as it marched its burden across the waste ground, toward the slag heap. He sighed.

"There is sorry I am for our dragon. Murder it will be, I think. But go and see it, I will. So no tricks from that Idris to make a dirty fight dirtier."

Bronwen hesitated.

"No fighting for you? You promise me?" she said.

"Is it a fool I am, girl, to be fighting fifty men, and more? Please to grant me some brains, now."

She moved doubtfully out of his way, and let him open the door. Then she snatched up a scarf and ran after him, tying it over her head as she went.

The crowd that was gathering on a piece of flat ground near the foot of the slag heap already consisted of something more like a hundred men than fifty, and there were more hurrying to join it. Several self-constituted stewards were herding people back to clear an oval space. At one end of it was the cage in which the red dragon crouched huddled, with a bad-tempered look. At the other, the as-

bestos hutch was set down, and its bearers withdrew. Idris noticed
Hwyl and Bronwen as they came up.

"And how much is it you are putting on your dragon?" he inquired, with a grin.

Bronwen said, before Hwyl could reply:

"Wicked, it is, and shamed you should be, Idris Bowen. Clip you
your dragon's wings to fight fair, and we will see. But betting
against a horseshoe in the glove, we are not." And she dragged Hwyl
away.

All about the oval the laying of bets went on, with the Welsh
dragon gaining favor all the time. Presently, Idris stepped out into the
open and held up his hands for quiet.

"Sport it is for you tonight. Supercolossal attractions as they are
saying in the movies, and never again, likely. So put you your money,
now. When the English law is hearing of this, no more dragon-fight-
ing, it will be—like no more to cockfight." A boo went up, mingled
with the laughter of those who knew a thing or two about cockfight-
ing that the English law did not. Idris went on: "So now the dragon
championship, I am giving you. On my right, the Red Dragon of
Wales, on his home ground. A People's dragon, see. For more than a
coincidence, it is, that the color of the Welsh dragon—" His voice
was lost for some moments in controversial shouts. It re-emerged,
saying: "—left, the decadent dragon of the imperialist exploiters of
the suffering Chinese people who, in their glorious fight for peace
under the heroic leadership—" But the rest of his introduction was
also lost among the catcalls and cheers that were still continuing
when he beckoned forward attendants from the ends of the oval, and
withdrew.

At one end, two men reached up with a hooked pole, pulled over
the contraption that enclosed the red dragon, and ran back hurriedly.
At the far end, a man knocked the peg from the asbestos door, pulled
it open, scuttled round behind the hutch and no less speedily out of
harm's way.

The red dragon looked round, uncertainly. It tentatively tried un-
furling its wings. Finding that possible, it reared up on its hind legs,

supporting itself on its tail, and flapped its pinions energetically, as though to dispel the creases.

The other dragon ambled out of its hutch, advanced a few feet, and stood blinking. Against the background of the waste ground and the slag heap it looked more than usually exotic. It yawned largely, with a fine display of fangs, rolled its eyes hither and thither, and then caught sight of the red dragon.

Simultaneously, the red dragon noticed the other. It stopped flapping and dropped to all four feet. The two regarded one another. A hush came over the crowd. Both dragons remained motionless, except for a slight waving of the last foot or so of their tails.

The oriental dragon turned its head a little on one side. It snorted slightly, and shriveled up a patch of weeds.

The red dragon stiffened. It suddenly adopted a pose gardant, one forefoot uplifted, with claws extended, wings raised. It huffed with vigor, vaporized a puddle, and disappeared momentarily in a cloud of steam. There was an anticipatory murmur from the crowd.

The red dragon began to pace round, circling the other, giving a slight flap of its wings now and then.

The crowd watched it intently. So did the other dragon. It did not move from its position, but turned as the red dragon circled, keeping its head and gaze steadily toward it.

With the circle almost completed, the red dragon halted. It extended its wings widely, and gave a full-throated roar. Simultaneously, it gushed two streams of fire and belched a small cloud of black smoke. The part of the crowd nearest to it moved back, apprehensively.

At this tense moment Bronwen Hughes began suddenly to laugh. Hwyl shook her by the arm.

"Hush, you! There is not funny, at all," he said, but she did not stop at once.

The oriental dragon did nothing for a moment. It appeared to be thinking the matter over. Then it turned swiftly round, and began to run. The crowd behind it raised a jeer, those in front waved their arms to shoo it back. But the dragon was unimpressed by arm-waving. It came on, with now and then a short spurt of flame from its nostrils.

The people wavered, and then scattered out of its way. Half a dozen men started to chase after it with sticks, but soon gave up. It was traveling at twice the pace they could run.

With a roar, the red dragon leaped into the air and came across the field, spitting flames like a strafing aircraft. The crowd scattered still more swiftly, tumbling over itself as it cleared a way.

The running dragon disappeared round the foot of the slag heap, with the other hovering above it. Shouts of disappointment rose from the crowd, and a good part of it started to follow, to be in at the death.

But in a minute or two the running dragon came into view again. It was making a fine pace up the mountainside, with the red dragon still flying a little behind it. Everybody stood watching it wind its way up and up until, finally, it disappeared over the shoulder. For a moment the flying dragon still showed as a black silhouette above the skyline, then, with a final whiff of flame, it, too, disappeared— and the arguments about paying up began.

Idris left the wrangling to come across to the Hugheses.

"So there is a coward your imperialist dragon is, then. And not one good huff, or a bite to him, either," he said.

Bronwen looked at him, and smiled.

"So foolish you are, Idris Bowen, with your head full of propaganda and fighting. Other things than to fight, there is, even for dragons. Such a brave show your red dragon was making, such a fine show, oh, yes—and very like a peacock, I am thinking. Very like the boys in their Sunday suits in Llangolwgcoch High Street, too—all dressed up to kill, but not to fight."

Idris stared at her.

"And our dragon," she went on. "Well, there is not a very new trick, either. Done a bit of it before now, I have, myself." She cast a sidelong glance at Hwyl.

Light began to dawn on Idris.

"But—but it is *he* you were always calling your dragon," he protested.

Bronwen shrugged.

"Oh, yes, indeed. But how to tell with dragons?" she asked.

She turned to look up the mountain.

"There is lonely, lonely the red dragon must have been these two thousand years—so not much bothering with your politics, he is, just now. More single with his mind, see. And interesting it will be, indeed, to be having a lot of baby dragons in Wales before long, I am thinking."

The George Business

□ □ □

by Roger Zelazny

Deep in his lair, Dart twisted his green and golden length about his small hoard, his sleep troubled by dreams of a series of identical armored assailants. Since dragons' dreams are always prophetic, he woke with a shudder, cleared his throat to the point of sufficient illumination to check the state of his treasure, stretched, yawned and set forth up the tunnel to consider the strength of the opposition. If it was too great, he would simply flee, he decided. The hell with the hoard; it wouldn't be the first time.

As he peered from the cave mouth, he beheld a single knight in mismatched armor atop a tired-looking gray horse, just rounding the bend. His lance was not even couched, but still pointing skyward.

Assuring himself that the man was unaccompanied, he roared and slithered forth.

"Halt," he bellowed, "you who are about to fry!"

The knight obliged.

"You're the one I came to see," the man said. "I have—"

"Why," Dart asked, "do you wish to start this business up again? Do you realize how long it has been since a knight and dragon have done battle?"

"Yes, I do. Quite a while. But I—"

"It is almost invariably fatal to one of the parties concerned. Usually your side."

"Don't I know it. Look, you've got me wrong—"

"I dreamt a dragon dream of a young man named George with whom I must do battle. You bear him an extremely close resemblance."

"I can explain. It's not as bad as it looks. You see—"

"*Is* your name George?"

"Well, yes. But don't let that bother you—"

"It *does* bother me. You want my pitiful hoard? It wouldn't keep you in beer money for the season. Hardly worth the risk."

"I'm not after your hoard—"

"I haven't grabbed off a virgin in centuries. They're usually old and tough, anyhow, not to mention hard to find."

"No one's accusing—"

"As for cattle, I always go a great distance. I've gone out of my way, you might say, to avoid getting a bad name in my own territory."

"I know you're no real threat here. I've researched it quite carefully—"

"And do you think that armor will really protect you when I exhale my deepest, hottest flames?"

"Hell, no! So don't do it, huh? If you'd please—"

"And that lance . . . You're not even holding it properly."

George lowered the lance.

"On that you are correct," he said, "but it happens to be tipped with one of the deadliest poisons known to Herman the Apothecary."

"I say! That's hardly sporting!"

"I know. But even if you incinerate me, I'll bet I can scratch you before I go."

"Now that would be rather silly—both of us dying like that—wouldn't it?" Dart observed edging away. "It would serve no useful purpose that I can see."

"I feel precisely the same way about it."

"Then why are we getting ready to fight?"

"I have no desire whatsoever to fight with you!"

"I'm afraid I don't understand. You said your name is George, and I had this dream—"

"I can explain it."

"But the poisoned lance—"

"Self-protection, to hold you off long enough to put a proposition to you."

Dart's eyelids lowered slightly.

"What sort of proposition?"

"I want to hire you."

"Hire me? Whatever for? And what are you paying?"

"Mind if I rest this lance a minute? No tricks?"

"Go ahead. If you're talking gold your life is safe."

George rested his lance and undid a pouch at his belt. He dipped his hand into it and withdrew a fistful of shining coins. He tossed them gently, so that they clinked and shone in the morning light.

"You have my full attention. That's a good piece of change there."

"My life's savings. All yours—in return for a bit of business."

"What's the deal?"

George replaced the coins in his pouch and gestured.

"See that castle in the distance—two hills away?"

"I've flown over it many times."

"In the tower to the west are the chambers of Rosalind, daughter of the Baron Maurice. She is very dear to his heart, and I wish to wed her."

"There's a problem?"

"Yes. She's attracted to big, brawny barbarian types, into which category I, alas, do not fall. In short, she doesn't like me."

"That *is* a problem."

"So, if I could pay you to crash in there and abduct her, to bear her off to some convenient and isolated place and wait for me, I'll come along, we'll fake a battle, I'll vanquish you, you'll fly away and I'll take her home. I am certain I will then appear sufficiently heroic in her eyes to rise from sixth to first position on her list of suitors. How does that sound to you?"

Dart sighed a long column of smoke.

"Human, I bear your kind no special fondness—particularly the

armored variety with lances—so I don't know why I'm telling you
this. . . . Well, I do know, actually. . . . But never mind. I could manage it, all right. But, if you win the hand of that maid, do you know
what's going to happen? The novelty of your deed will wear off after
a time—and you know that there will be no encore. Give her a year,
I'd say, and you'll catch her fooling around with one of those brawny
barbarians she finds so attractive. Then you must either fight him and
be slaughtered or wear horns, as they say."

George laughed.

"It's nothing to me how she spends her spare time. I've a girlfriend
in town myself."

Dart's eyes widened.

"I'm afraid I don't understand. . . ."

"She's the old baron's only offspring, and he's on his last legs.
Why else do you think an uncomely wench like that would have six
suitors? Why else would I gamble my life's savings to win her?"

"I see," said Dart. "Yes, I can understand greed."

"I call it a desire for security."

"Quite. In that case, forget my simple-minded advice. All right,
give me the gold and I'll do it." Dart gestured with one gleaming
vane. "The first valley in those western mountains seems far enough
from my home for our confrontation."

"I'll pay you half now and half on delivery."

"Agreed. Be sure to have the balance with you, though, and drop
it during the scuffle. I'll return for it after you two have departed.
Cheat me and I'll repeat the performance, with a different ending."

"The thought had already occurred to me.—Now, we'd better
practice a bit, to make it look realistic. I'll rush at you with the lance,
and whatever side she's standing on I'll aim for it to pass you on the
other. You raise that wing, grab the lance and scream like hell. Blow
a few flames around, too."

"I'm going to see you scour the tip of that lance before we rehearse
this."

"Right.—I'll release the lance while you're holding it next to you
and rolling around. Then I'll dismount and rush toward you with my

blade. I'll whack you with the flat of it—again, on the far side—a few times. Then you bellow again and fly away."

"Just how sharp is that thing, anyway?"

"Damned dull. It was my grandfather's. Hasn't been honed since he was a boy."

"And you drop the money during the fight?"

"Certainly.—How does that sound?"

"Not bad. I can have a few clusters of red berries under my wing, too. I'll squash them once the action gets going."

"Nice touch. Yes, do that. Let's give it a quick rehearsal now and then get on with the real thing."

"And don't whack too hard. . . ."

That afternoon, Rosalind of Maurice Manor was abducted by a green-and-gold dragon who crashed through the wall of her chamber and bore her off in the direction of the western mountains.

"Never fear!" shouted her sixth-ranked suitor—who just happened to be riding by—to her aged father who stood wringing his hands on a nearby balcony. "I'll rescue her!" and he rode off to the west.

Coming into the valley where Rosalind stood backed into a rocky cleft, guarded by the fuming beast of gold and green, George couched his lance.

"Release that maiden and face your doom!" he cried.

Dart bellowed, George rushed. The lance fell from his hands and the dragon rolled upon the ground, spewing gouts of fire into the air. A red substance dribbled from beneath the thundering creature's left wing. Before Rosalind's wide eyes, George advanced and swung his blade several times.

". . . and that!" he cried, as the monster stumbled to its feet and sprang into the air, dripping more red.

It circled once and beat its way off toward the top of the mountain, then over it and away.

"Oh George!" Rosalind cried, and she was in his arms. "Oh, George . . ."

He pressed her to him for a moment.

"I'll take you home now," he said.

*　　　*　　　*

That evening as he was counting his gold, Dart heard the sound of two horses approaching his cave. He rushed up the tunnel and peered out.

George, now mounted on a proud white stallion and leading the gray, wore a matched suit of bright armor. He was not smiling, however.

"Good evening," he said.

"Good evening. What brings you back so soon?"

"Things didn't turn out exactly as I'd anticipated."

"You seem far better accoutered. I'd say your fortunes had taken a turn."

"Oh, I recovered my expenses and came out a bit ahead. But that's all. I'm on my way out of town. Thought I'd stop by and tell you the end of the story.—Good show you put on, by the way. It probably would have done the trick—"

"But—?"

"She was married to one of the brawny barbarians this morning, in their family chapel. They were just getting ready for a wedding trip when you happened by."

"I'm awfully sorry."

"Well, it's the breaks. To add insult, though, her father dropped dead during your performance. My former competitor is now the new baron. He rewarded me with a new horse and armor, a gratuity and a scroll from the local scribe lauding me as a dragon slayer. Then he hinted rather strongly that the horse and my new reputation could take me far. Didn't like the way Rosalind was looking at me now I'm a hero."

"That is a shame. Well, we tried."

"Yes. So I just stopped by to thank you and let you know how it all turned out. It would have been a good idea—if it had worked."

"You could hardly have foreseen such abrupt nuptials.—You know, I've spent the entire day thinking about the affair. We *did* manage it awfully well."

"Oh, no doubt about that. It went beautifully."

"I was thinking . . . How'd you like a chance to get your money back?"

"What have you got in mind?"

"Uh—When I was advising you earlier that you might not be happy with the lady, I was trying to think about the situation in human terms. Your desire was entirely understandable to me otherwise. In fact, you think quite a bit like a dragon."

"Really?"

"Yes. It's rather amazing, actually. Now—realizing that it only failed because of a fluke, your idea still has considerable merit."

"I'm afraid I don't follow you."

"There is—ah—a lovely lady of my own species whom I have been singularly unsuccessful in impressing for a long while now. Actually, there are an unusual number of parallels in our situations."

"She has a large hoard, huh?"

"Extremely so."

"Older woman?"

"Among dragons, a few centuries this way or that are not so important. But she, too, has other admirers and seems attracted by the more brash variety."

"Uh-huh. I begin to get the drift. You gave me some advice once. I'll return the favor. Some things are more important than hoards."

"Name one."

"My life. If I were to threaten her she might do me in all by herself, before you could come to her rescue."

"No, she's a demure little thing. Anyway, it's all a matter of timing. I'll perch on a hilltop nearby—I'll show you where—and signal you when to begin your approach. Now, this time I have to win, of course. Here's how we'll work it. . . ."

George sat on the white charger and divided his attention between the distant cave mouth and the crest of a high hill off to his left. After a time, a shining winged form flashed through the air and settled upon the hill. Moments later, it raised one bright wing.

He lowered his visor, couched his lance and started forward. When he came within hailing distance of the cave he cried out:

"I know you're in there, Megtag! I've come to destroy you and make off with your hoard! You godless beast! Eater of children! This is your last day on earth!"

An enormous burnished head with cold green eyes emerged from the cave. Twenty feet of flame shot from its huge mouth and scorched the rock before it. George halted hastily. The beast looked twice the size of Dart and did not seem in the least retiring. Its scales rattled like metal as it began to move forward.

"Perhaps I exaggerated. . . ." George began, and he heard the frantic flapping of giant vanes overhead.

As the creature advanced, he felt himself seized by the shoulders. He was borne aloft so rapidly that the scene below dwindled to toy size in a matter of moments. He saw his new steed bolt and flee rapidly back along the route they had followed.

"What the hell happened?" he cried.

"I hadn't been around for a while," Dart replied. "Didn't know one of the others had moved in with her. You're lucky I'm fast. That's Pelladon. He's a mean one."

"Great. Don't you think you should have checked first?"

"Sorry. I thought she'd take decades to make up her mind—without prompting. Oh, what a hoard! You should have seen it!"

"Follow that horse. I want him back."

They sat before Dart's cave, drinking.

"Where'd you ever get a whole barrel of wine?"

"Lifted it from a barge, up the river. I do that every now and then. I keep a pretty good cellar, if I do say so."

"Indeed. Well, we're none the poorer, really. We can drink to that."

"True, but I've been thinking again. You know, you're a very good actor."

"Thanks. You're not so bad yourself."

"Now supposing—just supposing—you were to travel about. Good distances from here each time. Scout out villages, on the continent and in the isles. Find out which ones are well off and lacking in local heroes. . . ."

"Yes?"

"... And let them see that dragon-slaying certificate of yours. Brag a bit. Then come back with a list of towns. Maps, too."

"Go ahead."

"Find the best spots for a little harmless predation and choose a good battle site—"

"Refill?"

"Please."

"Here."

"Thanks. Then you show up, and for a fee—"

"Sixty-forty."

"That's what I was thinking, but I'll bet you've got the figures transposed."

"Maybe fifty-five and forty-five then."

"Down the middle, and let's drink on it."

"Fair enough. Why haggle?"

"Now I know why I dreamed of fighting a great number of knights, all of them looking like you. You're going to make a name for yourself, George."

A Hiss of Dragon

❑ ❑ ❑

by Gregory Benford & Marc Laidlaw

Incoming dragon!" Leopold yelled, and ducked to the left. I went
right.

Dragons come in slow and easy. A blimp with wings, this one
settled down like a wrinkled brown sky falling. I scrambled over
boulders, trying to be inconspicuous and fast at the same time. It did-
n't seem like a promising beginning for a new job.

Leopold and I had been working on the ledge in front of the
Dragon's Lair, stacking berry pods. This Dragon must have flown toward its Lair from the other side of the mountain spire, so our radio
tag on him didn't transmit through all the rock. Usually they're not
so direct. Most Dragons circle their Lairs a few times, checking for
scavengers and egg stealers. If they don't circle, they're usually too
tired. And when they're tired, they're irritable. Something told me I
didn't want to be within reach of this one's throat flame.

I dropped my berrybag rig and went down the rocks feet first. The
boulders were slippery with green moss for about 20 meters below
the ledge, so I slid down on them. I tried to keep the falls to under
four meters and banged my butt when I missed. I could hear Leopold
knocking loose rocks on the other side, moving down toward where
our skimmer was parked.

A shadow fell over me, blotting out Beta's big yellow disk. The
brown bag above thrashed its wings and gave a trumpeting shriek. It

had caught sight of the berry bags and knew something was up. Most likely, with its weak eyes, the Dragon thought the bags were eggers—off season, but what do Dragons know about seasons?—and would attack them. That was the optimistic theory. The pessimistic one was that the Dragon had seen one of us. I smacked painfully into a splintered boulder and glanced up. Its underbelly was heaving, turning purple: anger. Not a reassuring sign. Eggers don't bother Dragons that much.

Then its wings fanned the air, backwards. It drifted off the ledge, hovering. The long neck snaked around, and two nearsighted eyes sought mine. The nose expanded, catching my scent. The Dragon hissed triumphantly.

Our skimmer was set for a fast takeoff. But it was 200 meters down, on the only wide spot we could find. I made a megaphone of my hands and shouted into the thin mountain mist, "Leopold! Grab air!"

I jumped down to a long boulder that jutted into space. Below and a little to the left I could make out the skimmer's shiny wings through the shifting green fog. I sucked in a breath and ran off the end of the boulder.

Dragons are clumsy at level flight, but they can drop like a brick. The only way to beat this one down to the skimmer was by falling most of the way.

I banked down, arms out. Our gravity is only a third of Earth normal. Even when falling, you have time to think things over. I can do the calculations fast enough—it came out to nine seconds—but getting the count right with a Dragon on your tail is another matter. I ticked the seconds off and then popped the chute. It fanned and filled. The skimmer came rushing up, wind whipped my face. Then my harness jerked me to a halt. I drifted down. I thumped the release and fell free. Above me, a trumpeting bellow. Something was coming in at four o'clock and I turned, snatching for my blaser. Could it be that fast? But it was Leopold, on chute. I sprinted for the skimmer. It was pointed along the best outbound wind, flaps already down, a standard precaution. I belted in, sliding my feet into the pedals. I caught a dank, foul reek of Dragon. More high shrieking, closer. Leopold came running up, panting. He wriggled into the rear seat. A thumping of wings. A ceiling of wrinkled leather. Something hissing overhead.

Dragons don't fly, they float. They have a big green hydrogen-filled dome on their backs to give them lift. They make the hydrogen in their stomachs and can dive quickly by venting it out the ass. This one was farting and falling as we zoomed away. I banked, turned to get a look at the huffing brown mountain hooting its anger at us, and grinned.

"I take back what I said this morning," Leopold gasped. "You'll draw full wages *and* commissions, from the start."

I didn't say anything. I'd just noticed that somewhere back there I had pissed my boots full.

I covered it pretty well back at the strip. I twisted out of the skimmer and slipped into the maintenance bay. I had extra clothes in my bag, so I slipped on some fresh socks and thongs.

When I was sure I smelled approximately human, I tromped back out to Leopold. I was damned if I would let my morning's success be blotted out by an embarrassing accident. It was a hirer's market these days. My training at crop dusting out in the flat farmlands had given me an edge over the other guys who had applied. I was determined to hang on to this job.

Leopold was the guy who "invented" the Dragons, five years ago. He took a life form native to Lex, the bloats, and tinkered with their DNA. Bloats are balloonlike and nasty. Leopold made them bigger, tougher, and spliced in a lust for thistleberries that makes Dragons hoard them compulsively. It had been a brilliant job of bioengineering. The Dragons gathered thistleberries, and Leopold stole them from the Lairs.

Thistleberries are a luxury good, high in protein, and delicious. The market for them might collapse if Lex's economy got worse— the copper seams over in Bahinin had run out last month. This was nearly the only good flying job left. More than anything else, I wanted to keep flying. And *not* as a crop duster. Clod-grubber work is a pain.

Leopold was leaning against his skimmer, a little pale, watching his men husk thistleberries. His thigh muscles were still thick; he was clearly an airman by ancestry, but he looked tired.

"Goddamn," he said. "I can't figure it out, kid. The Dragons are hauling in more berries than normal. We can't get into the Lairs, though. You'd think it was mating season around here, the way they're attacking my men."

"Mating season? When's that?"

"Oh, in about another six months, when the puffbushes bloom in the treetops. The pollen sets off the mating urges in Dragons—steps up their harvest, but it also makes 'em meaner."

"Great," I said. "I'm allergic to puffbush pollen. I'll have to fight off Dragons with running eyes and a stuffy nose."

Leopold shook his head absently; he hadn't heard me. "I can't understand it—there's nothing wrong with my Dragon designs."

"Seems to me you could have toned down the behavior plexes," I said. "Calm them down a bit—I mean, they've outgrown their competition to the point that they don't even *need* to be mean anymore. They don't browse much as it is . . . nobody's going to bother them."

"No way—there's just not the money for it, Drake. Look, I'm operating on the margin here. My five-year rights to the genetic patents just ran out, and now I'm in competition with Kwalan Rhiang, who owns the other half of the forest. Besides, you think gene splicing is easy?"

"Still, if they can bioengineer *humans* . . . I mean, we were beefed up for strength and oxy burning nearly a thousand years ago."

"But we weren't blown up to five times the size of our progenitors, Drake. I made those Dragons out of mean sons of bitches—blimps with teeth is what they were. It gets tricky when you mess with the life cycles of something that's already that unstable. You just don't understand what's involved here."

I nodded. "I'm no bioengineer—granted."

He looked at me and grinned, a spreading warm grin on his deeply lined face. "Yeah, Drake, but you're good at what you do—really good. What happened today, well, I'm getting too old for that sort of thing, and it's happening more and more often. If you hadn't been there I'd probably be stewing in that Dragon's stomach right now—skimmer and all."

I shrugged. That gave me a chance to roll the slabs of muscle in my shoulders, neck, and pectorals—a subtle advertisement that I had enough to keep a skimmer aloft for hours.

"So," he continued, "I'm giving you full pilot rank. The skimmer's yours. You can fly it home tonight, on the condition that you meet me at the Angis Tavern for a drink later on. And bring your girl Evelaine, too, if you want."

"It's a deal, Leopold. See you there."

I whistled like a dungwarbler all the way home, pedaling my new skimmer over the treetops toward the city. I nearly wrapped myself in a floating thicket of windbrambles, but not even this could destroy my good mood.

I didn't notice any Dragons roaming around, though I saw that the treetops had been plucked of their berries and then scorched. Leopold had at least had the foresight, when he was gene tinkering, to provide for the thistleberries' constant replenishment. He gave the Dragons a throat flame to singe the treetops with, which makes the berries regrow quickly. A nice touch.

It would have been simpler, of course, to have men harvest the thistleberries themselves, but that never worked out, economically. Thistleberries grow on top of virtually unclimbable thorntrees, where you can't even maneuver a skimmer without great difficulty. And if a man fell to the ground . . . well, if it's on the ground, it has spines, that's the rule on Lex. There's nothing soft to fall on down there. Sky life is more complex than ground life. You can actually do something useful with sky life—namely, bioengineering. Lex may be a low-metal world—which means low-technology—but our bioengineers are the best.

A clapping sound, to the left. I stopped whistling. Down through the greenish haze I could see a dark form coming in over the treetops, its wide rubbery wings slapping together at the top of each stroke. A smackwing. Good meat, spicy and moist. But hard to catch. Evelaine and I had good news to celebrate tonight; I decided to bring her home smackwing for dinner. I took the skimmer down in the path of the smackwing, meanwhile slipping my blaser from its holster.

The trick to hunting in the air is to get beneath your prey so that you can grab it while it falls, but this smackwing was flying too low. I headed in fast, hoping to frighten it into rising above me, but it was no use. The smackwing saw me, red eyes rolling. It missed a beat in its flapping and dived toward the treetops. At that instant a snagger shot into view from the topmost branches, rising with a low farting sound. The smackwing spotted this blimplike thing that had leaped into its path but apparently didn't think it too threatening. It swerved about a meter under the bobbing creature—

And stopped flat, in midair.

I laughed aloud, sheathing my blaser. The snagger had won his meal like a real hunter.

Beneath the snagger's wide blimplike body was a dangling sheet of transparent sticky material. The smackwing struggled in the moist folds as the snagger drew the sheet upward. To the unwary smackwing that clear sheet must have been invisible until the instant he flew into it.

Within another minute, as I pedaled past the spot, the snagger had entirely engulfed the smackwing, and was unrolling its sticky sheet as it drifted back into the treetops. Pale yellow eyes considered me and rejected the notion of me as food. A ponderous predator, wise with years.

I flew into the spired city: Kalatin.

I parked on the deck of our apartment building, high above the jumbled wooden buildings of the city. Now that my interview had been successful, we'd be able to stay in Kalatin, though I hoped we could find a better apartment. This one was as old as the city—which in turn had been around for a great deal of the 1,200 years humans had been on Lex. As the wood of the lower stories rotted, and as the building crumbled away, new quarters were just built on top of it and settled into place. Someday this city would be an archaeologist's dream. In the meantime, it was an inhabitant's nightmare.

Five minutes later, having negotiated several treacherous ladders and a splintering shinny pole into the depths of the old building, I crept quietly to the wooden door of my apartment and let myself in, clutching the mudskater steaks that I'd picked up on the way home. It was dark and cramped inside, the smell of rubbed wood strong. I could hear Evelaine moving around in the kitchen, so I sneaked to the doorway and looked in. She was turned away, chopping thistle-berries with a thorn-knife.

I grabbed her, throwing the steaks into the kitchen, and kissed her.

"Got the job, Evey!" I said. "Leopold took me out himself and I ended up saving his—"

"It *is* you!" She covered her nose, squirming away from me. "What is that smell, Drake?"

"Smell?"

"Like something died. It's all over you."

I remembered the afternoon's events. It was either the smell of Dragon, which I'd got from scrambling around in a Lair, or that of urine. I played it safe and said, "I think it's Dragon."

"Well take it somewhere else. I'm cooking dinner."

"I'll hop in the cycler. You can cook up the steaks I brought, then we're going out to celebrate."

The Angis Tavern is no skiff joint, good for a stale senso on the way home from work. It's the best. The Angis is a vast old place, perched on a pyramid of rock. Orange fog nestles at the base, a misty collar separating it from the jumble of the city below.

Evelaine pedaled the skimmer with me, having trouble in her gown. We made a wobbly landing on the rickety side deck. It would've been easier to coast down to the city, where there was more room for a glide approach, but that's pointless. There are thick cactus and thornbushes around the Angis base, hard to negotiate at night. In the old days it kept away predators; now it keeps away the riffraff.

But not completely: two beggars accosted us as we dismounted, offering to shine up the skimmer's aluminum skin. I growled convincingly at them, and they skittered away. The Angis is so big, so full of crannies to hide out in, they can't keep it clear of beggars, I guess.

We went in a balcony entrance. Fat balloons nudged against the ceiling, ten meters overhead, dangling their cords. I snagged one and stepped off into space. Evelaine hooked it as I fell. We rode it down, past alcoves set in the rock walls. Well-dressed patrons nodded as we eased down, the balloon following. The Angis is a spire, broadening gradually as we descended. Phosphors cast creamy glows on the tables set into the walls. I spotted Leopold sprawled in a webbing, two empty tankards lying discarded underneath.

"You're late," he called. We stepped off onto his ledge. Our balloons, released, shot back to the roof.

"You didn't set a time. Evelaine, Leopold." Nods, introductory phrases.

"It seems quite crowded here tonight," Evelaine murmured. A plausible social remark, except she'd never been to an inn of this class before.

Leopold shrugged. "Hard times mean full taverns. Booze or sensos or tinglers—pick your poison."

Evelaine has the directness of a country girl and knows her own limitations; she stuck to a mild tingler. Service was running slow, so I went to log our orders. I slid down a shinny pole to the first bar level. Mice zipped by me, eating up tablescraps left by the patrons; it saves on labor. Amid the jam and babble I placed our order with a steward and turned to go back.

"You looking for work?" a thick voice said.

I glanced at its owner. "No." The man was big, swarthy, and sure of himself.

"Thought you wanted Dragon work." His eyes had a look of distant amusement.

"How'd you know that?" I wasn't known in the city.

"Friends told me."

"Leopold hired me today."

"So I hear. I'll top whatever he's paying."

"I didn't think business was that good."

"It's going to get better. Much better, once Leopold's out of the action. A monopoly can always sell goods at a higher price. You can start tomorrow."

So this was Kwalan Rhiang. "No thanks. I'm signed up." Actually,

I hadn't signed anything, but there was something about this man I didn't like. Maybe the way he was so sure I'd work for him.

"Flying for Leopold is dangerous. He doesn't know what he's doing."

"See you around," I said. A senso was starting in a nearby booth. I took advantage of it to step into the expanding blue cloud, so Rhiang couldn't follow and see where we were sitting. I got a lifting, bright sensation of pleasure, and then I was out of the misty confusion, moving away among the packed crowd.

I saw them on the stairway. They were picking their way down it delicately. I thought they were deformed, but the funny tight clothes gave them away. Offworlders, here for the flying. That was the only reason anybody came to Lex. We're still the only place men can seriously fly longer than a few minutes. Even so, our lack of machines keeps most offworlders away; they like it easy, everything done for them. I watched them pick their way down the stairs, thinking that if the desperation got worse, offworlders would be able to hire servants here, even though it was illegal. It could come to that.

They were short as children but heavyset, with narrow chests and skinny limbs. Spindly people, unaugmented for Lex oxy levels. But men like that had colonized here long ago, paying for it in reduced lifetimes. I felt as though I was watching my own ancestors.

Lex shouldn't have any oxy at all, by the usual rules of planetary evolution. It's a small planet, 0.21 Earth masses, a third gee of gravity. Rules of thumb say we shouldn't have any atmosphere to speak of. But our sun, Beta, is a K-type star, redder than Sol. Beta doesn't heat our upper atmosphere very much with ultraviolet, so we retain gases. Even then, Lex would be airless except for accidents of birth. It started out with a dense cloak of gas, just as Earth did. But dim old Beta didn't blow the atmosphere away, and there wasn't enough compressional heating by Lex itself to boil away the gases. So they stuck around, shrouding the planet, causing faster erosion than on Earth. The winds moved dust horizontally, exposing crustal rock. That upset the isostatic balance in the surface, and split open faults. Volcanoes poked up. They belched water and gas onto the surface, keeping the atmosphere dense. So Lex ended up with low gravity and a thick atmosphere. Fine, except that Beta's wan light also never pushed many heavy elements out this far, so Lex is metal-poor. Without iron and the rest you can't build machines, and without technology you're a backwater. You sell your tourist attraction—flying—and hope for the best.

One of the offworlders came up to me and said, "You got any sparkers in this place?"

I shook my head. Maybe he didn't know that getting a sendup by tying your frontal lobes into an animal's is illegal here. Maybe he didn't care. Ancestor or not, he just looked like a misshapen dwarf to me, and I walked away.

Evelaine was describing life in the flatlands when I got back. Leopold was rapt, the worry lines in his face nearly gone. Evelaine does that to people. She's natural and straightforward, so she was telling him right out that she wasn't much impressed with city life. "Farmlands are quiet and restful. Everybody has a job," she murmured. "You're right that getting around is harder—but we can glide in the updrafts, in summer. It's heaven."

"Speaking of the farmlands," I said, "an old friend of mine came out here five years ago. He wanted in on your operations."

"I was hiring like crazy five years ago. What was his name?"

"Lorn Kramer. Great pilot."

Leopold shook his head. "Can't remember. He's not with me now, anyway. Maybe Rhiang got him."

Our drinks arrived. The steward was bribable, though—Rhiang was right behind him.

"You haven't answered my 'gram," Rhiang said directly to Leopold, ignoring us. I guess he didn't figure I was worth any more time.

"Didn't need to," Leopold said tersely.

"Sell out. I'll give you a good price." Rhiang casually sank his massive flank on our table edge. "You're getting too old."

Something flickered in Leopold's eyes; he said nothing.

"Talk is," Rhiang went on mildly, "market's falling."

"Maybe," Leopold said. "What you been getting for a kilo?"

"Not saying."

"Tight lips and narrow minds go together."

Rhiang stood, his barrel chest bulging. "You could use a little instruction in politeness."

"From you?" Leopold chuckled. "You paid off that patent clerk to release my gene configs early. Was that polite?"

Rhiang shrugged. "That's the past. The present reality is that there may be an oversupply of thistleberries. Market isn't big enough for two big operations like ours. There's too much—"

"Too much of you, that's my problem. Lift off, Rhiang."

To my surprise, he did. He nodded to me, ignored Evelaine, and gave Leopold a look of contempt. Then he was gone.

I heard them first. We were taking one of the outside walks that corkscrew around the Angis spire, gawking at the phosphored streets below. A stone slide clattered behind us. I saw two men duck behind a jutting ledge. One of them had something in his hand that glittered.

"You're jumpy, Drake," Evelaine said.

"Maybe." It occurred to me that if we went over the edge of this spire, hundreds of meters into the thorn scrabble below, it would be very convenient for Rhiang. "Let's move on."

Leopold glanced at me, then back at the inky shadows. We strolled along the trail of volcanic rock, part of the natural formation that made the spire. Rough black pebbles slipped underfoot. In the distant star-flecked night, skylight called and boomed.

We passed under a phosphor. At the next turn Leopold looked back and said, "I saw one of them. Rhiang's right-hand man."

We hurried away. I wished for a pair of wings to get us off this place. Evelaine understood instantly that this was serious. "There's a split in the trail ahead," Leopold said. "If they follow, we'll know . . ." He didn't finish.

We turned. They followed. "I think I know a way to slow them down," I said. Leopold looked at me. We were trying to avoid slipping in the darkness and yet make good time. "Collect some of these obsidian frags," I said.

We got a bundle of them together. "Go on up ahead," I said. We were on a narrow ledge. I sank back into the shadows and waited. The two men appeared. Before they noticed me I threw the obsidian high into the air. In low gravity it takes a long time for them to come back down. In the darkness the two men couldn't see them coming.

I stepped out into the wan light. "Hey!" I yelled to them. They stopped, precisely where I thought they would. "What's going on?" I said, to stall.

The biggest one produced a knife. "This."

The first rock hit, coming down from over a hundred meters above. It slammed into the boulder next to him. Then three more crashed down, striking the big one in the shoulder, braining the second. They both crumpled.

I turned and hurried along the path. If they'd seen me throw they'd have had time to dodge. It was an old schoolboy trick, but it worked.

The implications, though, were sobering. If Rhiang felt this way, my new job might not last long.

I was bagging berries in the cavernous Paramount Lair when the warning buzzer in my pocket went off. A Dragon was coming in. I still had time, but not much. I decided to finish this particular bag rather than abandon the bagging-pistol. The last bit of fluid sprayed over the heap of berries and began to congeal instantly, its tremendously high surface tension drawing it around the irregular pile and sealing perfectly. I holstered the gun, leaving the bag for later. I turned—

A slow flapping boom. Outside, a wrinkled brown wall.

Well, I'd fooled around long enough—now I dived for safety. The Dragon's Lair was carpeted with a thick collection of nesting materials. None were very pleasant to burrow through, but I didn't have any choice. Behind me I could hear the Dragon moving around; if I didn't move out of his way in a hurry I might get stepped on. The emergency chute on my back tangled in a branch, just as the stench in the Lair intensified. I hurried out of it and went on. I'd just have to be sure not to fall from any great heights. I didn't worry about it, because my skimmer was parked on the ledge just outside the Lair.

I stuck my head up through the nest to judge my position. The bulk of the Dragon was silhouetted against the glare of the sky, which was clear of fog today. The beast seemed to be preening itself. That was something I never thought they did outside of the mating season—which was six months away.

I scrambled backward into the nest. The buzzer in my pocket went off again, though it was supposed to signal just once, for ten seconds. I figured the thing must have broken. It quieted and I moved on, thinking. For one thing, the Dragon that occupied this Lair was supposed to have been far from home right now—which meant that my guest didn't really belong here. Dragons never used the wrong Lair unless it was the mating season.

I frowned. Why did that keep coming up?

Suddenly there was a rush of wind and a low, thrumming sound. The light from outside was cut off. I poked my head into the open.

Another Dragon was lumbering into the Lair. *This* was really impossible. Two Dragons sharing a Lair—and the wrong one at that! Whatever their reasons for being here, I was sure they were going to start fighting pretty soon, so I burrowed deeper, moving toward the nearest wall.

My elbow caught on something. Cloth. I brushed it away, then looked again. A Dragonrobber uniform like my own. It was directly beneath me, half-buried in the nesting material. I caught my breath, then poked at the uniform. Something glittered near one empty sleeve: an identification bracelet. I picked it up, shifted it in the light, and read the name on it: *Lorn Kramer.*

Lorn Kramer! So he had been in Leopold's group after all. But that still didn't explain why he'd left his clothes here.

I tugged at the uniform, dragging it toward me. It was limp, but tangled in the nest. I jerked harder and some long, pale things rattled out of the sleeve.

Bones.

I winced. I was suddenly aware that my present situation must be somewhat like the one that had brought him here.

I looked into the Lair again. One of the Dragons was prodding its snout at the other, making low, whuffling sounds. It didn't look like a hostile gesture to me. In fact, it looked like they were playing. The other Dragon wheeled about and headed for the entrance. The first one followed, and in a minute both of them had left the Lair again—as abruptly and inexplicably as they had entered it.

I saw my chance. I ran across the Lair, grabbed my skimmer, and took off. I moved out, pedaling furiously away from the Dragons, and glanced down.

For a minute I thought I was seeing things. The landscape below me was blurred, though the day had been clear and crisp when I'd flown into the Lair. I blinked. It didn't go away, but got clearer. There was a cloud of yellowish dust spreading high above the forest, billowing up and around the Lairs I could see. Where had it come from?

I sneezed, passing through a high plume of the dust. Then my eyes began to sting and I sneezed again. I brought the skimmer out of the cloud, but by this time my vision was distorted with tears. I began to cough and choke all at once, until the skimmer faltered as I fought to stay in control, my eyes streaming.

I knew what that dust was.

Nothing affected me as fiercely as puffbush pollen: it was the only thing I was really allergic to.

I stopped pedaling.

It affected Dragons, too. It set off their mating urges.

But where was the damned stuff coming from? It was six months out of season. I started pedaling again, legs straining. I turned to get a better view.

A flash of light needled past my head, and I knew. Three skimmers shot into view from around the spire of Paramount Lair. The tip of one of my wings was seared away by a blaser. My skimmer lurched wildly, but I held on and brought it up just as the first skimmer came toward me. Its pilot was wearing a filtermask. Attached to the skimmer were some empty bags that must have held the puffbush pollen. But what I was looking at was the guy's blaser. It was aimed at me.

I reeled into an updraft, pulling over my attacker, grabbing for my own blaser. The skimmer soared beneath me, then careened into a sharp turn. It was too sharp. The guy turned straight into the path of his companion. The two skimmers crashed together with a satisfying sound, then the scattered parts and pilots fell slowly toward the tree-tops. Seconds later, the forest swallowed them up.

I looked for the third man, just as he came up beside me. The bastard was grinning, and I recognized that grin. It was Kwalan Rhiang's.

He nodded once, affably, and before I could remember to use my blaser, Rhiang took a single, precise shot at the chainguard of my skimmer. The pedals rolled uselessly. I was out of control. Rhiang lifted away and cruised out of sight, leaving me flailing at the air in a ruined skimmer.

I had exactly one chance, and this was to get back to the Lair I'd just abandoned. I was slightly higher than the opening, so I glided in, backpedaled for the drop—and crashed straight into the wall, thanks to my ruined pedals. But I made it in alive, still able to stand up and brush the dirt from my uniform. I stood at the mouth of the Lair, staring out over the forest, considering the long climb that lay below me.

And just then the Dragons returned.

Not one, this time—not even two. *Five* shadows wheeled overhead; five huge beasts headed toward the Lair where I was standing. And finally, five Dragons dropped right on top of me.

I leaped back just in time, scrambling into the blue shadows as the first Dragon thumped to the ledge. It waddled inside, reeking. I moved back farther. Its four friends were right behind. I kept moving back.

Well, at least now I knew *why* they were doing this. Kwalan Rhiang had been setting off their mating urges by dusting the Dragons with puffbush-pollen, messing up their whole life cycle, fooling with their already nasty tempers. It made sense. Anything less subtle might have gotten Rhiang into a lot of trouble. As it was, he'd doubtless fly safely home, waiting for Leopold's Dragons to kill off Leopold's men.

Out in the cavernous Lair, the Dragons began to move around, prodding at each other like scramblemice, hooting their airy courting sounds. The ground shook with their movement. Two seemed to be females, which suggested that I might look forward to some fighting between the other three. Great.

I fumbled at my pockets for something that might be of help. My warning buzzer had shattered in my rough landing; I threw it away. I still had my bagging-gun, but it wouldn't do me a lot of good. My blaser seemed okay. I unholstered it and began to move along the wall. If I went carefully, I might be able to get onto the outer ledge.

Two of the males were fighting now, lunging, the sounds of their efforts thundering around me. I made a short run and gained a bit of ground. One of the Dragons retreated from the battle—apparently the loser. I groaned. He had moved directly into my path.

A huge tail pounded at the ground near me and a female started backing my way, not looking at me. There was no place to go. And I was getting tired of this. I decided to warn her off. I made a quick shot at her back, nipping her in the hydrogen dome. She squawked and shuffled away, confused. I went on.

I stopped. There was a hissing sound behind me. Turning, I could see nothing but the Dragon I'd just shot. She didn't appear to be making the sound, but it was coming from her direction. I peered closer, through the blue gloom, and then saw where the noise was coming from.

Her hydrogen dome was deflating.

I nearly laughed aloud. Here was the answer to my problem. I could deflate the Dragons, leaving them stranded, unable to fly, while I climbed down this spire without fear of pursuit. I lifted my blaser and aimed at the male nearest the rear of the Lair. A near miss, then a hit. Hydrogen hissed out of his dome as well. Then I got the second female, and another male who was directly across from me.

One Dragon to go. The others were roaring and waddling. The Lair was full of the hissing sound.

I turned to my last opponent. He wasn't looking my way, but he was blocking my exit. I moved in closer and lifted my blaser.

Then he saw me.

I flung myself aside just as he bellowed and pounded forward, filling the entrance to the Lair, blocking out the sunlight. I rolled into the thorny nest. I fired once, hitting him in the snout. He swung his head toward me, pushing me around toward the outer ledge, bellowing. I fired again, and once more missed his hydrogen dome. I made a dash around his rump just as he spun my way, tail lashing against me. His dark little eyes narrowed as he sighted me, and his throat began to ripple.

My time was up. He was about to blast me with his throat flame.

The Dragon opened his mouth, belched hydrogen, and ignited it by striking a spark from his molars—

That was the wrong thing to do.

I saw it coming and ducked.

The cavern shuddered and blew up. The orange explosion rumbled out, catching the Dragons in a huge rolling flame. I buried myself in the nesting strands and grabbed onto the lashing tail of my attacker. Terrified by the blast, he took off. My eyebrows were singed, my wrists burned.

The world spun beneath me. A tendril of smoke drifted into view just below, mingled with flaming bits of nesting material and the leathery hide of Dragons. Then my view spun again and I was looking at the sky. It gradually dawned on me that I was clinging to a Dragon's tail.

It occurred to the Dragon at the same time. I saw his head swing toward me, snapping angrily. His belly was flashing purple. Every now and then he let out a tongue of flame, but he couldn't quite get at me. Meanwhile, I held on for my life.

The Dragon flew on, but my weight seemed to be too much for it. We were dropping slowly toward the trees, as easily as if I'd punctured his bony dome with my blaser. But it would be a rough landing. And I'd have to deal with the Dragon afterward.

I spied something rising from the trees below us. It shot swiftly into the air after a high-flying bulletbird, its transparent sheet rippling beneath its blimplike body. It was a huge snagger—as big as my own skimmer. I kicked on the Dragon's tail, dragging it sideways. The Dragon lurched and spun and then we were directly over the snagger.

I let go of the tail and dropped, my eyes closed.

In a second, something soft rumpled beneath me. I had landed safely atop the snagger. I opened my eyes as the Dragon—having lost my weight—shot suddenly upward. I watched it glide away, then looked down at the snagger, my savior. I patted its wide, rubbery body. My weight was pushing it slowly down, as if I were riding the balloons in the Angis Tavern. I looked forward to a comfortable trip to the ground.

"I like your style, kid."

I jumped, nearly losing my place on the snagger. The voice had come out of midair. Literally.

"You," I said. No more was necessary. He was banking around behind me.

Kwalan Rhiang had returned in his skimmer. He circled easily about me as I fell toward the treetops. He came in close, smiling, his huge legs pedaling him on a gentle course. I had to turn my head to keep an eye on him.

"I said before I'd top what Leopold was paying you," he shouted, his thick voice cutting the high air. "After today, I think I'd pay *double*. I could use someone like you."

I felt my face harden. "You bastard. You're responsible for what just happened. Why would I work for someone who's tried to kill me?"

He shrugged. "Gave you a chance to prove yourself. Come on, you're wasting your time with Leopold."

"And you're wasting your time with me."

He shrugged again, utterly sure of himself. "As you wish. I gave you a chance."

I nodded. "Now just go away."

"And leave you to tell Leopold about all this? You don't think I'm going to let you back alive, do you?"

I froze. Rhiang slid a blaser from its holster at his waist and aimed it at my head. His grin widened. The muzzle dropped a fraction, and I breathed a little easier.

"No," he said distantly, "why kill you straight off? Slow deaths are more interesting, I think. And harder to trace."

He aimed at the snagger. If he punctured it I'd drop into the trees. It was a long fall. I wouldn't make it.

I growled and grabbed for the gun at my waist, bringing it up before Rhiang could move. He stared at me for a moment, then started laughing. I looked at what I was holding.

"What're you going to do with that?" he said. "Bag me?"

It was my bagging-pistol, all right. I'd dropped the blaser back in the Lair. But it would still serve a purpose.

"Exactly," I said, and fired.

The gray fluid squirted across the narrow gap between us, sealing instantly over Rhiang's hands. He fired the blaser but succeeded only in melting the bag enough to let the weapon break away. It fell out of sight.

His eyes were wide. He was considering death by suffocation.

"No," he choked.

But I didn't fire at his head. I put the next bag right over his feet, sealing the pedal mechanism tight. His legs jerked convulsively. They slowed. Rhiang began to whimper, and then he was out of control. His skimmer turned and glided away as he hurried to catch any updraft he could. He vanished behind Paramount Lair, and was gone.

I turned back to observe the treetops. Rhiang might be back, but I doubted it. First he'd have a long walk ahead of him, over unpleasant terrain, back to his base . . . *if* he could maneuver his skimmer well enough to land in the treetops, and make the long, painful climb down.

But I didn't worry about it. I watched the thorntrees rise about me, and presently the snagger brought me gently to the ground. I dismounted, leaving the snagger to bob back into the air, and began to walk gingerly across the inhospitable ground, avoiding the spines. A daggerbush snapped at me. I danced away. It was going to be a rough walk out. Somewhere behind me, Rhiang might be facing the same problem. And he wanted me dead.

But I didn't have as far to go.

The Bully and
the Beast

◻ ◻ ◻

by Orson Scott Card

T he page entered the Count's chamber at a dead run. He had
long ago given up sauntering—when the Count called, he expected a page to appear immediately, and any delay at all
made the Count irritable and likely to assign a page to stable duty.

"My lord," said the page.

"My lord indeed," said the Count. "What kept you?" The Count
stood at the window, his back to the boy. In his arms he held a velvet gown, incredibly embroidered with gold and silver thread. "I
think I need to call a council," said the Count. "On the other hand, I
haven't the slightest desire to submit myself to a gaggle of jabbering
knights. They'll be quite angry. What do you think?"

No one had ever asked the page for advice before, and he wasn't
quite sure what was expected of him. "Why should they be angry, my
lord?"

"Do you see this gown?" the Count asked, turning around and
holding it up.

"Yes, my lord."

"What do you think of it?"

"Depends, doesn't it, my lord, on who wears it."

"It cost eleven pounds of silver."

The page smiled sickly. Eleven pounds of silver would keep the average knight in arms, food, women, clothing, and shelter for a year with six pounds left over for spending money.

"There are more," said the Count. "Many more."

"But who are they for? Are you going to marry?"

"None of your business!" roared the Count. "If there's anything I hate, it's a meddler!" The Count turned again to the window and looked out. He was shaded by a huge oak tree that grew forty feet from the castle walls. "What's today?" asked the Count.

"Thursday, my lord."

"The day, the day!"

"Eleventh past Easter Feast."

"The tribute's due today," said the Count. "Due on Easter, in fact, but today the Duke will be certain I'm not paying."

"Not paying the tribute, my lord?"

"How? Turn me upside down and shake me, but I haven't a farthing. The tribute money's gone. The money for new arms is gone. The travel money is gone. The money for new horses is gone. Haven't got any money at all. But gad, boy, what a wardrobe." The Count sat on the sill of the window. "The Duke will be here very quickly, I'm afraid. And he has the latest in debt collection equipment."

"What's that?"

"An army." The Count sighed. "Call a council, boy. My knights may jabber and scream, but they'll fight. I know they will."

The page wasn't sure. "They'll be very angry, my lord. Are you sure they'll fight?"

"Oh, yes," said the Count. "If they don't, the Duke will kill them."

"Why?"

"For not honoring their oath to me. Do go now, boy, and call a council."

The page nodded. Kind of felt sorry for the old boy. Not much of a Count, as things went, but he could have been worse, and it was pretty plain the castle would be sacked and the Count imprisoned and the women raped and the page sent off home to his parents. "A council!" he cried as he left the Count's chamber. "A council!"

*   *   *

In the cold cavern of the pantry under the kitchen, Bork pulled a huge keg of ale from its resting place and lifted it, not easily, but without much strain, and rested it on his shoulders. Head bowed, he walked slowly up the stairs. Before Bork worked in the kitchen, it used to take two men most of an afternoon to move the huge kegs. But Bork was a giant, or what passed for a giant in those days. The Count himself was of average height, barely past five feet. Bork was nearly seven feet tall, with muscles like an ox. People stepped aside for him.

"Put it there," said the cook, hardly looking up. "And don't drop it."

Bork didn't drop the keg. Nor did he resent the cook's expecting him to be clumsy. He had been told he was clumsy all his life, ever since it became plain at the age of three that he was going to be immense. Everyone knew that big people were clumsy. And it was true enough. Bork was so strong he kept doing things he never meant to do, accidentally. Like the time the swordmaster, admiring his strength, had invited him to learn to use the heavy battleswords. Bork hefted them easily, of course, though at the time he was only twelve and hadn't reached his full strength.

"Hit me," the swordmaster said.

"But the blade's sharp," Bork told him.

"Don't worry. You won't come near me." The swordmaster had taught a hundred knights to fight. None of them had come near him. And, in fact, when Bork swung the heavy sword the swordmaster had his shield up in plenty of time. He just hadn't counted on the terrible force of the blow. The shield was battered aside easily, and the blow threw the sword upward, so it cut off the swordmaster's left arm just below the shoulder, and only narrowly missed slicing deeply into his chest.

Clumsy, that was all Bork was. But it was the end of any hope of his becoming a knight. When the swordmaster finally recovered, he consigned Bork to the kitchen and the blacksmith's shop, where they needed someone with enough strength to skewer a cow end to end and carry it to the fire; where it was convenient to have a man who, with a double-sized ax, could chop down a large tree in half an hour, cut it into logs, and carry a month's supply of firewood into the castle in an afternoon.

A page came into the kitchen. "There's a council, cook. The Count wants ale, and plenty of it."

The cook swore profusely and threw a carrot at the page. "Always changing the schedule! Always making me do extra work." As soon as the page had escaped, the cook turned on Bork. "All right, carry the ale out there, and be quick about it. Try not to drop it."

"I won't," Bork said.

"He won't," the cook muttered. "Clever as an ox, he is."

Bork manhandled the cask into the great hall. It was cold, though outside the sun was shining. Little light and little warmth reached the inside of the castle. And since it was spring, the huge logpile in the pit in the middle of the room lay cold and damp.

The knights were beginning to wander into the great hall and sit on the benches that lined the long, pock-marked slab of a table. They knew enough to carry their mugs—councils were always well-oiled with ale. Bork had spent years as a child watching the knights practice the arts of war, but the knights seemed more natural carrying their cups than holding their swords at the ready. They were more dedicated to their drinking than to war.

"Ho, Bork the Bully," one of the knights greeted him. Bork managed a half-smile. He had learned long since not to take offense.

"How's Sam the stableman?" asked another, tauntingly.

Bork blushed and turned away, heading for the door to the kitchen.

The knights were laughing at their cleverness. "Twice the body, half the brain," one of them said to the others. "Probably hung like a horse," another speculated, then quipped, "Which probably accounts for those mysterious deaths among the sheep this winter." A roar of laughter, and cups beating on the table. Bork stood in the kitchen, trembling. He could not escape the sound—the stones carried it echoing to him wherever he went.

The cook turned and looked at him. "Don't be angry, boy," he said. "It's all in fun."

Bork nodded and smiled at the cook. That's what it was. All in fun. And besides, Bork deserved it, he knew. It was only fair that he be treated cruelly. For he had earned the title Bork the Bully, hadn't he? When he was three, and already massive as a ram, his only friend, a beautiful young village boy named Winkle, had hit upon the idea of becoming a knight. Winkle had dressed himself in odds and ends of leather and tin, and made a makeshift lance from a hog prod.

"You're my destrier," Winkle cried as he mounted Bork and rode him for hours. Bork thought it was a fine thing to be a knight's horse. It became the height of his ambition, and he wondered how one got started in the trade. But one day Sam, the stableman's son, had taunted Winkle for his make-believe armor, and it had turned into a fist fight, and Sam had thoroughly bloodied Winkle's nose. Winkle screamed as if he were dying, and Bork sprang to his friend's defense, walloping Sam, who was three years older, along the side of his head.

Ever since then Sam spoke with a thickness in his voice, and often lost his balance; his jaw, broken in several places, never healed properly, and he had problems with his ear.

It horrified Bork to have caused so much pain, but Winkle assured him that Sam deserved it. "After all, Bork, he was twice my size, and he was picking on me. He's a bully. He had it coming."

For several years Winkle and Bork were the terror of the village. Winkle would constantly get into fights, and soon the village children learned not to resist him. If Winkle lost a fight, he would scream for Bork, and though Bork was never again so harsh as he was with Sam, his blows still hurt terribly. Winkle loved it. Then one day he tired of being a knight, dismissed his destrier, and became fast friends with the other children. It was only then that Bork began to hear himself called Bork the Bully; it was Winkle who convinced the other children that the only villain in the fighting had been Bork. "After all," Bork overheard Winkle say one day, "he's twice as strong as anyone else. Isn't fair for him to fight. It's a cowardly thing for him to do, and we mustn't have anything to do with him. Bullies must be punished."

Bork knew that Winkle was right, and ever after that he bore the burden of shame. He remembered the frightened looks in the other children's eyes when he approached them, the way they pleaded for

mercy. But Winkle was always screaming and writhing in agony, and
Bork always hit the child despite his terror, and for that bullying
Bork was still paying. He paid in the ridicule he accepted from the
knights; he paid in the solitude of all his days and nights; he paid by
working as hard as he could, using his strength to serve instead of
hurt.

But just because he knew he deserved the punishment did not
mean he enjoyed it. There were tears in his eyes as he went about his
work in the kitchen. He tried to hide them from the cook, but to no
avail. "Oh, no, you're not going to cry, are you?" the cook asked.
"You'll only make your nose run and then you'll get snot in the soup.
Get out of the kitchen for a while!"

Which is why Bork was standing in the doorway of the great hall
watching the council that would completely change his life.

"Well, where's the tribute money gone to?" demanded one of the
knights. "The harvest was large enough last year!"

It was an ugly thing, to see the knights so angry. But the Count
knew they had a right to be upset—it was they who would have to
fight the Duke's men, and they had a right to know why.

"My friends," the Count said. "My friends, some things are more
important than money. I invested the money in something more important than tribute, more important than peace, more important than
long life. I invested the money in beauty. Not to create beauty, but to
perfect it." The knights were listening now. For all their violent pre-
occupations, they all had a soft place in their hearts for true beauty.
It was one of the requirements for knighthood. "I have been entrusted
with a jewel, more perfect than any diamond. It was my duty to place
that jewel in the best setting money could buy. I can't explain. I can
only show you." He rang a small bell, and behind him one of the bet-
ter-known secret doors in the castle opened, and a wizened old
woman emerged. The Count whispered in her ear, and the woman
scurried back into the secret passage.

"Who's she?" asked one of the knights.

"She is the woman who nursed my children after my wife died.
My wife died in childbirth, you remember. But what you don't know

is that the child lived. My two sons you know well. But I have a third child, my last child, whom you know not at all, and this one is not a son."

The Count was not surprised that several of the knights seemed to puzzle over this riddle. Too many jousts, too much practice in full armor in the heat of the afternoon.

"My child is a daughter."

"Ah," said the knights.

"At first I kept her hidden away because I could not bear to see her—after all, my most beloved wife had died in bearing her. But after a few years I overcame my grief, and went to see the child in the room where she was hidden, and lo! She was the most beautiful child I had ever seen. I named her Brunhilda, and from that moment on I loved her. I was the most devoted father you could imagine. But I did not let her leave the secret room. Why, you may ask?"

"Yes, why!" demanded several of the knights.

"Because she was so beautiful I was afraid she would be stolen from me. I was terrified that I would lose her. Yet I saw her every day, and talked to her, and the older she got, the more beautiful she became, and for the last several years I could no longer bear to see her in her mother's cast-off clothing. Her beauty is such that only the finest cloths and gowns and jewels of Flanders, of Venice, of Florence would do for her. You'll see! The money was not ill-spent."

And the door opened again, and the old woman emerged, leading forth Brunhilda.

In the doorway, Bork gasped. But no one heard him, for all the knights gasped, too.

She was the most perfect woman in the world. Her hair was a dark red, flowing behind her like an auburn stream as she walked. Her face was white from being indoors all her life, and when she smiled it was like the sun breaking out on a stormy day. And none of the knights dared look at her body for very long, because the longer they looked the more they wanted to touch her, and the Count said, "I warn you. Any man who lays a hand on her will have to answer to me. She is a virgin, and when she marries she shall be a virgin, and a king will pay half his kingdom to have her, and still I'll feel cheated to have to give her up."

"Good evening, my lords," she said, smiling. Her voice was like the song of leaves dancing in the summer wind, and the knights fell to their knees before her.

None of them was more moved by her beauty than Bork, however. When she entered the room he forgot himself; there was no room in his mind for anything but the great beauty he had seen for the first time in his life. Bork knew nothing of courtesy. He only knew that, for the first time in his life, he had seen something so perfect that he could not rest until it was his. Not his to own, but his to be owned by. He longed to serve her in the most degrading ways he could think of, if only she would smile upon him; longed to die for her, if only the last moment of his life were filled with her voice saying, "You may love me."

If he had been a knight, he might have thought of a poetic way to say such things. But he was not a knight, and so his words came out of his heart before his mind could find a way to make them clever. He strode blindly from the kitchen door, his huge body casting a shadow in the torchlight that seemed to the knights like the shadow of death passing over them. They watched in uneasiness that soon turned to outrage as he came to the girl, reached out, and took her small white hands in his.

"I love you," Bork said to her, and tears came unbidden to his eyes. "Let me marry you."

At that moment several of the knights found their courage. They seized Bork roughly by the arms, meaning to pull him away and punish him for his effrontery. But Bork effortlessly tossed them away. They fell to the ground yards from him. He never saw them fall; his gaze never left the lady's face.

She looked wonderingly in his eyes. Not because she thought him attractive, because he was ugly and she knew it. Not because of the words he had said, because she had been taught that many men would say those words, and she was to pay no attention to them. What startled her, what amazed her, was the deep truth in Bork's face. That was something she had never seen, and though she did not recognize it for what it was, it fascinated her.

The Count was furious. Seeing the clumsy giant holding his daughter's small white hands in his was outrageous. He would not endure it. But the giant had such great strength that to tear him away would mean a full-scale battle, and in such a battle Brunhilda might be injured. No, the giant had to be handled delicately, for the moment.

"My dear fellow," said the Count, affecting a joviality he did not feel. "You've only just met."

Bork ignored him. "I will never let you come to harm," he said to the girl.

"What's his name?" the Count whispered to a knight. "I can't remember his name."

"Bork," the knight answered.

"My dear Bork," said the Count. "All due respect and everything, but my daughter has noble blood, and you're not even a knight."

"Then I'll become one," Bork said.

"It's not that easy, Bork, old fellow. You must do something exceptionally brave, and then I can knight you and we can talk about this other matter. But in the meantime, it isn't proper for you to be holding my daughter's hands. Why don't you go back to the kitchen like a good fellow?"

Bork gave no sign that he heard. He only continued looking into the lady's eyes. And finally it was she who was able to end the dilemma.

"Bork," she said, "I will count on you. But in the meantime, my father will be angry at you if you don't return to the kitchen."

Of course, Bork thought. Of course, she is truly concerned for me, doesn't want me to come to harm on her account. "For your sake," he said, the madness of love still on him. Then he turned and left the room.

The Count sat down, sighing audibly. "Should have got rid of him years ago. Gentle as a lamb, and then all of a sudden goes crazy. Get rid of him—somebody take care of that tonight, would you? Best to do it in his sleep. Don't want any casualties when we're likely to have a battle in the morning."

The reminder of the battle was enough to sober even those who were on their fifth mug of ale. The wizened old woman led Brunhilda away again. "But not to the secret room, now. To the chamber next to mine. And post a double guard outside her door, and keep the key yourself," said the Count.

When she was gone, the Count looked around at the knights. "The treasury has been emptied in a vain attempt to find clothing to do her justice. I had no other choice."

And there was not a knight who would say the money had been badly spent.

The Duke came late in the afternoon, and demanded the tribute, and the Count refused, of course. There was the usual challenge to come out of the castle and fight, but the Count, outnumbered ten to one, merely replied, rather saucily, that the Duke should come in and get him. The messenger who delivered the sarcastic message came back with his tongue in a bag around his neck. The battle was thus begun grimly: and grimly it continued.

The guard watching on the south side of the castle was slacking. He paid for it. The Duke's archers managed to creep up to the huge oak tree and climb it without any alarm being given, and the first notice any of them had was when the guard fell from the battlements with an arrow in his throat.

The archers—there must have been a dozen of them—kept up a deadly rain of arrows. They wasted no shots. The squires dropped dead in alarming numbers until the Count gave orders for them to come inside. And when the human targets were all under cover, the archers set to work on the cattle and sheep milling about in their open pens. There was no way to protect the animals. By sunset, all of them were dead.

"Dammit," said the cook. "How can I cook all this before it spoils?"

"Find a way," said the Count. "That's our food supply. I refuse to let them starve us out."

So all night Bork worked, carrying the cattle and sheep inside, one by one. At first the villagers who had taken refuge in the castle tried to help him, but he could carry three animals inside the kitchen in the time it took them to drag one, and they soon gave it up.

The Count saw who was saving the meat. "Don't get rid of him tonight," he told his knights. "We'll punish him for his effrontery in the morning."

Bork only rested twice in the night, taking naps for an hour before the cook woke him again. And when dawn came, and the arrows began coming again, all the cattle were inside, and all but twenty sheep.

"That's all we can save," the cook told the Count.

"Save them all."

"But if Bork tries to go out there, he'll be killed!"

The Count looked the cook in the eyes. "Bring in the sheep or have him die trying."

The cook was not aware of the fact that Bork was under sentence of death. So he did his best to save Bork. A kettle lined with cloth and strapped onto the giant's head; a huge kettle lid for a shield. "It's the best we can do," the cook said.

"But I can't carry sheep if I'm holding a shield," Bork said.

"What can I do? The Count commanded it. It's worth your life to refuse."

Bork stood and thought for a few moments, trying to find a way out of his dilemma. He saw only one possibility. "If I can't stop them from hitting me, I'll have to stop them from shooting at all."

"How!" the cook demanded, and then followed Bork to the black-smith's shop, where Bork found his huge ax leaning against the wall.

"Now's not the time to cut firewood," said the blacksmith.

"Yes it is," Bork answered.

Carrying the ax and holding the kettle lid between his body and the archers, Bork made his way across the courtyard. The arrows pinged harmlessly off the metal. Bork got to the drawbridge. "Open up!" he shouted, and the drawbridge fell away and dropped across the moat. Bork walked across, then made his way along the moat toward the oak tree.

In the distance the Duke, standing in front of his dazzling white tent with his emblem of yellow crosses on it, saw Bork emerge from the castle. "Is that a man or a bear?" he asked. No one was sure.

The archers shot at Bork steadily, but the closer he got to the tree the worse their angle of fire and the larger the shadow of safety the kettle lid cast over his body. Finally, holding the lid high over his head, Bork began hacking one-handed at the trunk. Chips of wood flew with each blow; with his right hand alone he could cut deeper and faster than a normal man with both hands free.

But he was concentrating on cutting wood, and his left arm grew tired holding his makeshift shield, and an archer was able to get off a shot that slipped past the shield and plunged into his left arm, in the thick muscle at the back.

He nearly dropped the shield. Instead, he had the presence of mind to let go of the ax and drop to his knees, quickly balancing the kettle lid between the tree trunk, his head, and the top of the ax handle. Gently he pulled at the arrow shaft. It would not come backward. So he broke the arrow and pushed the stub the rest of the way through his arm until it was out the other side. It was excruciatingly painful, but he knew he could not quit now. He took hold of the shield with his left arm again, and despite the pain held it high as he began to cut again, girdling the tree with a deep white gouge. The blood dripped steadily down his arm, but he ignored it, and soon enough the bleeding stopped and slowed.

On the castle battlements, the Count's men began to realize that there was a hope of Bork's succeeding. To protect him, they began to shoot their arrows into the tree. The archers were well-hidden, but the rain of arrows, however badly aimed, began to have its effect. A few of them dropped to the ground, where the castle archers could easily finish them off; the others were forced to concentrate on finding cover.

The tree trembled more and more with each blow, until finally Bork stepped back and the tree creaked and swayed. He had learned from his lumbering work in the forest how to make the tree fall where he wanted it; the oak fell parallel to the castle walls, so it neither bridged the moat nor let the Duke's archers scramble from the tree too far from the castle. So when the archers tried to flee to the safety of the Duke's lines, the castle bowmen were able to kill them all.

One of them, however, despaired of escape. Instead, though he already had an arrow in him, he drew a knife and charged at Bork, in a mad attempt to avenge his own death on the man who had caused it. Bork had no choice. He swung his ax through the air and discovered that men are nowhere near as sturdy as a tree.

In the distance, the Duke watched with horror as the giant cut a man in half with a single blow. "What have they got!" he said. "What is this monster?"

Covered with the blood that had spurted from the dying man, Bork walked back toward the drawbridge, which opened again as he approached. But he did not get to enter. Instead the Count and the fifty mounted knights came from the gate on horseback, their armor shining in the sunlight.

"I've decided to fight them in the open," the Count said. "And you, Bork, must fight with us. If you live through this, I'll make you a knight!"

Bork knelt. "Thank you, my Lord Count," he said.

The Count glanced around in embarrassment. "Well, then. Let's get to it. Charge!" he bellowed.

Bork did not realize that the knights were not even formed in a line yet. He simply followed the command and charged, alone, toward the Duke's lines. The Count watched him go, and smiled.

"My Lord Count," said the nearest knight. "Aren't we going to attack with him?"

"Let the Duke take care of him," the Count said.

"But he cut down the oak and saved the castle, my lord."

"Yes," said the Count. "An exceptionally brave act. Do you want him to try to claim my daughter's hand?"

"But my lord," said the knight, "if he fights beside us, we might have a chance of winning. But if he's gone, the Duke will destroy us."

"Some things," said the Count, with finality, "are more important

than victory. Would you want to go on living in a world where per-
fection like Brunhilda's was possessed by such a man as that?"

The knights were silent, then, as they watched Bork approach the
Duke's army, alone.

Bork did not realize he was alone until he stood a few feet away from
the Duke's lines. He had felt a strange exhilaration as he walked
across the fields, believing he was marching into battle with the
knights he had long admired in their bright armor and deft instru-
ments of war. Now the exhilaration was gone. Where were the others? Bork was afraid.

He could not understand why the Duke's men had not shot any arrows at him. Actually, it was a misunderstanding. If the Duke had
known Bork was a commoner and not a knight at all, Bork would
have had a hundred arrows bristling from his corpse. As it was, however, one of the Duke's men called out, "You, sir! Do you challenge
us to single combat?"

Of course. That was it—the Count did not intend Bork to face an
army, he intended him to face a single warrior. The whole outcome
of the battle would depend on him alone! It was a tremendous honor,
and Bork wondered if he could carry it off.

"Yes! Single combat!" he answered. "Your strongest, bravest
man!"

"But you're a giant!" cried the Duke's man.

"But I'm wearing no armor." And to prove his sincerity, Bork took
off his helmet, which was uncomfortable anyway, and stepped forward. The Duke's knights backed away, making an opening for him,
with men in armor watching him pass from both sides. Bork walked
steadily on, until he came to a cleared circle where he faced the Duke
himself.

"Are you the champion?" asked Bork.

"I'm the Duke," he answered. "But I don't see any of my knights
stepping forward to fight you."

"Do you refuse the challenge, then?" Bork asked, trying to sound
as brave and scornful as he imagined a true knight would sound.

The Duke looked around at his men, who, if the armor had allowed, would have been shuffling uncomfortably in the morning sunlight. As it was, none of them looked at him.

"No," said the Duke. "I accept your challenge myself." The thought of fighting the giant terrified him. But he was a knight, and known to be a brave man; he had become Duke in the prime of his youth, and if he backed down before a giant now, his duchy would be taken from him in only a few years; his honor would be lost long before. So he drew his sword and advanced upon the giant.

Bork saw the determination in the Duke's eyes, and marveled at a man who would go himself into a most dangerous battle instead of sending his men. Briefly Bork wondered why the Count had not shown such courage; he determined at that moment that if he could help it the Duke would not die. The blood of the archer was more than he had ever wanted to shed. Nobility was in every movement of the Duke, and Bork wondered at the ill chance that had made them enemies.

The Duke lunged at Bork with his sword flashing. Bork hit him with the flat of the ax, knocking him to the ground. The Duke cried out in pain. His armor was dented deeply; there had to be ribs broken under the dent.

"Why don't you surrender?" asked Bork.

"Kill me now!"

"If you surrender, I won't kill you at all."

The Duke was surprised. There was a murmur from his men.

"I have your word?"

"Of course. I swear it."

It was too startling an idea.

"What do you plan to do, hold me for ransom?"

Bork thought about it. "I don't think so."

"Well, what then? Why not kill me and have done with it?" The pain in his chest now dominated the Duke's voice, but he did not spit blood, and so he began to feel some hope.

"All the Count wants you to do is go away and stop collecting tribute. If you promise to do that, I'll promise that not one of you will be harmed."

The Duke and his men considered this in silence. It was too good to believe. So good it was almost dishonorable even to consider it. Still—there was Bork, who had broken the Duke's body with one blow, right through the armor. If he chose to let them walk away from the battle, why argue?

"I give my word that I'll cease collecting tribute from the Count, and my men and I will go away in peace."

"Well, then, that's good news," Bork said. "I've got to go tell the Count." And Bork turned away and walked into the fields, heading for where the Count's tiny army waited.

"I can't believe it," said the Duke. "A knight like that, and he turns out to be generous. The Count could have his way with the King, with a knight like that."

They stripped the armor off him, carefully, and began wrapping his chest with bandages.

"If he were mine," the Duke said, "I'd use him to conquer the whole land."

The Count watched, incredulous, as Bork crossed the field.

"He's still alive," he said, and he began to wonder what Bork would have to say about the fact that none of the knights had joined his gallant charge.

"My Lord Count!" cried Bork, when he was within range.

He would have waved, but both his arms were exhausted now. "They surrender!"

"What?" the Count asked the knights near him. "Did he say they surrender?"

"Apparently," a knight answered. "Apparently he won."

"Damn!" cried the Count. "I won't have it!"

The knights were puzzled. "If anybody's going to defeat the Duke, *I* am! Not a damnable commoner! Not a giant with the brains of a cockroach! Charge!"

"What?" several of the knights asked.

"I said charge!" And the Count moved forward, his warhorse plodding carefully through the field, building up momentum.

Bork saw the knights start forward. He had watched enough mock battles to recognize a charge. He could only assume that the Count hadn't heard him. But the charge had to be stopped—he had given his word, hadn't he? So he planted himself in the path of the Count's horse.

"Out of the way, you damned fool!" cried the Count. But Bork stood his ground. The Count was determined not to be thwarted. He prepared to ride Bork down.

"You can't charge!" Bork yelled. "They surrendered!"

The Count gritted his teeth and urged the horse forward, his lance prepared to cast Bork out of the way.

A moment later the Count found himself in midair, hanging to the lance for his life. Bork held it over his head, and the knights laboriously halted their charge and wheeled to see what was going on with Bork and the Count.

"My Lord Count," Bork said respectfully. "I guess you didn't hear me. They surrendered. I promised them they could go in peace if they stopped collecting tribute."

From his precarious hold on the lance, fifteen feet off the ground, the Count said, "I didn't hear you."

"I didn't think so. But you *will* let them go, won't you?"

"Of course. Could you give a thought to letting me down, old boy?"

And so Bork let the Count down, and there was a peace treaty between the Duke and the Count, and the Duke's men rode away in peace, talking about the generosity of the giant knight.

"But he isn't a knight," said a servant to the Duke.

"What? Not a knight?"

"No. Just a villager. One of the peasants told me, when I was stealing his chickens."

"Not a knight," said the Duke, and for a moment his face began to turn the shade of red that made his knights want to ride a few feet further from him—they knew his rage too well already.

"We were tricked then," said a knight, trying to fend off his lord's anger by anticipating it.

The Duke said nothing for a moment. Then he smiled. "Well, if he's not a knight, he should be. He has the strength. He has the courtesy. Hasn't he?"

The knights agreed that he had.

"He's the moral equivalent of a knight," said the Duke. Pride assuaged, for the moment, he led his men back to his castle. Underneath, however, even deeper than the pain in his ribs, was the image of the Count perched on the end of a lance held high in the air by the giant, Bork, and he pondered what it might have meant, and what, more to the point, it might mean in the future.

Things were getting out of hand, the Count decided. First of all, the victory celebration had not been his idea, and yet here they were, riotously drunken in the great hall, and even villagers were making free with the ale, laughing and cheering among the knights. That was bad enough, but worse was the fact that the knights were making no pretense about it—the party was in honor of Bork.

The Count drummed his fingers on the table. No one paid any attention. They were too busy—Sir Alwishard trying to keep two village wenches occupied near the fire, Sir Silwiss pissing in the wine and laughing so loud that the Count could hardly hear Sir Braig and Sir Umlaut as they sang and danced along the table, kicking plates off with their toes in time with the music. It was the best party the Count had ever seen. And it wasn't for him, it was for that damnable giant who had made an ass of him in front of all his men and all the Duke's men and, worst of all, the Duke. He heard a strange growling sound, like a savage wolf getting ready to spring. In a lull in the bedlam he suddenly realized that the sound was coming from his own throat.

Get control of yourself, he thought. The real gains, the solid gains were not Bork's—they were mine. The Duke is gone, and instead of me paying him tribute from now on, he'll be paying me. Word would get around, too, that the Count had won a battle with the Duke. After all, that was the basis of power—who could beat whom in battle. A duke was just a man who could beat a count, a count someone who could beat a baron, a baron someone who could beat a knight.

But what was a person who could beat a duke?

"You should be king," said a tall, slender young man standing near the throne.

The Count looked at him, making a vague motion with his hidden hand. How had the boy read his thoughts?

"I'll pretend I didn't hear that."

"You heard it," said the young man.

"It's treason."

"Only if the king beats you in battle. If *you* win, it's treason *not* to say so."

The Count looked the boy over. Dark hair that looked a bit too carefully combed for a villager. A straight nose, a pleasant smile, a winning grace when he walked. But something about his eyes gave the lie to the smile. The boy was vicious somehow. The boy was dangerous.

"I like you," said the Count.

"I'm glad." He did not sound glad. He sounded bored.

"If I'm smart, I'll have you strangled immediately."

The boy only smiled more.

"Who are you?"

"My name is Winkle. And I'm Bork's best friend."

Bork. There he was again, that giant sticking his immense shadow into everything tonight. "Didn't know Bork the Bully had any friends."

"He has one. Me. Ask him."

"I wonder if a friend of Bork's is really a friend of mine," the Count said.

"I said I was his best friend. I didn't say I was a good friend." And Winkle smiled.

A thoroughgoing bastard, the Count decided, but he waved to Bork and beckoned for him to come. In a moment the giant knelt before the Count, who was irritated to discover that when Bork knelt and the Count sat, Bork still looked down on him.

"This man," said the Count, "claims to be your friend."

Bork looked up and recognized Winkle, who was beaming down at him, his eyes filled with love, mostly. A hungry kind of love, but Bork wasn't discriminating. He had the admiration and grudging respect of the knights, but he hardly knew them. This was his childhood friend, and at the thought that Winkle claimed to be his friend

Bork immediately forgave all the past slights and smiled back. "Winkle," he said. "Of course we're friends. He's my *best* friend."

The Count made the mistake of looking in Bork's eyes and seeing the complete sincerity of his love for Winkle. It embarrassed him, for he knew Winkle too well already, from just the moments of conversation they had had. Winkle was nobody's friend. But Bork was obviously blind to that. For a moment the Count almost pitied the giant, had a glimpse of what his life must be like, if the predatory young villager was his best friend.

"Your majesty," said Winkle.

"Don't call me that."

"I only anticipate what the world will know in a matter of months."

Winkle sounded so confident, so sure of it. A chill went up the Count's spine. He shook it off. "I won one battle, Winkle. I still have a huge budget deficit and a pretty small army of some fairly lousy knights."

"Think of your daughter, even if *you* aren't ambitious. Despite her beauty she'll be lucky to marry a duke. But if she were the daughter of a king, she could marry anyone in all the world. And her own lovely self would be a dowry—no prince would think to ask for more."

The Count thought of his daughter, the beautiful Brunhilda, and smiled.

Bork also smiled, for he was also thinking the same thing.

"Your majesty," Winkle urged, "with Bork as your right-hand man and me as your counselor, there's nothing to stop you from being king within a year or two. Who would be willing to stand against an army with the three of us marching at the head?"

"Why three?" asked the Count.

"You mean, why me. I thought you would already understand that—but then, that's what you need me for. You see, your majesty, you're a good man, a godly man, a paragon of virtue. You would never think of seeking power and conniving against your enemies and spying and doing repulsive things to people you don't like. But kings *have* to do those things or they quickly cease to be kings."

Vaguely the Count remembered behaving in just that way many times, but Winkle's words were seductive—they *should* be true.

"Your majesty, where you are pure, I am polluted. Where you are fresh, I am rotten. I'd sell my mother into slavery if I had a mother and I'd cheat the devil at poker and win hell from him before he caught on. And I'd stab any of your enemies in the back if I got the chance."

"But what if my enemies aren't your enemies?" the Count asked.

"Your enemies are *always* my enemies. I'll be loyal to you through thick and thin."

"How can I trust you, if you're so rotten?"

"Because you're going to pay me a lot of money." Winkle bowed deeply.

"Done," said the Count.

"Excellent," said Winkle, and they shook hands. The Count noticed that Winkle's hands were smooth—he had neither the hard horny palms of a village workingman nor the slick calluses of a man trained to warfare.

"How have you made a living, up to now?" the Count asked.

"I steal," Winkle said, with a smile that said I'm joking and a glint in his eye that said I'm not.

"What about me?" asked Bork.

"Oh, you're in it, too," said Winkle. "You're the king's strong right arm."

"I've never met the king," said Bork.

"Yes you have," Winkle retorted. "That is the king."

"No he's not," said the giant. "He's only a count."

The words stabbed the Count deeply. *Only* a count. Well, that would end. "Today I'm only a count," he said patiently. "Who knows what tomorrow will bring? But Bork—I shall knight you. As a knight you must swear absolute loyalty to me and do whatever I say. Will you do that?"

"Of course I will," said Bork. "Thank you, my Lord Count." Bork arose and called to his new friends throughout the hall in a voice that could not be ignored. "My Lord Count has decided I will be made a knight!" There were cheers and applause and stamping of feet. "And

the best thing is," Bork said, "that now I can marry the Lady Brunhilda."

There was no applause. Just a murmur of alarm. Of course. If he
became a knight, he was eligible for Brunhilda's hand. It was un-
thinkable—but the Count himself had said so.

The Count was having second thoughts, of course, but he knew no
way to back out of it, not without looking like a word breaker. He
made a false start at speaking, but couldn't finish. Bork waited, expectantly. Clearly he believed the Count would confirm what Bork
had said.

It was Winkle, however, who took the situation in hand. "Oh,
Bork," he said sadly—but loudly, so that everyone could hear.
"Don't you understand? His majesty is making you a knight out of
gratitude. But unless you're a king or the son of a king, you have to
do something exceptionally brave to earn Brunhilda's hand."

"But, wasn't I brave today?" Bork asked. After all, the arrow
wound in his arm still hurt, and only the ale kept him from aching unmercifully all over from the exertion of the night and the day just
past.

"You were brave. But since you're twice the size and ten times the
strength of an ordinary man, it's hardly fair for you to win Brunhilda's hand with ordinary bravery. No, Bork—it's just the way
things work. It's just the way things are done. Before you're worthy
of Brunhilda, you have to do something ten times as brave as what
you did today."

Bork could not think of something ten times as brave. Hadn't he
gone almost unprotected to chop down the oak tree? Hadn't he attacked a whole army all by himself, and won the surrender of the
enemy? What could be ten times as brave?

"Don't despair," the Count said. "Surely in all the battles ahead of
us there'll be *something* ten times as brave. And in the meantime,
you're a knight, my friend, a great knight, and you shall dine at my
table every night! And when we march into battle, there you'll be,
right beside me—"

"A few steps ahead," Winkle whispered discreetly.

"A few steps ahead of me, to defend the honor of my county—"

"Don't be shy," whispered Winkle.

"No, not my county. My kingdom. For from today, you men no longer serve a count! You serve a king!"

It was a shocking declaration, and might have caused sober reflection if there had been a sober man in the room. But through the haze of alcohol and torchlight and fatigue, the knights looked at the Count and he did indeed seem kingly. And they thought of the battles ahead and were not afraid, for they had won a glorious victory today and not one of them had shed a drop of blood. Except, of course, Bork. But in some corner of their collected opinions was a viewpoint they would not have admitted to holding, if anyone brought the subject out in the open. The opinion so well hidden from themselves and each other was simple: Bork is not like me. Bork is not one of us. Therefore, Bork is expendable.

The blood that still stained his sleeve was cheap. Plenty more where that came from.

And so they plied him with more ale until he fell asleep, snoring hugely on the table, forgetting that he had been cheated out of the woman he loved; it was easy to forget, for the moment, because he was a knight, and a hero, and at last he had friends.

It took two years for the Count to become King. He began close to home, with other counts, but soon progressed to the great dukes and earls of the kingdom. Wherever he went, the pattern was the same. The Count and his fifty knights would ride their horses, only lightly armored so they could travel with reasonable speed. Bork would walk, but his long legs easily kept up with the rest of them. They would arrive at their victim's castle, and three squires would hand Bork his new steel-headed ax. Bork, covered with impenetrable armor, would wade the moat, if there was one, or simply walk up to the gates, swing the ax, and begin chopping through the wood. When the gates collapsed, Bork would take a huge steel rod and use it as a crow, prying at the portcullis, bending the heavy iron like pretzels until there was a gap wide enough for a mounted knight to ride through.

Then he would go back to the Count and Winkle.

Throughout this operation, not a word would have been said; the nly activity from the Count's other men would be enough archery hat no one would be able to pour boiling oil or hot tar on Bork while he was working. It was a precaution, and nothing more—even if they set the oil on the fire the moment the Count's little army approached, it would scarcely be hot enough to make water steam by the time Bork was through.

"Do you surrender to his Majesty the King?" Winkle would cry.

And the defenders of the castle, their gate hopelessly breached and terrified of the giant who had so easily made a joke of their defenses, would usually surrender. Occasionally there was some token resistance—when that happened, at Winkle's insistence, the town was brutally sacked and the noble's family was held in prison until a huge ransom was paid.

At the end of two years, the Count and Bork and Winkle and their army marched on Winchester. The King—the real king—fled before them and took up his exile in Anjou, where it was warmer anyway. The Count had himself crowned king, accepted the fealty of every noble in the country, and introduced his daughter Brunhilda all around. Then, finding Winchester not to his liking, he returned to his castle and ruled from there. Suitors for his daughter's hand made a constant traffic on the roads leading into the country; would-be courtiers and nobles vying for positions filled the new hostelries that sprang up on the other side of the village. All left much poorer than they had arrived. And while much of that money found its way into the King's coffers, much more of it went to Winkle, who believed that skimming off the cream meant leaving at least a quarter of it for the King.

And now that the wars were done, Bork hung up his armor and went back to normal life. Not quite normal life, actually. He slept in a good room in the castle, better than most of the knights. Some of the knights had even come to enjoy his company, and sought him out for ale in the evenings or hunting in the daytime—Bork could always be counted on to carry home two deer himself, and was much more convenient than a packhorse. All in all, Bork was happier than he had ever thought he would be.

Which is how things were going when the dragon came and changed it all forever.

Winkle was in Brunhilda's room, a place he had learned many routes to get to, so that he went unobserved every time. Brunhilda, after many gifts and more flattery, was on the verge of giving in to the handsome young adviser to the King when strange screams and cries began coming from the fields below. Brunhilda pulled away from Winkle's exploring hands and, clutching her half-open gown around her, rushed to the window to see what was the matter.

She looked down, to where the screams were coming from, and it wasn't until the dragon's shadow fell across her that she looked up. Winkle, waiting on the bed, only saw the claws reach in and, gently but firmly, take hold of Brunhilda and pull her from the room. Brunhilda fainted immediately, and by the time Winkle got to where he could see her, the dragon had backed away from the window and on great flapping wings was carrying her limp body off toward the north whence he came.

Winkle was horrified. It was so sudden, something he could not have foreseen or planned against. Yet still he cursed himself and bitterly realized that his plans might be ended forever. A dragon had taken Brunhilda who would be his means of legitimately becoming king; now the plot of seduction, marriage, and inheritance was ruined.

Ever practical, Winkle did not let himself lament for long. He dressed himself quickly and used a secret passage out of Brunhilda's room, only to reappear in the corridor outside it a moment later. "Brunhilda!" he cried, beating on the door. "Are you all right?"

The first of the knights reached him, and then the King, weeping and wailing and smashing anything that got in his way. Brunhilda's door was down in a moment, and the King ran to the window and cried out after his daughter, now a pinpoint speck in the sky many miles away. "Brunhilda! Brunhilda! Come back!" She did not come back. "Now," cried the King, as he turned back into the room and sank to the floor, his face twisted and wet with grief, "Now I have nothing, and all is in vain!"

My thoughts precisely, Winkle thought, but I'm not weeping about it. To hide his contempt he walked to the window and looked out. He saw, not the dragon, but Bork, emerging from the forest carrying two huge logs.

"Sir Bork," said Winkle.

The King heard a tone of decision in Winkle's voice. He had learned to listen to whatever Winkle said in that tone of voice. "What about him?"

"Sir Bork could defeat a dragon," Winkle said, "if any man could."

"That's true," the King said, gathering back some of the hope he had lost. "Of course, that's true."

"But will he?" asked Winkle.

"Of course he will. He loves Brunhilda, doesn't he?"

"He said he did. But Your Majesty, is he really loyal to you? After all, why wasn't he here when the dragon came? Why didn't he save Brunhilda in the first place?"

"He was cutting wood for the winter."

"Cutting wood? When Brunhilda's life was at stake?"

The King was outraged. The illogic of it escaped him—he was not in a logical mood. So he was furious when he met Bork at the gate of the castle.

"You've betrayed me!" the King cried.

"I have?" Bork was smitten with guilt. And he hadn't even meant to.

"You weren't here when we needed you. When *Brunhilda* needed you!"

"I'm sorry," Bork said.

"Sorry, sorry, sorry. A lot of good it does to say you're sorry. You swore to protect Brunhilda from any enemy, and when a really dangerous enemy comes along, how do you repay me for everything I've done for you? You hide out in the forest!"

"What enemy?"

"A dragon," said the King, "as if you didn't see it coming and run out into the woods."

"Cross my heart, Your Majesty, I didn't know there was a dragon coming." And then he made the connection in his mind. "The dragon—it took Brunhilda?"

"It took her. Took her half-naked from her bedroom when she leaped to the window to call to you for help."

Bork felt the weight of guilt, and it was a terrible burden. His face grew hard and angry, and he walked into the castle, his harsh footfalls setting the earth to trembling. "My armor!" he cried. "My sword!"

In minutes he was in the middle of the courtyard, holding out his arms as the heavy mail was draped over him and the breastplate and helmet were strapped and screwed in place. The sword was not enough—he also carried his huge ax and a shield so massive two ordinary men could have hidden behind it.

"Which way did he go?" Bork asked.

"North," the King answered.

"I'll bring back your daughter, Your Majesty, or die in the attempt."

"Damn well better. It's all your fault."

The words stung, but the sting only impelled Bork further. He took the huge sack of food the cook had prepared for him and fastened it to a belt, and without a backward glance strode from the castle and took the road north.

"I almost feel sorry for the dragon," said the King.

But Winkle wondered. He had seen how large the claws were as they grasped Brunhilda—she had been like a tiny doll in a large man's fingers. The claws were razor sharp. Even if she were still alive, could Bork really best the dragon? Bork the Bully, after all, had made his reputation picking on men smaller than he, as Winkle had ample reason to know. How would he do facing a dragon at least five times his size? Wouldn't he turn coward? Wouldn't he run as other men had run from *him?*

He might. But Sir Bork the Bully was Winkle's only hope of getting Brunhilda and the kingdom. If he could do anything to ensure that the giant at least *tried* to fight the dragon, he would do it. And so, taking only his rapier and a sack of food, Winkle left the castle by another way, and followed the giant along the road toward the north.

And then he had a terrible thought.

Fighting the dragon was surely ten times as brave as anything Bork had done before. If he won, wouldn't he have a claim on Brunhilda's hand himself?

It was not something Winkle wished to think about. Something would come to him, some way around the problem when the time came. Plenty of opportunity to plan something—*after* Bork wins and rescues her.

Bork had not rounded the second turn in the road when he came across the old woman, waiting by the side of the road. It was the same old woman who had cared for Brunhilda all those years that she was kept in a secret room in the castle. She looked wizened and weak, but there was a sharp look in her eyes that many had mistaken for great wisdom. It was not great wisdom. But she did know a few things about dragons.

"Going after the dragon, are you?" she asked in a squeaky voice. "Going to get Brunhilda back, are you?" She giggled darkly behind her hand.

"I am if anyone can," Bork said.

"Well, anyone can't," she answered.

"*I* can."

"Not a prayer, you big bag of wind!"

Bork ignored her and started to walk past.

"Wait!" she said, her voice harsh as a dull file taking rust from armor. "Which way will you go?"

"North," he said. "That's the way the dragon took her."

"A quarter of the world is north, Sir Bork the Bully, and a dragon is small compared to all the mountains of the earth. But I know a way you can find the dragon, if you're really a knight."

"What is it?" Bork asked. It would simplify everything if he had a sure way of finding where Brunhilda was being kept captive.

"Light a torch, man. Light a torch, and whenever you come to a fork in the way, the light of the torch will leap the way you ought to go. Wind or no wind, fire seeks fire, and there is a flame at the heart of every dragon."

"They *do* breathe fire, then?" he asked. He did not know how to fight fire.

"Fire is light, not wind, and so it doesn't come from the dragon's mouth or the dragon's nostrils. If he burns you, it won't be with his breath." The old woman cackled like a mad hen. "No one knows the truth about dragons anymore!"

"Except you."

"I'm an old wife," she said. "And I know. They don't eat human beings, either. They're strict vegetarians. But they kill. From time to time they kill."

"Why, if they aren't hungry for meat?"

"You'll see," she said. She started to walk away, back into the forest.

"Wait!" Bork called. "How far will the dragon be?"

"Not far," she said. "Not far, Sir Bork. He's waiting for you. He's waiting for you and all the fools who come to try to free the virgin." Then she melted away into the darkness.

Bork lit a torch and followed it all night, turning when the flame turned, unwilling to waste time in sleep when Brunhilda might be suffering unspeakable degradation at the monster's hands. And behind him, Winkle forced himself to stay awake, determined not to let Bork lose him in the darkness.

All night, and all day, and all night again Bork followed the light of the torch, through crooked paths long unused, until he came to the foot of a dry, tall hill, with rocks and crags along the top. He stopped, for here the flame leaped high, as if to say, "Upward from here." And in the silence he heard a sound that chilled him to the bone. It was Brunhilda, screaming as if she were being tortured in the cruelest imaginable way. And the screams were followed by a terrible roar. Bork cast aside the remnant of his food and made his way to the top of the hill. On the way he called out, to stop the dragon from whatever it was doing.

"Dragon! Are you there!"

The voice rumbled back to him with a power that made the dirt shift under Bork's feet. "Yes indeed."

"Do you have Brunhilda?"

"You mean the little virgin with the heart of an adder and the brain of a gnat?"

In the forest at the bottom of the hill, Winkle ground his teeth in fury, for despite his designs on the kingdom, he loved Brunhilda as much as he was capable of loving anyone.

"Dragon!" Bork bellowed at the top of his voice, "Dragon! Prepare to die!"

"Oh dear! Oh dear!" cried out the dragon. "Whatever shall I do!"

And then Bork reached the top of the hill, just as the sun topped the distant mountains and it became morning. In the light Bork immediately saw Brunhilda tied to a tree, her auburn hair glistening. All around her was the immense pile of gold that the dragon, according to custom, kept. And all around the gold was the dragon's tail.

Bork looked at the tail and followed it until finally he came to the dragon, who was leaning on a rock chewing on a tree trunk and smirking. The dragon's wings were clad with feathers, but the rest of him was covered with tough gray hide the color of weathered granite. His teeth, when he smiled, were ragged, long, and pointed. His claws were three feet long and sharp as a rapier from tip to base. But in spite of all this armament, the most dangerous thing about him was his eyes. They were large and soft and brown, with long lashes and gently arching brows. But at the center each eye held a sharp point of light, and when Bork looked at the eyes that light stabbed deep into him, seeing his heart and laughing at what it found there.

For a moment, looking at the dragon's eyes, Bork stood transfixed. Then the dragon reached over one wing toward Brunhilda, and with a great growling noise he began to tickle her ear.

Brunhilda was unbearably ticklish, and she let off a bloodcurdling scream.

"Touch her not!" Bork cried.

"Touch her what?" asked the dragon, with a chuckle. "I will not."

"Beast!" bellowed Bork. "I am Sir Bork the Big! I have never been defeated in battle! No man dares stand before me, and the beasts of the forest step aside when I pass!"

"You must be awfully clumsy," said the dragon.

Bork resolutely went on. He had seen the challenges and jousts—

it was obligatory to recite and embellish your achievements in order to strike terror into the heart of the enemy. "I can cut down trees with one blow of my ax! I can cleave an ox from head to tail, I can skewer a running deer, I can break down walls of stone and doors of wood!"

"Why can't I ever get a handy servant like that?" murmured the dragon. "Ah well, you probably expect too large a salary."

The dragon's sardonic tone might have infuriated other knights; Bork was only confused, wondering if this matter was less serious than he had thought. "I've come to free Brunhilda, dragon. Will you give her up to me, or must I slay you?"

At that the dragon laughed long and loud. Then it cocked its head and looked at Bork. In that moment Bork knew that he had lost the battle. For deep in the dragon's eyes he saw the truth.

Bork saw himself knocking down gates and cutting down trees, but the deeds no longer looked heroic. Instead he realized that the knights who always rode behind him in these battles were laughing at him, that the King was a weak and vicious man, that Winkle's ambition was the only emotion he had room for; he saw that all of them were using him for their own ends, and cared nothing for him at all.

Bork saw himself asking for Brunhilda's hand in marriage, and he was ridiculous, an ugly, unkempt, and awkward giant in contrast to the slight and graceful girl. He saw that the King's hints of the possibility of their marriage were merely a trick, to blind him. More, he saw what no one else had been able to see—that Brunhilda loved Winkle, and Winkle wanted her.

And at last Bork saw himself as a warrior, and realized that in all the years of his great reputation and in all his many victories, he had fought only one man—an archer who ran at him with a knife. He had terrorized the weak and the small, but never until now had he faced a creature larger than himself. Bork looked in the dragon's eyes and saw his own death.

"Your eyes are deep," said Bork softly.

"Deep as a well, and you are drowning."

"Your sight is clear." Bork's palms were cold with sweat.

"Clear as ice, and you will freeze."

"Your eyes," Bork began. Then his mouth was suddenly so dry

that he could barely speak. He swallowed. "Your eyes are filled with light."

"Bright and tiny as a star," the dragon whispered. "And see: your heart is afire."

Slowly the dragon stepped away from the rock, even as the tip of his tail reached behind Bork to push him into the dragon's waiting jaws. But Bork was not in so deep a trance that he could not see.

"I see that you mean to kill me," Bork said. "But you won't have me as easily as that." Bork whirled around to hack at the tip of the dragon's tail with his ax. But he was too large and slow, and the tail flicked away before the ax was fairly swung.

The battle lasted all day. Bork fought exhaustion as much as he fought the dragon, and it seemed the dragon only toyed with him. Bork would lurch toward the tail or a wing or the dragon's belly, but when his ax or sword fell where the dragon had been, it only sang in the air and touched nothing.

Finally Bork fell to his knees and wept. He wanted to go on with the fight, but his body could not do it. And the dragon looked as fresh as it had in the morning.

"What?" asked the dragon. "Finished already?"

Then Bork felt the tip of the dragon's tail touch his back, and the sharp points of the claws pressed gently on either side. He could not bear to look up at what he knew he would see. Yet neither could he bear to wait, not knowing when the blow would come. So he opened his eyes, and lifted his head, and saw.

The dragon's teeth were nearly touching him, poised to tear his head from his shoulders.

Bork screamed. And screamed again when the teeth touched him, when they pushed into his armor, when the dragon lifted him with teeth and tail and talons until he was twenty feet above the ground. He screamed again when he looked into the dragon's eyes and saw, not hunger, not hatred, but merely amusement.

And then he found his silence again, and listened as the dragon spoke through clenched teeth, watching the tongue move massively in the mouth only inches from his head.

"Well, little man. Are you afraid?"

Bork tried to think of some heroic message of defiance to hurl at the dragon, some poetic words that might be remembered forever so that his death would be sung in a thousand songs. But Bork's mind was not quick at such things; he was not that accustomed to speech, and had no ear for gallantry. Instead he began to think it would be somehow cheap and silly to die with a lie on his lips.

"Dragon," Bork whispered, "I'm frightened."

To Bork's surprise, the teeth did not pierce him then. Instead, he felt himself being lowered to the ground, heard a grating sound as the teeth and claws let go of his armor. He raised his visor, and saw that the dragon was now lying on the ground, laughing, rolling back and forth, slapping its tail against the rocks, and clapping its claws together. "Oh, my dear tiny friend," said the dragon. "I thought the day would never dawn."

"What day?"

"Today," answered the dragon. It had stopped laughing, and it once again drew near to Bork and looked him in the eye. "I'm going to let you live."

"Thank you," Bork said, trying to be polite.

"Thank me? Oh no, my midget warrior. You won't thank me. Did you think my teeth were sharp? Not half so pointed as the barbs of your jealous, disappointed friends."

"I can go?"

"You can go, you can fly, you can dwell in your castle forever for all I care. Do you want to know why?"

"Yes."

"Because you were afraid. In all my life, I have only killed brave knights who knew no fear. You're the first, the very first, who was afraid in that final moment. Now go." And the dragon gave Bork a push and sent him down the hill.

Brunhilda, who had watched the whole battle in curious silence, now called after him. "Some kind of knight you are! Coward! I hate you! Don't leave me!" The shouts went on until Bork was out of earshot.

Bork was ashamed.

Bork went down the hill and, as soon as he entered the cool of the forest, he lay down and fell asleep.

Hidden in the rocks, Winkle watched him go, watched as the dragon again began to tickle Brunhilda, whose gown was still open as it had been when she was taken by the dragon. Winkle could not stop thinking of how close he had come to having her. But now, if even Bork could not save her, her cause was hopeless, and Winkle immediately began planning other ways to profit from the situation.

All the plans depended on his reaching the castle before Bork. Since Winkle had dozed off and on during the day's battle, he was able to go farther—to a village, where he stole an ass and rode clumsily, half-asleep, all night and half the next day and reached the castle before Bork awoke.

The King raged. The King swore. The King vowed that Bork would die.

"But Your Majesty," said Winkle, "you can't forget that it is Bork who inspires fear in the hearts of your loyal subjects. You can't kill him—if he were dead, how long would you be king?"

That calmed the old man down. "Then I'll let him live. But he won't have place in this castle, that's certain. I won't have him around here, the coward. Afraid! Told the dragon he was afraid! Pathetic. The man has no gratitude." And the King stalked from the court.

When Bork got home, weary and sick at heart, he found the gate of the castle closed to him. There was no explanation—he needed none. He had failed the one time it mattered most. He was no longer worthy to be a knight.

And now it was as it had been before. Bork was ignored, despised, feared; he was completely alone. But still, when it was time for great strength, there he was, doing the work of ten men, and not thanked for it. Who would thank a man for doing what he must to earn his bread?

In the evenings he would sit in his hut, staring at the fire that pushed a column of smoke up through the hole in the roof. He remembered how it had been to have friends, but the memory was not happy, for it was always poisoned by the knowledge that the friendship did not outlast Bork's first failure. Now the knights spat when they passed him on the road or in the fields.

The flames did not let Bork blame his troubles on them, however. The flames constantly reminded him of the dragon's eyes, and in their dance he saw himself, a buffoon who dared to dream of loving a princess, who believed that he was truly a knight. Not so, not so. I was never a knight, he thought. I was never worthy. Only now am I receiving what I deserve. And all his bitterness turned inward, and he hated himself far more than any of the knights could hate him.

He had made the wrong choice. When the dragon chose to let him go, he should have refused. He should have stayed and fought to the death. He should have died.

Stories kept filtering into the village, stories of the many heroic and famous knights who accepted the challenge of freeing Brunhilda from the dragon. All of them went as heroes. All of them died as heroes. Only Bork had returned alive from the dragon, and with every knight who died Bork's shame grew. Until he decided that he would go back. Better to join the knights in death than to live his life staring into the flames and seeing the visions of the dragon's eyes.

Next time, however, he would have to be better prepared. So after the spring plowing and planting and lambing and calving, where Bork's help was indispensable to the villagers, the giant went to the castle again. This time no one barred his way, but he was wise enough to stay as much out of sight as possible. He went to the one-armed swordmaster's room. Bork hadn't seen him much since he accidentally cut off his arm in sword practice years before.

"Come for the other arm, coward?" asked the swordmaster.

"I'm sorry," Bork said. "I was younger then."

"You weren't any smaller. Go away."

But Bork stayed, and begged the swordmaster to help him. They worked out an arrangement. Bork would be the swordmaster's personal servant all summer, and in exchange the swordmaster would try to teach Bork how to fight.

They went out into the fields every day, and under the swordmaster's watchful eye he practiced sword-fighting with bushes, trees, rocks—anything but the swordmaster, who refused to let Bork near him. Then they would return to the swordmaster's rooms, and Bork would clean the floor and sharpen swords and burnish shields and repair broken practice equipment. And always the swordmaster said, "Bork, you're too stupid to do anything right!" Bork agreed. In a summer of practice, he never got any better, and at the end of the summer, when it was time for Bork to go out in the fields and help with the harvest and the preparations for winter, the swordmaster said, "It's hopeless, Bork. You're too slow. Even the bushes are more agile than you. Don't come back. I still hate you, you know."

"I know," Bork said, and he went out into the fields, where the peasants waited impatiently for the giant to come carry sheaves of grain to the wagons.

Another winter looking at the fire, and Bork began to realize that no matter how good he got with the sword, it would make no difference. The dragon was not to be defeated that way. If excellent swordplay could kill the dragon, the dragon would be dead by now—the finest knights in the kingdom had already died trying.

He had to find another way. And the snow was still heavy on the ground when he again entered the castle and climbed the long and narrow stairway to the tower room where the wizard lived.

"Go away," said the wizard, when Bork knocked at his door. "I'm busy."

"I'll wait," Bork answered.

"Suit yourself."

And Bork waited. It was late at night when the wizard finally opened the door. Bork had fallen asleep leaning on it—he nearly knocked the magician over when he fell inside.

"What the devil are you—you waited!"

"Yes," said Bork, rubbing his head where it had hit the stone floor.

"Well, I'll be back in a moment." The wizard made his way along a narrow ledge until he reached the place where the wall bulged and a hole opened onto the outside of the castle wall. In wartime, such holes were used to pour boiling oil on attackers. In peacetime, they were even more heavily used. "Go on inside and wait," the wizard said.

Bork looked around the room. It was spotlessly clean, the walls were lined with books, and here and there a fascinating artifact hinted at hidden knowledge and arcane powers—a sphere with the world on it, a skull, an abacus, beakers and tubes, a clay pot from which smoke rose, though there was no fire under it. Bork marveled until the wizard returned.

"Nice little place, isn't it?" the wizard asked. "You're Bork, the bully, aren't you?"

Bork nodded.

"What can I do for you?"

"I don't know," Bork said. "I want to learn magic. I want to learn magic powerful enough that I can use it to fight the dragon."

The wizard coughed profusely.

"What's wrong?" Bork asked.

"It's the dust," the wizard said.

Bork looked around and saw no dust. But when he sniffed the air, it felt thick in his nose, and a tickling in his chest made him cough, too.

"Dust?" asked Bork. "Can I have a drink?"

"Drink," said the wizard. "Downstairs—"

"But there's a pail of water right here. It looks perfectly clean—"

"Please don't—"

But Bork put the dipper in the pail and drank. The water sloshed into his mouth, and he swallowed, but it felt dry going down, and his thirst was unslaked. "What's wrong with the water?" Bork asked.

The wizard sighed and sat down. "It's the problem with magic, Bork old boy. Why do you think the King doesn't call on me to help him in his wars? He knows it, and now you'll know it, and the whole world probably will know it by Thursday."

"You don't know any magic?"

"Don't be a fool! I know all the magic there is! I can conjure up monsters that would make your dragon look tame! I can snap my fingers and have a table set with food to make the cook die of envy. I can take an empty bucket and fill it with water, with wine, with gold—whatever you want. But try spending the gold, and they'll

hunt you down and kill you. Try drinking the water and you'll die of
thirst."

"It isn't real."

"All illusion. Handy, sometimes. But that's all. Can't create anything except in your head. That pail, for instance—" And the wizard
snapped his fingers. Bork looked, and the pail was filled, not with
water, but with dust and spider webs. That wasn't all. He looked
around the room, and was startled to see that the bookshelves were
gone, as were the other trappings of great wisdom. Just a few books
on a table in a corner, some counters covered with dust and papers
and half-decayed food, and the floor inches deep in garbage.

"The place is horrible," the wizard said. "I can't bear to look at it."
He snapped his fingers, and the old illusion came back. "Much nicer,
isn't it?"

"Yes."

"I have excellent taste, haven't I? Now, you wanted me to help you
fight the dragon, didn't you? Well, I'm afraid it's out of the question.
You see, my illusions only work on human beings, and occasionally
on horses. A dragon wouldn't be fooled for a moment. You understand?"

Bork understood, and despaired. He returned to his hut and stared
again at the flames. His resolution to return and fight the dragon
again was undimmed. But now he knew that he would go as badly
prepared as he had before, and his death and defeat would be certain.
Well, he thought, better death than life as Bork the coward, Bork the
bully who only has courage when he fights people smaller than himself.

The winter was unusually cold, and the snow was remarkably
deep. The firewood ran out in February, and there was no sign of an
easing in the weather.

The villagers went to the castle and asked for help, but the King
was chilly himself, and the knights were all sleeping together in the
great hall because there wasn't enough firewood for their barracks
and the castle, too. "Can't help you," the King said.

So it was Bork who led the villagers—the ten strongest men,
dressed as warmly as they could, yet still cold to the bone in the

wind—and they followed in the path his body cut in the snow. With his huge ax he cut down tree after tree; the villagers set the wedges and Bork split the huge logs; the men carried what they could but it was Bork who made seven trips and carried most of the wood home. The village had enough to last until spring—more than enough, for, as Bork had expected, as soon as the stacks of firewood were deep in the village, the King's men came and took their tax of it.

And Bork, exhausted and frozen from the expedition, was carefully nursed back to health by the villagers. As he lay coughing and they feared he might die, it occurred to them how much they owed to the giant. Not just the firewood, but the hard labor in the farming work, and the fact that Bork had kept the armies far from their village, and they felt what no one in the castle had let himself feel for more than a few moments—gratitude. And so it was that when he had mostly recovered, Bork began to find gifts outside his door from time to time. A rabbit, freshly killed and dressed; a few eggs; a vast pair of hose that fit him very comfortably; a knife specially made to fit his large grip and to ride with comfortable weight on his hip. The villagers did not converse with him much. But then, they were not talkative people. The gifts said it all.

Throughout the spring, as Bork helped in the plowing and planting, with the villagers working alongside, he realized that this was where he belonged—with the villagers, not with the knights. They weren't rollicking good company, but there was something about sharing a task that must be done that made for stronger bonds between them than any of the rough camaraderie of the castle. The loneliness was gone.

Yet when Bork returned home and stared into the flames in the center of his hut, the call of the dragon's eyes became even stronger, if that were possible. It was not loneliness that drove him to seek death with the dragon. It was something else, and Bork could not think what. Pride? He had none—he accepted the verdict of the castle people that he was a coward. The only guess he could make was that he loved Brunhilda and felt a need to rescue her. The more he tried to convince himself, however, the less he believed it.

He had to return to the dragon because, in his own mind, he knew he should have died in the dragon's teeth, back when he fought the dragon before. The common folk might love him for what he did for them, but he hated himself for what he was.

He was nearly ready to head back for the dragon's mountain when the army came.

"How many are there?" the King asked Winkle.

"I can't get my spies to agree," Winkle said. "But the lowest estimate was two thousand men."

"And we have a hundred and fifty here in the castle. Well, I'll have to call on my dukes and counts for support."

"You don't understand, Your Majesty. These *are* your dukes and counts. This isn't an invasion. This is a rebellion."

The King paled. "How do they dare?"

"They dare because they heard a rumor, which at first they didn't believe was true. A rumor that your giant knight had quit, that he wasn't in your army anymore. And when they found out for sure that the rumor was true, they came to cast you out and return the old King to his place."

"Treason!" the King shouted. "Is there no loyalty?"

"I'm loyal," Winkle said, though of course he had already made contact with the other side in case things didn't go well. "But it seems to me that your only hope is to prove the rumors wrong. Show them that Bork is still fighting for you."

"But he isn't. I threw him out two years ago. The coward was even rejected by the dragon."

"Then I suggest you find a way to get him back into the army. If you don't, I doubt you'll have much luck against that crowd out there. My spies tell me they're placing wagers about how many pieces you can be cut into before you die."

The King turned slowly and stared at Winkle, glared at him, gazed intently in his eyes. "Winkle, after all we've done to Bork over the years, persuading him to help us now is a despicable thing to do."

"True."

"And so it's your sort of work, Winkle. Not mine. *You* get him back in the army."

"I can't do it. He hates me worse than anyone, I'm sure. After all, I've betrayed him more often."

"You get him back in the army within the next six hours, Winkle, or I'll send pieces of you to each of the men in that traitorous group that you've made friends with in order to betray me."

Winkle managed not to look startled. But he *was* surprised. The King had somehow known about it. The King was not quite the fool he had seemed to be.

"I'm sending four knights with you to make sure you do it right."

"You misjudge me, Your Majesty," Winkle said.

"I hope so, Winkle. Persuade Bork for me, and you live to eat another breakfast."

The knights came, and Winkle walked with them to Bork's hut. They waited outside.

"Bork, old friend," Winkle said. Bork was sitting by the fire, staring in the flames. "Bork, you aren't the sort who holds grudges, are you?"

Bork spat into the flames.

"Can't say I blame you," Winkle said. "We've treated you ungratefully. We've been downright cruel. But you rather brought it on yourself, you know. It isn't *our* fault you turned coward in your fight with the dragon. Is it?"

Bork shook his head. "My fault, Winkle. But it isn't my fault the army has come, either. I've lost my battle. You lose yours."

"Bork, we've been friends since we were three—"

Bork looked up so suddenly, his face so sharp and lit with the glow of the fire, that Winkle could not go on.

"I've looked in the dragon's eyes," Bork said, "and I know who you are."

Winkle wondered if it was true, and was afraid. But he had courage of a kind, a selfish courage that allowed him to dare anything if he thought he would gain by it.

"Who I am? No one knows anything as it is, because as soon as it's known it changes. You looked in the dragon's eyes years ago, Bork. Today I am not who I was then. Today you are not who you were then. And today the King needs you."

"The King is a petty count who rode to greatness on my shoulders. He can rot in hell."

"The other knights need you, then. Do you want them to die?"

"I've fought enough battles for them. Let them fight their own."

And Winkle stood helplessly, wondering how he could possibly persuade this man, who would not be persuaded.

It was then that a village child came. The knights caught him lurking near Bork's hut; they roughly shoved him inside. "He might be a spy," a knight said.

For the first time since Winkle came, Bork laughed. "A spy? Don't you know your own village, here? Come to me, Laggy." And the boy came to him, and stood near him as if seeking protection from the giant. "Laggy's a friend of mine," Bork said. "Why did you come, Laggy?"

The boy wordlessly held out a fish. It wasn't large, but it was still wet from the river.

"Did you catch this?" Bork said.

The boy nodded.

"How many did you catch today?"

The boy pointed at the fish.

"Just the one? Oh, then I can't take this, if it's all you caught."

But as Bork handed the fish back, the boy retreated, refused to take it. He finally opened his mouth and spoke. "For you," he said, and then he scurried out of the hut and into the bright morning sunlight.

And Winkle knew he had his way to get Bork into the battle.

"The villagers," Winkle said.

Bork looked at him quizzically.

And Winkle *almost* said, "If you don't join the army, we'll come out here and burn the village and kill all the children and sell the adults into slavery in Germany." But something stopped him; a memory, perhaps, of the fact that he was once a village child himself. No, not that. Winkle was honest enough with himself to know that what stopped him from making the threat was a mental picture of Sir Bork striding into battle, not in front of the King's army, but at the head of the rebels. A mental picture of Bork's ax biting deep into the gate of

the castle, his huge crow prying the portcullis free. This was not the
time to threaten Bork.

So Winkle took the other tack. "Bork, if they win this battle, which
they surely will if you aren't with us, do you think they'll be kind to
this village? They'll burn and rape and kill and capture these people
for slaves. They hate us, and to them these villagers are part of us,
part of their hatred. If you don't help us, you're killing them."

"I'll protect them," Bork said.

"No, my friend. No, if you don't fight with us, as a knight, they
won't treat you chivalrously. They'll fill you full of arrows before
you get within twenty feet of their lines. You fight with us, or you
might as well not fight at all."

Winkle knew he had won. Bork thought for several minutes, but it
was inevitable. He got up and returned to the castle, strapped on his
old armor, took his huge ax and his shield, and kept his sword belted
at his waist, and walked into the courtyard of the castle. The other
knights cheered, and called out to him as if he were their dearest
friend. But the words were hollow and they knew it, and when Bork
didn't answer they soon fell silent.

The gate opened and Bork walked out, the knights on horseback
behind him.

And in the rebel camp, they knew that the rumors were a lie—the
giant still fought with the King, and they were doomed. Most of the
men slipped away into the woods. But others, particularly the lead-
ers who would die if they surrendered as surely as they would die if
they fought, stayed. Better to die valiantly than as a coward, they
each thought, and so as Bork approached he still faced an army—
only a few hundred men, but still an army.

They came out to meet Bork one by one, as the knights came to
the dragon on his hill. And one by one, as they made their first cut or
thrust, Bork's ax struck, and their heads flew from their bodies, or
their chests were cloven nearly in half, or the ax reamed them end to
end, and Bork was bright red with blood and a dozen men were dead
and not one had touched him.

So they came by threes and fours, and fought like demons, but still

Bork took them, and when even more than four tried to fight him at once they got in each other's way and he killed them more easily.

And at last those who still lived despaired. There was no honor in dying so pointlessly. And with fifty men dead, the battle ended, and the rebels laid down their arms in submission.

Then the King emerged from the castle and rode to the battle-ground, and paraded triumphantly in front of the defeated men.

"You are all sentenced to death at once," the King declared.

But suddenly he found himself pulled from his horse, and Bork's great hands held him. The King gasped at the smell of gore; Bork rubbed his bloody hands on the King's tunic, and took the King's face between his sticky palms.

"No one dies now. No one dies tomorrow. These men will all live, and you'll send them home to their lands, and you'll lower their trib-ute and let them dwell in peace forever."

The King imagined his own blood mingling with that which al-ready covered Bork, and he nodded. Bork let him go. The King mounted his horse again, and spoke loudly, so all could hear. "I for-give you all. I pardon you all. You may return to your homes. I con-firm you in your lands. And your tribute is cut in half from this day forward. Go in peace. If any man harms you, I'll have his life."

The rebels stood in silence.

Winkle shouted at them "Go! You heard the king! You're free! Go home!"

And they cheered, and long-lived-the-King, and then bellowed their praise to Bork.

But Bork, if he heard them, gave no sign. He stripped off his armor and let it lie in the field. He carried his great ax to the stream, and let the water run over the metal until it was clean. Then he lay in the stream himself, and the water carried off the last of the blood, and when he came out he was clean.

Then he walked away, to the north road, ignoring the calls of the King and his knights, ignoring everything except the dragon who waited for him on the mountain. For this was the last of the acts Bork would perform in his life for which he would feel shame. He would not kill again. He would only die, bravely, in the dragon's claws and teeth.

The old woman waited for him on the road.

"Off to kill the dragon, are you?" she asked in a voice that the years had tortured into gravel. "Didn't learn enough the first time?" She giggled behind her hand.

"Old woman, I learned everything before. Now I'm going to die."

"Why? So the fools in the castle will think better of you?"

Bork shook his head.

"The villagers already love you. For your deeds today, you'll already be a legend. If it isn't for love or fame, why are you going?"

Bork shrugged. "I don't know. I think he calls to me. I'm through with my life, and all I can see ahead of me are his eyes."

The old woman nodded. "Well, well, Bork. I think you're the first knight that the dragon won't be happy to see. We old wives know, Bork. Just tell him the truth, Bork."

"I've never known the truth to stop a sword," he said.

"But the dragon doesn't carry a sword."

"He might as well."

"No, Bork, no," she said, clucking impatiently. "You know better than that. Of all the dragon's weapons, which cut you the deepest?"

Bork tried to remember. The truth was, he realized, that the dragon had never cut him at all. Not with his teeth nor his claws. Only the armor had been pierced. Yet there had been a wound, a deep one that hadn't healed, and it had been cut in him, not by teeth or talons, but by the bright fires in the dragon's eyes.

"The truth," the old woman said. "Tell the dragon the truth. Tell him the truth, and you'll live!"

Bork shook his head. "I'm not going there to live," he said. He pushed past her, and walked on up the road.

But her words rang in his ears long after he stopped hearing her call after him. The truth, she had said. Well, then, why not? Let the dragon have the truth. Much good may it do him.

This time Bork was in no hurry. He slept every night, and paused to hunt for berries and fruit to eat in the woods. It was four days before he reached the dragon's hill, and he came in the morning, after a good night's sleep. He was afraid, of course; but still there was a pleasant feeling about the morning, a tingling of excitement about the meeting with the dragon. He felt the end coming near, and he relished it.

Nothing had changed. The dragon roared; Brunhilda screamed. And when he reached the top of the hill, he saw the dragon tickling her with his wing. He was not surprised to see that she hadn't changed at all—the two years had not aged her, and though her gown still was open and her breasts were open to the sun and the wind, she wasn't even freckled or tanned. It could have been yesterday that Bork fought with the dragon the first time. And Bork was smiling as he stepped into the flat space where the battle would take place.

Brunhilda saw him first. "Help me! You're the four hundred and thirtieth knight to try! Surely that's a lucky number!" Then she recognized him. "Oh, no. You again. Oh well, at least while he's fighting you I won't have to put up with his tickling."

Bork ignored her. He had come for the dragon, not for Brunhilda.

The dragon regarded him calmly. "You are disturbing my nap time."

"I'm glad," Bork said. "You've disturbed me, sleeping and waking, since I left you. Do you remember me?"

"Ah yes. You're the only knight who was ever afraid of me."

"Do you really believe that?" Bork asked.

"It hardly matters what I believe. Are you going to kill me today?"

"I don't think so," said Bork. "You're much stronger than I am, and I'm terrible at battle. I've never defeated anyone who was more than half my strength."

The lights in the dragon's eyes suddenly grew brighter, and the dragon squinted to look at Bork. "Is that so?" asked the dragon.

"And I'm not very clever. You'll be able to figure out my next move before I know what it is myself."

The dragon squinted more, and the eyes grew even brighter.

"Don't you want to rescue this beautiful woman?" the dragon asked.

"I don't much care," he said. "I loved her once. But I'm through with that. I came for you."

"You don't love her anymore?" asked the dragon.

Bork almost said, "Not a bit." But then he stopped. The truth, the old woman had said. And he looked into himself and saw that no matter how much he hated himself for it, the old feelings died hard. "I love her, dragon. But it doesn't do me any good. She doesn't love me. And so even though I desire her, I don't want her."

Brunhilda was a little miffed. "That's the stupidest thing I've ever heard," she said. But Bork was watching the dragon, whose eyes were dazzlingly bright. The monster was squinting so badly that Bork began to wonder if he could see at all.

"Are you having trouble with your eyes?" Bork asked.

"Do you think *you* ask the questions here? I ask the questions."

"Then ask."

"What in the world do I want to know from *you*?"

"I can't think of anything," Bork answered. "I know almost nothing. What little I do know, you taught me."

"Did I? What was it that you learned?"

"You taught me that I was not loved by those I thought had loved me. I learned from you that deep within my large body is a very small soul."

The dragon blinked, and its eyes seemed to dim a little.

"Ah," said the dragon.

"What do you mean, 'Ah'?" asked Bork.

"Just 'Ah,'" the dragon answered. "Does every *ah* have to mean something?"

Brunhilda sighed impatiently. "How long does this go on? Everybody else who comes up here is wonderful and brave. You just stand around talking about how miserable you are. Why don't you fight?"

"Like the others?" asked Bork.

"They're so brave," she said.

"They're all dead."

"Only a coward would think of that," she said scornfully.

"It hardly comes as a surprise to you," Bork said. "Everyone knows I'm a coward. Why do you think I came? I'm of no use to anyone, except as a machine to kill people at the command of a King I despise."

"That's my father you're talking about!"

"I'm nothing, and the world will be better without me in it."

"I can't say I disagree," Brunhilda said.

But Bork did not hear her, for he felt the touch of the dragon's tail on his back, and when he looked at the dragon's eyes they had stopped glowing so brightly. They were almost back to normal, in fact, and the dragon was beginning to reach out its claws.

So Bork swung his ax, and the dragon dodged, and the battle was on, just as before.

And just as before, at sundown Bork stood pinned between tail and claws and teeth.

"Are you afraid to die?" asked the dragon, as it had before.

Bork almost answered *yes* again, because that would keep him alive. But then he remembered that he had come in order to die, and as he looked in his heart he still realized that however much he might fear death, he feared life more.

"I came here to die," he said. "I still want to."

And the dragon's eyes leaped bright with light. Bork imagined that the pressure of the claws lessened.

"Well, then, Sir Bork, I can hardly do you such a favor as to kill you." And the dragon let him go.

That was when Bork became angry.

"You can't do this to me!" he shouted.

"Why not?" asked the dragon, who was now trying to ignore Bork and occupied itself by crushing boulders with its claws.

"Because I insist on my right to die at your hands."

"It's not a right, it's a privilege," said the dragon.

"If you don't kill me, then I'll kill you!"

The dragon sighed in boredom, but Bork would not be put off. He began swinging the ax, and the dragon dodged, and in the pink light of sunset the battle was on again. This time, though, the dragon only fell back and twisted and turned to avoid Bork's blows. It made no effort to attack. Finally Bork was too tired and frustrated to go on.

"Why don't you fight!" he shouted. Then he wheezed from the exhaustion of the chase.

The dragon was panting, too. "Come on now, little man, why don't you give it up and go home. I'll give you a signed certificate testifying that I asked you to go, so that no one thinks you're a coward. Just leave me alone."

The dragon began crushing rocks and dribbling them over its head. It lay down and began to bury itself in gravel.

"Dragon," said Bork, "a moment ago you had me in your teeth. You were about to kill me. The old woman told me that truth was my only defense. So I must have lied before, I must have said something false. What was it? Tell me!"

The dragon looked annoyed. "She had no business telling you that. It's privileged information."

"All I ever said to you was the truth."

"Was it?"

"Did I lie to you? Answer—yes or no!"

The dragon only looked away, its eyes still bright. It lay on its back and poured gravel over its belly.

"I did then. I lied. Just the kind of fool I am to tell the truth and still get caught in a lie."

Had the dragon's eyes dimmed? Was there a lie in what he had just said?

"Dragon," Bork insisted, "if you don't kill me or I don't kill you, then I might as well throw myself from the cliff. There's no meaning to my life, if I can't die at your hands!"

Yes, the dragon's eyes were dimming, and the dragon rolled over onto its belly, and began to gaze thoughtfully at Bork.

"Where is the lie in that?"

"Lie? Who said anything about a lie?" But the dragon's long tail was beginning to creep around so it could get behind Bork.

And then it occurred to Bork that the Dragon might not even know. That the dragon might be as much a prisoner of the fires of truth inside him as Bork was, and that the dragon wasn't deliberately toying with him at all. Didn't matter, of course. "Never mind what the lie is, then," Bork said. "Kill me now, and the world will be a better place!"

The dragon's eyes dimmed, and a claw made a pass at him, raking the air by his face.

It was maddening, to know there was a lie in what he was saying and not know what it was. "It's the perfect ending for my meaningless life," he said. "I'm so clumsy I even have to stumble into death."

He didn't understand why, but once again he stared into the dragon's mouth, and the claws pressed gently but sharply against his flesh.

The dragon asked the question of Bork for the third time. "Are you afraid, little man, to die?"

This was the moment, Bork knew. If he was to die, he had to lie to the dragon now, for if he told the truth the dragon would set him free again. But to lie, he had to know what the truth was, and now he didn't know at all. He tried to think of where he had gone astray from the truth, and could not. What had he said? It was true that he was clumsy; it was true that he was stumbling into death. What else then?

He had said his life was meaningless. Was that the lie? He had said his death would make the world a better place. Was that the lie?

And so he thought of what would happen when he died. What hole would his death make in the world? The only people who might miss him were the villagers. That was the meaning of his life, then—the villagers. So he lied.

"The villagers won't miss me if I die. They'll get along just fine without me."

But the dragon's eyes brightened, and the teeth withdrew, and Bork realized to his grief that his statement had been true after all. The villagers wouldn't miss him if he died. The thought of it broke his heart, the last betrayal in a long line of betrayals.

"Dragon, I can't outguess you! I don't know what's true and what isn't! All I learn from you is that everyone I thought loved me doesn't. Don't ask me questions! Just kill me and end my life. Every pleasure I've ever had turns to pain when you tell me the truth."

And now, when he had thought he was telling the truth, the claws broke his skin, and the teeth closed over his head, and he screamed. "Dragon! Don't let me die like this! What is the pleasure that your truth won't turn to pain? What do I have left?"

The dragon pulled away, and regarded him carefully. "I told you, little man, that I don't answer questions. I ask them."

"Why are you here?" Bork demanded. "This ground is littered with the bones of men who failed your tests. Why not mine? Why not mine? Why can't I die? Why did you keep sparing my life? I'm just a man, I'm just alive, I'm just trying to do the best I can in a miserable world and I'm sick of trying to figure out what's true and what isn't. End the game, dragon. My life has never been happy, and I want to die."

The dragon's eyes went black, and the jaws opened again, and the teeth approached, and Bork knew he had told his last lie, that this lie would be enough. But with the teeth inches from him Bork finally realized what the lie was, and the realization was enough to change his mind. "No," he said, and he reached out and seized the teeth, though they cut his fingers. "No," he said, and he wept. "I have been happy. I have." And, gripping the sharp teeth, the memories raced through his mind. The many nights of comradeship with the knights in the castle. The pleasures of weariness from working in the forest and the fields. The joy he felt when alone he won a victory from the Duke; the rush of warmth when the boy brought him the single fish he had caught; and the solitary pleasures, of waking and going to sleep, of walking and running, of feeling the wind on a hot day and standing near a fire in the deep of winter. They were all good, and they had all happened. What did it matter if later the knights despised him? What did it matter if the villagers' love was only a fleeting thing, to be forgotten after he died? The reality of the pain did not destroy the reality of the pleasure; grief did not obliterate joy. They each happened in their time, and because some of them were dark it did not mean that none of them was light.

"I have been happy," Bork said. "And if you let me live, I'll be happy again. That's what my life means, doesn't it? That's the truth, isn't it, dragon? My life matters because I'm alive, joy or pain, whatever comes, I'm alive and that's meaning enough. It's true, isn't it, dragon! I'm not here to fight you. I'm not here for you to kill me. I'm here to make myself alive!"

But the dragon did not answer. Bork was gently lowered to the ground. The dragon withdrew its talons and tail, pulled its head away, and curled up on the ground, covering its eyes with its claws.

"Dragon, did you hear me?"

The dragon said nothing.

"Dragon, look at me!"

The dragon sighed. "Man, I cannot look at you."

"Why not?"

"I am blind," the dragon answered. It pulled its claws away from its eyes. Bork covered his face with his hands. The dragon's eyes were brighter than the sun.

"I feared you, Bork," the dragon whispered. "From the day you told me you were afraid, I feared you. I knew you would be back. And I knew this moment would come."

"What moment?" Bork asked.

"The moment of my death."

"Are you dying?"

"No," said the dragon. "Not yet. You must kill me."

As Bork looked at the dragon lying before him, he felt no desire for blood. "I don't want you to die."

"Don't you know that a dragon cannot live when it has met a truly honest man? It's the only way we ever die, and most dragons live forever."

But Bork refused to kill him.

The dragon cried out in anguish. "I am filled with all the truth that was discarded by men when they chose their lies and died for them. I am in constant pain, and now that I have met a man who does not add to my treasury of falsehood, you are the cruelest of them all."

And the dragon wept, and its eyes flashed and sparkled in every hot tear that fell, and finally Bork could not bear it. He took his ax and hacked off the dragon's head, and the light in its eyes went out. The eyes shriveled in their sockets until they turned into small, bright diamonds with a thousand facets each. Bork took the diamonds and put them in his pocket.

"You killed him," Brunhilda said wonderingly.

Bork did not answer. He just untied her, and looked away while she finally fastened her gown. Then he shouldered the dragon's head and carried it back to the castle, Brunhilda running to keep up with him. He only stopped to rest at night because she begged him to. And when she tried to thank him for freeing her, he only turned away and refused to hear. He had killed the dragon because it wanted to die. Not for Brunhilda. Never for her.

At the castle they were received with rejoicing, but Bork would not go in. He only laid the dragon's head beside the moat and went to his hut, fingering the diamonds in his pocket, holding them in front of him in the pitch blackness of his hut to see that they shone with their own light, and did not need the sun or any other fire but themselves.

The King and Winkle and Brunhilda and a dozen knights came to Bork's hut. "I have come to thank you," the King said, his cheeks wet with tears of joy.

"You're welcome," Bork said. He said it as if to dismiss them.

"Bork," the King said. "Slaying the dragon was ten times as brave as the bravest thing any man has ever done. You can have my daughter's hand in marriage."

Bork looked up in surprise.

"I thought you never meant to keep your promise, Your Majesty."

The King looked down, then at Winkle, then back at Bork. "Occasionally," he said, "I keep my word. So here she is, and thank you."

But Bork only smiled, fingering the diamonds in his pocket. "It's enough that you offered, Your Majesty. I don't want her. Marry her to a man she loves."

The King was puzzled. Brunhilda's beauty had not waned in her years of captivity. She had the sort of beauty that started wars. "Don't you want *any* reward?" asked the King.

Bork thought for a moment. "Yes," he said. "I want to be given a plot of ground far away from here. I don't want there to be any count, or any duke, or any king over me. And any man or woman or child who comes to me will be free, and no one can pursue them. And I will never see you again, and you will never see me again."

"That's all you want?"

"That's all."

"Then you shall have it," the King said.

*   *   *

Bork lived all the rest of his life in his little plot of ground. People did come to him. Not many, but five or ten a year all his life, and a village grew up where no one came to take a king's tithe or a duke's fifth or a count's fourth. Children grew up who knew nothing of the art of war and never saw a knight or a battle or the terrible fear on the face of a man who knows his wounds are too deep to heal. It was everything Bork could have wanted, and he was happy all his years there.

Winkle, too, achieved everything he wanted. He married Brunhilda, and soon enough the King's sons had accidents and died, and the King died after dinner one night, and Winkle became King. He was at war all his life, and never went to sleep at night without fear of an assassin coming upon him in the darkness. He governed ruthlessly and thoroughly and was hated all his life; later generations, however, remembered him as a great King. But he was dead then, and didn't know it.

Later generations never heard of Bork.

He had only been out on his little plot of ground for a few months when the old wife came to him. "Your hut is much bigger than you need," she said. "Move over."

So Bork moved over, and she moved in.

She did not magically turn into a beautiful princess. She was foul-mouthed and nagged Bork unmercifully. But he was devoted to her, and when she died a few years later he realized that she had given him more happiness than pain, and he missed her. But the grief at her dying did not taint any of the joy of his memory of her; he just fingered the diamonds, and remembered that grief and joy were not weighed in the same scale, one making the other seem less substantial.

And at last he realized that Death was near; that Death was reaping him like wheat, eating him like bread. He imagined Death to be a dragon, devouring him bit by bit, and one night in a dream he asked Death, "Is my flavor sweet?"

Death, the old dragon, looked at him with bright and understanding eyes, and said, "Sweet and salt, bitter and rich. You sting and you soothe."

"Ah," Bork said, and was satisfied.

Death poised itself to take the last bite. "Thank you," it said.

"You're welcome," Bork answered, and he meant it.

Gregory Benford describes himself as a scientist first and a writer second, but the high quality of his science fiction indicates that he is equally proficient in both fields. From the novel *Timescape,* a novel where scientists of the future try to warn the past not to make the same mistakes, to the epic Galactic Center series, his work explores the human will to survive and the nature of man's role in the universe. He has won the Nebula award twice, and received the U.N. Medal in Literature in 1990.

Ray Bradbury has remained at the forefront of speculative fiction for the last half century, writing hundreds of short stories that deal with man's ambition and shortcomings. Space exploration and extrapolations of what future societies might be like are major themes in his work. Among his many collections are *The Martian Chronicles, The Illustrated Man,* and *Dark Carnival.* His novel *Fahrenheit 451* is his best-known satire of a repressive government where firemen start fires instead of fighting them. He has also written screenplays, poetry and mystery novels, and has won several awards for his work, including the Nebula Grand Master award in 1988.

Although best known for his Nebula and Hugo award-winning science fiction novels *Ender's Game* and *Speaker for the Dead,* **Orson Scott Card** is also an accomplished fantasy and horror writer. Among his other achievements are two Locus awards, a Hugo award for nonfiction, and a World Fantasy award. Currently he is working on the Tales of Alvin Maker series, which chronicles the history of an alternate 19th century America where magic works. The Alvin Maker series, like the majority of his work, deals with messianic characters and their influence on the world around them. His short fiction has been collected in the anthology *Maps in a Mirror.*

L. Sprague de Camp has been writing since the 1930s, and has more than three dozen novels, dozens of short stories and many nonfiction works to show for his efforts. Known early on for his space opera novels, he was first critically recognized for novel *Lest Darkness Fall,* about one man's attempt to change history during the

Roman Empire. In his wide-ranging career he has written everything from Conan pastiches to books on writing science fiction. He has also edited more than a dozen fantasy anthologies and manuscripts, working with authors such as Christopher Stasheff and the late Robert E. Howard.

While **Gordon R. Dickson** is also primarily known for his science fiction, there is a strong thread of fantasy underlying much of his work. Here, he has taken one of the basic plot ideas, that of one person facing a menace to his race or society, and given it a twist as only he can. The novella "St. Dragon and the George" was expanded into the novel *The Dragon and the George* in 1976, and became the beginning of the Dragon Knight series of novels, which continue with *The Dragon Knight, The Dragon on the Border, The Dragon at War,* and *The Dragon, the Earl, and the Troll.* A three-time winner of the Hugo award, he was the president of the Science Fiction Writers of America from 1969–1971.

David Drake is one of the foremost writers of military science fiction. His Hammer's Slammers series, about a group of mercenaries hiring themselves out in a far-reaching space empire, is an excellent character study of the men and women who make a career out of war. But he can also write about ancient history as well, as evidenced by his novels *Killer, The Dragon Lord,* and *Ranks of Bronze,* in which the gritty details of Roman military life come alive against the decaying atmosphere of the Empire. Besides his writing, he is also a proficient editor, having worked on almost twenty anthologies. He lives in North Carolina.

Alan Dean Foster was born in New York City and raised in Los Angeles. He has a bachelor's degree in Political Science and a Master of Fine Arts in Cinema from UCLA. He has traveled extensively around the world, from Australia to Papua New Guinea. He has also written fiction in just about every genre, and is known for his excellent movie novelizations, which include *Alien, The Thing,* and *Outland.* Currently, he lives in Prescott, Arizona, with his wife, assorted dogs, cats, fish, javelina and other animals, where he is working on several new novels and media projects.

Esther Friesner's latest novel in *Child of the Eagle* from Baen Books. While known primarily for writing humorous fantasy novels, her more serious works are excellent combinations of literary figures, history and magic. She has written over twenty novels and co-edited two fantasy collections. Other fiction of hers appears in *Excalibur, The Book of Kings,* and numerous appearances in *Fantasy and Science Fiction* and other prose magazines. She lives in Madison, Connecticut.

Marc Laidlaw's fiction has appeared in *Scare Care,* the *Shadows* and *New Terrors* series and *Isaac Asimov's Science Fiction Magazine.*

Ursula K. Le Guin is considered one of the most influential authors in the science fiction and fantasy field. Her Earthsea novels have been favorably compared to Tolkien's work for their intricate detailing of a fantasy world. Like Tolkien, Le Guin makes her worlds come alive through the use of language, and accomplishes this end as well as he did. Her work in the field has been critically acclaimed as well, garnering her four Nebula awards, five Hugo awards, three Jupiter awards, and the Gandalf award. She has taught writing courses all around the world, and currently lives in Portland, Oregon.

Anne McCaffrey is one of the best-selling science-fiction writers in the world. Her Doona, Pern, and Rowan series have all won worldwide acclaim. A winner of both the Hugo and Nebula awards, her recent novels include *Freedom's Landing* and *Power Play.* She has also collaborated with some of the best authors in the field, including S.M. Stirling, Mercedes Lackey, and Margaret Ball. Her work is concerned with all aspects of the human condition, from birth to death and everything in between. She currently lives in Ireland.

Mickey Zucker Reichert is a pediatrician whose twelve science fiction and fantasy novels include *The Legend of Nightfall, The Unknown Soldier,* and the Renshai trilogy. Her latest release from DAW Books is *Prince of Demons,* the second in The Renshai Chronicles trilogy, based on Norse religious myths. Her short fiction has appeared in numerous anthologies. Her claims to fame: she *has* performed brain surgery, and her parents *really are* rocket scientists.

Joan D. Vinge's stories weave mythology, fantasy and science-fiction into amazing tapestries of characterization set against a backdrop of wonderfully alien worlds. Her degree in anthropology figures prominently in her work, which explores relationships between different cultures. She has written over a dozen novels, including several movie novelizations. Her best-known work is the Snow Queen series, which stands at three books, *The Snow Queen, World's End,* and *The Summer Queen.*

Influenced by the novels of H.G. Wells, the theme of humans dealing with catastrophe is prominent in the work of **John Wyndham** (1903–1969). The novel *Day of the Triffids* is his best-known work dealing with this subject. Alien invasion, telepathy, mutation and fantastic events occurring in everyday life are also explored in his work, usually as the catalyst for change in the Earth of his novels. Certainly the included story is no exception.

Roger Zelazny (1937–1995) burst onto the science-fiction writing scene as part of the "New Wave" group of writers in the mid to late 1960s. His novels *This Immortal* and *Lord of Light* met universal praise, the latter winning a Hugo award for best novel. His work is notable for his lyrical style and innovative use of language both in description and dialogue. His most recognized series is the Amber novels, about a parallel universe which is the true world with all others, Earth included, being mere shadows of Amber. Besides the Hugo, he was also awarded three Nebulas, three more Hugos and two Locus awards.